Kiss The Sky

Dale Greenlee

Dreams do come true.

Dale Greenlee

JGC/United Publishing Corps • Rockford, Illinois
www.jgcunited.com

Kiss The Sky

Dale Greenlee

Library of Congress Card Number: 2008921838
ISBN: 978-0-910941-33-4

Printed in the United States of America
by Worzalla, Stevens Point, Wisconsin

Acknowledgments

I wish to give a special thank you to the following people, without whom *Kiss The Sky* would still be only a dream:

• My beautiful wife Linda — my life partner, my best friend, the spiritually strongest person I know. Your love and encouragement sustain me.

• My darling daughters, Amanda and Julie — you are the joy of my life, and the inspiration for AJ Clark.

• My parents, Wayne and Vivian — you gave me life and love, determination, and the joy of reading. Your support makes all things possible.

• My family and friends — your encouragement and support are greatly appreciated.

• And my editor, publisher, literary coach, and friend, John Gile, and his wife and partner Renie — your wisdom and guidance were invaluable in making my dream a reality.

Dale Greenlee

• Editor's note: A percentage of the proceeds from the book will go to cancer research in honor of Dale's wife Linda, a two time cancer survivor, and in honor of Dale's parents, Wayne and Vivian, both cancer survivors.

".…'scuse me while I kiss the sky."

Jimi Hendrix   Purple Haze   1967

"Don't it always seem to go
      That you don't know what you've got
         'Til it's gone?
They paved paradise —
      And put up a parking lot."

Joni Mitchell   Big Yellow Taxi   1970

CHAPTER 1

A pipe burst and steam shot into the Wisconsin sky. An emergency siren shredded the air with its high pitched squeal.

Peter Rudi stood on a steel grating three stories in the air, watching his personal Dante's Inferno. Chaos spread before him as steam billowed into the air. Liquids sprayed from exposed piping next to massive tanks, and men in blue coveralls and hard hats scurried back and forth in a Keystone Cops ballet.

Rudi pounded his fist on the stainless steel guardrail and muttered out loud, "I don't have time for this!"

Peter Rudi was the plant manager of the GF Products state of the art manufacturing facility, nestled among verdant fields and dairy farms in southern Wisconsin. Normally he found the view of the factory and the surrounding countryside relaxing and inspiring.

Today he wondered if anyone could keep his factory from being destroyed, taking his career down with it. His breakthroughs in animal food supplements would be negated by this disaster.

Nobody knew what to do and everyone blamed everyone else. Tempers ran high as intelligence and cooperation took the day off. Devastation stared down strong men and they blinked. If ever a clear head was needed to steer the course, it was now.

Down on the production floor, Clark was fed up with the chaos. Wham! The clipboard hit the concrete, and the babbling stopped. Twenty goggled eyes stared at the yellow clad Clark. "Get a grip! We need to act decisively, but carefully. Be quick, but don't hurry."

As his employees hustled to and fro, Rudi spotted a stationary figure creating an area of calm in the center of disorder. Outfitted in a yellow visitor hardhat, yellow all weather gear and goggles, the visitor was the one the GF Products personnel were taking their orders from. He would lean close to give instructions, point, and off they went.

Heads topped with blue hard hats nodded. "Who covers storage tanks seven and eight?" asked Clark. A gloved hand went up. "Go close the manual inlet valve on the steam cleaning line."

Clark distributed assignments with the efficiency of a New York traffic cop. The disaster at the GF Products factory had to be stopped, and stopped now. An old-timer spoke up. "How do we know you're right?"

He'd verbalized what the others were thinking. Clark smiled. "Cuz someone's gotta be right, and I'm the one." That produced a laugh. "And how do you know I'm not right? You looking to place blame or take credit?"

The old-timer shook his head and raised his hands in mock surrender. "Neither. I just don't want this place to blow. I can't change jobs and go through one of them retraining programs."

Clark caught the twinkle in his eye and answered with confidence. "We'll get the leaks stopped, and I don't think you need retraining. You just have to ask yourself if you trust me. Do you trust me?"

It was the old-timer's turn to smile, displaying tobacco stained teeth. "I reckon we ain't got no choice." He looked at the circle of men. "Fellas, get a move on. Time's a wastin'."

His blessing sparked the group into action. The collective energy of a defined goal was palpable as the men scattered to their respective assignments. Clark spoke half out loud, "Let the healing begin."

Rudi retreated to his office to escape the mind numbing noise. He needed to sort out the problem and plan a recovery. Final production tests had broken down this morning due to equipment malfunctions, but he had no idea what caused the failures.

Sitting on the corner of his desk, Peter rubbed his temples and closed his eyes. What was it Swen had said? The control valves on the water pretreatment system had gone haywire and the pump on tank seven seized up causing a production shutdown. Maintenance put in a rush call for the valve representative to come to the plant.

Then the wheels came off the buggy. Two steam lines ruptured, mixers quit for no reason, and product-sampling valves began opening randomly. A small fire broke out and confusion became the norm. This was the chaos occurring around tanks seven, eight and twelve.

Delays hurt Rudi's timetable and his budget. Maintenance and repair costs had increased 36% in the last month, just as the project was yielding results. His reviews and bonuses were dependent upon stemming the tide of bad luck.

The intercom sprang to life with a click. "Mr. Rudi, Mr. Swenson of maintenance just called to say the leaks are stopped and they're working on the valves now. He said to tell you the representative from the Ultra Valve Company, AJ Clark, was a great help. And he said he'd keep you posted on their progress."

"Well, well, the Man In Yellow saves the day," responded Rudi.

"What, sir?" came the reply through the intercom.

"Nothing. That's great news. Be sure to buzz me the second you hear anything from Swenson. Oh, and tell Swenson when he checks in I want to meet this Clark fellow before he leaves and thank him for his help."

"Very good, sir. And sir, your wife called earlier. I said we had a plant emergency and you couldn't be reached. She wasn't particularly happy, sir."

Rudi sighed and had an unkind thought. *That woman is never happy.* "Don't worry, Tammy. That's my problem, not yours. Please get me the regional FDA and regional EPA phone numbers."

"Sure, Mr. Rudi. Right away."

Peter stretched and rubbed the back of his neck. Responsibility and promotions were great, if the pressure didn't kill you. When he moved to southern Wisconsin from New Jersey to accept the position of managing a cutting edge technology plant for GF Products, he thought he was walking down the yellow brick road to prestige and riches.

He didn't realize the road was full of land mines. Steering his career and his personal life had become a wild ride. It certainly wasn't as simple as the driver's education adage of hands at ten and two.

CHAPTER 2

Two hours later, Harold Swenson shook his head in awe. He'd never really considered women inferior, but he thought there were some things men were just better at. Like mechanical things. Women didn't work on cars, fix appliances or rewire their houses.

"Mr. Swenson, where should I put this gear?"

Harold's eyes snapped up to meet the beautiful brown eyes of Miss AJ Clark. He'd been admiring her very attractive backside as she peeled off the yellow rain pants, slicker, and the rest of the protective equipment. He blushed, fearing she could read his thoughts concerning the fit of her navy slacks.

"Oh, here, I'll take that stuff, please, and I'll put it away," he stammered.

AJ smiled and handed everything over. Young, attractive, intelligent, and female, she knew she was an anomaly in the industrial world. She sought to be treated equally, but knew men treated her differently.

"Miss, you can go to the lobby while I put this away." Harold cocked his head down the hallway indicating the direction of the lobby.

Another dazzling smile. "Thanks. I'll wait for you there," responded AJ.

Harold gave a lingering look at AJ as she walked away from him. That woman could sure be a distraction. And an attraction. His face broke into a half grin, half smirk. Maybe a little industrial accident once in a while ain't such a bad thing after all. You get to meet some darn interesting people.

Entering the well-appointed reception area, AJ Clark noticed the only other visitor was a gentleman dressed in a suit sitting on a black leather couch. He was dressed a shade too well for the typical industrial salesman. Maybe he was with a government or state agency.

Or maybe he was with a non-domestic valve manufacturer. That would make him a competitor and AJ strove to know her competition. Foreign

4

manufacturers were eating into Ultra Valve's market share.

AJ casually leaned on the reception counter as Harold Swenson entered the lobby. She tried to appear nonchalant as she fiddled with the pen and the guest register on the counter.

"Miss Clark, you sure solved our actuator problems. Adding more pressure to the supply line gave us...."

AJ listened to Swenson while she scanned the guest register . During her indoctrination with Ultra, dubbed Sales 101, she became a legend for her ability to pick up information from notes on desks and bulletin boards. The joke was she could read the serial number on a dollar bill in a McDonald's as she drove by and talked on her cell phone.

A glance at the register told her the man in the lobby was probably Emile Bouhler of the Biomet Company. The spot for city had been left blank. His contact was listed as Peter Rudi. AJ returned her attention to Harold Swenson, concluding the visitor was probably not a competitor. But her curiosity was aroused and her antennae were sensing for clues.

She looked at Swenson, realizing he'd stopped talking. "So Harold, do you think the Packer's draft picks will help them this year?" As Harold began his response, the door to the corner office opened and a dark haired fit looking man in his late forties strode purposefully toward them.

"Swenson," the man called across the lobby. "Is our problem under control?" As he talked, Rudi gave AJ an appraising once over. By the look in his eyes, he liked what he saw.

"Sure, Mr. Rudi. We've got it under control, pretty much, thanks to Miss Clark here. She sure knows her stuff. She got the system shut down and prevented a lot more damage."

AJ held out her hand. "Hello Mr. Rudi. I'm AJ Clark of Ultra Valve. And really, Harold pretty much had the problems figured out. We had to shut the system down to allow for repair of the leaks. We also had to make some control signal adjustments to stabilize the operating systems."

Rudi smiled as he held AJ's hand a bit longer than necessary. "So you were the one helping our men out there today?"

"Yes, sir. You have a great maintenance crew."

"Well, we certainly appreciate the fine service. The response of you and your company during this critical situation will be duly noted."

"Thank you, sir. But I want to mention I feel this was more than an accident." AJ thought for a moment to choose the proper wording. "The manner in which the system went out of sync points to something other than random mechanical failures."

Rudi's eyes narrowed. "Are you trying to imply this catastrophe was an act of sabotage? I assure you our security is first rate and our internal controls second to none."

"I'm sure that's the case. But I feel all possibilities should be considered." As AJ spoke, she noticed Rudi stiffen as his gaze shifted to a spot behind her. She realized he had noticed the visitor in the lobby, and it had a sobering effect.

"Well," Rudi responded, now very matter of fact. "We do appreciate your efforts. Swenson, if there is anything else we need to do, carry on. Remember, the process is what counts. Now, if you'll excuse me."

Swenson mumbled a "Yes, Sir" as Rudi dismissed them both and turned to the receptionist. "Tammy, I'm going down to the record vault. Tell Mr. Bouhler I'll be with him in twenty minutes." Rudi gave a barely perceptible nod across the lobby, turned on his heels and strode through a glass doorway and out of sight.

It felt as if the air had gone out of the building, leaving the lobby in a vacuum. "Well, Harold, I guess we're finished for the day," AJ commented to break the awkward silence. "I'll fax you the parts list for the 3 inch and 4 inch control valves for your reference. Just call my office to set up a follow-up call to check on the system."

Harold stood with his arms crossed and a befuddled look on his face. He looked like a ten-year-old who'd been dropped off at camp watching his parents drive away. Rudi's abrupt exit had certainly unnerved him.

"OK, Harold," coaxed AJ. "I'll call you tomorrow, just to be sure there are no hidden surprises anywhere."

"Yeah, sure, that would be great," Harold mumbled. "Thanks again for all of your help. You really bailed us out."

"No problem. Keep the faith. I'll see you soon."

AJ gave a wave to the receptionist and turned toward the front door. She noticed Bouhler watching her with more than casual interest as she exited. The intense stare of the stranger was unsettling.

Walking to her car, AJ fought the conflicting feelings of satisfaction over a job well done and a nagging uneasiness concerning Mr. Rudi's behavior. Normally, she would be ecstatic because her coolness under fire had literally saved the day. Her system knowledge demonstrated her value to the customer and would surely lock in Ultra Valve for substantial future business.

But the usual feeling of triumph after a job well done was missing. There were too many loose ends and unexplained occurrences to suit AJ. She believed the problems at the plant were too diverse to be coincidence.

This was a new factory, so metal fatigue and normal wear and tear could not have caused the pipeline breaks. The pump, control valve, and sampling valve problems all seemed to be caused by faulty adjustments.

AJ didn't believe in bad luck or coincidence, and she didn't think the problems of GF Products were the result of either. She couldn't shake the feeling that tampering was involved in the disaster. And the reaction of Mr. Rudi to that guy in the lobby! Was that weird, or what?

AJ Clark trusted her intuition. She prided herself on her product knowledge and organizational skills, but it was her "sixth sense" that often told her when to push for an order and when to listen for market information.

Tangible results of her success were her salary increase, growing commissions, and the new Jeep Grand Cherokee she drove as a reward for being the Ultra salesperson of the year. Not bad for a young woman in a male dominated industry.

Mulling over the days' events, AJ noticed a black Mercedes CL550 as the only other car in a visitors' spot, with license plates proclaiming Georgia as the peach state. With no other guests in the lobby, AJ assumed this could be the stranger's car. It was highly unusual to see Georgia plates in Wisconsin. Someone traveling that far would typically fly, not drive. Maybe he had recently moved north and hadn't changed his plates yet.

As she slid into her red Jeep, AJ memorized the license number using her own formula. The number TC2332 became Ty Cobb/Michael Jordan/ Magic Johnson. Ty Cobb for TC, with the additional reminder that it's a Georgia plate, since Cobb was called the Georgia Peach. Jordan was number 23 and Magic was number 32. The license number was now filed away for future reference. You never know when you need to recall a fact.

CHAPTER 3

R eleasing his tether to earth, Jimmy Wickland willed himself to make it over the bar to the other side. Arching his back and throwing his arms over his head, he had a euphoric thought. *I'm gonna make it.*

Jimmy was wrong by six centimeters as gravity and poor timing conspired to defeat him. His heart sank as he fell helplessly, his body accelerating toward the landing pad. Staring skyward, he waited for the inevitable end to his fall. His last thought was about the mistakes he'd made. All he could do now was look up at the Norwegian sky and wait for the impact.

They say what doesn't kill you makes you stronger. I'm not dead, so I'll be stronger next time. This thought gave Jimmy hope as he sat alone on his small island of infield grass, apart from the groups of chattering competitors. He approached no one, and no one approached him.

Swaying slowly forward and backward, he sat cross-legged with hands resting on his ankles. His facial features were hidden by his orange hooded sweatshirt, exposing only half-closed eyes and a mouth set in a thin line.

The sun hung low in the horizon as his event drew to a close. The ebb and flow of the international track meet swirled around the stadium in Oslo, Norway, but this solitary figure appeared unaffected by the starter's guns, final lap bells, and mass adrenaline of the crowd.

In a world of product endorsements and designer sweat suits, this world-class athlete was conspicuous in his attire. The solid orange sweatshirt and matching baggy sweatpants screamed J. C. Penney. The lack of Nike, Adidas or Under Armour emblems would make him at home stretching on your local high school track, not with the elite of the track and field world.

Underneath this unassuming exterior raged the fire of a man possessed.

As he rocked back and forth, his mind played a closed loop film of his body hurtling high over the crossbar. In his mind, he never landed. He sailed over the bar into the azure sky and then took off again. Concentration wasn't required for landing, you just fell. But clearing the bar took concentration and coordination of every body part.

Picturing his vault a thousand times imprinted his technique in his brain and in every muscle of his body. The coordination of his body became automatic. It was his Vision of Success.

Sports psychologists worked with athletes on positive mental images to improve performance, so Jimmy began doing it himself with some success. Of course, he thought with a smile, it didn't hurt to have R. Kelly urging him on with "I Believe I Can Fly" through his personal stereo.

He was just about ready. As his time grew near, the tingling began in his feet and spread to his calves and thighs. He uncrossed his ankles and placed the soles of his shoes against each other, pressing his knees to the ground. Holding his feet together, he gave his back a thorough stretch by leaning forward to touch his nose to the side of his shoes. The tingling spread up his back to his neck just as he cleared the bar one more time in his mind's eye.

The tap on his back and the "Jimmy, you're up next," came at just the right time.

"Thanks," he mumbled as he peeled off his orange sweats and discarded his headphones. One straight knee bend to lay his palms flat on the ground for good luck and he was ready. Jimmy hefted his fiberglass pole and walked to the runway.

He had to clear the bar this time. He tried to block out thoughts of his last miss. But the memory of falling onto the inflatable landing pad nagged at his confidence.

CHAPTER 4

W hen Jimmy Wickland failed to clear 19'6" on his third attempt, a grayhaired gentleman in the stands smiled openly, barely concealing his excitement. His tenth row seat at the south curve of the stadium gave him a perfect vantage point to observe the approach and form of each contestant.

The gentleman made copious notes on each vaulter's physical attributes, style, form and attitude. He pinpointed the strengths and weaknesses of each competitor. His graphs of speed, strength, timing, and technique enabled him to predict the limits and progress of each of the top twenty pole vaulters in the world. For the past four years, he had been remarkably accurate in his estimates of which vaulters would improve their heights and by how much.

Except for this American. He was too short, too slow, and of average technique. He was repeatedly injured during the last few years with everything from pulled muscles to stress fractures. Yet he recovered quickly and his personal best continued to improve. Until now.

Wickland had not improved since the Millrose Games four months ago. The man chuckled with satisfaction. Vindication was its own reward. The American could not continue to climb, while his protégé would soar to the clouds.

The old man, Gregory Krug, closed his eyes and allowed himself to drift back several decades to a stadium filled to overflowing. He felt the excitement as the Reich's greatest athletes prepared to show the world the accomplishments of a unified society. The rhythmic chant of the opening ceremonies still rang in his ears!

The power was overwhelming. How could anyone or anything stand in their way? And yet, the Third Reich had been robbed of so many things.

Their goals unfulfilled, their progress dismantled, and their followers destroyed or scattered to the four corners of the earth.

But the time was at hand for absolving past failures with world record accomplishments. The high-water mark for the Reich could still be reached, and the world would take notice. In a few months the stage would be set, and he was ready. His decades of focus would result in a world record at the grandest event on the planet. The thought drove him forward with his experiments.

His research was indeed extensive. He had successfully genetically influenced the strength versus mass ratio of the major muscle groups. He acquired specialized drugs to enhance athletic performance. These improvements were coupled with his own unorthodox experiments in electrical muscle stimulation. The data from his original experiments, beginning in 1943, had enlightened him to the capacity of muscles to tolerate shock.

Thinking back bathed him in the warmth of nostalgia. Those were the days when he enjoyed total autonomy over his experimental subjects. He recalled the feeling of absolute power as he pushed his subjects past their physical limits, with death as the usual result.

Those crude, yet informative experiments laid the foundation for the lifetime of work that followed. While most people cringed at its mention, he had fond remembrances of Auschwitz. Those were his halcyon days as a member of the Third Reich.

Gregory Krug had seen great changes in his life. Europe had dominated the world of his youth. But now the world obsessed over all things American. American television, American clothing, American sports, and American movies filled the landscape like an Anglo cancer. From Coca Cola to Hershey to Nike, the world was one huge billboard for America.

Krug's name had changed more than a few times to avoid recognition. He had been Dr. Helmut Gregor, Dr. Fritz Fischer, and Pedro Stammer, among others. He had lived in Argentina, Paraguay, Brazil, and Uruguay.

But he missed all things German, and he missed the name he was unable to use for over fifty years, Dr. Josef Mengele — a name recognized the world over for inhumanity and excess, which infuriated him. He was an innovator, a brilliant scientist. Others didn't have the courage to do what he had done. Nor the courage to admit openly what they felt in their hearts.

Josef Mengele was born in 1911 to Karl and Walburga Mengele in Gunzburg, Germany. Mengele's youth was filled with colds, flu, and various childhood diseases. He spent much of his time reading or at home with his strict disciplinarian mother.

Young Josef enjoyed the study of science and had a curious mind. While not interested in team sports, he liked individual endeavors, such as mountain climbing and driving, when he was able. The individual struggle fascinated him.

Mengele grew up in a society where euthanasia was taught as a way to eliminate people who were an economic drain on the state. Nationalism ran high in the aftermath of the First World War as Germans sought to regain pride in themselves and their heritage. Aryan purity and superiority were preached in schools and from pulpits.

Clinics disposed of the physically and mentally infirm with lethal injections and poisoned food. *The Release of the Destruction of Life Unworthy of Life*, the 1920 German book authored by jurist Karl Binding and psychologist Alfred Hoche, promoted mercy killing as an acceptable way to deal with physical and social deviates. Bavarian psychiatrists viewed sterilization and euthanasia as acceptable, and German films of the day showed mercy killing in a favorable light.

Viewing other humans as less valuable than Aryans was hammered into young Mengele. Believing it was acceptable to experiment with humans gave him an absolutely remorseless attitude toward taking life. When the Nazi's came to power in Germany, Mengele reveled in the opportunity to conduct human experiments as he wished.

When Heinrich Himmler placed him in the Auschwitz concentration camp, it was as if Dr. Josef Mengele's entire life had pointed toward that moment. Mengele had the power of life and death over enemies of the Third Reich. He used that power gleefully.

Mengele particularly enjoyed meeting the trains as they arrived with cattle cars packed with Jews, Gypsies, and political undesirables. With a flick of his wrist, he sent them left to death or right to forced labor and experimentation. In the shadow of the smokestacks of the crematoriums, Josef Mengele had the giddy, unquestioned power over those who came before him.

And the twins! "Zwillinge, Zwillinge," he would shout as the trains arrived. Twins fascinated Mengele. In the camp, the Angel of Death, as the prisoners called him, found a special spot to keep his twins. He spared them from the gas chamber and made them call him Uncle.

In return, Mengele froze them, injected dye into their eyes, poisoned them, shocked them, and performed all varieties of atrocities. All in the name of science. The more than 3,000 twins passing through Auschwitz yielded notebooks full of data that SS Hauptsfuehrer Josef Mengele smuggled out of the Fatherland when he fled following the defeat of Germany. This was the foundation of his work.

And what a body of work it was. As he moved from country to country in South America, he continued to read and study. There was also the occasional human subject. But Josef Mengele constantly feared discovery by the Nazi hunters. In the 1970's, Simon Weisenthal and other Jewish avenging harpies vowed to bring the "Nazi murderers" to justice.

The German Bund in South America provided a relatively safe haven for Mengele, Martin Bormann, and other high visibility Nazi war criminals. But the pressure of hiding became unbearable. The Israeli Mossad, the CIA, the international press, and the independent researchers made even the remote jungles of South America unsafe.

So Mengele had to die. ODESSA, the Nazi organization that bankrolled his and other escapes, helped arrange his demise. A Mengele cousin was found with approximately the same build as Josef. Dental work was altered, officials bribed, and a stroke suffered in 1979 while swimming took the life of the most notorious Nazi still at large. DNA reports confirmed it, and the world press rehashed the crimes of the sixty-eight year old "Angel of Death".

Soon Dr. Josef Mengele was forgotten. Old news. Relegated to the scrap heap of once huge stories — the Kennedy assassination, Elvis sightings, and the breakup of the Beatles. As years passed, a new generation couldn't remember Vietnam, let alone the Second World War. The existence of Nazis seemed as ancient to them as the Civil War seemed to their parents. No one looked back. Everyone looked forward toward technology and profits.

Absolutely no one was looking for a dead war criminal in the Caribbean Islands. One of the Windward Islands in the Lesser Antilles, St. Lucia, proved to be the perfect spot for Gregory Krug.

With support from the ill gotten gains of ODESSA, citizen Krug set up a very private and very complete research laboratory at the south end of the island. During the next twenty-five years the Doctor made a number of amazing discoveries.

CHAPTER 5

Jimmy Wickland was mad. Not depressed, not frustrated. Just mad. He slammed his pole down and tore off his wrist wraps. He'd hit the bar going up. If you knock the bar off, it doesn't matter how high you vault. Third place wasn't so bad. But that would not get him to his goal. He plopped down on the grass next to his bag and loosened his shoes.

A few other vaulters and high jumpers came by to commiserate. "Too bad, Dude." "Tough break, man." "You'll get it next time." Hand slaps and knuckle raps were the athletes' way of hugging to support one another.

Jimmy took it all in the spirit in which it was given. He began to cool down, and he knew he would need to analyze his performance. First he had to update his bag.

Grabbing the oversized orange bag with University of Tennessee emblazoned on the side, Jimmy gripped the tape on the side of the bag that said 'OSLO' in black block letters. With a tug, he ripped the tape from the bag, exposing 'FRANKFORT' on the tape beneath.

Six months ago, he listed all the competitions he would enter. The tape a few layers down said 'CHICAGO', site of the Olympics. It was the return of the Olympic Games to the United States, and Jimmy Wickland planned to attend the party.

"Jimmy, old boy. You better kick it in gear if you expect to go to Chi Town to represent the good old U. S. of A." Talking to himself was something he accepted. Grams told him it was okay. She always said, "Who knows more about you than you? So why not talk to the one who knows you best?" Besides, when he was on the road at the meets, Jimmy needed to hear a familiar voice.

Grams encouraged him to set his goals high when he was growing up. She read him stories about Billy Mills, the runner from the University of

Kansas. Mills had overcome many obstacles on his way to an Olympic gold medal. As a Native American Indian, Mills had to overcome prejudice, as well as the rigors of distance running.

Born in South Dakota and orphaned at the age of twelve, the seven-sixteenths Oglala Sioux took up track while attending the Haskell Institute, a Native American boarding school in Lawrence, Kansas. Mills' philosophy of life was based on an adage which Grams wrote on an index card and posted on young Jimmy's wall when he was still in grade school.

Your life is a gift to you from God.
What you do with your life is your gift back to God.
Choose your gifts wisely.

That note was still there. Grams told Jimmy that Billy Mills wrote down his goals. Mills had written down his greatest personal goal: "Gold medal, 10,000 meter run", and had lived every day working toward that goal. He visualized the details of the race and pushed himself, mentally and physically, to succeed. In 1964 he reached his goal in Tokyo, becoming the only American ever to win the gold medal in the Olympic 10,000 meters.

Motivated by Mills' story, Jimmy listed his goals, also. Setbacks were cause to evaluate and work to improve. All these thoughts passed through his mind as he began unlacing his shoes. He had time to think, as he changed shoes and put on his sweat suit.

Reaching into his bag, Jimmy pulled out his plastic squeeze bottle. Rubbing his sore left quadriceps with his left hand, he gave the bottle a vigorous shake with his right before tilting his head back and taking a long swallow.

He welcomed the bittersweet taste of the green liquid. This was Grams' special mixture. Jimmy knew he performed better when he loaded up on Grams' "plant juice". He was running low and watered it down to make it last through this trip. He'd be glad to get back to Tennessee to Grams' home cooking and to replenish his supply.

Slipping his headset on, Jimmy cranked up the volume and massaged his leg. He would forget the bad performance and concentrate on the future.

CHAPTER 6

As AJ pulled onto Interstate 90 toward Madison, she thought, all in all, it had been quite a day. She used her training to avert an industrial disaster and surely made a customer for life. Dad would be proud.

He would also be proud of her company car. Most salespeople drove sedans or mini-vans. But AJ negotiated the Jeep after her record sales performance the previous year. She had insisted it be a Jeep. Dad had believed there were only three acceptable vehicle brands — Jeep, Ford and John Deere. They were original American companies worthy of loyalty.

With a forty-five minute drive ahead of her, AJ indulged herself by following up a hunch. She hit the speed-dial for her office on her cell phone and put her Bluetooth on her right ear.

After two rings she heard, "Ultra Valve, for the Ultimate Valve solutions. How may I direct your call?"

"Hi Barb. Phones busy today?"

"AJ, how's it going? I've sent lots of people to your voice mail. I told them all you were on a big trouble shooting call and you might not be able to check your messages until late today."

AJ checked the time on the Jeep's digital clock, which registered 4:11. "Thanks, Barb. I'll check my messages in a minute. But I need to speak to John Cline, please."

"Can do. Now you be careful on the drive home. There are lots of crazy drivers out there."

As the receptionist and unofficial office mom, Barbara Rutledge took it upon herself to remind outside salespersons to drive carefully when they called in. She told smokers not to smoke, gave unsolicited fashion advice, and admonished those who didn't keep their work areas neat and tidy. Her mothering was tolerated because she made brownies for every office birthday and her heart was in the right place. AJ listened to the company propaganda recording while on hold.

"John Cline. May I help you?"

It was rumored within the company that John was older than dirt and twice as dry. In truth, he was just in his late fifties. But his many years of experience and his claim that he had forgotten more about valves than any of the bunch of "young whippersnappers" would ever know gave him an air of Methuselah. He seemed to revel in the role of the old curmudgeon. He was a valuable asset as the inside sales manager and a throwback to the days when employees stayed with one company for their entire careers.

"Hey, Valve God. How's the desk jockey today?"

The joy was evident in Cline's voice as he responded. "Well, AJ! What did they do, close the golf courses today, so you thought you better call in?"

"No," replied AJ. "Actually, I was at the pool all day, and I've got to get home to wash the chlorine out of my hair."

John gave one of his deep laughs. "And I'm stuck here in the office. Busier than a one legged man in a butt kicking contest."

John Cline was also the self proclaimed King of Clichés, the Prince of Puns. Some of the salesmen dissed him behind his back, but AJ thought it was cute, and it made conversations with John interesting.

"I know, life's tough all over. Hey, I need a favor. Can you help me?"

"Fire away. Your wish is my command."

"Ever hear of a company called Biomet? I don't know what they do or where they're located. I ran across a guy from Biomet at GF Products today and I want to be sure he's not a competitor."

John thought for a moment. "You know, it sounds vaguely familiar. Let me check the Thomas Register. I'm sending you to the land of hold for a minute."

AJ listened to Ultra's continuous loop recording detailing the company products and services. John Cline searched the Thomas Register Internet site for AJ's information while he fielded another phone call. The Thomas Register had an encyclopedia type listing of all industrial manufacturers cross-referenced by company name and products.

After dispatching the other call, Cline returned to AJ. "I'm back with the goods. There are only two listings for Biomet. A bunch of listings with names that are close, but just two exact listings. One is Biomet Incorporated, a maker of biological testing equipment out of Phoenix. The other is Biomet Products and Services, a manufacturer and distributor of animal feed supplements out of Des Moines. They don't exactly sound like valve companies."

"Probably not, John. But can I have their phone numbers anyway?"

"Of course, Super Saleswoman. Y'all can write and drive?"

"In my sleep." AJ jotted down the phone numbers as her Jeep continued toward Madison. She was glad both Biomet companies were in time zones she could call now. She wanted to satisfy her curiosity.

"Thanks, Valve Guru. You're the Man."

"Don't mention it, kiddo. Now, some of us have to get back to work. My call light is lit, and it may be one of your customers looking for the RIGHT answer for a change."

AJ couldn't resist smiling. John actually made work fun. "OK, John. Bring home another order."

After pushing END to disconnect, AJ dialed the number for Biomet in Des Moines. She learned they were an up and coming force in animal feed supplements, had six branch offices, but they did not have, nor did they ever have, an employee named Emile Bouhler. So much for that Biomet.

The second Biomet took two calls with the same result. Phoenix referred her to its Chicago office. There was no Mr. Bouhler in their records, and no, they did not have an office or a representative in Georgia.

After the last phone call, AJ reflected on what she had learned. She knew she had read the name correctly as Biomet. Maybe it was a division of someone else, or a subsidiary. But her intuition and the Thomas Register told her something was fishy. Mr. Rudi's reaction to the visitor was too strange to be ignored. There was more to Biomet that met the eye.

Checking the mile marker, AJ realized she was only fifteen minutes from home. She looked forward to this evening so she could get to the health club and work out. Long workdays and hours spent in the car took their toll. A workout would be invigorating, both physically and mentally, and get her started on the weekend. Biomet and Bouhler could wait for another day.

CHAPTER 7

S weat rolled down his forehead and into his eyes. Kirk wiped it away with the back of his hand and looked at the screen. He was staying at 82 RPM's and had only three minutes to go on the Lifecycle. He continued to pump his legs at an even pace.

"You are the sunshine of my life, and I will always thi...ink of you," crooned Philippe as he rode next to Kirk. "You are the apple of my eye, and I want you to go home with me...ee!"

"Hey, Philippe," Kirk gulped for air as he rode. "Did anybody ever mention you sound like a prison singer?"

Philippe smiled in anticipation. "No, Kirk. Pray tell, what does a prison singer sound like?"

Kirk waited for a two count then answered. "You're always behind a few bars and you can't find the right key."

Philippe pedaled furiously and replied, "Yuck, yuck. You're a regular Chris Rock. Maybe we'll get you a TV show."

Both men continued pedaling as they looked around the health club. The after work crowd was filtering in to fill up the bikes, treadmills, weight machines, and aerobics classes. The stationary bikes gave a perfect view of the entire club, as well as a view of Lake Monona through the picture windows on their right.

"Whoa, check it out," Philippe said in a stage whisper. "Blond Rackasaurous at nine o'clock."

Kirk looked to the left where Philippe indicated and saw a very well endowed woman walking toward the Nautilus equipment. Her fully expanded red sports bra and skintight black spandex shorts left little to the imagination. Her walk was calculatingly casual as she looked from side to side to see who was checking her out.

"No way, Philippe. Too much 'tude. She thinks she's all that and a Happy Meal. Plus, I have a sneaking suspicion her conspicuous assets are store-bought."

Philippe made a snorting sound and replied, "Oh, so now you're Mr. conservative, real deal, looking for Ms. Goodbar. I think you've got Long and Lean on the brain, man. You don't even like to TALK about chicks anymore. You take the fun out of the meat market."

The Long and Lean Philippe referred to was the young woman they nicknamed after seeing her at the club. Kirk had fixated on her for weeks after he first laid eyes on her at Madison's Scandinavian Health Club.

In Kirk's eyes, she was the most beautiful woman on earth. And she didn't act like she knew it! She was five foot ten, light brown, shoulder length hair, a catlike body, and a beautiful face.

"OK, Casanova," instructed Philippe. "Forget what I want to see. Long and Lean is in the house. Let's see if you can keep it in your pants today."

Kirk looked across the club and saw the object of his affection. She and another young woman were striding from the Number Two aerobics room to the free weight area. The two women were engaged in animated conversation. Then, Long and Lean took off her baseball cap and ran her fingers through her hair, glancing toward Kirk. Her perfect teeth, full lips, high cheekbones and sparkling brown eyes made Kirk's heart jump.

Thud! Kirk's right foot slipped off the pedal and banged into the side of the Lifecycle. He grunted loudly as he struggled to keep his balance and fought to regain a cycling rhythm. There were stares and a few snickers from the treadmills and bikes.

Philippe chuckled. "Oh, that was a smooth move, Kirk. I bet Long and Lean wants to dance with the guy that almost fell off the stationary bike."

Kirk's face was cherry red as he looked down and pedaled. The beep of his bike told him his program had ended. He punched in six additional minutes and cranked up to 90 RPM. He looked up to see Long and Lean with her cap back on, positioning herself to bench press as her workout partner prepared to spot for her.

Philippe swung off his bike. "Look, man, I've got to split. But you've got to talk to her. Cuz, you got it bad. And I don't want you to hurt yourself."

Kirk nodded and gave a wry smile. "Maybe today's the day. Anyway, have a good weekend."

"You too, dude. Later."

Kirk looked at the bike's monitor and realized he had five minutes to formulate a plan to approach Long and Lean. He could do that. He had certainly taken on tougher assignments.

CHAPTER 8

A J loved to exercise. A good workout made her feel physically and mentally alive. As she did flys facing the mirror, she could feel the burn in her deltoids and forearms. She knew she looked good in her red UW hat, red gym shorts and gray UW cropped t-shirt. In the mirror, she could see the tall guy approaching who had been watching her for days.

"Hey, Sarah, here he comes," whispered AJ to her workout partner.

As she bent to pick up the 15-pound dumbbells, Sarah replied. "Well I hope so. You two have been eyeing each other forever."

"Hi ladies," chimed Kirk. "How's the workout going?" Kirk hoped he sounded casual and cool.

"Not bad," responded Sarah. "For a Friday, we're hitting it pretty hard."

Kirk was trying not to stare at AJ, but he wasn't having much success. "So, did you go to UW?"

AJ rolled her head from side to side stretching her neck and replied, "Yes, I was a Badger. How about you?'

Kirk was excited they were conversing. "I went to Pepperdine in Malibu, California. I've only been in the Midwest a few years. My name's Kirk Vail, like the ski resort in Colorado."

Smiling, AJ responded. "I'm AJ Clark, same as the candy bar in your exclusive grocery stores."

That got a laugh out of Kirk. As the two made small talk, Sarah winked at AJ from behind Kirk. She gave her the thumbs up sign as she made an exaggeration of checking out Kirk's derriere and the back of his legs.

"So," said Kirk, working up the courage for the big question. "How about having dinner or coffee or something tomorrow. You pick the spot."

AJ had been waiting for him to get to the point. She gave him one of her million dollar smiles. "Sure. That would be nice."

"Well great!" Kirk paused as he tried to contain his excitement. "Hey, I also wanted to ask you if you do any sports. You look like an athlete. I played some volleyball in college. How about you?"

AJ rummaged through her duffle bag for her water bottle. "I played basketball in college and loved it. But while I was growing up, I tried everything. Dad had me in tennis, swimming, soccer, volleyball, ballet, gymnastics, softball, track and racquetball. Shoot, he even had me in hockey and tae kwon do."

"Wow, your old man sounds like one pushy SOB," said Kirk. "How did you ever put up with him?"

Like a cold front crashing down from Canada, the atmosphere between them turned icy. Without a word, AJ spun around, snatched her bag from the floor and began speed walking away.

Kirk looked at Sarah, who could only shrug. Trotting after AJ, Kirk called out. "Wait, please wait."

AJ reached the stairway leading down to the main level when Kirk caught up. "Please wait," he said again.

With one hand on the railing, AJ stopped and looked back over her shoulder at Kirk. A single tear slowly rolled down her cheek, curved along her jaw and seemed to suspend on the edge of her chin. Gravity finally broke it free and Kirk watched the water droplet fall in seemingly slow motion. Looking back into AJ's eyes, he saw physical pain.

"Don't you ever say anything about my father, do you hear me?" she whispered. "You didn't even know him." AJ blinked to hold back the tears. She quick stepped down the stairs with Kirk right behind.

"I'm sorry, I'm sorry, I'm sorry," whispered Kirk as he followed her, hoping not to attract the attention of the two attendants working the check-in counter.

Head down, AJ plowed ahead to the exit. Only a group of chattering twenty-somethings blocking the door caused her to stop.

Kirk stepped to her right and leaned down in an attempt to make eye contact. "Whatever I said, I take it back a thousand times. If I hurt your feelings, I didn't mean to."

AJ placed her hand on the visor of her cap to shield her eyes from view as Kirk issued his whispered plea. The doorway was now clear but AJ remained frozen.

Kirk held his arms toward her with his palms up, a beseeching look on his face. "You said we could get together tomorrow. We can talk then and straighten this out. Please. I'll meet you anyplace, anytime."

Kirk held his breath as AJ still refused to look in his direction. The world stood still as he waited for her response.

She began to speak as Kirk strained to hear. "Tomorrow's okay. Listen carefully." Rapid-fire instructions followed. "Pele AM at Wilt Butkus Greeley First President." She paused. "Hope you can make it." With that, AJ darted through the door and was gone into the night.

CHAPTER 9

K irk stared at the door, trying to figure out what had just happened. What was she talking about and where had he gone so terribly wrong?

A tap on his shoulder brought Kirk back to reality. "All right, big boy. Never fear, help is here." Kirk turned to look into the eyes of AJ's friend, Sarah.

Kirk exhaled. "I feel like I've been hit by a train. What was that all about?"

Sarah took Kirk by the arm and steered him away from the exit. "AJ's cool. She has her own secret lingo and it takes time to understand."

Kirk shook his head. "I'm totally lost. Why did she get so mad and what was she talking about before she left?"

Sarah looked up at Kirk and attempted to fill in the blanks. "AJ is my friend and a great person. But she is emotionally on edge. Her father died a few months ago. They were real close, so when you made that crack about her old man, she flipped. You're lucky she talked at all on the way out."

Kirk scratched his head and looked at Sarah. "I'm sure sorry about her dad, but what was that gibberish when she left?"

"That was Clarkspeak. She has her own shortcut language. She cut you some slack and is giving you a chance to meet her tomorrow. But you have to figure out where and when. So, do you remember what she said?"

Kirk thought a minute. "I'm pretty sure I remember it." He recited what he thought he had heard.

"Here's how it works," interpreted Sarah. "Pele AM. You know who Pele is, right?"

"Well, duh," answered Kirk. "He was like the greatest soccer player ever."

"Good man. So, what was his number?"

Now Kirk looked confused. "His number? Like his ranking or something?"

"No, Einstein. What number did he wear on his jersey? Do you know?"

Kirk admitted he didn't.

Sarah continued his education. "For starters, Pele wore number 10. So Pele AM, means ten in the morning. Wilt Butkus Greeley First President, means Wilt Chamberlain, Dick Butkus, Horace Greeley and the first president was George Washington. Get it?"

Kirk thought he was catching on. "Sure, Wilt wore number 13, I think Butkus was number 50, but Horace Greeley?"

"Right with Wilt. Wrong with Butkus. He was number 51 with the Bears. And Horace Greeley had that famous quote, 'Go West, young man'. So you need to be at 1351 West Washington Street tomorrow at ten AM. Make sense?"

Kirk's face split into a smile. "That is so cool. So there must be a restaurant or something at that address?"

Sarah shrugged. "With AJ, you never know. But now you know a little Clarkspeak, which is more that most guys know with her. From here on, you're on your own." Sarah gave Kirk a serious look. "AJ's a good friend, so play nice."

Kirk nodded and thanked Sarah for her help. His mind was racing as he left the health club. Long and Lean was one intriguing lady.

CHAPTER 10

The next morning, the quiet of the bedroom was broken by a soft click. Two stereo speakers jumped to life, emitting cheers and claps of a huge crowd. As the throng cheered, the inert form on the bed began to stir. A long arm reached to the floor and groped from side to side until the hand closed upon the object it sought.

Meanwhile, the crowd noise gave way to an announcer speaking in dramatic tones. "It's the Colts' ball, fourth and ten on their own forty yard line with only seconds on the clock. Manning takes the snap from the shotgun and looks downfield. He has two receivers going long, but here comes the rush! Manning pump fakes once, sidesteps one tackler and lets it go long!"

Kirk sat up in bed and pump faked with Peyton Manning, and then fired a perfect spiral with the nerf football. The flight path carried the ball through the bedroom door, down the hall and through the florescent orange bicycle tire hanging from the ceiling. As the football passed through the center of the suspended tire, an electronic sensor started the next recording.

"Touchdown! Harrison caught the ball in the end zone after streaking behind the strong safety. Touchdown for the Colts! What an unbelievable pass." The crowd went wild, filling the room with cheers. Kirk knew he had exactly forty-five seconds before the tape changed.

He rolled out of bed and strode down the hall, ducking to avoid the tire. Yanking open the refrigerator, he pushed the cold pizza aside to get at the orange juice. As he drank from the quart container, the cheering ended and a new voice was heard.

"The Cavaliers trail by three with under a minute to play. LeBron looks inside from the top of the key. He cradles the ball in his right hand, rocker steps, dribbles right, stutter steps and goes up for an eighteen footer."

As the announcer spoke, Kirk reached on top of the kitchen cupboards and grabbed one of his mini basketballs. Holding the juice carton in his left hand, he dribbled twice and moved into the living room.

"LeBron James rises above the defender and releases the shot..."

Kirk flipped a one handed jump shot at the basket mounted on the far wall. The shot was long, hitting the back of the rim and bouncing off. "Brick!" grunted Kirk.

He tossed the empty juice container over his left shoulder, banking it into the wastebasket in the corner. The satisfaction of sinking the shot far outweighed the slight problem of OJ spattered on the kitchen drywall. Kirk grabbed another ball from the top of the living room lampshade — an excellent storage place — and pivoted to face the basket.

"James gets his own rebound, squares up from fifteen feet out, the shot is up..."

Kirk flicked his wrist and watched the multicolored ball rotate with perfect backspin as it swished through the net. Another electric eye recorded the successful shot.

"And it's good! The Cavs pull within one. The Spurs inbound the ball and look to advance up court."

Kirk flipped a ball up off the floor with his toes, grabbed it in midair and fired a behind-the-back pass toward the wall.

"LeBron knifes in and steals the ball! He drives hard for the hoop as the clock ticks down."

Kirk's left hand swallowed the ball as it came back toward him after banking off of the wall. With one hard dribble, he leaped the coffee table and did his best impression of a three-step NBA drive to the hoop.

"Soaring, LeBron double clutches and comes in for the reverse..."

Kirk stretched to his full six foot seven inches and extended his arm far above his head as he hammered the ball home.

"Dunk!" The sound of pandemonium filled the room. Shouts and whistles filled the air. "The Cleveland Cavaliers win by one with LeBron James scoring forty-five points." Ten seconds of cheering followed, after which the big screen TV came to life with Sports Center on ESPN.

Listening to a recap of scores, Kirk filled a mixing bowl with cereal, sliced bananas, and milk. Returning to the living room, he paused in front of the full-length mirror to admire himself. Resplendent in checkered blue and white boxer shorts, Kirk felt he had the perfect body. Others might disagree.

His shoulders were a bit on the narrow side, his arms quite long and his chest of average proportions. Nothing here to inspire comparisons to Rambo or Arnold. Kirk's muscle tone was in his long tanned legs. He had well defined thighs and bulging calves. His foundation was a pair of feet his friends described as snowshoes or skis. Kirk didn't think size sixteen feet were that big a deal, and there was nothing he could do to change them anyway.

Kirk never worried too much about what other people thought. His personal attitude was summed up as he looked in the mirror and made his usual proclamation. "Kirk, you BAD!"

CHAPTER 11

K irk Vail had the best job in America. In fact, he had the two best jobs in America. He often wondered how he had gotten so lucky. Most people work long and hard their entire lives and don't land that job of jobs. They never experience the career they hope and pray for. But Kirk, not long out of college, had the perfect vocation.

He had never heard of the Green Star Sports Equipment Company until they contacted him his senior year in college. But they had impressed him with their personnel and their "game plan". They were launching a campaign to promote their Green Star athletic shoe line worldwide.

The new employees would get in on the ground floor of an exciting new venture. Their slogan, "Shoes of the Stars", would be backed with plenty of green, both for product promotion and for the employees.

In fact, that's where the name came from. The company founders had brainstormed possible names during a corporate strategy meeting. One member suggested Super Flyer Shoes, which the group thought juvenile and a blatant rip-off of the old PF Flyers. Another suggested Blue Ball Jets. You know, like Red Ball Jets, only these are for guys who can't get a date. Well, that cracked everybody up, but it didn't get the group any closer to a name.

A visually strong name was needed that was simple and meaningful. One founder noted that stars were popular in logos. Everyone that laces up a pair of sneakers, whether four or forty, wants to be a star. We'll bill our product as "Shoes for the Stars". Good idea, they all said. A star will be a good visual for the logo and letterheads.

But what color stars? Silver was too Dallas Cowboy, and gold didn't show up well on the product. Someone suggested using a red star. The senior member of the group removed the enormous cigar from his mouth, exhaled a cloud of smoke, and in a gravely serious voice said, "The Red Star stands for the Soviet Union. Gentlemen, no matter what the state of that country or countries, we will NOT be using the red star for anything!"

The ensuing silence lasted over three minutes as the chastised members examined their fingernails, looked thoughtful, and avoided eye contact. The senior member, known as the General, broke the awkward silence with a puff of smoke and a single word. "Green."

The members waited expectantly, relieved the silence was broken. A rare smile crossed the General's lips. "Green Star. Yup, I like it. Shoes of the stars, with lots of green cash. The corporation has the money to put into this project. And who knows? If we handle it properly, this venture could be a cash cow while we meet our primary goals."

When the General stood, the other members rose immediately. With a cloud of smoke, the assignment was issued.

"Green Star it is. Flesh it out, fluff it up. I want a market strategy, procedures to interface with other operations, and a prospective employee profile developed so we can begin an internal and external talent search. The works, on my desk by fifteen hundred hours tomorrow. Gentlemen, get to work."

After exiting the meeting room, the General allowed himself a slight grin as he marched down the corridor. He liked the name, he liked the logo, and he especially liked the project concept. Plus, tonight he could tell Edna, his wife of twenty-seven years, that he had chosen green to match her eyes. He could make big points, and it wasn't even Saturday night!

Now, if the snotnoses back there just do their jobs, he'd have a program with some zest to it. He was warming to the prospect of running this operation. His earlier doubts were melting away, replaced by an excitement he hadn't felt in years. He might have to head home early to give Edna the good news.

Back in meeting room D, the five remaining members, four young men and a woman, sat looking at each other. One cursed and exclaimed loudly, "Twenty-four hours! He wants a complete plan in twenty-four hours. Who does he think he is?"

"Why, he's Da Man," responded the Blue Ball proponent. "And I, for one, don't intend to disappoint Da Man."

"Agreed," said the Red Star suggestee. "I'm just glad we're over the creative hump."

The female member attempted to get the group back on task. "OK, guys. To accomplish this we need two groups. One to develop the strategy and the other to set up the interface procedures. Then we can all get together to design an employee qualification profile."

As her co-founders agreed and began deciding who should work with whom, she couldn't help but reflect on her position. *How can the General refer to us as "Gentlemen" so blatantly? And that cigar smoke! My hair and clothes are going to reek. When I'm in his position, there will definitely be no smoking in the entire building.*

CHAPTER 12

Kirk switched from ESPN to CNN as he finished his breakfast. He was so excited he couldn't sit still. He was having brunch with an angel at 10 o'clock today!

Thank goodness AJ's friend, Sarah, had deciphered Clarkspeak for him or he wouldn't have a clue what she had said. With two great jobs, all he was missing was a lovely lady in his life.

The Green Star gig was going great. Kirk got to travel on his expense account to ballgames, hang out with athletes, coaches, and team owners, and he got all of the free athletic gear he wanted. And the other job was so cool! Every kid wants to be a James Bond, and Kirk was no exception. Doing something mysterious and sometimes dangerous sure kept the adrenaline flowing. The beep from his pager brought him back to reality. Job Two was calling. He needed to check in and file this week's report, but first, brunch with AJ.

Finding her was proving to be a challenge. Kirk had driven up and down West Washington Street three times with mounting frustration. There was no 1351 address. It was an odd numbered address, so it should be on the south side of the street.

There was an Amoco service station which said 1185 on a corner, the next block was residential with house numbers from 1211 to 1275, and what had to be the thirteen hundred block was all taken up by the LaFollette Middle School.

The school had a huge sign, but no address posted. Where was the restaurant? Maybe Sarah had steered him wrong, or maybe he had heard something wrong.

Out of desperation, Kirk pulled into the school parking lot, which had quite a few cars in it for a Saturday. As he entered the building, he heard noise down the hallway. The double doors to the gym were propped open, so he stepped in to check things out. A crowd of parents and siblings sat in the bleachers on one side of the gym watching young girls play basketball.

Kirk scanned the crowd, and then glanced at the team benches across the way. Standing at the red team's bench was AJ Clark, hands on hips, shouting encouragement.

In five seconds, Kirk took in all of the details. Sparkling white Nike low-cut basketball shoes with red accents, white socks with red Nike logo, and form-fitting red sweatpants with two white stripes and a swoosh on the side. A white short sleeve three-button shirt with UW Badgers embroidered in red on the left breast, hair in a ponytail held with a red and white ribbon, and the face of a goddess smiling and calling out to her team.

Kirk stared as he soaked up every detail concerning the way AJ looked and moved. He memorized the curves and contours of her body and face, her sights and sounds and colors. A timeout was called and her team circled around her, their heads coming to AJ's shoulders.

The looks in the girls' eyes as they listened to their assignments were pure awe, and maybe even love. Then, hands held together, they shouted, "Go Red!" and the team headed back to the court.

Kirk watched the players walk to the far end of the court, and glanced back at AJ just in time to see a ball hurtling his way. He caught the basketball chest high after one bounce.

"Nice catch. I see you found us," teased AJ.

"No problem, great directions," responded Kirk.

AJ pointed to the bench next to her. "If you know a jump ball from a double dribble, I need an assistant coach today."

Kirk palmed the ball and held it straight out. "I'm your man!" As he walked around the court to meet AJ, he had two thoughts. *How can anyone so beautiful be so dang cool? And I hope my heart stops pounding so fast. I feel like I'm going to explode.*

CHAPTER 13

A J and Kirk rehashed the game over lunch at the Einstein Bagel Shop.
Munching on her veggie bagel with veggie spread, AJ expounded on
the advantages of changing defenses to keep the opposition off balance.
Kirk was thrilled to share in the afterglow of the victory.

"Those girls play hard," Kirk observed. "I think they would run through
a brick wall for you."

AJ smiled. "They're a nice bunch. They play to win."

"You make it sound like it's the girls, but it's your effort that makes the
team a success. You're too modest."

AJ finished her apple juice before responding "Dad always said, 'Plan
your work and work your plan'. I guess it rubbed off on me. I work hard
because I want them prepared for our games."

Kirk looked into her eyes. "I bet you work hard at everything, judging
by how you work out and by how you work with your team. So tell me,
what does AJ Clark do with the rest of her time?"

AJ found Kirk easy to talk to. She told him about her job, with its
challenges and variety. About college and her degree in Business
Administration from the University of Wisconsin. About accepting a sales
job with Ultra Valve Incorporated and about being trained in Houston for
three months. She described in detail the catastrophe she helped avert last
week at the GF Products plant outside of Beloit.

Realizing she was rambling, AJ stopped in mid-sentence. "Enough about
my job, what about yours?"

Kirk gave a quick laugh. "Not as exciting as yours. No factory disasters.
I work for Green Star Athletics. I cover the Midwest and deal with sporting
goods stores, colleges, and pro teams. Decent pay, decent fringe benefits,
and great perks. Maybe if you play your cards right, I can get you out of

your Nike clothes and into Green Star gear."

AJ saw the twinkle in his hazel eyes as Kirk talked about getting her out of her clothes! She was amused, not offended.

"Well," she countered, "that would depend on what Green Star has to offer. But I think that is a conversation for another day. Time for me to head home."

As they gathered up their trash, AJ let out an exclamation. "I hate that!"

Startled, Kirk looked around quickly to see what had happened. "What's wrong?"

Pointing to the television in the corner, AJ countered. "Look at that! Isn't that disgusting?"

Kirk was confused. There was a basketball game on TV. There was nothing on or around the television that Kirk viewed as disgusting. "AJ, what's wrong? I don't see anything."

AJ stuffed her trash into the receptacle and nodded toward the television. "The uniform colors, Kirk. Look at that. Minnesota is playing IU, and the Gophers have on YELLOW uniforms! They're the home team, and the Home Team Wears White! It's Rule Number One. But, noooo. Teams now wear yellow, gray, tan, and other unbelievably inappropriate colors."

Kirk saw the serious look in AJ's eyes. He wasn't sure if this was comical or a sign of some tragically misplaced passion. "While I agree the yellow jerseys look ugly, what's the big deal? And what rule number one are you talking about?"

"Dad's Rule Number One. Home team wears white. It represents honoring tradition and history. Consistency and trust. Doing the right thing and values we can rely on." AJ's staccato response felt like a lecture.

CHAPTER 14

K irk felt the Dad thing coming on again, just as it had at the health club. He wasn't sure he wanted to go there after what happened last time.

AJ noticed people were staring at them now. She also realized she was probably over the top when it came to memories of Dad. She needed to check her mouth at the door next time. And heed some of Dad's other advice: "Engage brain before engaging tongue."

"Sorry. I got carried away," she said sheepishly. "Let's get outta here."

As they walked to their cars, Kirk decided AJ was even prettier when her face was flushed.

When they had crossed the parking lot, AJ appeared to have her emotions under control and Kirk felt it safe to talk. "Ms. Clark, thank you for the basketball lesson and for joining me for lunch."

They turned to face each other next to AJ's Jeep. AJ extended her hand to Kirk. "Thanks for lunch. I'm glad you found the school. I think my team likes you."

"Well, I hope the coach feels the same way. How about doing something tonight?" Kirk was involuntarily holding his breath awaiting a response.

"Oh, I can't. I've got plans. But I'd like to another time."

Kirk had prepared for this. He had written it on an index card, which he memorized in the Einstein Bagel restroom before they left. He forged ahead and hoped for the best.

"How about tomorrow? It's Sunday and I've got a plan. Meet me at Red Grange Eric Montross Glendale Street. Time to meet is Joe DiMaggio Winston Churchill. I'll supply a meal, so come hungry." Kirk had a grin on his face like a first grader with his first report card.

"Not bad." AJ couldn't help but like his smile and his effort. She cocked her head to one side and gave him her *you're making some progress, but you aren't home free yet* look.

"Well, have you figured it out?"

"Sure. Grange was 77, the Galloping Ghost at Illinois. Montross was a hoopster, wore double zero. So it's 7700 Glendale Street. DiMaggio, the Yankee Clipper, was number 5. And Churchill lived at Number 10 Downing Street in London. So we're meeting at 5:10?"

"Well, close, but not exactly. I was going for P.M. with Churchill, since he was the Prime Minister. The time is 5 PM." Kirk was disappointed AJ had known everything so quickly. He was hoping to stump her.

However, her wide smile and hand shake told him he had done well. "Congratulations, that's really good! I mean it. I like it a lot. You could have thrown in, Astronaut John... and Over Hill, Over... to go for Glendale. But you did your research. I'm impressed. I'll be there tomorrow."

Kirk was still holding AJ's hand. It was strong, yet soft. Warm and comfortable. He self-consciously let go of her, and met her gaze. "I look forward to it," he said in a low voice.

After their goodbyes, AJ reviewed the day as she drove to her apartment. Kirk Vail was an interesting guy. And her team thought he was cute. She smiled to herself as she made the last turn home.

CHAPTER 15

H e waited patiently this time. He sat still in the dark with no real sense of time. But he knew she was close. He could almost smell her.

Footsteps in the hall preceded the rattling of a key in the lock. His pulse quickened as he crawled toward the hall from the bedroom. He didn't want to alert her to his presence. She would hang her coat on the hall tree stand and go to the kitchen. That would be his opportunity to attack from behind.

AJ hummed softly as she entered her apartment and draped her red and white jacket on the hall tree stand. She dropped her playbook on the seat and went into the kitchen.

He crept down the hall, pausing to listen. The refrigerator door opened, followed by the distinctive sound of glass pitchers bumping aluminum cans as AJ searched for something cold to drink. He had reached the kitchen doorway and snuck a quick look. She had her back to the doorway!

He bent his legs, poised to spring. This was it.

AJ turned and faced the doorway and crouched low. She had caught sight of reflected movement in the glass door of the oven. She held her arms forward with her hands turned up in a defensive stance.

He came around the doorway and leaped! AJ caught him in midair and fell backwards, holding him to her chest. He wiggled and then began licking her face.

"Freethrow!" AJ squealed. "How's my baby? You thought you could surprise me, huh?"

The attacker was perfectly content to continue licking AJ's chin, cheeks, nose, and eyebrows. Freethrow was a 14-pound Bichon Frise, a dog who believed the sun rose and set on AJ Clark. He was a shaggy white bundle of love with uncommon intelligence. He and AJ played the attack game when she came home, and it tickled her that Freethrow actually seemed to understand.

After a few minutes of wrestling, AJ stood up. "Quiz time."

Freethrow faced his master expectantly. AJ's father had trained the dog to respond to various commands, and AJ continued the training. One of the fun tasks was asking Freethrow if basketball players were good free throw shooters.

"How is Reggie Miller on free throws?"

Freethrow stood on his hind legs and held both paws up. This was a thumbs up for the Indiana Pacers sharpshooter.

"Wilt?"

Freethrow lay down and covered his eyes with his paws. That summed up Wilt Chamberlain's erratic free throw shooting.

"Rick Barry?"

One of the NBA's all time great shooters drew another two paws up from Freethrow.

"Last one. Shaq?"

Freethrow loved this one. He rolled over on his back and played dead. AJ always got a kick out of this.

As she rubbed Freethrow's exposed belly, AJ talked to her dog in a soothing tone. "You are such a good baby. We'll go for a walk in a little bit. We won our game today. And I had lunch with the man I told you about."

Freethrow had a limited vocabulary, but he sensed when AJ was happy, and that made him happy as well. Besides, if she rubbed his belly, he was as close to heaven as a dog could get.

When AJ was four, she lost her mother in a car accident. Her father, Sam Clark, was devastated. How could he go on? But he had to, for his daughter's sake. So he became father, mother, teacher, and friend to his daughter.

One thing he thought would help was a pet. At the local pet shop, Sam asked the owner to recommend a dog. He told the store owner his parameters were no shedding, small housedog size, but calm, big dog temperament. Sam didn't want a yippy poodle type.

"You want a Bichon," said the storeowner.

When Sam confessed he didn't know what the heck the owner was talking about, he was handed a tiny white furry puppy that easily fit in the palm of his hand. Sam learned the Bichon Frise breed was descended from the Water Spaniel. Originating in Spain, the breed developed as a companion dog in France. During the reign of Henry III in the 1570's, the ruler so loved his Bichons he tied a basket around his neck with ribbons in order to carry a pup with him at all times.

So when AJ was four years old, the Clarks acquired their first Bichon which they aptly named Rebound. As a high school basketball coach, Sam Clark helped AJ opt for a basketball related name. When Rebound passed away after fourteen years, the second Bichon, Freethrow, entered the Clarks' lives.

Now Freethrow was AJ's alone. She loved him for what he was and for the memories of Dad he gave her every day. Freethrow could and would do anything for AJ.

CHAPTER 16

The weekend had been uncommonly enjoyable. Sunday dinner with Kirk was fun and relaxing. Good conversation with occasional zingers and lots of laughs. AJ hadn't laughed much since Dad passed away. She went through work some days on autopilot. If she thought too much, she hurt too much.

This week was flying by. A regional meeting in Elk Grove Village on Monday, sales calls in East Chicago and Gary, Indiana, on Tuesday, and today she was working from Lafayette to Indianapolis. Her morning appointments had gone well. As she drove toward Indy, she knew she was ahead of schedule, so she decided to take the scenic route. Exiting off of Interstate 65, she took Highway 28 east to state road 421 south.

Dad said this was the way to travel. Blacktop two lanes running string straight between cornfields. Farms with red barns, skyscraper silos, white houses and white picket fences.

AJ could hear Dad's voice as he talked about the country. "Holsteins in the fields and Durocs in the pigpen. John Deere in the barns and steeples on the churches. This is AMERICA!"

AJ would giggle when Dad got started, but his enthusiasm was contagious. When he talked about country living, basketball, or American history, he was like a preacher afire. The car was his pulpit and AJ his congregation. She had heard his "The Midwest is the Heartland of America" theme almost as often as his "Offense wins games, Defense wins Championships" dissertation.

Father and daughter crisscrossed the Midwest from Ohio to Kansas for AAU tournaments, and just to travel for fun. Sam Clark believed the automobile windshield was the window to the world.

AJ slowed as she entered Kirkin, Indiana, a town Dad would have loved. Addresses like 101 Main Street. The TAKA Dive Tank Shop, where you could get scuba gear and gossip. Memory Lane Antiques, next to White Lion Antiques. Three dogs sitting in the shade at the Amoco Station. And a diner where the food was really homemade.

She remembered the diner in Darien, Wisconsin. Dad had driven 20 miles out of their way to go there because it had the best lunch specials and a piece of pie filled half a plate. Funny, but he was right. Best cherry pie she ever had.

In a blink, Kirkin was in the rearview mirror. The blacktop stretched south toward Indianapolis framed in a Carolina Blue sky with marshmallow clouds. Dad loved clouds. He and AJ would compete to see what animal shapes they could see in the clouds. The contests always ended with both of them seeing a llama.

It had become the family joke years ago. They were sharing Animal Crackers after a soccer game and Dad was perturbed there were no llamas in the box. He researched all animal cracker manufacturers and found no one included the llama in their menagerie.

So the beleaguered llama became the family game animal. Cruising down Highway 421 at fifty-five miles per hour, AJ spotted a lone cloud to her left with definite llama proportions. She smiled as memories flooded through her, and then she broke down.

Braking suddenly, she swerved into a farm lane, stopping her car in a cloud of dust. With her face in her hands, AJ wept uncontrollably. Her shoulders shook as she sobbed.

Time passed. One minute? Ten? She rubbed her eyes, and then rubbed her scalp, and then her neck. Her mind said *Quit it* but her heart said *Cry your eyes out*. She dug for a Kleenex to blow her nose as she rolled down her window. Cars whizzed by and birds called from the fence posts. AJ couldn't clear her mind.

She punched a speed dial number on her cell phone and watched it dance across the display. A baritone voice answered on the second ring. "Hi Grandpa," AJ managed to respond.

"Well, Hello Baby Girl!" The delight in Grandpa Clark's voice was evident. When AJ didn't answer, concern shown in his voice. "What's the matter, honey?"

AJ sniffed. "Grandpa, I miss Dad so much. I think I'm doing fine and then I just can't stand it. Sometimes I think I'm cracking up."

Russell Clark leaned forward in his easy chair with the phone cradled on his shoulder. He looked at his hands as he rubbed them together. Eight decades of farming were etched in those hands. Almost a century of hard work and love.

His hands were powerful, but weathered and scarred. Just like his heart.

He missed his son terribly, but he had to be strong.

"I know you miss him. We all miss your Dad. When you lose someone you love, there's a hole in your heart. It won't go away, but it will shrink and, after a while, it won't hurt so much."

"But Grandpa, sometimes I *want* to hurt. Hurting and thinking about Dad help me remember everything. I don't want to forget, like I've forgotten Mom."

Grandpa Clark looked at the paneled wall of his farmhouse family room. They called it the wall of fame. Sports pictures, prom pictures, and graduation photos. His family was displayed in new and old reproductions. "You won't forget," he said tenderly. "Your Dad will always be a part of you. Your Mom is too."

AJ's breathing slowed as she calmed down. "But I can hardly remember Mom. What if I start to forget Dad, too?"

Russell Clark's voice was smooth and stable. "I guarantee you won't forget. Remember how he bragged you were the best mathematician in third grade? You could figure shooting percentages in your head. You would sit on the bench at the games and do running stats. You can't forget that."

AJ smiled at that thought. She remembered one game when, during a timeout, her Dad had turned to her and said, "AJ, what do we need to get back in this game?"

His high school team was down by 5, and little AJ piped up, "We need a two and a three, Daddy. And two defensive stops."

She could still see the look of pride on his face as he turned back to his team. "See, fellas. From the mouths of babes." He drew up a play and they went on to win in overtime.

AJ and Grandpa traded reminiscences for a few minutes, and AJ knew she could make it through another day. It wouldn't be easy, but she would make it. "Thanks, Grandpa. I really needed to talk."

"Any time, AJ. Anytime. Now, keep that car between the white lines. I don't want to have to drive down there and pull you out of a cornfield."

Now AJ was able to smile. "For sure, Grandpa. When I get to Indy, I'll look up AJ Foyt and have a race."

They both laughed and said their goodbyes. Hanging up the phone, Russell Clark sat back in his chair and looked at the wall of fame. He let his mind travel back over the years as he thought about the son and the daughter-in law he had lost. He intertwined his fingers and held on tight. And he had a good cry.

CHAPTER 17

K irk couldn't believe Tyrese King wanted five million dollars to wear Green Star sneakers! Or rather, his agent wanted 10% of five million dollars to have Tyrese lace up the Green Star Viper, an all-leather, over priced Taiwanese made piece of crap. These guys would wear sandals if the price were right. If you were 6 foot ten with mad hops, it wasn't the shoes. But eighth grade consumers would plunk down their folk's hard earned cash to wear the hottest new shoe.

He continued his presentation in the Timberwolves plush conference room. His pitch to the agent and the team PR director was a slick power point presentation filled with demographic pie charts and name recognition data. It promised TV and print ads, as well as a major promo with two of the largest sporting goods chains. The promised exposure would help both the player and the team.

Yeh right, thought Kirk. This all meant diddly to anyone in the room. It was a dance he had learned to do. It was like dinner and a show. If you just came out with the offer, someone felt like a whore. Even though everyone knew where you were headed, you had to act like the journey was important. But all that mattered was the destination. And it had a dollar sign taped to the door.

"Kirk, will the store promotions be timed to coincide with when the Timberwolves play in those cities?"

"Well, Frederick, we had initially considered that. But our researchers feel that, with the impact of the NBA game of the week, it would be more forceful to do nationwide promos when the Wolves are featured. We would get the most bang for thc buck that way."

Frederick Blackwell gave a thoughtful nod and picked imaginary lint from the perfect crease in his charcoal gray trousers. His crossed legs showed tasseled loafers and stylish gray and black patterned socks. He had told Tyrese what he thought he could get out of Green Star, and he was aching to hear the offer. But he knew the drill, so he feigned interest and made what he hoped sounded like meaningful comments.

The meeting lasted another hour, followed by lunch with plans to meet at the arena a half-hour before tip-off. Kirk could meet Mr. King after the game for a few minutes before the team left for Utah. This gave Kirk the afternoon to pursue Job Two.

When he was hired, Kirk thought Job One sounded interesting. Dealing with the sports world would be more like play than work. To most young guys, hanging out at arenas and sports stores was not work.

But it was Job Two that captivated him. The cloak and dagger element intrigued him. He would be an undercover agent working to ferret out criminals in the sports world.

The primary crimes investigated involved gambling and drugs. The mega-dollars involved in sports made it a favorite for gamblers. Always looking for an edge, gamblers sought inside information and influence. You could fix a ballgame easier than you could pull four aces at a high stakes poker game. And where there was gambling and money, there were drugs.

Kirk was trained in the methods of the flesh peddlers who used college and professional athletes for profit. He had been educated about the myriad assortment of performance enhancing and recreational drugs currently available. He felt like a pharmacist by the time he completed his company training. He knew ten slang names for Cocaine, not to mention its chemical makeup and countries of origin.

He also learned the two big vices, gambling and drugs, attracted other crimes like ants to a picnic. It seems infidelity, prostitution, classroom cheating, extortion, money laundering, battery, and even murder tag along like an underworld Wheel of Fortune. Vanna, I'd like to buy a vowel to spell Point Spread. I think I can get Joe Quarterback to throw a few incomplete passes near the end of the game to protect my bet on the under.

Kirk entered this dark underbelly of the sports world for Green Star. Job One provided his cover, Job Two provided the adrenaline. Kirk's contacts broke the Minnesota test score scandal, leading to the suspension of five basketball players and the retiring of the coach. And it had been Kirk who helped close the noose on the Cincinnati Bengal who molested and intimidated his girlfriend.

As he entered the Downtown Tap, Kirk did a mental recap of his goal. Place a bet on the Timberwolves and find out where the money goes from Minnesota. He'd been cultivating his contacts in the Twin Cities and was close to learning about their hierarchy. He was sure the cash went to Chicago, but he didn't know the flow path from the bookies to the big bosses. By placing gradually larger losing bets, he hoped to loosen a few tongues.

CHAPTER 18

G regory Krug sat in the shade on the veranda and reviewed his notes. The Caribbean breeze on the island of St. Lucia was a perfect 80 degrees. Krug was master of all he surveyed, and he loved it. His twenty room colonial mansion sat on the hillside facing the ocean, giving him an expansive view of the oval track below to the left and the research lab to the right.

The running track boasted the latest synthetic running surface and circled the high jump, pole vault, and long jump pits. The research lab was a long, low slung building housing a weight room, training room, test labs, chemical process room, electronic equipment, offices, and file storage area.

Excellent facilities and hard work yielded excellent results. Krug's discoveries, if made public, would bring him critical acclaim and awards. Of course, he would be hard pressed to explain some of his research tactics, as well as the various quantum leaps in his chain of discovery.

"Borrowing" research data of others didn't bother Krug. The end justified the means. But not everyone saw things that way.

Looking at the track, Krug saw his protégé warming up for his afternoon workout. Jogging in exaggerated high steps across the grass infield in only shorts and track shoes was the culmination of Krug's work. Rickie Armendariz was a genetic wonder. A superb physical specimen, he stood 6 feet 2 inches tall, with a body carefully sculpted for speed and strength. In the vernacular, he was cut!

Armendariz was strong without being massive, fast without losing strength. As he swung his arms and high stepped, every muscle in his shoulders, back, arms and thighs seemed to sing, "Look at me." The grace and beauty of the finely honed athlete was like a beautiful weapon, poised for action. Krug's years of work would soon payoff.

"Herr Krug?"

The interruption startled the doctor. He turned to see his nurse holding a tray. "Yes, Gertrude, is it time?"

"Yes, Herr Krug. It is time for your shots. Do you care to do them here or inside?"

Gertrude knew you always asked Herr Krug what he preferred, even when you knew the answer. Gertrude had been hired because she was of German descent and not a security threat. She had lived on the island with Krug for the past five years and knew her role well.

She also knew there was something quite special about these shots. Though only in her mid thirties, Gertrude hoped the doctor would share some of his secrets with her.

"We'll do the shots here," directed Krug. "It is such a beautiful day."

Dressed in a loose fitting white shirt, lightweight cotton slacks and sandals, Krug stood and faced away from Gertrude, leaning on the glass topped table. As Gertrude pulled his shirt up to mid-back and slid his slacks and shorts below his buttocks, she marveled at the supple condition of his skin.

She overheard a conversation once in which the age of Herr Krug had been noted as near one hundred. Herr Krug's was not the paper thin, dry skin of someone that age. His skin had the appearance of a man of sixty-five.

As she prepared the first injection, Gertrude asked, "Are you ready, Herr Krug?"

"Yes, Gertrude. Make me young."

This exchange was their ritual. As she administered three injections into his buttocks, the verbal ritual was repeated each time.

After his shots were completed, Krug stood at the edge of the veranda to watch Rickie's workout. Armendariz was doing intervals — running a lap around the track, walking half a lap, running a lap, etc. He seemed to never slow or become fatigued.

A rap on the open French doors behind him caused Krug to turn toward the house.

"Good morning, Mister Krug. A package just came in. It's postmarked Atlanta, so I thought you would want it immediately." Bill Schultz stood in the doorway, hat in one hand, and Fed Ex envelope in the other, like a schoolboy waiting to be called on. As a personal assistant, Schultz had seen the dark side of Krug, and he worked hard not to provoke him. He had patented subservient behavior and it served him well.

"Wonderful, William. Let's have a look."

The two sat as Krug opened the envelope and perused the contents.

Ten minutes of silence ensued,with Schultz knowing better than to interrupt or comment. Krug flipped through pages and mumbled to himself. Finally, he looked up.

"William, this is the final data from Wisconsin. Bouhler has done an exemplary job. We'll have the lab review this, and we can clean up some loose ends. You know how I hate loose ends."

Indeed, Bill Schultz knew how Gregory Krug handled loose ends. He was sure he'd be making a phone call for Mr. Krug with instructions to clean up this loose end. He wondered what it would cost and if he would need to travel to make the arrangements. Never a dull moment on the island.

CHAPTER 19

AJ Clark's furrowed brow expressed her dissatisfaction. "Dick, I can't. There isn't enough time to make the call and keep my other appointments. I'm in Kenosha, Wisconsin." Sitting in the lobby of Quartz Manufacturing and talking to her boss, who was about to screw up her day, was not her idea of a productive endeavor.

AJ listened closely on her cell phone to be sure she didn't miss anything being said in Houston. "This is not a debate, Clark. I've committed a salesperson to be at Fermilab this afternoon, and you're it!" Dick Stile's tone convinced AJ there was no changing his mind.

"Fine," she replied into her cell. "I'll be there, but I wish you had consulted with me to check my schedule. You don't have to take the heat from the rest of my customers when I cancel on them"

The ensuing silence told AJ she may have gone too far. To Dick Stiles, national sales manager for Ultra Valve, anything short of blind obedience was a major insurrection. He wanted your feedback, as long as you agreed with him 100%, and did so in the proper subservient manner.

Mustering her most contrite voice, AJ softly purred into the phone. "Sorry, Dick. It's been a rough week. I'll give Fermilab a sales pitch they'll never forget. We'll solve their problems and they'll be thankful for the opportunity to deal with a professional organization like Ultra Valve."

"Great," responded Stiles, his anger partially diffused. "That's my girl. Go get 'em, Tiger."

When Stiles hung up, breaking the phone connection from Houston, AJ held her cell phone at arms length and stared at it. "My girl? You jerk!!" she said aloud before snapping the phone shut and literally throwing it into her briefcase. The salesmen sitting in the lobby on both sides gave startled looks at her outburst.

Standing, AJ smiled sweetly at them, spun on her heels and strode toward the glass doors leading to the parking lot. She was unaware every eye in the lobby was fixed on her long legs as her heels tapped a staccato beat across the slate floor. She was already planning the actions required for the rest of the day.

AJ made a mental list of her tasks. She made the phone calls necessary to reschedule appointments as she drove south toward Illinois on Interstate 94. She made notes concerning the rescheduled appointments, literature to be mailed, and items to be quoted. As she clipped her gold Cross pen to her notepad, her thoughts turned to the last item on her list.

PREPARE FOR FERMILAB was on her mind in capital letters. She flipped her call book open to Fermilab and set it on the seat next to her. While driving sixty-five down the interstate, AJ glanced back and forth from the road to her book, gradually taking in more details from the info sheet. She noted the key personnel names, which style of valves they use, and helpful sales tips.

The head of plant engineering had a son playing football at Ohio State University. AJ made a friend of him when she mentioned she didn't think Michigan's gridiron tradition could hold a candle to that of the Buckeyes.

Still traveling sixty-five, she reached into the back seat with her right hand to dig out the appropriate literature for the sales call. Her literature box sat in the back with brochures tabbed and arranged by category.

The large green interstate sign told her she had five miles to her exit. In half an hour she would be at Fermilab, ready to do her thing for Ultra and Dick Stiles.

CHAPTER 20

Fermilab was commissioned by the Atomic Energy Commission in 1967 to encompass 6,800 acres of farmland surrounding the town of Weston, near Batavia, Illinois. Now in the western suburbs of Chicago, in the 1960's it was a rural community. It was the height of the Cold War and an effort was under way for superiority in all fields of technology.

The construction of an electron accelerator ring allowed Fermilab to create the highest energy beam in the world. Not to mention the record for the largest proton-antiproton collision luminosity.

Driving onto the property, AJ thought how fortunate it was that the massive electron ring was buried underground, leaving the surface with the look of a national park. Green meadows, stands of pine trees, deer, and even buffalo greeted visitors during the winding drive to the administration building. It was hard to believe all this existed just outside of Chicago.

Approaching the main building of Fermilab was awe-inspiring. The tuning fork shaped structure rose fifteen stories into the blue Illinois sky. Two outer walls of concrete curved gracefully inward toward each other, with glass front and back walls displaying the inside of the building, giving it the look of a giant greenhouse.

The interior of the building was, in fact, teeming with plants. Large pots and planters appeared on every landing and every balcony of the inner atrium. AJ took all this in as she parked in the visitors' lot and made her way to the lobby. Gazing up, she thought for once the government allowed form and function to co-exist in a pleasing manner.

The namesake of Fermilab, Enrico Fermi, was one of the greatest physicists of the Twentieth Century. An Italian by birth, Fermi won the 1938 Nobel Prize for physics for his nuclear process work. While a professor at the University of Rome, he was the first to split the atom.

Like his contemporaries in Germany who fled Adolf Hitler, Fermi left Italy to escape the Fascist regime of Benito Mussolini. Making the United States his adopted home allowed Enrico Fermi to develop the first atomic pile at the University of Chicago. He became part of the team during World War II that developed the atomic bomb as part of the Manhattan Project at Los Alamos, New Mexico.

After the war, Fermi continued his pioneering research on the actions of high-energy particles until his death in 1954. For his great contributions to the war effort, a grateful United States awarded him a small bit of immortality by naming the massive complex in Illinois after him.

As AJ was signing the guest register and making small talk with the receptionist, she noticed a man on the far side of the lobby who looked familiar. As he turned to the side, she realized it was Mr. Bouhler, whom she had seen at GF Products.

As she stared, he sensed her eyes on him and turned away. AJ glanced at the registration book and then looked back in time to see Bouhler walking briskly away down a long corridor.

Inspecting the register, AJ saw neither a Mr. Bouhler under the name column, nor Biomet under the company column of the guest register. "Miss," AJ asked the receptionist. "Would you know who the man was in the brown jacket? He was at the far end of the lobby." AJ pointed where Bouhler had exited.

"Well, honey, let me see." The receptionist put on her glasses and slowly scanned the register, methodically comparing it to a sheet on her clipboard. AJ guessed, based on her age that the receptionist may have known Enrico Fermi personally.

After what seemed an eternity, the receptionist looked up at AJ and smiled. "Cox."

"Pardon me?" exclaimed AJ, a bit startled. "What did you say?"

"Well honey, don't get your shorts all bunched up. I said his name is Cox. Duane Cox. Says so right here. Works for Southern Physics Incorporated."

Regaining her composure, AJ dug for more information. "If you don't mind me asking, where does that hallway go?"

Peering over her glasses, the receptionist looked AJ up and down. "You got a special interest in the gentleman, honey? I'm not being nosey, mind you. But you're asking a lot of questions."

AJ fought for patience. "I thought he was someone I once met. Never did get his name the first time. I was wondering where he went and who he's seeing here."

The receptionist gave a conspiratorial smile. "Well, girl-to-girl, I'll tell you. That hall goes to the neutron therapy facility. That's where they use the atomic stuff on people. Pretty amazing what they can do. Shrink tumors, excite muscles, things like that."

AJ nodded thoughtfully. "Interesting. My business keeps me on the other side of the building. I guess I never fully understood all that goes on here."

"You and everybody else, honey. We don't just split atoms anymore. We're helping people, not destroying things," the receptionist said with pride.

"And who would Mr. Cox be seeing over in the neutron therapy facility?"

At that moment, two men dressed in dark suits and wielding bulging leather briefcases stepped to the receptionist's desk. "Excuse me, Ma'am," said the taller of the two. "We're late for our appointment and we need your assistance."

AJ reluctantly backed away as the two men signed in and phone calls were made. She stood in the lobby trying to make sense of the whole situation. Bouhler or Cox? Or none of the above. Who was this guy? And why did she have such a strange feeling about him?

A tap on the shoulder and an insistent voice interrupted AJ's thoughts. "Miss Clark?" AJ looked up into the long thin face of a bald man wearing a white lab coat two sizes too large. "Are you all right, Miss Clark? You seem to be in a daze. I'm Herbert Lange, and I'm supposed to show you the valves."

Extending her hand to shake his, AJ apologized. "I'm sorry, Mr. Lange. I guess my mind was wandering."

Lange continued unperturbed. "Very well. Please come with me. We're so glad you're here today."

With that, AJ switched gears into sales mode. For the next two hours, her mind would be completely occupied with Ultra Valve and the applications for her products at Fermilab.

After her business was completed, AJ stopped at the receptionist desk to sign out. She really wanted to get more information about Bouhler. But the young man on duty was preoccupied with the stack of paperwork in front of him. He merely grunted when AJ set her visitor's badge on the desk and said goodbye.

As she wrote the time in the appropriate sign-out column of the register, AJ noted that Duane Cox had not signed out yet. She also noticed Cox had written so sloppily in the column marked "Company Contact" that there was no way a name could be deciphered.

Walking to the parking lot, she chided herself for letting her imagination run away from her. She often wrote illegibly herself on guest registers so her competitors couldn't see whom she was visiting. And now she was wondering if the guy in the lobby was Bouhler. He had been across the lobby and left quickly when she looked at him. She told herself to leave mysteries to the novelists.

In the parking lot, she felt a magnetic pull to her left as she neared her car. Turning slightly, she looked down the next row of vehicles and stopped in her tracks. A black Mercedes CL550 stared at her from between a blue Ford Taurus and a white Chrysler Town and Country van.

Slowly walking closer, AJ focused on the license plate. TC2332. Ty Cobb/Michael Jordan/Magic Johnson, on a Georgia plate. A chill shot through her body. It was the same car from GF Products. So it *was* the same man in the lobby!

Walking to the driver's side of the Mercedes, AJ looked through the windows into the front and back seats, not knowing exactly what she was looking for. The inside of the car was as clean as the day it came off the assembly line. Nothing to give any clues about the owner.

After circling the Mercedes, AJ went to her Jeep, tossed her notebook and Ultra Valve binder onto the front seat, and took out her cell phone. Pacing back and forth in the parking lot, she called her office.

"Barb, this is AJ." Cutting off the response of the receptionist in mid sentence, AJ continued. "I'm in a rush and I need John Cline right now!"

"Well, sure, AJ. Let me transfer you," replied Barb in a hurt tone.

AJ waited impatiently for John to pick up his line.

"John Cline. May I help you?"

"Hey, Valve Gypsy. I need some help." As AJ spoke, she leaned against the back of her Jeep.

"Fire away, AJ. You sound like you've got ants in your pants and bees in your bonnet."

"Remember when I had you check on the Bouhler guy from Biomet and we came up empty? Well it gets weirder. I swear I saw him today at Fermilab using a different name and a different company."

"Now, AJ. Why would anyone do that? Are you sure?" John trusted AJ's instincts, but this was certainly off the wall.

"Humor me," she responded. "Fire up your computer and check on a Duane Cox at a company called Southern Physics."

John chatted with AJ while he did the net search. He came up with four variations of company names close to Southern Physics. He said he'd check two and AJ could check the other two. They could find out what the companies did and if they had a Duane Cox as an employee. Hanging up with Cline and sitting in her vehicle, AJ made her phone calls.

CHAPTER 21

While AJ worked the phone lines, 100 yards away the man she was looking for was looking at her. From a second story plate glass window which gave a panoramic view of the visitors' parking lot, he watched her circle his car. He observed her pacing, then leaning against her vehicle staring at his Mercedes while she talked on the phone. He began to punch numbers on his own phone, then stopped.

Alerting the boss to a potential problem sometimes backfired. He certainly didn't want to be the one singled out for a security leak. That was bad for one's health. This may be a situation where a wait and see attitude was the best approach.

Having talked himself out of setting off any alarms, Bouhler slid his phone into his jacket pocket and watched as AJ finally drove away. Besides, he thought. I can take care of her myself. There's no time for distractions. It's almost time to clean up loose ends.

AJ's mind was whirling. The companies she and John checked on knew nothing of Duane Cox and none of them admitted having any business relationship with Fermilab. As she gunned her Jeep in and out of the Chicagoland traffic, she felt boxed out. It was like basketball, where you could see the ball but your opponent kept you from reaching your goal.

Here the goal was knowledge, and AJ was not one to be denied. She had to find out what was going on with Bouhler/Cox. With her curiosity and instincts driving her forward, she gave little thought to what she would do once she learned more. She focused on solving the next step in the equation.

She punched a speed dial. "Kirk, it's AJ."

Kirk Vail cradled his cell phone on his right shoulder as he walked down the aisle of the Shoe Circus store in Madison. "Hey, AJ. What's up?

Good to hear your voice. I'm doing the retail store swing today and I need your friendly vibes to keep me from sliding into the doldrums."

"Kirk, are you free tonight? Something is really eating at me. I need help solving a mystery."

"Just call me Colonel Mustard. Give me a clue, and we'll head to the parlor with a rope." Kirk tried to be clever, and hoped he wasn't falling on his face. There was nothing he would rather do than spend time with AJ.

"Down, Rover. No ropes. Let's grab dinner somewhere and talk." They made their plan for the evening and set the time to meet.

"See you at Bill Russell/Gale Sayers," AJ instructed.

It was Kirk's turn to smile. "Reading that as 6:40 this evening. Six for the Boston Celtic great, Bill Russell, and 40 for the incomparable Chicago Bear running back, Gale Sayers." The note of triumph was evident in Kirk's voice.

"Right you are, Kirk. Except, to allow for the fact that you sometimes run late, it could be 6:48. Sayers wore number 48 when he played at the University of Kansas. Know thy numbers exactly."

With a chuckle, Kirk replied, "Yes, oh Doctor of Numerology. No later than 6:48."

Kirk went back to work and AJ drove with a lighter heart. Collaboration was good for the mind. And good for the soul.

CHAPTER 22

As AJ drove with a vengeance toward Madison, a young man in Tennessee was running through the woods with the same single-minded determination. Jimmy Wickland zigzagged around trees and hurtled stumps. He pumped his arms, then leaped a stream, jarring his knee in the process. He ran as if chased by demons.

And in fact he was. Demons of his own making. They were the twin brothers of high expectations and unfulfilled promise. His demons propelled him forward as surely as if they were flesh and blood pursuers.

When he cut too close to an old weathered pine, Jimmy' felt his arm torn open by the jagged bark. Blood ran down his triceps to his elbow, but he ignored it, dug for a higher gear, and accelerated. A glance at his watch told him he needed a strong sprint to finish on time.

The final two hundred yards were on a torturous uphill grade with loose sandy soil. He clawed as much as ran the final yards, popping through the trees into the open air like a cork rising out of water. A slap on the guardian granite boulder and a press on his watch signaled the end of the run. As he jogged in place for his cool down, Jimmy looked out at his favorite sight in the whole world.

Reelfoot Lake stretched before him like a glistening blue highway. The lake covered 23,000 acres, stretching fifteen miles long and almost seven miles across at the widest point. Nestled in the northwest corner of Tennessee where Kentucky shakes hands with Missouri, the Reelfoot region has a quiet isolation seldom found in the twenty-first century. It's a mix of north and south, old and new. With swamps and bayous, some areas were reminiscent of Louisiana. Yet vacationers have said on clear spring evenings the wooded hills reflected in the lake remind them of Wisconsin or Michigan.

The lake gave him a feeling of oneness. He was truly at home when he was near the water. Part Native American, part Spanish, part French, and part English, Jimmy had learned the hard way that he didn't often fit in. But at Reelfoot Lake, all was right with his world.

The lake, Grams, and her plant juice made him whole. The demons were still with him, but here he could stay a step ahead. The turmoil was pushed beneath the surface. For a while.

Like Jimmy's family, Reelfoot Lake had a tumultuous past. The lake was created by the New Madrid Earthquakes, a series of tremors from December 16, 1811, until March 8, 1812. The repeated quakes rocked the Mississippi Valley when the area was virgin forest with a few scattered white settlements. It was the Spanish and French village of New Madrid, on the Mississippi River in present day Missouri, which gave the earthquakes their name.

During the three-month period, the earth and the Mississippi River were torn with violent contractions. Fissures opened in the earth, the ground swelled, and sulfur filled the air. During the particularly hard shocks in February, the Mississippi ran backwards, flowing north for the only time in history.

Twenty-foot waves raced upstream, crashing across the banks as the riverbed turned. When the violence subsided, what had been a wooded valley, miles from the Mississippi, became Reelfoot Lake. This now tranquil lake had been forged by the hammer and anvil of Mother Nature.

So, too, had Jimmy been tempered by adversity. He was left to live with his Grams after his mother died and his father deserted him. Raised by his grandmother, he was called Injun and Geronimo by the white kids in school.

He never understood what his family had done wrong. The white kids were part French and English and German and Scotch. But nobody made fun of them and called them half-breeds. Yet the fact that he was one-quarter Native American seemed to label him for life.

Leaning against the boulder and looking at his beloved lake, Jimmy wished it could always be like this. The physical exertion of a workout and the smooth blue water melted his tension away. As he stretched his arms overhead, he noticed the blood on his arm. Gingerly touching the wound, he saw it was wide but not deep.

He knew what Grams would do. She would put her plant paste on the cut, lay a wet leaf over it, and bind it with a cloth strip. Then she would make him drink a glass of her plant juice before bed. From experience, Jimmy knew that in 24 hours his wound would be barely a memory.

When he was twelve, he cut himself with his Buck knife on purpose just to see how fast he could heal. It was the maddest Grams ever got. She threatened to let him bleed to death.

She tended to him because he was all she had. But she exacted a promise from him to honor the power they had. She said their bodies and the plants she used were sacred. You did not abuse them. They were to be used for good.

As he grew, he channeled his energy into athletics. He focused on track because of its individual nature. You had to count on yourself, not on your teammates. To Jimmy, that was enough.

With a last look at the lake, he turned to begin the three-mile run home. The straight route didn't take long. He would do his power jumping after Grams bandaged his arm. No sense losing any more blood than necessary.

Focusing on track earned him a scholarship to the University of Tennessee. A multi-event man in high school, he gravitated to the pole vault in college. He came to love the intricacies and the challenge of the vault.

In the sprints, technique couldn't overcome blazing speed. It was the same in the field events with strength. But the vault took speed, strength, coordination, intelligence, and technique. It was a difficult event to master, which eliminated a lot of the track jocks.

Having won the SEC championship twice while in college and having gotten to the NCAA finals his senior year, Jimmy felt he had a legitimate shot at the Olympics. Since graduating with his Biology degree last year, he had concentrated on track full time. Without big name sponsorships, he proudly wore his University of Tennessee sweats to the international meets. He was part of the Tennessee Track Club. Total membership of four.

As he neared home, he thought about Grams and the sacrifices she made for him. At her age, she should be retired. But she worked two jobs and took in laundry as well.

Grams never complained about her lot in life. As a Native American married to a Hispanic immigrant, Lily Eagle Eye became Lily Morales. Named for the beautiful flower, Lily had an inner strength which was apparent to all she met.

Her only daughter, Juanita Morales, married a local building contractor named Edward Wickland. The Wicklands could trace their family tree back to England on one side and France on the other.

The marriage of Edward Wickland to Juanita Morales caused an uproar in Lake County, Tennessee. Though not operating as openly as in earlier times, the Ku Klux Klan reared its ugly head. To his credit, Ed Wickland didn't back down from the commitment to the woman he loved, and the wedding proceeded as planned.

But family bliss was short lived. Ed found less and less work for his company. Nothing you could trace to the Klan, mind you, but decent projects were tougher and tougher to come by.

Juanita died in a car accident when Jimmy was eight months old, and at that point, Ed threw in the towel. He had loved Juanita, but he was worn out. He turned the baby over to Grandma Lily and moved to Florida to get rich in the building boom.

From that day on, Jimmy Wickland was the sole reason for Lily Morales' existence. The loss of her husband six years before to pneumonia, and the loss of her darling Juanita, left a void in her heart only baby Jimmy could fill.

In the years that followed, she vowed that she would do whatever it took to give her grandson a better life.

Loping along with the easy gait of one who has run thousands of miles, Jimmy saw the house a quarter mile away. Grams was walking across the yard as sheets flapped in the breeze. She had all four clotheslines full, looking like sails on a schooner. Jimmy took to the ditch so Grams wouldn't see him. He ran slightly hunched, arms swinging low, to avoid detection.

He needed to clean the cut before Grams saw it. It upset her if he was injured. He would come around the house from the back and rinse the wound off using the hose outside. Then Grams could work her magic and make him better.

As he ran, Jimmy remembered his first serious talk with Grams about the special plants with the healing powers. He was in seventh grade and it was shortly after he cut himself with his knife. Grams sat him down on the living room couch, giving him her full attention.

"Jimmy, have you studied the great explorers in school? Those who came to America?"

"Sure, Grams. Like Columbus, Amerigo Vespucci, and Coronado, right?"

"That's right, Jimmy. It's time for me to tell you a story in history that affects our family. You and me. It's a story not written in any history book. It is very important that you listen closely."

Jimmy nodded, confused but excited.

"I'm going to tell the story as it was told to me by my mother when I was about your age. And her mother told her, and her grandmother told her mother."

Lily cradled her grandson's head in her hands and kissed him lightly on the forehead. "Lean back and close your eyes and picture the story as I tell it to you."

"It began with an explorer, Juan Ponce de Leon, centuries ago. New lands and new discoveries lay before him. He sailed with The Great One as a young man when the New World was discovered. During that now famous voyage, he had seen Captain Columbus rule his crew with an iron hand to keep the nonbelievers in check. When others thought they would sail off the edge of the earth, the Bold One made history with his discoveries. He proved the weak would not inherit the earth!

"Juan was determined to unlock the mystery of life. He was influenced by a legacy of folklore about The Fountain of Youth that would save humanity from the never-ending sleep of death. His obsession was to succeed where all others had failed.

"The man who fearlessly faced battle, tempestuous storms, and danger in strange distant lands, cringed at the thought of his own inevitable aging.

"As the fire of youth gave way to the wisdom of maturity, Juan recognized the ultimate truth of life. As winter follows fall, so do we all pass from this life. It is the law of God and nature and cannot be changed. Or can it? Juan was no common man, so could he therefore not accomplish the most uncommon of deeds?

"If he, Juan Ponce de Leon, the Lion of Castile, could find the secret of the ages, his name would go down in history as the greatest explorer of all time! He must continue the search northward to find the slayer of demon dreams, the elixir of the ages....the Fountain of Youth!"

Jimmy opened his eyes to sneak a peek at his grandmother. She had her eyes closed and her hands clasped in her lap.

"Jimmy Wickland, I know you're looking at me."

Jimmy squeezed his eyes closed and looked down.

"It would take a brave man to sail into the unknown, wouldn't it Jimmy?"

"Yes, ma'am."

Lily Morales smiled. "You're right. It was very difficult. The Spaniards enlisted help from our ancestors. Sometimes with force. The Europeans called this the New World, but our ancestors had lived here for thousands of years. Ponce de Leon and his men were the first men from the Old World to set foot on this land."

"And they were looking for the Fountain of Youth?"

Lily touched his cheek. "Yes, my angel," she said, as she continued the story.

CHAPTER 23

"Hernando d'Escalente Fontaneda was second in command to Ponce de Leon and had been halfway around the world with the Lion of Castile. When they sighted land, the excitement swept through the ship. The natives in what is now Cuba told the Spaniards tales of a life-renewing river flowing in the land to the North. Ponce de Leon believed this was the rejuvenating river Jordan he sought.

"Sailing north and finding new land was another exciting discovery for Ponce de Leon. The beauty of the land heightened his excitement. He named the sheltered bay of their landing the Bay of the Holy Cross. As the Captain's personal rowboat touched down high on the beach, Juan Ponce de Leon was first to set foot on what appeared to be a large island. When the ship's chaplain, Father Antonio, disembarked, the Captain knelt, gave thanks to God, and claimed the land for King Ferdinand.

"The April air was filled with the fragrance of the many flowers near the white sand beach, and it was near the time of the Spanish feast of Pasqua de Flores. Father Antonio said Mass in a clearing, where a small stone pillar displaying a cross and a coat of arms was erected. Standing in front of the pillar, the Captain declared the land would henceforth be known as La Florida, Spanish for the flower, in honor of the flowers and the sacred feast.

"Exploring up the coast, the Spaniards had contacted friendly natives who agreed, after some coercion, to lead them to the Fountain of Eternal Youth. Moving inland with their horses and mules, They set up a base camp. The excitement of exploration gave way to frustration after unsuccessful sorties into the swamps and underbrush.

"Ponce de Leon lost confidence in his guides. La Florida, indeed! The land of flowers had given way to a land not fit for a mule. They wandered through a maze of backwater jungle that yielded nothing but sickness and death. Juan Ponce de Leon was hot, tired, and angry. It was their third day on foot away from the base camp in this godforsaken place.

"He began to think that, if the Fountain of Youth existed here, it was a joke by the Almighty. Who would want to live here, especially forever? The swamp land didn't support the weight of horses, insects were the size of rodents, and the air was so heavy it was a labor to breathe."

Jimmy interrupted her. "Grams, I'm hot. Are we going to find the Fountain of Youth or not? I could sure use a drink from that fountain right now. How about you?"

"Sure. Thank you, Jimmy."

He stood and walked to the kitchen with his arms extended stiffly in front of him, doing his best Frankenstein impression. In a low voice, he said, "Find the Fountain of Youth. Find the Fountain of Youth."

Jimmy returned with two glasses of water. "Here's yours, Grams. Straight from the Tennessee Fountain of Youth known as our faucet."

They brought their glasses to their lips at the same time and took a long drink of water with thoughts of the Fountain of Youth dancing in their heads.

Grams picked up the tale of Ponce de Leon's search.

"Hernando had pushed the native guides relentlessly for the past two days. Finally they stood in a clearing, facing a small natural pool.

"The still surface of the water was broken at one end by bubbles. Water entered the pool from an unseen underground source, bubbling to the surface before mixing with the rest of the water in the pool. The movement of the water kept one end of the pool clear, while the rest of the surface was covered with algae and lily pads.

"The Spanish explorer believed he had found the legendary Fountain of Youth. It was a day he knew would go down in history. with the name of Juan Ponce de Leon immortalizes as a conqueror.

"He turned to see the guides huddled back in the trees, whispering to one another. Hernando told Ponce de Leon that the guides said this was the Fountain of Eternal Youth, the Water of No Age, but they would not step closer because only the shaman, their Holy Man, could approach the water.

"Ponce de Leon grew angry. He would not be ruled by legend or fear.

"Juan Ponce de Leon, the Lion of Castile, walked to the waters edge, removed his helmet and knelt. The clearing grew silent, as if even the birds knew this was a solemn moment. The Spanish soldiers and their native guides waited breathlessly in the trees, straining to see a transformation.

"Ponce de Leon made the sign of the cross on his chest and spoke in a strong, clear voice. He claimed the discovery of the Fountain of Youth for

King Ferdinand and Spain and the Holy Father and he said it would be theirs forever.

"The captain bowed his head and said a silent prayer, asking for strength and wisdom in the administration of the power he would soon possess. The power over aging, and possibly even power over death itself! He scooped his helmet full of the sacred water and held it high.

"Would a Fountain of Youth be a blessing or a curse? One New World Indian legend told of a Fountain of Youth created halfway between heaven and earth. But it only brought sorrow and grief, for all who drank from it outlived their children and their friends. The legend says the fountain was destroyed because it brought only harm.

"Reality or simply legend? Good or evil? What was the Fountain of Youth? These were the thoughts racing through the mind of Ponce de Leon as he held his helmet aloft. The time for reflection was over. It was time for action.

"The knight of Spain brought the helmet to his lips and drank fully of the cool liquid. He paused, and drank again. Water trickled down his graying beard.

"Standing, he took a third drink, and then poured the remaining water from his helmet onto his hands. Discarding his helmet, he rubbed his wet hands on his face, massaging his wrinkled brow and cheeks.

"Juan Ponce de Leon stood next to the spring in the open clearing, with sunlight just breaking through the scattered clouds. He looked up, rays of sun bathing him, and held his arms straight out to the side with his palms turned upward.

"To his men, the visage of their leader had an eerie quality. They were mesmerized, as they waited for tangible results of the power of the rejuvenating waters.

"The Captain wished for a change, prayed for a change. But he felt nothing. Who knew how the water worked?

"Turning toward his clustered troops, he made a decision. He bid them come and drink from the Fountain of Youth."

"Silver shields with embossed red lions clattered to the ground, swords and battle-axes clanked as men surged to the waters' edge. Some dropped to their stomachs and buried their faces in the healing water. Others knelt, using hands or helmets as goblets for the precious liquid. All drank voraciously, guzzling and splashing noisily.

"After a few minutes, silence once again descended over the clearing. While they awaited the beginning of the miracles, men with wet faces and beards intently stared at their companions looking for signs of change. Did anyone look younger or more full of vitality? Did anyone feel different?

"Eager eyes looked for a transformation, but no miracles happened. Gray hair and grizzly features remained the same. Aching joints and old war wounds sent their same constant message of pain. Men sat in small groups and whispered among themselves.

"Juan Ponce de Leon, Hernando d'Escalente Fontaneda and Father Antonio stood together and discussed the lack of miraculous developments.

"Ponce de Leon's shoulders sagged under the weight of disappointment.

"Hernando herded the dejected troops into the trees to gather their weapons. Their weariness was evident in the dragging steps and the downcast faces."

Lily and Jimmy finished their glasses of water. Grams spoke first. "Feel anything?"

"Other than satisfying my thirst?" Jimmy smacked his lips. "Nope, Grams. Nothing. Just like Ponce de Leon. I guess stronger and faster is up to me. Got to keep working out if I'm going to be the next Billy Mills."

Lily took Jimmy's hand and rubbed the spot where he'd cut himself with his knife. She traced the barely discernable mark where there should have been a major scar.

"The Fountain of Youth isn't really water from a fountain. There is no water that heals or makes us younger. That is a myth. But it isn't the end of the story."

Lily paused, wanting to tell the ending exactly as it was relayed to her by her mother. "The Spaniards came to take from the New World. Gifts are to be given, not taken. There was a special gift in Florida. A magical gift."

Lily held Jimmy's hand as she told him of this gift.

"As the great Ponce de Leon and his troops prepared to depart, across the clearing, hidden from view, was Olatheta, shaman of the Arawaks, smiling behind his wooden mask. He wore the mask of the turtle. The turtle was sturdy and tough, pulled in his appendages for defense, and lived a long fruitful life. The shaman valued these qualities.

"The Arawak tribe had lived in harmony with the land forever. Their history began and ended with the land, water, plants, and animals that surrounded them. They didn't 'own' the land or water, as these bearded newcomers claimed to. You could no more own the land than you could own the sky or the stars.

"Olatheta himself had lived with his tribe on the peninsula more than 70 years. Yet his eyes were clear, his skin was smooth, and he had the strength of a young warrior. He had followed the progress of the white devils as they tramped noisily through his land. He heard them call his land of Teresta by the name Florida, and he cursed their foolishness.

"As he crouched, hidden in the jungle, Olatheta watched the Spaniards vacate the clearing and leave the pond behind. Still smiling at the cruelest of jokes, he whispered to himself. 'So close, so very close.'

"As he chewed on the plant he had pulled from the waters' edge before the Spaniards intrusion, he whispered with satisfaction. 'It's not the water. No, no, it's not the water!'

"Chewing the leaves of the sacred plant, he swallowed the sweet juice that kept him young. He knew the secret and he had the power. The white devils would have neither."

Lily looked into the earnest eyes of her grandson, hoping this all made sense. "It's a plant that has a special power, Jimmy. Like a Fountain of Youth of sorts, the plant helps us heal faster. The plant doesn't make us younger, but it can help keep us from aging as fast."

Jimmy didn't know what to say. It was a lot to grasp.

"Our Native American ancestors passed on the secret of the power of the plant. When you cut yourself, I use the plant to help you heal. But part of the power is keeping it a secret. We use but don't abuse the plant. And we never, never tell anyone else what the plants can do."

Jimmy still had not spoken as he tried to grasp what his grandmother was saying. He knew Grams helped him heal fast, but talking about it seemed surreal. It was like something out of a Superman or Batman movie.

Grams grasped his hand. "Do you understand? Do you see the power and how cautiously it must be treated?"

Jimmy still did not speak.

"I need to know that you understand. What do you think of the power of the plant?"

Jimmy knew only one word that expressed his thoughts. "Cool!"

CHAPTER 24

At 6:43 p.m., Kirk strode into Chili's and looked left and right for AJ. Spotting her waving to him, he headed for her booth.

Sliding into the opposite side, Kirk bumped AJ's knees with his. "Sorry. Booths aren't built for long legs," he said by way of apology.

Giving Kirk's knee a gentle nudge with hers, AJ replied, "Not a problem. Cozy works for me."

Kirk looked at AJ in her white blouse and blue business blazer and couldn't help but comment. "You look fantastic! I'd buy whatever you're selling if I were a customer. Doesn't seem fair to the competition."

With a slight blush, AJ responded in her best Mae West accent. "You're not so bad yourself, big boy. For a shoe peddler, I mean."

They both laughed. While AJ had come straight from work, Kirk had changed into a navy sweater vest over a white short sleeve golf shirt and navy slacks. It was an outfit he felt comfortable in, and with AJ he had learned color combinations mattered.

While Kirk drank a Corona, AJ nursed a margarita and told her story about Emile Bouhler and Duane Cox. She took her time, trying to include every important detail. Kirk asked few questions, preferring to just listen. When she finished the part about the phone calls to Southern Physics with no results, AJ took a long drink from her glass and sat silently looking into Kirk's eyes. Breaking the silence, she said, "You know, Kirk. You are either a really good listener, or you've gone brain dead while I've spun my tale and you don't know what to say."

Kirk smiled and leaned forward. "I'm a really good listener. Especially when the story comes from you. Now for the questions."

"Fire away, Mr. Prosecutor. I'm looking for some help here."

"First and foremost, are you absolutely sure it's the same guy? That's the crux of your whole argument. If Bouhler isn't Cox, there's nothing to discuss. Lots of people look alike. In fact, I myself have been mistaken for

Brad Pitt a number of times."

AJ reached across the table and cupped Kirk's chin in her hand. Turning his head from side to side, she made a show of examining him closely. "I'll take that under further consideration. More evidence is needed."

Kirk ran his hand through his hair and struck what he hoped looked like a model type pose, looking off into space. "Other than the height difference, hair color difference, and the total dissimilarity of facial bone structure, Brad and I could pass for twins. Of course, he wishes he had my nose!"

AJ liked Kirk's self-deprecating manner. Most of the guys she had dated seemed to believe they were God's gift to women. "Well, I'm sure he envies your personality."

The waitress interrupted them with a dinner order request. After the orders were placed, AJ began again in a serious tone. "I *know* it's the same man. I'm really good with faces. And what about the car? It's the same car, same plate."

"I'll agree the car is the same. All I'm saying is, maybe Bouhler was at Fermilab somewhere and you didn't see him. Maybe he didn't sign in or he went into a different entrance. Then this guy Cox could be who he says is."

AJ persisted. "Well then, why can't we find anything out about either company or find evidence of either guy? It's creepy, I tell you. And Bouhler had a spooky effect on the plant manager at GF Products. It was not a typical vendor/customer relationship." AJ spoke with passion and conviction.

Kirk took out a pen and flipped his paper placemat over on the table. Using it as a worksheet, he drew a line across the middle from left to right. "Let's say they are one and the same. What do we know?"

Kirk wrote Emile Bouhler as a heading for the top half and Duane Cox as a heading for the bottom half. With AJ dictating, he filled in company names, locations, car information, and even what Bouhler was wearing each time AJ had seen him. Her attention to detail amazed Kirk.

After filling in Peter Rudi as the contact at GF Products, Kirk asked AJ whom Cox was visiting at Fermilab.

AJ shook her head. "I don't know. And it's killing me. I just know what department he headed for."

"Well, let's fill in motive." Kirk looked at AJ intently. "We're dealing with two motives here."

"Two motives? I don't get it."

"We want to find out the motive this Bouhler/Cox person has for having two identities, if that's the case." After a pause, Kirk continued. "But we need to establish what your motive is in spending time chasing down a guy you've seen twice in lobbies for a total of five minutes."

AJ was taken aback. She leaned back in the booth. "I'm not sure I like your tone or insinuation."

Kirk felt the chill in AJ's voice and worked to recover. "Please don't misunderstand me. I'm just trying to facilitate, and I don't know what the goal is. Do you think this guy is a threat to your business?"

AJ took a minute to let herself calm down. "Well, no. He doesn't appear to be a competitor."

"Is he a physical threat? When you say he's creepy, do you feel threatened by him?"

"Not really," AJ admitted. "There's just something about him I can't peg. Both times I've gotten really bad vibes."

Kirk toyed with his pen. "Let's see. That leaves national defense. Miss Clark, is this man a communist sympathizer or a terrorist, ready to pull down democracy and the American way of life from his base of operations here in the Midwest?" Kirk used his best southern Senator voice when asking the question, hoping to lighten the mood.

Kirk's impression had the desired effect. AJ laughed and gave Kirk a soft kick in the shin. "All right. Maybe, just maybe, I'm jumping to conclusions here. It does seem a bit silly when you say it out loud."

With the mood lightened, Kirk made a few more notes with arrows trying to show relationships between GF Products and Fermilab. "No, AJ, You're right. It's not your imagination. Something about this situation is fishy. You have good instincts. These events just don't make sense."

AJ reached out and took Kirk's hands, holding his long fingers in hers. "Thanks, Kirk. I needed someone to hash this out with. I'm glad you met me here tonight."

Kirk had something he'd wanted to ask AJ since the first time they met, so he figured this was the time. "OK, AJ, I've got another, more personal question for you."

AJ played along. "All right, Kirk. Ask away. I'll see what I can do to satisfy your curiosity."

Kirk took a deep breath. "We've known each other for a while now and I'm curious. I'd like to know what AJ stands for."

Kirk's honest, sincere tone caught AJ off guard. The banter was gone. "Well, Mr. Kirk Vail. That's a long story, and one I don't tell often."

Kirk waved two fingers at their waitress as she passed, the universal signal for more drinks. "Well, Miss AJ Clark. I have the time, and I have the interest."

AJ found herself looking into Kirk's eyes and thinking that here was a guy worth spending time with. Opening up couldn't hurt.

"Before I give up the well guarded secret about my name, I have to give a little background."

AJ looked down, playing with her glass for a full fifteen seconds before looking up. "You've heard me talk about my Dad. I think you know how I feel about him." AJ could never bring herself to say her "late" Dad. Somewhere in the deep recesses of her mind, she never accepted the fact that he was gone from her life.

"Sure, AJ. I know how you feel about him." Kirk sensed that had he used the term "felt" in the past tense rather than "feel" in the present tense, the conversation would have ended right there.

AJ sipped her margarita, relaxed a bit, and continued. "My Dad was big time into sports. Played them all in high school — football, basketball, baseball, track. He was a farm kid, and he went from a tiny grade school to a big high school in Beloit. East High was a state power in sports, and Dad excelled. Captained all the teams and had big plans for college."

"Sounds like quite the athlete," responded Kirk.

"Sure was. If you go to East High today you'll see Sam Clark's name plastered all over the record books. So the University of Kansas recruited him to play basketball. They even had Wilt Chamberlain call Dad to encourage him to head to KU."

Kirk nodded his understanding. "How could you say no to that?"

"You're right. The coaches told Dad that if he agreed to play for Kansas, they'd have a chance to win a national championship. Things looked great."

Kirk wasn't sure where the story was going, but he could feel the intensity of feeling radiating from AJ.

"Dad was excited about Kansas, but he had a problem. He loved my Mom. She went to East High, too. He told me he knew he loved her before he ever talked to her. The school colors were black and red, and Dad said nobody looked as good as Mom did in a black and red pleated skirt."

Kirk was warming to the story. "So how did they hook up?"

"Dad was walking down the hall his sophomore year with one of his friends, Rich Watson. It was a Friday in the fall, so the guys had their football jerseys on. Coming toward them in her cheerleading outfit was my Mom, Leslie Wilson. She stopped and called Rich over across the hall to talk."

"Dad knew Rich was friends with Leslie since they had the same homeroom and sat next to each other alphabetically. Dad leaned against the lockers across from them and watched them whisper to each other. He felt like a fifth wheel and was about to move on when Rich returned."

Kirk looked at AJ and said, "I know how that feels if you like someone and you think they don't know you exist."

AJ gave Kirk a soft kick under the table and continued. "So Dad and Watson start walking again, and Dad tells Rich how lucky he is because Leslie Wilson likes him. But Rich turns to Dad with a strange look on his face and says, 'No, Leslie likes You!'"

"Wow," said Kirk, "I bet your Dad was blown away."

AJ nodded. "To say the least. Happiest day of his life, he used to say. So they started dating, and that brings us to their senior year. Dad wanted to go to Kansas more than anything, but Mom couldn't afford out of state tuition. She was planning on going to the University of Wisconsin at Whitewater. Affordable, close to home, but 500 miles from Lawrence, Kansas. And 500 miles back then was a long, long way."

Kirk waved for two more drinks, then turned back to AJ. "No kidding. No e-mail, no cheap long distance calls, no supersaver air fares."

"Right. Mom asked Dad why he couldn't go to Whitewater or the University of Wisconsin in Madison. The coaches there were begging Dad to stay close to home and play for them. They both said he would be a huge star. But, Dad chose Kansas. He wanted to be a Jayhawk."

Kirk was dying to know what this had to do with AJ's name, but he held his tongue. "So what happened next?"

AJ leaned back and crossed her arms. "Mom broke up with my Dad."

"She what?" Kirk was expecting a "This is how they worked it out" ending to the story. "I don't get it."

"Mom decided it was too far away to keep a relationship going, so after Dad signed the letter of intent with Kansas in the spring, she told him she couldn't go out with him anymore."

Kirk shook his head. "Wom..." He caught himself just in time, before he uttered the second syllable. "I mean, how could she do that to him?"

AJ smiled, knowing what he meant. "She thought it was for his own good. He could concentrate on basketball and school without worrying about the girl he left behind. But Dad took it hard. One night he was so upset, he went to the hayloft in the barn and worked himself into a frenzy. He did hundreds of pushups, jumped rope till he practically dropped, and then began dunking on the old hoop my Grandpa hung up in the barn for him. With the lights on in the barn, Dad could practice all night."

AJ paused. "On one of the dunks, Dad came down at a bad angle, slipped on the uneven barn floor, and wrenched his knee. Torn ACL and torn MCL. It wasn't like now. Back then, a torn knee was tough to recover from."

"What a bummer. Did he have surgery?" Kirk asked.

"Yes. But since he had ligament and cartilage damage, it was a difficult operation. He was hurting physically and mentally. And he didn't know what Kansas would do."

Kirk had his elbows on the table and his chin cradled in his hands. "Did your Mom feel guilty?"

"Of course. She blamed herself for his injury. She and Dad got back together, and she spent the summer helping him rehabilitate. But his knee never came back 100%. Kansas, however, honored his scholarship and Dad had a wonderful four years.

"He was primarily a practice player, but he learned to coach basketball and discovered his calling. He became a great high school coach and history teacher when he graduated. He loved KU because of the way they had treated him."

Kirk looked into AJ's eyes. "What about your mom?"

"Mom got her degree from UW Whitewater. Mom and Dad took the train back and forth when they could. When they graduated, they got married and settled down in Beloit."

Kirk added his Corona bottle to the growing glass forest on their table and looked at AJ intently. "Great love story. I mean it. But where does your name fit in?"

AJ toyed with her margarita glass. "When Mom and Dad were picking out names for the baby before I was born, Mom chose Amanda. She loved the TV show Gunsmoke, and she thought Amanda Blake, who played Miss Kitty, was a very strong character."

"Amanda is a beautiful name," added Kirk.

"Dad said he wanted to pick the middle name. He told Mom that Julie Andrews' performance in *Sound of Music* was his favorite, so he chose Julie as my middle name."

Kirk held both hands over his head and practically shouted. "Glory Halleluiah, you are Amanda Julie Clark! A sweeter name has never been spoken."

AJ suspected the Coronas were having an effect on Kirk. Never the less, she couldn't help but laugh at his exuberance. "That's not my whole name. Now, it's time for the rest of the story."

Kirk leaned forward and whispered in a conspiratorial tone. "Are you in the witness relocation program or something?"

AJ shook her head. "No, silly. But after my birth, Dad was the one who filled out the paperwork at the hospital. A week later Mom saw that my full, legal name was Amanda Julie Hawk Clark. Dad planned on writing my name as Amanda J. Hawk Clark. He so loved Kansas he wanted his daughter to be a Jayhawk."

Kirk shook his head. "Man, I heard once there was a kid named Bucky Badger Bowman. But I didn't think people actually did stuff like that."

AJ finished her margarita. "Well, it hit the fan. Mom told Dad she understood his love for KU. She loved the school, too. But she was NOT having her daughter called J. Hawk. So she started calling me AJ right from the start. And it stuck."

Suddenly, AJ noticed they were two of the last people in the restaurant, and chairs were being set on top of tables. "And now we better hit it. If we stay much longer, we'll be recruited for kitchen duty."

Kirk laid money for the meal and a tip on the table, stood, and extended his hand. "Amanda Julie, thank you for sharing the story of your name. Now, a few more questions..."

Standing, AJ took Kirk's hand, turned and pulled his arm around her shoulder. Looking up at him, she said, "Another time, another place. For now, let's see if we can get you home in one piece."

As they walked into the parking lot with their bodies pressed next to each other, they were much closer than they had been hours before. Kirk stumbled and leaned heavily on AJ. When she looked up into his eyes, she had a quick thought and inadvertently spoke aloud. "Gretzky."

Kirk paused in mid-stride, giving AJ a quizzical look. "What did you say?"

"Nothing, Kirk. Just mumbling," replied AJ.

Kirk pointed to his car. "Let's steer this ship to safe harbor. Lead on, fair maiden. I seem to have lost my bearings."

AJ laughed as she held tight to Kirk's waist and felt his arm draped across her shoulders. Dad was right. Someday she would meet a Gretzky.

Wayne Gretzky, number 99, the Great One, hockey player for the ages. Anything that is 99 per cent right, Dad called a Gretzky. Nothing was perfect, but only 1 per cent short of perfection is extraordinary.

He told her someday she would find her Gretzky. He wouldn't be perfect, but he'd be a keeper. AJ was getting that feeling about Kirk, and she liked it.

CHAPTER 25

Josef Mengele, alias Gregory Krug, was in a particularly buoyant mood. It had been three weeks since the last package arrived from Wisconsin and he was sure he had all the data he needed from GF Products. The enzyme formulas Bouhler obtained proved to be extremely useful in the development of food supplements. The diet he had devised for Rickie was the most nutritionally efficient in the world.

He thought back to his early experiments and was amazed at his progress. Mengele spent years experimenting with a plethora of chemical and natural food supplements with the two-pronged goal of increasing physical performance and retarding the aging process. In the days of the Third Reich in Germany, he had worked to turn the Aryans into a true master race of superior soldiers and athletes. And he worked to make the Fuehrer immortal.

Now he was working to develop the world's greatest athlete — an athlete to shatter a world record at the Olympics as he unfurled the power of the Fourth Reich. And Mengele was stretching his own life to the limits.

On behalf of Adolf Hitler, legions of fervent Nazis searched the world over for the Fountain of Youth. The magic water was never discovered, but the Third Reich experienced a time of unbridled experimentation in which Mengele flourished. His diabolical experiments laid the foundation for his future discoveries.

His dogged determination and focus over the past decades yielded fantastic results. Of course, blackmail and threats created a cooperative group of contributors to the cause. Peter Rudi of GF Products had been convinced to share the technical secrets from his vault through a combination of money and intimidation. The carrot and the stick. Mengele smiled at the thought of the stick as a motivating tool.

Heinrich Himmler taught him that the carrot, a positive motivator, was a good way to start someone as a collaborator. But it was the stick, the threat of physical violence, which provided total domination. Fear was the ultimate control weapon.

Of course, there came a point when a person lost value to the cause. When that point came, the non-essential was pruned, like a dead branch from a tree. Mengele looked out to sea and smiled again. It was time to prune. Summer was arriving and the climax was fast approaching It was time to clean up loose ends.

"Gertrude! Get William in here. Now!" he called.

Within minutes, William Schultz stood before Mengele. "Afternoon, Mr. Krug. Gertrude said you needed me."

"Yes, William. It's time to begin the cleanup process. Contact The Gardener for me. Here is a list of the first weeds to be plucked."

Schultz accepted the paper and looked at the list of code names. "Usual payment terms?"

"Yes, but stress the importance of discretion. We don't need any scrutiny at this point. We remain invisible until we decide to be seen."

Schultz nodded his agreement. "Of course, sir. But then, with The Gardener, you never have to worry. He's the best."

"Of course," said Mengele. "That's why he works for me."

With that, Josef Mengele turned away to look out to sea. Schultz knew he was dismissed, so he turned and left the room to make the arrangements. Heaven help those on the list. Their fate was sealed.

CHAPTER 26

The Gardener changed his name so many times he could hardly remember his given name. After his life evolved into one of traveling invisibly, he wanted the distinction of standing out. He wanted to make a name for himself as a paid assassin, and toyed with various monikers.

The Jackal was the most famous assassin ever, so he thought of using the Wolf, the Cheetah, or the Fox. Did he want to imply strength, speed or cunning? No, he decided, animal names were not for him.

How about the Blade, the Flame, or the Hammer? All had a deadly ring, but they were also over the top. He certainly didn't want to be thought of as a skateboarding, surfer-dude assassin. He wanted his clientele to be the elite who appreciated discretion and efficiency.

While sitting alone contemplating what to charge a wealthy client the name came to him. The Gardener. It was subtle. He will uproot your problems, prune the antagonists, and plant them six feet under. The Gardener will quietly do your dirty work while you keep your hands clean. He liked it.

The Gardener was born William Clayton Farnsworth the Third in Calcutta, India, in March of 1969, to a beautiful Indian girl of seventeen. The father, William Clayton Farnsworth the Second, grandson of the Duke of Dartmoor, had been raised on the family estate in southern England. Young Farnsworth decided that if the Beatles could go to India to find their true spirit, he could do the same.

It wasn't with Maherishi Maheyogi or Ravi Shankar that Farnsworth found enlightenment. Instead, he found his awakening in the arms of the beautiful flower, Irindi Patel. But after six months in India, Farnsworth began to tire of curry and of his Indian companion, especially when he realized Irindi was beginning to show with child.

Farnsworth's father warned him that the free love the hippies advocated wasn't really free. Payment would come due. And that point was fast approaching. So Farnsworth packed his bags and charged home to bloody old England. He had done his part to further split British/Indian relations.

Left holding the bag, or, in this case, the child, was young Irindi. Her outraged family sold her into prostitution. They wanted no part of a tainted baby. As Irindi delivered her child in a brothel on a filthy back street of Calcutta, she thought about the brutal life that lay before her and her baby son. In an act of defiance, she named her child for his father.

As he grew up roaming the teeming streets of Calcutta, little William developed an affinity for languages and dialects. He discovered he could mimic an English accent, or American, Scottish, German, French, Arabic, and many more. He would entertain his mother and her friends with his impressions.

When he spoke, he actually looked the part he was playing. His skin color and facial features allowed him to pass for almost any nationality except Scandinavian. Local gangsters soon noticed his chameleon-like abilities.

India's very active underworld fashioned themselves after the Italian Mafia. They organized themselves into 'families' and had a council to settle disputes. William, using the name Daruka Patel, joined a south Calcutta crime family at the age of twelve. With a feeling of belonging for the first time, he performed his tasks with gusto. His communication skills made him a favorite message runner.

By the time he was fifteen, he spent most of his time working the docks. He acted as part translator, part negotiator. He used different names and various accents, depending on the audience. Control of the dock area was critical when importing drugs and exporting prostitutes as part of India's female slave trade.

William learned to fight and how to handle weapons as part of his training. Again, he found he had a natural aptitude. His uniquely nondescript appearance added to his effectiveness. Not short, not tall, not thin, not fat. Using benign facial expressions, he would disarm his target into assuming he was harmless, and then strike.

At seventeen years old, he killed his first man. He'd been sent to a warehouse to meet with a particularly stubborn Spanish buyer. The Spaniard had not paid the full amount due for his shipment of young girls. Using a Hispanic alias and his skills of negotiation, William sought to solve the problem.

The buyer was adamant about not paying more. And when he made foul-mouthed comments about the Indian girls and the entire Indian race, William thought of his poor mother's life and something inside him snapped.

Agreeing to settle for the lower payment, William joked with the Spaniard and walked out of the second story office onto the landing inside the warehouse. With a shake of his hand and a slap on the shoulder, William wished the man well. Then, with the quickness of a cat, he ripped two pens from the bigger man's shirt pocket, rammed one into the man's left ear, and drove the other deep into his right eye.

The look on the Spaniard's face burned into William's brain indelibly. It was a look of total shock, horror and surprise. William whispered, "You underestimate me!" As the Spaniard raised his hands to his face, William tripped him and gave a push. The scream was muffled as the victim bounced down the wooden stairs. There was a thud when he hit the concrete floor, followed by silence.

After checking to be sure the Spaniard was dead, William felt a rush of power as he left the warehouse. Taking a life was the ultimate trip. He liked the feeling. As for remorse? None. He saw his life as an effort to climb over others. There was no reason to feel sorry for those who got in the way.

That murder launched his career — from family hits, to contract work, to international projects. The money and power were addictive. As was the game. He enjoyed the planning and the deception. And he loved the look in the victim's eyes when they realized they were about to die. That was the ultimate high.

That is how the back street urchin from Calcutta became the Gardener, the most feared and hunted assassin in the world. Sitting in his villa in Milan, he reviewed his next assignment.

He was glad to see the Americans on the list. Americans made the easiest targets — open borders, no travel restrictions, and a culturally diverse population. You had to bungle a job completely to raise suspicions in the United States.

CHAPTER 27

The Gardner passed through customs in Detroit without incident using his Pakistani passport . Since the 9/11 disasters and the War in Iraq, security was tighter but certainly not inpenetrable. Americans varied their security with their crazy color-coded system. And in first class, they gave you real steel forks but a plastic knife. Didn't they know the damage you could do with a steel fork?

His incessant babbling about an upcoming interview for an engineering position with Daimler Chrysler apparently bored the customs official to tears. With lots of smiling and nodding, the Gardner made his way through the airport to a hotel, changed identities, rented a silver Taurus, and drove to Wisconsin. There he staked out his assignment and went shopping.

I love America, thought the Gardner. Where else could you walk into Wal-Mart or Target and buy anything you need to assassinate someone and have them say "Welcome", 'Thank You", and "Have A Nice Day"? His supplies included a short piece of steel pipe, latex gloves, a spring, wire, washers, super glue, and a cheap knife. He preferred German knives, but he'd learned to use the most common items to make tracing next to impossible.

After scouting the area for a week, he finalized his plan. With an unsuspecting target, the biggest challenge was determining the method. This target was a creature of habit. Same routines. Went to work at the same time, came home the same time, mowed the grass every Saturday, etc.

When Peter Rudi fired up his Toro lawnmower at 10:01 a.m. on Saturday, he was thinking about work. He liked mowing his half-acre lot because it gave him time to think. Mowing was mindless, back and forth, almost hypnotic, except around the house and the pool, where he had to pay attention. Rudi picked this lot because of it's privacy. Surrounded by trees on all sides, it made him feel like he was in his own little kingdom.

The Gardener pilfered a few fallen oak branches from the surrounding woods earlier in the week. He experimented with these, whittling tiny arrow-like projectiles. The gun he fabricated had the power to fire a wooden projectile through half-inch thick cardboard, plenty of velocity for the job at hand.

Peter Rudi lit his cigar and began the mowing ritual. Saturday's were the best. His wife always went shopping or to the club. He was alone with his thoughts and his Toro. Wearing shorts, tee shirt, Packers' cap, and dirty tennis shoes, he looked like thousands of men in southern Wisconsin on this sunny weekend morning. Except he was about to die.

After twenty minutes, Rudi had finished the side yard and was starting on the back. On his third pass along the tree line, he felt a tap on his shoulder.

The Gardener had circled through the woods, checking every angle. There was no one around, nothing to worry about. The homemade gun was ready. The tap on the shoulder started a slow motion sequence for the Gardener. This is what he loved.

Rudi turned, a bit startled. He took the cigar from his mouth and with a quizzical look, began to speak above the roar of the Toro. "What are you..."

The Gardener raised his arm with the homemade gun, smiled, and shot Peter Rudi in the right eye, stopping him in mid sentence. The wooden stake drove through Rudi's eye, severing the optic nerve, tearing through the cerebrum, nicking the corpus callosum, and lodging in the back of the skull. Rudi's left eye showed the surprise and utter terror the Gardener loved to see. Then, with a gasp, Peter Rudi fell backwards, clutching at his eye with one hand.

As Rudi lay convulsing, the Gardener stepped around him and pulled the catch bag away from the lawnmower. Grass began to spew out onto Rudi as the mower continued to run. Reaching into his pocket, the former street urchin from Calcutta tossed a few broken sticks around the mower.

One last look at the victim gave the story of the obituary. *Peter Rudi, executive for GF Products, died tragically Saturday morning in a freak accident. Rudi was trying to unclog his lawnmower when a stick, propelled by the mower blade, struck him in the eye. Services will be on Tuesday.*

Adjusting his fishing cap, the Gardener turned away and headed through the woods to his rental car. His mind framed the picture of Peter Rudi, sprawled on his back, with one hand clutching his face, and the other stretched out to the side, still clutching a cigar. Grass was strewn across his legs and torso. Another job well done.

CHAPTER 28

A J stared at the receptionist, stunned and not fully comprehending what she had just been told. "What did you say?"

The receptionist replied in a stage whisper. "Like I just said, the flag is at half mast and the black crepe paper is everywhere because Mr. Rudi died last week."

"You mean, Peter Rudi, the plant manager?" AJ's mind didn't seem to be in gear.

"Well, yes, of course. Peter Rudi, the boss. Everyone is still in shock. It was so strange."

AJ gripped the edge of the receptionist's desk with both hands. "How did it happen?"

"Just a minute." After answering the phone twice and transferring both calls, the receptionist turned back to AJ. "We can still hardly believe what happened. Mr. Rudi was killed mowing his grass. Is that bizarre, or what?"

AJ struggled to maintain patience. "What exactly happened?"

Tammy Andrews, receptionist at GF Products for the past two years, enjoyed nothing more than gossip. She loved knowing something others didn't, and relished the opportunity to share. "Well, what I heard is, Mr. Rudi was mowing his grass, and he reached down to clear a plug of grass out of the mower spout. You know how grass bunches up sometimes? My father always said to be real careful around power equipment."

AJ gave her a keep going nod.

"So, anyway, I guess Mr. Rudi left the mower running, leaned down to clear out some grass, and BAM, a stick comes flying out from the mower. Instant eye-kabob." Tammy gave a nervous laugh at her attempted humor.

The strength drained from AJ's legs. Taking a step, she sat down heavily in the chair at the side of the receptionist's desk.

"I know what you're feeling," said a concerned Tammy. "We were all shocked when we heard it. Mr. Rudi was so important and so in charge. Hey, you don't look so good. Can I get you a glass of water or something?"

AJ waved her hand by way of declining. "A stick in the eye killed him?"

"Yup." Tammy warmed to the tale. "Frank in engineering said it was a one in ten million shot. Now, I don't know how he calculated that, but that's what he said. That stick came straight out of the mower and went right smack into the middle of his eye and into his brain. His wife came home and found him laying in the yard, dead as a doornail."

AJ had to get out of the lobby. Saying goodbye, she made it to the parking lot and leaned against her car. She felt like she might be sick, but after a few moments the feeling passed.

She struggled to clear her head. A one in ten million shot. Dad said if something seemed too coincidental to be a coincidence, it probably wasn't. She needed to talk to Kirk.

With her cell phone cradled against her shoulder, AJ put the Cherokee into gear and pulled out of the GF Products parking lot. Tapping the steering wheel impatiently, she listened to Kirk's voice mail message. "Kirk, it's AJ. Call me right away. Thanks."

Five minutes later, AJ's phone began to vibrate on the seat next to her. She saw "Kirk" on the caller ID. Opening the phone to connect, she started right in.

"Kirk, Peter Rudi of GF Products is dead, and I don't think it was an accident. This proves something strange is going on. We have to get to the bottom of it."

"Well, hi to you, too," replied Kirk. "Now slow down, and tell me again what's going on."

AJ glanced left, gunned the Jeep to change lanes and started over. "All right, all right. You remember Peter Rudi? He was the first one I saw Bouhler with at GF Products."

"Right. You said he acted strange in the lobby," responded Kirk.

"Yup. And now he's dead. The receptionist said he was killed mowing his grass." AJ related the entire story as she had heard it.

"So, AJ," Kirk paused. "What are you saying?"

"I think Peter Rudi was murdered. I think someone stabbed him in the eye and tried to make it look like an accident." AJ held her breath while she waited for Kirk's reply. She so wanted him to believe her.

Kirk sensed that AJ needed his support. "I agree with you. It's way too coincidental. Can we get more details?"

AJ breathed a sigh of relief. Kirk didn't think she was off her rocker. They discussed plans to get more information. AJ agreed to go to the library and check the newspaper reports, and Kirk said he would talk to a friend who worked in the state police department.

Kirk shifted his cell phone to his other ear. "AJ, I'm on my way to Memphis for the Olympic qualifying meet. I'll be gone for four days. Are you going to be all right?"

"Sure. I'll be fine. I feel better now that we've talked."

"OK. I'll make some calls from Memphis and see what I can find out. See what you can find out at the library. You might also search for any articles in the past year or so about GF Products and Rudi."

They finalized their strategy and said goodbye.

CHAPTER 29

W̲hile AJ and Kirk talked, the Gardener completed his surveillance in a posh neighborhood in Hinsdale, Illinois. Hinsdale had one of the highest per capita income levels in Illinois, and it showed. Homes worth millions and landscaping to match were the norm.

Only a half hour from Fermilab, Hinsdale was home to many of the Fermilab executives and top scientists. The Gardener watched his target and determined the appropriate method of separation from this world. He marveled at the wealthy. Their pomposity left them no street smarts. Ego had taken over where self-preservation previously existed.

Matthew Clement had climbed the Fermilab ladder quickly. His expensive tastes, however, outpaced his pay. His greed allowed Mengele to snare him. Clement rationalized that corporate secrets eventually got out anyway, so why not profit by sharing his knowledge?

Clement had no idea that he had become excess baggage, to be discarded like yesterday's newspaper. At thirty-nine years old, he had the world by the tail. But everything he valued — house, car, worldly possessions — would soon become superfluous. Too bad he hadn't realized what was really important in life.

Tonight, all that mattered to Clement was the fantastic party he would be attending the following evening. The limo, his date, and the who's who guest list were what counted. He was on the A list. Too bad he was also on the list of the former street urchin, William Clayton Farnsworth. And all that mattered to the Gardener was completing his contracts.

Two days later, Kirk had learned a lot. He realized that Memphis was more Louisiana than Tennessee. Growing up in California and then living in the Midwest, his vision of Tennessee was of mountains and country music. Knoxville and Nashville.

But, Memphis was hot and southern. Beale Street jazz and southern hospitality. The winding Mississippi River provided stop you in your tracks humidity. Almost a New Orleans feel.

Kirk Vail worked the track meet from two angles. As the Green Star rep, he schmoozed the athletes. As an undercover agent, he tracked the drugs and gambling that stalked the sport of track and field.

He also picked up more details concerning the death of Peter Rudi. Through the agency, he'd gotten a copy of the police report, complete with photos. The local police declared it an unfortunate accident. But after reviewing the file, Kirk had to admit AJ might be on the right track.

The photos showed Rudi lying face up next to his lawn mower. A stick protruded from his right eye, blood was streaked across his face and grass was scattered across his legs and torso. What Kirk found interesting was that Rudi still held a cigar in his left hand, outstretched to the side. His right arm lay across his chest, where he apparently had reached for the stick before dying.

The position of the mower made the chain of events perplexing. Rudi lay by the left side of the lawn mower, where the grass catcher was located. Supposedly, he took the end of the catcher off to unclog some grass, and was struck in the eye while leaning down.

It seemed to Kirk a person would be more likely to be struck in the left eye if he leaned that low. But the real kicker was how could you have a cigar in your left hand?

Kirk acted it out in his hotel room a dozen times. If you leaned over on the left side of a mower to unhook the grass catcher, you used your left hand. No way would you have a cigar in your left hand. No, you'd either have it in your right hand or clamped between your teeth.

The angle of entry of the stick was just too perfect. Straight into the eye of a man bent over the mower defied the odds. The close-up photos of the stick showed, at least to Kirk, a pointed end too symmetrical to have been cut by a mower blade. It looked like a whittling stick.

Maybe AJ was right. Maybe there was something terribly wrong with this picture. He'd have the company do more digging and he'd let AJ know Rudi's death looked fishy. But for the next two days, he would be totally occupied with the Olympic Track Trials.

CHAPTER 30

It was four in the afternoon on Friday when AJ found out. She had finished her last sales call in Appleton and stopped at a Starbucks to get a caramel machiato. Standing in line, she watched the television above the checkout. The CNN announcer was silently mouthing words as the split screen showed a huge building with the word "Fermilab" on the front. Stepping around the people ahead of her, AJ reached up and turned up the volume.

"...are piecing together what happened. Matthew Clement, executive director of the Fermilab neutron therapy division, died last evening after returning to his home in Hinsdale, Illinois. Clement had been the keynote speaker at the 'Executives Under Forty' banquet held at the Drake Hotel in downtown Chicago. Police were called to investigate when Mr. Clement failed to arrive at work today."

AJ's eyes were glued to the screen. She was totally oblivious to the nasty looks from customers forced to make their way around her.

The picture shifted to a uniformed policeman standing in the front yard of a large brick home. The sidewalk in front of the million-dollar mansion was lined with reporters and neighborhood gawkers. Everyone strained to see what had happened to the Fermilab executive.

An attractive blond newswoman stepped into the picture, looked directly into the camera and began to speak. "Officer Hanson, can you describe what you found when you arrived at the Matthew Clement home this afternoon?"

A twenty-six year veteran of the Hinsdale police force, Edward Richard Hanson was ill at ease as the blond talking-head thrust the microphone in front of him.

Officer Hanson blinked and began to speak. "Responding to the call from Fermilab that Mr. Clement didn't come to work, we tried the doorbell with no response. The doors were all locked. We checked the entire perimeter and everything appeared normal."

Chelsea Lang, runway model turned television reporter, couldn't let her audience change the channel. Her producer screamed in her earpiece to "get to the good stuff."

"What did you find after you forced entry into the Clement home?" she asked.

"The first floor was empty," Hanson said. "We called out, but received no answer. So we checked the second floor, and that's when we found him."

The reporter tried to hide her exasperation as she probed. "And what condition was Mr. Clement in when you found him?"

Ed Hanson suppressed an incredulous laugh. "Why, he was dead! Why else would the news people be here?"

With her producer's vitriol spewing in her ear, Chelsea pushed on. "Officer Hanson, so Mr. Clement was dead. Can you tell us what room he was in and *exactly* what he was wearing and what the scene looked like?"

Ed Hanson gazed into the camera and in his most official voice produced the details America wanted. "At 3:27 p.m., we found Mr. Matthew Clement lying on the floor of the second story bathroom, off of the master bedroom of his home. The deceased was lying on his side, wearing only a pair of black dress slacks. They were bunched down around his ankles."

Chelsea Lang's smile corresponded to the producer saying, "Now we're getting somewhere!"

"Officer Hanson, are you saying Matthew Clement lay dead in his own bathroom, wearing no shirt, no shoes, no socks, and no underwear? Just slacks around his ankles?" Chelsea hoped she was usung the appropriate breathless voice to convey her shock to the viewing audience.

Ed Hanson knew his fifteen minutes of fame had arrived and was glad he'd shaved closely and carefully that morning. "Yes, Ma'am. No unders. No boxers, no briefs, no nothing. In my younger days we called that 'going commando.' Mr. Clement was naked as a jaybird, except for those expensive slacks."

A Starbucks customer who thought coffee was more important than breaking news bumped AJ. The look in her eyes made him back off and leave the TV to her.

"Officer Hanson, what was the cause of death?"

Hanson gave the official consensus, hoping his wife was taping this. "Mr. Matthew Clement had returned home after a banquet, undressed to just his slacks, and while removing them, became entangled and fell. His right temple struck the sharp marble corner of the vanity and Mr. Clement died on the bathroom floor from the blow. The coroner describes it as blunt blow trauma to the temporal lobe."

Taking a cue from her producer, Chelsea Lang probed for further details. "Is there any evidence of foul play?"

"No, ma'am. The alarms were set in the house, and all of the doors and windows were secured. No signs of forced entry or foul play. The blood alcohol level of Mr. Clement was 0.12, which can sure make you unsteady. It's a freak accident, but exactly that. An accident. Heck, we've all had that happen, where you almost fall getting dressed or undressed. Mr. Clement, unfortunately, didn't catch himself in time."

AJ didn't hear anything else. She didn't know how long she stood in Starbucks, people moving too and fro around her. She was in the eye of a hurricane. She stood in a vacuum, waiting to be sucked into the storm. Not knowing why terrible things were happening, but knowing they were connected.

Peter Rudi and Matthew Clement. Emile Bouhler and Duane Cox. Life wasn't making sense. She had that boxed in feeling. She didn't have any answers. There was no audience help, no fifty-fifty chance.

Time to phone a friend.

Kirk's voice mail message said it all. "Hi, this is Kirk Vail. I'm in Memphis at the Olympic track trials. I'm not sure when I'll get to my messages, but I'll get back to you as soon as I can."

AJ left a frantic message saying call her. She paced around the parking lot of Starbucks like a caged animal. Who to talk to? She had to talk to someone. Then it hit her. John Cline! He was the coolest under fire and AJ trusted his judgment.

She dialed the office, tapping on the hood of her car with her free hand. When Barb told her John had taken a day off, AJ practically screamed. But Barb knew where he was. He was on his boat in Door County. He docks it at Sister Bay. Twenty-four foot sailboat named Cash Bar.

After thanking Barb for the information, AJ called her friend Sarah and asked her to take Freethrow for a walk because she'd be late getting home. Firing up the Jeep, she did the mental math. Appleton to Green Bay, Green Bay to the tip of Door County. She figured two hours and twenty minutes. She calmed down a fraction. Dad always said, "In times of stress focus on a short-term goal."

Sister Bay, here I come.

CHAPTER 31

John Cline sat on the built-in couch inside his Pearson sailboat and stared at the half empty bottle of Paul Masson brandy. Half empty or half full? Definitely half empty, soon to be all empty. The irregular sound of rain hitting canvas, wood, and water, darkened his mood. Clouds had blanketed the bay all day, and now rain.

His plans for a three-day sailing weekend looked like a bust. Like most of his plans lately, this one was going south fast. When both his friends cancelled on him, he bull-headedly decided to come alone, even though he knew he should have at least one more hand on deck.

As he grabbed his cigarettes from the galley counter, John thought, *It's just as well. It's raining and I'd probably wreck the boat trying to sail her by myself.* After lighting an unfiltered Camel, which he hated but couldn't quit, he put on his rain gear and went topside. Standing in the light rain, he let his mind wander.

Why is it called a rain slicker? Slicker than what? Teflon? Now, that's some slick stuff. That's why they make spatulas and valve seats out of it.

Who invented smoking? Can you imagine someone rolling up big leafs, lighting them on fire, and sucking on them? Doesn't make much sense.

Why does rain seem so depressing when you're alone, when it was the absolute best thing about football practice in high school? Why did the guy I bought this boat from pick Cash Bar as the name? Was he an alcoholic or a liquor distributor? Why didn't I change the name? Thank goodness it wasn't named Last Chance or End of the Road. But that's exactly what it feels like to me.

John stared westward into the bay and watched the rain pepper the water like thousands of tiny stones. With water streaming down his hat and shoulders, he had another random thought. *Am I killing myself an inch at a time? Am I doing with cigarettes and alcohol what I don't have the guts to do with a Smith and Wesson 45?*

A shiver ran down his spine at the thought. He turned to go below and flicked his cigarette over the side of the boat. It hit the rope railing and fell back onto the deck. *Missed again*, he thought, as he hunched his shoulders forward and trudged down the steep steps. Closing the hatch and shedding his rain gear, John Cline sat down to finish his brandy and play solitaire.

He knew he wouldn't win at solitaire, but finishing the brandy was a sure bet. One for two. Fifty percent. Best percentage he'd hit this year.

As he shuffled the cards, John wondered if he was suffering from depression. He thought of that old joke; a recession is when your neighbor loses his job, but a depression is when you lose yours.

When your friends feel down, you try to be sympathetic. But when you feel down, the world is coming to an end.

Driving up from Madison this morning was depressing. Something about Door County got to him lately. Cutesy towns with cutesy names. Egg Harbor, Fish Creek, Whitefish Bay, Baileys Harbor. It seemed to smack of the fat cats' playground. The common man didn't have cottages in Door County. The Door County peninsula was the thumb of Wisconsin, sticking into Lake Michigan.

More like sticking it to the regular folks. Catch a glimpse of how the other half lives! Come to Door County and see what you dream about, but will never have. Unlike the Hotel California, you can come in, but you can't STAY!

CHAPTER 32

For hundreds of years, Native Americans of the Potawatomi and Chippewa tribes fished the waters of Green Bay. The peninsula sheltered the waters from the tempestuousness of Lake Michigan, providing a haven for marine life.

In the 1600's, exploration of the region by Europeans brought the Frenchmen Robert de LaSalle and Jean Nicolet to the lower peninsula. Their reports of timber, game, and fish paved the way for trappers and traders. Ships loaded with valuable furs provided motivation for more adventurers.

The northern stretch of the peninsula received its first permanent white settlers in 1844. Increase Claflin and his wife Mary decided to brave isolation for the opportunity to claim land for themselves. Within eleven years, the communities of Baileys Harbor on the Lake Michigan side and Fish Creek on the Green Bay side were established as refueling stops for ships plying trade across the lake.

Cordwood shipped out of the refueling stops provided new job opportunities and growth for the area. Harvesting the natural resources of timber and fish provided a living for most of the early settlers.

By the early 1900's, greatly improved transportation provided an avenue for tourists to visit the scenic area for outdoor recreation and water activities. Steam ships and automobiles brought a growing stream of Midwesterners looking to spend their disposable income on leisure.

From the time the peninsula had been acquired by the United States from the British in 1783, the territory had fallen under numerous names. The peninsula had been part of the Northwest Territory, Indiana Territory, Illinois Territory, Michigan Territory and Wisconsin Territory. In 1848, it became part of Brown County in the State of Wisconsin.

Finally, after gaining enough citizens to qualify as a county, on February 11, 1851, the peninsula became Door County. As a tip of land jutting into mighty Lake Michigan, the area was truly a doorway to the lake. Tourism became the primary revenue source. For those entering the area in the new millennium, the thumb of Wisconsin was a doorway to nature and recreational splendor.

For AJ, the doorway this evening was wet. What started out as an overcast afternoon when she left Appleton turned into a steady drizzle. The slow moving traffic on Highway 42 gave her time to reminisce about happier days in Door County. She had read that over six million tourists visited the peninsula annually. It was the Cape Cod of the Midwest.

Coming here with her Dad had always been a special treat for AJ. They would rent a pontoon boat and spend lazy hot summer days fishing, and tubing on the bay. Walks along the beach, skipping stones on the water, and watching the sunset were special times. And the card games at night in the cabin were marathon matches with friends and neighbors.

She recalled a story Dad told about Reverend Andrew Iverson. Iverson had walked across the ice of the frozen bay in the 1850's from Green Bay to the peninsula to pick a spot to establish a new community. The reverend and his followers called the town Ephraim. Dad explained that Ephraim was the youngest son of Joseph in the Bible and that one of the twelve tribes of Israel was descended from him.

Dad explained Ephraim was also a name for the northern kingdom of Israel. He thought it was clever of the reverend to name a northern settlement on the peninsula after a northern kingdom of Israel. Dad liked to tell the story about the walk across the ice. He would embellish it with howling wind sounds and shiver as if freezing to death.

When he ended the story, Dad always made sure you got the message. Anything you believed in was worth going after, and anything worth going after was sure to have hardships along the way. Were you willing to walk miles across the ice to reach your goal? If not, then it wasn't a worthwhile goal.

AJ only had a mile to go to see if John Cline could help solve her own personal mystery. While the wipers of the Jeep kept cadence, AJ hummed along with the Beach Boys on the radio. "No surfing today. Say Hey, rain delay, we'll come back another day." She spotted the line of boats and began to read the names.

CHAPTER 33

John took a sip of brandy and shuffled the cards. He had tried six kinds of solitaire and hadn't come close to winning a game. Why did people play solitaire? It was a waste of time for people who had nothing but time to waste.

Thinking of his own life, John knew he now had way too much time on his hands. He loved work and the rewards of helping customers and fellow employees. But since his divorce, nights and weekends were torturous. Non-productive free time made him angry and frustrated.

He was also starting to feel prejudiced again. It made him so mad he could spit. When he grew up in rural Minnesota, everybody got along. True, it wasn't a hugely diverse population, but differences in people didn't seem to matter.

Then John Cline was drafted. It was 1971 and a crazy time in the world. Riots were breaking out in the U.S., and he would be sent to Vietnam. It was in the army where John Cline became a bigot.

His galvanizing experience occurred during basic training at Fort Jackson, South Carolina. From the first day, he felt that blacks and whites were treated differently. Sometimes it was subtle, but often it was blatant. He knew it wasn't right and he tried to speak up a couple of times.

Big mistake. It seems Alabama crackers and New York brothers weren't interested in the input from the kid from Minnesota. He wasn't part of either group, and it hurt.

Then the incident occurred. A white private walked into the TV room where three black PFC's were watching Soul Train. After loudly disparaging the show, the white private changed the channel. Heated words were exchanged and a shoving match ensued.

The white soldier threw the first punch and fled the TV room. The three black soldiers chased him, disappearing onto the stairway landing. There were shouts and the sound of someone tumbling down the stairs. The result was a white private with a broken leg, dislocated shoulder and a face that looked like ground beef. And John Cline, idly shooting pool by himself at the end of the rec room, was the only witness.

During the investigation, the black soldiers contended the white private initiated the fight and had fallen down the steps, injuring himself. The injured white private claimed the blacks attacked him for no reason and threw him down the stairs. Every white on the base screamed for revenge for the malicious attack, while every black denounced the charges as a railroad job.

John Cline was caught in the maelstrom. He had not seen what happened in the stairway, but he was threatened, and called derogatory names. He was accused of conspiracy by one side, and pressured to backup the story of the other side.

Cline was pushed to his limits. He was treated as a stereotype and he had to choose a side. For the first time in his life he picked his side based on something he hadn't worried about much previously, the color of his skin. But from then on, it mattered. John Cline was black. The whites treated him horribly, so he testified against the white private, saying he fell down the stairs.

The rest of his tour of duty was a blur. Nam did things to a person you didn't talk about. He crawled into tunnels and slit the throats of VC. He used grenades to clear out huts, knowing there could be women and children inside. And he learned to hate whites, lumping them all together with a prejudice he couldn't prevent.

But that was decades years ago. He'd returned to the Midwest and made a life for himself. It took time, but he had gotten back to being himself. No prejudging people. He had a family, a good job, and a warm circle of friends.

Then Pam left him, and his world crumbled. They had grown apart, she said. No, there was no one else, she said. Then, after the divorce, she took the kids and moved in with the guy who miraculously appeared out of nowhere.

John leaned back and rubbed his eyes. After Pam left, he saw the world differently. Things made him mad that hadn't mattered before. Now, he didn't like being alone, he didn't like being black, and he didn't like getting older. Actually, he didn't like much of anything.

"Hey, anybody home?"

The voice startled John. Who would be out in the rain on a night like this looking for him?

"Who is it?" he called, as he worked to slide back the hatch.

"Let me in, before I catch pneumonia!"

He recognized AJ's voice and laughed. "Well, look what the cat dragged in. It's a might wet for sitting on deck, so come below, and welcome aboard."

While John secured the hatch, AJ shook off the rain and removed her coat. Hanging AJ's coat on a hook, John asked, "So, what brings you out here tonight? I suppose you've got a huge project you want old John to take care of for you."

The look on her face told him something serious was going on.

"John, I need someone to talk to. I think I've stumbled onto some sort of industrial espionage, and I don't know what to do. Do you have some time to talk?"

The intense, sincere look in AJ's eyes melted John's heart. Since the day she started work, John had liked AJ Clark. She was smart, caring, and paid attention to detail. They developed a strong mentoring relationship, and John was protective of her.

Looking around the boat and back at AJ, John gave a mock sigh. "As you can see, the party is raging. But for you, I'll put the celebration on hold."

"Thanks, John. I appreciate it. I'm a bit rattled right now."

"AJ, no problem. Besides, the three greatest mysteries of the last 100 years are: Who stole the Lindbergh baby, who really shot President Kennedy, and what has AJ Clark gotten herself involved in? If I can solve one of the three, I'll die a happy man."

A load was lifted from AJ's shoulders, knowing she had someone else to confide in. She hoped John Cline was as understanding as Kirk had been.

She told her story, trying to be as unemotional as possible. Since John had helped her check on the companies related to Bouhler and Cox, he knew the background for her concern. As she retold the story, AJ again felt her instincts were correct. She knew she wasn't imagining things. But what was it all about and what could they do about it?

CHAPTER 34

K irk enjoyed track meets. Multiple activities occurring simultaneously and the buzz of the crowd challenged the senses. The warm Memphis air and sunny sky were great for the spectators.

The Olympic trials were progressing mostly as expected. The favorites were winning the sprints, distance races, and most of the field events. But there was real excitement around the pole vault pit. The leader, from UCLA, had been bragging all week in the papers that he was going to break the record of 20' 1 3/4" , held by the international pole vault great, Sergei Bubka of the USSR.

Bubka won the gold medal in the 1988 Olympics. He set world records thirty-five times and had won six consecutive world championships. His dominance in the sport was evident by the fact that he still held the indoor and outdoor pole vault world records, even though he was now long retired.

The pole vault was particularly interesting during this Olympic year. The Americans were mounting a real challenge for a gold medal, and there was a murmur in the track community of a new world record. No one had broken the six-meter mark since Bubka.

In a sport of statistics, the six-meter pole vault was akin to the ten second hundred meter dash and the four minute mile. Fans loved records that were easy to relate to.

The pole vault record had meaning for the world and America. The world related to the six-meter mark, while Americans related to the twenty-foot mark. Even for the Americans uninterested in metrics, the pole vault was going to be worth watching this year.

The United States had reason to be excited about the prospect of renewing dominance. When the pole vault was instituted in the modern Olympic Games in 1896, the winner was an American, William Hoyt, with a vault of 10'10", or 3.30 meters.

For the next seventy-two years, the US dominated the event, winning the gold in every Olympics. Bob Seagren's winning vault in 1968 in Mexico City was a shining moment in American sports. His height of 5.40 meters, not quite eighteen feet, was the high water mark in the event for the US. He was the last American to stand on the platform to receive the pole vault gold medal, until Nick Hysong of the US won the gold in 2000 in Atlanta.

Since 1968, the event had been dominated by a succession of Europeans. The Soviets, Germans, Polish and French had continued to raise the bar, with the rest of the world lagging behind. In the U.S., the lucrative team sports attracted the superior athletes needed to excel at this difficult event. Often the Western Hemisphere seemed to concede the pole vault while concentrating on other events.

Not this year. The U.S. wanted to repeat and to dominate again. The UCLA vaulter crowed to the press about his superiority and his preparation. And now he battled the unassuming kid from Tennessee, Jimmy Wickland, as the rest of the contestants failed to clear the bar.

Kirk found the vault intriguing. There was an intimidation factor in track you couldn't feel unless you were near the event. The icy stares, sunglasses, and strutting bravado were all part of the psych factor. The UCLA hotshot was pulling out all the stops as he preened prior to each vault.

Wickland, on the other hand, adopted the ignore strategy. He paid little attention to anything, just waiting to be called. Both athletes cleared 19' 3", then 19' 4 1/2". At 19' 6", both failed on their first attempt. They were attempting to clear 5.98 meters, a mark that would have won the last four Olympics.

After his opponent kicked off the bar on his second attempt, Jimmy knew this was it. His second vault was often his best. He knew what he had to do. He needed to push off harder and twist a bit more as he shot skyward. He tugged at his orange and blue shorts to be sure they didn't bind, and he hefted his pole.

Staring down the rubberized runway surface, Jimmy exhaled twice and rocked slightly. He said a simple silent prayer, ending in, "Let me fly and kiss the sky." One final deep breath and he was off. Thundering down the runway with his pole held skyward, Jimmy felt like he was jousting. He'd had that conversation with a teammate once. Jimmy made a comment about taping pillows on the end of the poles and jousting with each other. The strange look he received convinced him to keep his private thoughts to himself.

As he neared the pit, he aimed the pole toward the metal vault box and raised his arms. As the pole bent, he felt the tension build as he moved forward. Just as he was beginning to experience the lift, the pole snapped.

Jimmy careened forward, the shattered end of the pole catching him hard across the shoulder. As he cartwheeled to the side, his leg struck the stanchion and he tried to pull himself into a tuck. As he rolled over the edge of the inflatable landing surface, the fans at the near side of the stadium came to their feet.

Even though no fan ever admits it, the specter of violence at a sporting event is part of the attraction. The Romans hadn't packed the Coliseum and the Hippodrome with jugglers and poets. It was blood and gore they wanted. Auto races have crashes, hockey has glorified fights, and football has high-speed collisions. In track, a vault or hurdle mishap pumped adrenaline through the crowd like the pulsing music of a rock concert.

Jimmy landed with a skid and a thud. The stadium gasped as everyone strained to see the extent of his injuries. Officials from the corners of the infield sprinted over to see how seriously he was injured.

Blood streaked down Wickland's left shoulder and his right leg was bent beneath him at an odd angle. When he attempted to rise, an official pushed him back down and told him to lie still. Looking around, Jimmy took a quick mental inventory of his body parts.

One official called loudly, "Everyone back! Let's get a stretcher over here." Again, Jimmy tried to get up, but was assured he needed to remain stationary.

The crowd applauded as four men carried Wickland from the infield on a stretcher. Giving a weak wave, Jimmy laid his head back and wondered how badly he was injured.

Placed on a table in the locker room beneath the stands, Jimmy was approached by a gray haired man dressed all in white. "Hello, Mr. Wickland. I'm Dr. Charles Jacobs, and I'd like to take a look to see what we have done to ourselves today."

Jimmy liked the doctor's calm demeanor and hoped he was as competent as he was likeable. His easy-going attitude allayed Jimmy's fears.

"Now, son," said Dr. Jacobs. "I've worked on all kinds of people and a few animals in my day. Don't you worry. I've been around the barn a few times and I can say with authority, I think you'll live."

Jimmy let out a laugh. Hopefully this grandfather MD practiced on more people than horses.

Dr. Jacobs took the large plastic Olympic pass that hung on a lanyard around his neck and flipped it over his shoulder out of the way. He began examining Jimmy's shoulder.

"Frank," Dr. Jacobs said to the assistant trainer who was hovering behind him. "Go get two wet towels and a couple of ice packs."

"Yes, sir," replied Frank as he hurried to fetch the supplies.

"Now, Mr. Wickland. From where I stood, it looked as though your pole broke in half. Did you do anything different on that vault?"

"No, Dr. Jacobs. I planted the pole as usual. When I gave the final push to elevate, the pole snapped. Maybe it was a manufacturing defect. My pole wasn't that old."

Dr. Jacobs chuckled. "My grandson works for a company that manufactures motor parts, and he's always telling me quality is dead. Their rejection rate on parts keeps going up."

Frank returned with the towels and the cold packs. While he worked on Jimmy, Dr. Jacobs kept a constant banter.

"This might sting a bit. I want to clean this blood off your shoulder so I can see what we've got here."

Dr. Jacobs probed while Jimmy winced and groaned through the examination. While Frank bandaged the affected areas, the doctor left the locker room for a few minutes. The trainer applied ice packs and elastic wraps where needed.

When he returned, Dr. Jacobs pulled a metal folding chair up next to the table and took a seat. Crossing his legs, he looked Jimmy in the eye. "Mr. Wickland, we have some good news, some bad news, and some great news."

After a pause, in which Jimmy's eyes said, "Please continue," the doctor removed his glasses and began cleaning them. "Let's start with the good news. It doesn't look like you have any permanent debilitating injuries. No surgery, no hospital stay, no nurses fawning over you."

Jimmy nodded, waiting for the rest of the news.

"The bad news is you are pretty well banged up. You have a couple of serious abrasions that will take time to heal and will be quite painful. Your right shin is badly skinned up, your shoulder will be quite stiff for a while, and your left knee has a moderate sprain."

Jimmy listened intently as Dr. Jacobs continued. "So that's the bad news. It will take time to heal, but the good news is that you will be good as a new penny in time."

Leaning up on his elbows, Jimmy exhaled. "OK, Doc. But you said there was some great news, too."

"Oh, yes. I almost forgot." Dr. Jacobs's eyes twinkled. "You're going to the Olympics!"

Jimmy's eyes threatened to burst from his head. "You must be kidding. Are you serious?!"

Dr. Jacobs nodded. "Two of you qualified for the Olympics. The young stud from UCLA will be carrying the U.S. Olympic hopes. And a banged up young man from Tennessee will be going along to carry his pole. You're last completed jump qualified you for a trip to Chicago. I wish you the best."

After a pause, Dr. Jacobs continued, "That's the great news. The downside is you're going to be awfully sore for quite a while. I don't know how well you'll be able to train or if you'll be able to compete."

Jimmy sat up on the table and looked at the doctor with the intensity of a laser. "Doc, I'll compete. Make no mistake about that. I WILL be ready for the Olympics."

Having seen that look in athletes' eyes before, Dr. Jacobs had no doubt that if heart alone could make it happen, Jimmy Wickland would be wearing gold someday. Giving Jimmy's good shoulder a squeeze, Jacobs replied, "I know you'll be ready, son."

After giving a series of instructions to the trainer, Dr. Jacobs turned back to Jimmy. "Mr. Wickland, I want you to lay back down here for a half hour with ice on the injured areas. We'll get some painkillers for you in a few minutes. You'll be bandaged up and out of here in a bit."

"But I want you to take it easy for a week to let your body heal before you begin rigorous training again. You're lucky you didn't do any serious damage."

With a wink, the doctor turned and left the training room.

CHAPTER 35

In the hall, Dr. Jacobs was met by a phalanx of media. Cameramen and news reporters all jabbered at once asking the condition of Jimmy Wickland.

Holding up his hand for silence, Dr. Jacobs made a show of taking off his glasses and slowly cleaning them. When he had them repositioned on his nose to his satisfaction, he addressed the crowd.

"Folks, I'm only going to do this once, so get your cameras rolling and have your pencils ready." Straightening his jacket, he looked directly at the nearest camera.

"I'm Dr. Charles Jacobs. I have just examined young Jim Wickland, the pole vaulter from Tennessee who gave you the highlight film you'll be using tonight."

There was laughter from the crowd and a number of nodding heads. "When his pole broke, Mr. Wickland suffered a number of injuries, including class two abrasions, a moderate sprain to his left knee, and a contusion of the right shoulder. In my opinion, he'll heal up as good as new. But it will take some time."

Dr. Jacobs waved off the questions from the reporters. "I'm sure you heard young Mr. Wickland made the Olympic team, which makes all of us very proud. He is excited about the prospect of representing his country. The challenge for him is going to be working toward full recovery in time to compete in Chicago. That's all I have for now. Thank you."

Reporters shouted questions and waved their notepads as Dr. Jacobs turned and walked down the tunnel toward the stadium. Reporters continued to call after him. He turned and reiterated, "Folks, if you'll excuse me. We have other Olympic trial events to finish, and I need to be on the field."

As he marched resolutely into the sunlight, a tall gentleman fell in step with him. "Dr. Jacobs?"

Turning to look up at the man's face, the doctor exclaimed, "Well, Kirk Vail!" He shook Kirk's hand as they walked. "I haven't seen you in a month of Sundays, son. In fact, I still remember the first time we met. You sprained your wrist in a volleyball tournament years ago."

"Your memory is perfect, as usual. It's good to see you, Dr. Jacobs."

"Walk with me, Kirk." Dr. Jacobs headed to the infield of the track with Kirk in tow.

As they walked, Kirk asked about Jimmy Wickland. "He's banged up, Kirk. But I tell you, he's tough. He'll recover fine, though I doubt if he can recover in time to be really competitive in the Olympics. He took quite a tumble."

Kirk gave a laugh. "I know. It looks like that shot will make the Sports Center highlights for months. When the pole snapped and he went flying, I figured he was sure to break something."

"You're exactly right. He was fortunate. No broken bones and no serious joint injury. He has a long road to a full recovery. But at least his dream of making the Olympics has been realized. How many of us can say we've reached our dreams?"

As they neared a group of officials, Kirk knew it was time to say farewell. "Thanks for the insight, Doc. And thanks for the help on the previous cases."

Dr. Jacobs stopped and looked up at Kirk. "Keep up the good work. The problems in sports need to be cleaned up. I know it's often a convoluted path to the truth, so if I can help, I'm glad to lend assistance."

Kirk smiled. "It's a never-ending battle. Please keep me posted of any developments."

With a smile and a wink, Dr. Jacobs replied. "You'll be the first to know."

As he walked back to the stands, Kirk looked at the scene around him. He knew the huge pressure to compete and the restricted time frame till the Olympics would tempt Wickland to use performance-enhancing drugs. It was a situation Kirk would monitor closely.

Just then an announcement came over the loudspeakers declaring the qualifiers for the Olympics in the high jump and the pole vault. When Jimmy Wickland's name was announced, there was an eruption from the crowd. Here in Memphis, Wickland was the only Tennessee participant to qualify, so the hopes and dreams of the local fans fell on his shoulders.

There was a chorus of applause, whistling and cheering that drowned out the announcements that followed. Kirk hoped the kid could handle the pressure he was going to be under.

After Dr. Jacobs left, Jimmy reflected on his accomplishment. He made the Olympic team. That, in itself, was a dream come true. He sat up, flexed his shoulder, and winced at the pain.

He reached to the floor and hauled his gym bag up on the table. He ripped off the piece of tape showing "Memphis", exposing the tape beneath reading "Chicago" with the five Olympic rings drawn next to it. He was going to the Olympic Games! Grams will be proud.

Rummaging in his bag and looking around to be sure no one was nearby, he pulled out a jar containing a thick green ointment. Peeling back the bandages the trainer had applied, Jimmy massaged the ointment into his shoulder muscles. There was an immediate feeling of relief as he applied the healing salve.

After replacing the bandage, he repeated the procedure with his abrasions. After he finished, he took the mixture and massaged his injured knee, taking time to be sure and cover the joint from every angle. He felt warmth within the joint beginning to radiate outward. He could almost feel the healing taking place.

Jimmy smiled as he worked on his knee. *I'll be ready for the Olympics. There is no way anything can keep me from fulfilling my dream. There are more goals underneath the Chicago tape I intend to reach.*

A roar from the stadium interrupted his thoughts. There were cheers and foot stomping. The door to the training room flew open and Frank, the trainer, leaned in.

"Wickland, they're cheering for you, man. The crowd is going nuts. I thought you'd want to know what all the noise was about."

"Hey, thanks. I guess I got the sympathy vote," answered Jimmy.

Frank shook his head. "It's more than that. Listen."

As he strained to hear above the crowd noise, Jimmy could faintly hear the tune "Rocky Top", the Tennessee anthem.

Frank, who'd gone to the University of Memphis and who had a brother attending the University of Tennessee, smiled at Jimmy. "Tennessee rocks! The whole state will be pulling for you!"

"Thanks. I'll do my best."

After Frank left and the cheers and music finally died down, Jimmy thought about Grams. She was always saying, "Enjoy the trip. It's the journey, not the destination that brings the most enjoyment."

He'd gotten goose bumps listening to the crowd. It couldn't get any better than this. *I wonder if they'll play Rocky Top after the National Anthem when I win in Chicago?*

CHAPTER 36

John Cline looked at AJ as she finished her tale of suspected intrigue. He patiently listened to AJ's theory as the two of them sat on the vinyl bench seats of his boat. "I think you're on to something," said John. "What you've told me goes way beyond coincidence.

AJ was relieved John didn't think she was losing her mind. She vacillated from thinking there was a deadly conspiracy to paranoia over worrying about something that was none of her business. With Kirk unavailable, she needed someone to confide in.

"Thanks, John. I appreciate your taking this seriously. When I tell this story, it just sounds so strange. But I know something is terribly wrong. I know the deaths of Peter Rudi of GF Products and Matthew Clement of Fermilab are connected somehow."

John stood and went to the galley to rinse out his cup. "AJ, let me dig into this for you. I want to search on the Internet under companies and persons' names. There has to be a connection somewhere."

AJ was relieved to have help. "That would be great. You're the best!"

John smiled as he wiped off the tiny stainless steel galley counter. "Flattery will get you everything. I know you think I sit with my feet up all day, while you're out in the field doing all the work. So I might as well put that time to use."

Laughing, AJ stood. "I really needed someone to talk to tonight. I hated to bother you on your boat."

"Hey, AJ. That's what I'm here for. I'm a support guy, working in the background while you close the deals. Someday, when you're rich and famous, I'll get the award for best supporting valve salesman, and my life will be complete."

"Thanks, John." AJ took her coat from the hook. "I've got to head back to Madison. A friend's checking on my dog and you need to get back to your plans."

"Sure," said John. "Leave me here in Door County, in the rain, all alone, with an inexplicable mystery on my mind. I'll have nightmares tonight."

AJ smiled. "Oh, I think you'll be all right."

As they stood facing each other, there was an awkward silence. AJ finally took a step forward and gave John a quick hug. "Thanks."

She turned and was up the steps and gone before John could respond. He stood with his arms hanging by his sides, the silence broken by the patter of rain on the deck coming through the open hatch.

Two realizations hit John simultaneously. He needed to close the hatch so the rain didn't get in the boat. And AJ Clark smelled better than anything he had smelled in a long time. He knew what to do about the hatch. But he wasn't sure what to do about his feelings toward AJ.

CHAPTER 37

The next afternoon, Kirk felt a tap on his shoulder as he stood in the Memphis sun enjoying the track meet. "I'm sorry. No shoe peddlers allowed."

Kirk turned. "Well, Dr. Jacobs. Good to see you again."

"I'm glad you're here today. I've got something interesting to tell you." Dr. Jacobs motioned Kirk to follow him across the infield. When they were safely away from stray ears, the doctor turned to Kirk.

"I examined the pole vaulter, Wickland, earlier this afternoon. Very interesting results."

Kirk's curiosity was aroused. "What is it, Dr. Jacobs? Is he going to have to pull out of the Olympics?"

Dr. Jacobs shook his head. "Quite the contrary. His injuries look unbelievably good. His abrasions look like they've had a week to heal, not just twenty-four hours."

"You're kidding!" said Kirk.

"No, I'm not kidding. His skin has practically healed overnight. He seems to have very little pain in his shoulder and knee, which should be aching for weeks. I've been in medicine so long I thought I'd seen it all. But this boy is the fastest healer, I mean by far the fastest healer, I have ever seen."

Kirk crossed his arms and thought for a moment. "What's the significance of that?"

Dr. Jacobs chewed on the stem of his glasses as he thought. "The healing of Jimmy Wickland is simply miraculous. I asked if he always heals this fast, and he got a funny look on his face. He said it had something to do with his Native American heritage. But something tells me there's a lot he's not telling me."

"Doc, do you think he's taking some sort of drug?"

"No, it isn't that," responded the physician. "I checked his urine sample and there's nothing unusual. But there is something strange going on. I thought you might want to keep an eye on his progress. I know you monitor the illegal and the strange goings on in sports."

Kirk thought for a moment. "Do you have any hunches on what caused Wickland's speedy recovery?"

"Coincidentally, a colleague of mine in Atlanta was telling me about a statistical analysis that may be relevant. She's with the government, and she discovered a number of anomalies concerning the northwest corner of Tennessee, which is where Wickland is from. You ought to give her a call."

"What kind of anomalies are you talking about?"

Dr. Jacobs smiled and replied, "Kirk, I don't want to bias your opinion of her data. You need to see it for yourself." With that, Dr. Jacobs pulled out a business card and handed it to Kirk.

Kirk looked at the card. "All right, Doc. I'll check it out. Thanks for the lead."

"Don't mention it." A bell sounded as eight runners began their final lap. "Now, I must get back to my athletes. I'll keep an eye on Wickland and keep you posted on any developments."

Kirk reflected on the past few days as he walked back to the stands. All in all, it had been an interesting Olympic trial meet with intriguing leads to follow up. He'd also signed five athletes to do Green Star ads. Who said you couldn't do two jobs at once?

Suddenly, he thought about AJ. He'd been so busy, he hadn't talked to her in days. He made a mental note to give her a call. Glancing at the card Dr. Jacobs had given him, Kirk knew this was a call he needed to make right away. He wanted to get to the bottom of the miracle healer Jimmy Wickland.

CHAPTER 38

J immy stood at the window of his Memphis hotel room and stared at the Mighty Mississippi. Big Muddy meandered past him like molten lava on its way to the Gulf. Inexorable with its progress and inscrutable with its depth, the lifeblood river of America flowed south with the same certainty that his blood flowed through his veins. To stop the flow meant death.

Death was something Jimmy rarely thought about. His were the thoughts of youth and excitement. But thoughts of death knocked on his subconscious today.

What if something happened to Grams? What would he do without her? He couldn't bear the thought. He remembered when she told him about the power of the plant that grew along Reelfoot Lake. That it healed and slowed down aging. He prayed every day since then that God and the plant would protect Grams.

It was a day when his thoughts should be filled with joy, knowing he was going to the Olympics. Instead he wondered about the plant and how long it would continue to work.

When Grams told him the story of Ponce de Leon and her Arawak ancestors, young Jimmy had asked the logical question. "Grams, how did the plants get from Florida all the way to Tennessee?"

"The shaman of the small tribe foresaw the conquests of the white man. Their weapons, armor, and attitude would spell the end of the Indian tribes as they then existed. So he set a doctrine that was passed down through each generation to move away from the invaders. To fight would be futile.

"The small band slowly migrated northwest to Georgia over many decades, avoiding the warlike Creek tribes and finding harmony with the Cherokee. They intermarried, yet maintained their ancestry."

"What about the plants, Grams? I guess they took some along?"

"They tried, but it was easier said than done. The plants survived for a time in clay pots, but they never flourished anywhere they were planted. It seems the ponds and lakes they tried were missing something. So a gathering party was sent periodically back to the sacred pond in Florida to get more plants."

It made sense to Jimmy. They had studied agriculture in school and the teacher explained why rice, cotton, wheat, and corn grow only in certain climates and soils. "Okay," he said. "Our ancestors were in Georgia. How did they get to northwest Tennessee?"

Jimmy was startled by the sad look on his grandmother's face.

"That, my angel, is the saddest part of the story. It is a story that hurts to tell."

Grams had a faraway look in her eyes. "The Cherokee called it Nunna dual Tsuny. It literally translates as Trail Where They Cried. Your history book will call it the Trail of Tears."

Jimmy sat perfectly still, afraid Grams would cry. He had never seen her like this.

"Georgia was growing, and settlers wanted the Native Americans' land. In 1830 the U.S. government passed the Indian Removal Act, and President Andrew Jackson signed it. But the Cherokee tribe formed the independent Cherokee Nation, and went to the Supreme Court to fight the law."

"It looked like they might get to stay on the lands they had lived on for centuries, but a few Cherokee signed a treaty agreeing to move. President Jackson sent troops to the Cherokee Nation in Georgia in 1838 to forcibly move them to what is now Oklahoma. So men, women, and children were removed from their land and herded on a thousand mile walk west."

"Grams, you've got to be kidding! How could they do that?"

The innocence of her grandson's question hurt her. She would mourn this day as more of his innocence was lost to the reality of a harsh world.

"Believe me, Jimmy, men have abused and enslaved other men for thousands of years. Thousands died along the Trail Where They Cried. But four of our ancestors decided to cut the trip short. A group of Cherokee camped on the Illinois side of the Mississippi River, waiting to cross into Missouri the next day. The soldiers on guard paid little attention during the night.

"Two Cherokee, friends for life and determined not to end up on a reservation, took their wives and snuck out of the encampment, stole a raft, and headed down the Mississippi. All they took were the clothes on their backs and four clay pots filled with the healing plant. They made it to the big curve in the river where Kentucky and Tennessee meet. They abandoned the raft and hiked away from the river till they saw the most beautiful sight they had ever seen — Reelfoot Lake."

"Wow, Grams! So they put the plants along the edge of the lake, and they lived?"

"Lived and thrived. And we've used the plant for our own purposes ever since. And we pretty much have gotten along with everyone else. Except for one thing."

Jimmy stared at Grams. "What thing?"

"My grandfather and my father would never take or handle a twenty dollar bill. They hated Andrew Jackson for what he did to our people, so they refused to accept anything with his picture on it. Local merchants called them crazy old Indians when they had to give them a pile of ten dollar bills as change."

Jimmy smiled for the first time that day. "I'm going to do the same thing, Grams. No twenties for me."

Lily Morales, the last pureblood of Native American ancestry in her family, gave her grandson some sage advice. "No, Jimmy, I saw the problems and the confrontation that brings. Do what I do."

With that, she slipped off her right shoe and held it out so Jimmy could see inside. There was a faded twenty dollar bill taped inside her shoe.

"Old Hickory may have put his foot down on our people, but I put my foot down on him every day!"

Jimmy thought back to that day and leaned forward on the balls of his feet as he looked out of the hotel window. He liked to put a little more pressure on the Jacksons in his shoes. Just for old time's sake.

CHAPTER 39

J ack Ward started out the day happy. But now he was turning mad. And it made him angry that he was mad. He prided himself on his positive attitude. But some things just got under his skin.

He was happy because, when Jimmy Wickland qualified for the Olympics, it meant great things for northwest Tennessee. Jack had gotten a call from the mayor this morning saying reporters were coming to do stories on Jimmy. If Wickland did well in the Olympics, there would be a flood of publicity. TV crews, People magazine, and money for the town.

What made Jack mad was the assignment he'd been handed. The mayor told Jack to clean up the kudzu. Jack considered himself a law enforcement officer first and a maintenance man second. But in small towns, the job descriptions were extremely broad. Jack was technically the town sheriff, but his duties also included overseeing the town maintenance crew.

Cleaning up kudzu was easier said than done. Kudzu was a fast growing, green leafed vine that had been introduced to this country from the Philippines in the 1930's by the U.S. Department of Agriculture. The plant was billed as a cure-all ground cover for weak soil to prevent erosion. The southern United States had many such areas. The red clay on the washed out hillsides seemed ideal locations to introduce the Asian plant.

Roadside planting of kudzu in Georgia, Alabama, and Mississippi worked wonders. Barren roadside slopes were replaced with attractive lush carpets of green. Unfortunately, no one told the kudzu where to stop.

Kudzu was much more aggressive than first believed. It grew over fence posts, strangled shrubs, and climbed fifty-foot trees. It slowly spread like molten lava, devouring forests and even homes. Under the right conditions, kudzu can grow up to a foot a day. Jack heard the man who had suggested bringing kudzu to the United States had his house in Alabama engulfed by the rogue plant. Now that was justice.

Over the past seventy years, kudzu had spread its tentacles north as far as Tennessee. It was an eyesore for tourists and locals alike. Knowing the history of the plant caused Jack to snort at the mayor's order. Control kudzu? Maybe. Eradicate kudzu? Not in his lifetime.

But an order was an order. So Jack Ward had driven his squad car to the municipal building to work out a solution. That's when his anger boiled over.

Bubba Baker sat in an ancient swivel chair with his feet on the cluttered desk. He was a big man, at six foot four and three hundred plus pounds, amply filling out his "Drink More Beer" t-shirt. His Tennessee Titans' hat was tilted back on his balding head as he read the sports page.

Jack Ward, in his pressed khaki slacks and crisp navy long sleeve shirt, stood in the doorway looking at Bubba. Not bothering to remove his feet, Bubba gave a nod. Jack knew Baker acted this way to get his goat, but Jack's temper took over nonetheless.

"Bubba, get your feet off the desk! And how many times do I have to tell you not to wear shirts like that? No liquor or cigarette names on shirts at work. I bought you two plain t-shirts."

Bubba grudgingly pulled his sneaker-clad feet off of the desk.

"Those shirts got no pockets for my smokes. Besides, chief, who cares what we wear anyway?"

Knowing this discussion would go nowhere, Jack changed the subject to removing the kudzu. He explained to Bubba what the mayor expected.

Bubba laughed. "Chief, it would be easier to catch the Easter Bunny than get rid of kudzu. Why didn't you tell the mayor to go chop some kudzu himself? Lord knows, that man never did a day's worth of work in his life."

Baker's attitude infuriated Ward. "Bubba! I'm sick and tired of your backtalk! I've got a million things to do, and I'm assigning the kudzu to you. Cut it, kill it, get rid of it. Do whatever you have to do. Do you understand?"

Bubba stood up, towering over the smaller man. "Hey, man, don't get all bent out of shape. I think it's a stupid waste of time."

Jack thrust out his chin. "You're not supposed to think about it. Just do it. If excuses were dollars, you'd be a millionaire."

Bubba gave a crooked smile and a mock salute, knowing how to get Jack's goat. "Roger, wilco, over and out. I'll wipe the mighty kudzu out today."

With an exasperated shake of his head, Ward turned and stormed out of the office. "Idiot," said Bubba, softly enough that Ward couldn't hear but loud enough to make himself feel better.

Bubba, born Earl Richard Baker, had never liked being bossed around, especially by little sawed off Jack Ward. Get rid of the kudzu! Who does he think he is? People have been fighting kudzu for years without success.

Too bad there wasn't some miracle cure for kudzu. Like in those sci-fi movies. "Make it so, Number One," Bubba said out loud, waving his right arm like a wand. "No more kudzu."

He jerked the small refrigerator door open and pulled out a can of Coca Cola. Digging the last doughnut out of the box on the fridge with his free hand, he lowered himself back into his chair, armed for some serious brainwork. Bubba did his best thinking on a full stomach.

Chewing and thinking, Bubba weighed the options for getting rid of the kudzu. Chopping or digging it out did no good. There was too much of it and you couldn't get the roots out anyway. Burning it had been tried, with poor results. Besides, if a fire got out of control, he would really be up a creek.

Then it hit him. He knew how to get rid of the kudzu. Down in the old storage shed, they had a bunch of fifty-five gallon drums of old chemicals. Bubba stood and hitched up his pants. He would head over to the shed and see what he could use. He licked his fingers and jammed his flashlight into his back pocket.

The walk to the storage shed gave Bubba time to think about the chemicals. The barrels had those big, multi-colored, diamond shaped warning stickers on the side. He knew in the back of the shed there were old barrels that were supposed to kill anything. What could be wrong with that? The stuff was free. Been there forever.

Spraying the stuff would be easy. He could get out of town in the municipal truck with the fertilizer sprayer and milk this job for weeks. He was warming to the kudzu assignment. Maybe old stuffed shirt Jack Ward had done him a favor.

Bubba rummaged through the shed, looking at bags and barrels. In the far corner, he found what he was looking for. Pulling back the corner of a dust covered tarp, he aimed his flashlight at the rusted barrels. The skull and crossbones made him smile.

With a red shop rag, he wiped off the first barrel. Dichloro-diphenyl trichloroethane was stenciled across the top. DDT. Bubba remembered his dad saying it was originally used as an insecticide. But it was found to be too toxic, so it was outlawed. He'd heard if it weren't diluted, it would kill plants as well as insects.

He wished he had some of that Agent Orange stuff from Vietnam. Dad said it was the best for defoliating where the Cong hid. But Bubba would make do with what he had.

More rummaging uncovered barrels of concentrated Roundup for weed control. He read it had isopropylamine salt as an active ingredient. Bubba knew salt would kill plants.

He also knew what gasoline would do. He'd dumped a can of gas on old man Lundquist's prize lawn when he was a kid because Lundquist yelled at him when he cut through his yard. He chuckled at the memory of Mr. Lundquist having to replace the dead spot with sod.

Bubba had an idea for his kudzu cocktail. He figured if he mixed DDT with concentrated Roundup and gasoline, he'd have a concoction that would wipe out kudzu. As he was figuring out where to start spraying, he had another thought. *Maybe I can patent this if it works the way I think it will. Would that be cool, or what?*

For the next week, Bubba spent six hours a day spraying the kudzu with his concoction. He covered the roadsides, the edges of the campgrounds, and along the edge of the lake. He especially liked working along the lake. He would spray for twenty minutes, then take a thirty-minute break.

In the low wetlands along the lake, there were lots of plants growing in the water. He gave those a good spraying, even though it wasn't kudzu. He figured getting rid of those weeds would clean up the lake for the swimmers, boaters, and fishermen.

Bubba was a man on a mission. He liked the feeling of purpose each day as he took the municipal truck out on the road. He had covered most of the obvious kudzu areas, and was starting over for a second application.

The fact that he was spraying a toxin that wouldn't break down didn't enter Bubba's mind. He was getting results. The plant life he sprayed began turning brown and dying. He didn't know three kids and two adults in the campground had developed debilitating diarrhea.

Striking a pose, Bubba held the spray wand out like a sword. This would be a great cover shot for People Magazine. Bubba Baker Cures Kudzu! Or maybe, Bubba Baker Conquers Kudzu!

As he went back to work, he thought he might get a haircut tonight and see if they had blue jeans on sale at the Value Mart. You never know when someone will want to take your picture.

CHAPTER 40

It had been a week since AJ talked to John Cline on the boat. John had checked into names and companies on the Internet from every possible angle and had come up with absolutely nothing on Bouhler or Cox. He told AJ he was coming up emptier than a tip glass at a piano bar on a snowy Monday night.

Whoever this Bouhler/Cox guy was, he was leaving a vapor trail. Inquiries at Fermilab and GF Products had been stonewalled. Since the deaths, no one was saying anything.

AJ was frustrated. And she was miffed at Kirk. He didn't seem interested in her search. All he wanted to talk about was the Olympic trials and some pole vaulter from Tennessee. Kirk talked about strange healing powers and possible drug connections. AJ really didn't understand why he was so excited.

For the first time since she had met Kirk, AJ felt he was hiding something. When she asked him why a shoe salesman was so interested in the recovery of a pole vaulter, Kirk clammed up. He was acting very strange.

Then there was her work. AJ was leaving for a two-day training seminar in Los Angeles. Technical training was continuous and important to success in sales. Maybe getting away would do her some good, but she was obsessed with following up on her instincts.

After packing her bags and leaving Freethrow with Sarah, AJ caught the commuter flight from Madison to O'Hare Airport in Chicago. While waiting for her flight to California, she picked up a USA Today. The article on the front page of the business section made her gasp.

Her hands began to shake. There was a picture of a smiling man dressed in a lab coat. The caption read, "Eli Lilly Pharmaceutical Research Genius Dies". The article detailed the career of Daniel Wu, head of research at Eli Lilly, who chaired the group developing growth enhancement hormones.

Mr. Wu had died the previous evening in his fashionable Carmel, Indiana, home under bizarre circumstances. While working in his basement on a remodeling project, Mr. Wu had apparently electrocuted himself. The police had ruled it an accidental death. His house had been locked and there was no evidence of foul play.

As if through a fog, AJ's mind registered the boarding call for her flight. Daniel Wu's death could not be a coincidence! Another scientist dying in his home? Why is this happening and what do these men have in common?

Walking like a zombie, AJ started toward the gate. Her mind was racing. There had to be a connection. She knew Bouhler had something to do with this.

Watching AJ from across the crowded concourse was Emile Bouhler. He knew she was going to cause trouble ever since he saw her snooping around at Fermilab. He had been tailing her while he debated what to do. He needed to find out what she knew and who else was involved.

Seeing her reaction to the USA Today headline answered one question. He was going to follow her to Los Angeles. He had to stay close to AJ Clark.

His life depended on it.

The flight to California was a blur. AJ replayed her two encounters with Bouhler/Cox over and over in her mind. She developed a monster headache as she kept coming up with dead ends.

In the meeting the next day, AJ scribbled notes having nothing to do with the speaker's presentation. She wrote with a fury, drawing lines and highlighting key words. The harder she thought, the more confused she became.

After the meeting, the training group was taken to Disneyland as a reward for being attentive during the less than exhilarating presentations. While most headed to the rides, AJ joined a small contingent going to see the Walt Disney Story on Main Street USA.

The part of the presentation called "Great Moments with Mr. Lincoln" held fond memories for AJ. It was the first place her dad had taken her on their first Disney visit. Dad loved history, and he never missed an opportunity to give AJ a lesson.

As Abraham Lincoln delivered his Gettysburg Address, AJ sat up with a start and almost shouted "Eureka!" Everything came together as she stared at the the life-size, talking Lincoln.

Lincoln's movements and speech were controlled by someone off stage. That was it! Bouhler was working for someone using high tech electronics and nutritional supplements to enhance and control humnan performance and behavior! But for what?

AJ felt she was on the right track, but where did it lead? What was the goal? Political influence? Financial gain? Some military purpose? Athletics?

Both soldiers and athletes required strength and stamina. AJ stood and said her "excuse me's" as she worked her way out of her row in the theater.

Exiting the building into the brilliant sunlight, she paused to let her eyes adjust, then strode toward a bank of pay phones. She had left her cell phone at the hotel, and she needed to call Kirk right now.

Leaning against the wall of the pavilion, unseen by AJ, was Emile Bouhler. In tan slacks, a blue windbreaker, yellow Lakers cap, and Rayban sunglasses, he watched AJ walk resolutely to the phones. Reaching into his pocket, Bouhler took the earpiece of an electronic listening device and inserted it in his left ear.

Using a magazine as a shield from observers, Bouhler casually pointed the small device toward AJ. He twisted a knob to increase the volume.

AJ reached Kirk on the second ring. "Kirk Vail. Green Star Athletics. How may I help you?"

"Hi, Kirk. It's AJ."

The pleasure in Kirk's voice was evident. "Hi, AJ! How are things in sunny California?"

AJ tried to control the excitement in her voice. "I've just had an epiphany. The answer to the mystery just hit me."

"Slow down, AJ. Answer about what?" Kirk shifted his cell phone trying to clear up the reception.

AJ gave Kirk a rapid-fire account of her analysis of the relationship of the deaths of the scientists, the Bouhler/Cox connection, and the idea of some sinister manipulation of body and mind. She outlined her theory, admitting she had no clue as to motive nor any thoughts as to who might be behind it.

Responding with a series of grunts and "Uh-huhs", Kirk waited until AJ had finished before framing a response. "AJ, are you saying you think someone is trying to turn people into robots?"

"No, No! Not robots. You weren't listening." AJ repeated the key points of her theory again, twisting the telephone cord with her free hand.

Bouhler strained to hear the one sided conversation. The listening device created gaps in reception. It reminded Bouhler of the days spent with his father in the tiny living room in his boyhood home in Argentina, straining to hear the fortunes of the Argentine National Soccer team on the radio above the static.

Bouhler could tell from the bits and pieces of conversation that this woman had somehow stumbled into the middle of their plan. She was piecing together a vague outline similar to Krug's real plan. She had to be eliminated.

AJ told Kirk they had to go to the authorities with what they knew. They needed to let the police investigate.

After a pause, Kirk answered. "Earth to AJ. Let's think about this. While I believe you, I don't see any hard evidence that we can present to anyone else. We'd be treated like harebrains if we went to the police."

"Harebrained? Is that what you think this is?" AJ was practically shouting into the receiver. "I thought you believed me?"

Kirk tried to rebuild the bridge. "Bad choice of words. But we need to get hard data. I know some people that can help us. But we can't run off halfcocked."

AJ tried to calm herself. Her mind told her Kirk was right, but her emotions said to act now. She took a deep breath and leaned back.

Rule number seven. Dad's rule seven struck her as weird at first, but it made sense. Rule seven was, "Unlock both doors of double doors". Dad hated it when he entered a store or restaurant, and one of the two double doors was locked.

You could hurt yourself jerking on a locked door or rushing to push on a door that didn't give. The moral of the rule was, take the time to do things right. Check details before you move on to the next step of a task.

As usual, Dad was right. AJ needed to get more data before she did anything else. She needed to unlock the other door.

"You're right, Kirk. We need to see if we can get some more information to support my harebrained idea. Thanks for bringing me back to reality."

Kirk breathed a sigh of relief. "OK. Let's keep checking on what we know. I'm on the road tomorrow, so let's get together when we both get back to Wisconsin."

"Sounds great," said AJ. "I fly back tomorrow, and I have appointments in Sauk City north of Madison the next day. But I'll be back in time for dinner, if someone wants to escort me."

While AJ and Kirk made their plans, Bouhler made plans of his own. He knew he had to do this himself. He needed to clean up his mess.

"Kirk, pick me up at Hondo Pistol Pete, and we'll grab dinner."

Kirk laughed. He was glad AJ was back to her old self, using Clarkspeak. "Let me be sure I'm straight on this. Hondo has to be John Hondo Havlicek, number seventeen for the Celtics. Pistol Pete, the greatest scorer in hoops history, wore number 23 at LSU, but since you're using Hondo, I'm going with the Pistol's pro number, 44."

It was AJ's turn to laugh. "Good Kirk! You've been reading the basketball books I've been giving you."

Kirk continued. "So, we have 1744. That would be military time, so that's 5:44 p.m. Am I the answer man?"

AJ laughed. And Bouhler grunted. He knew she would be going to Sauk City when she returned to Wisconsin. He knew her vehicle, the red Jeep. He would be ready for her. He had to be. He couldn't call Krug and admit he had a loose end.

After saying goodbye to Kirk, AJ called John Cline. "Hey, Valve Buddha. What's up in Mad Town?"

John chuckled. "As I live and breathe! It's the Wonder Woman of Disneyland. Have they got you replacing Cinderella as the hostess for Mickey?"

"Not yet," responded AJ. "They have to alter the costume first. So while they work on that, could you do me a favor?"

John readily agreed, and made notes as AJ gave him the information on Dr. Wu to research. "I'll get on it right away. Since our discussion on my boat, I've been pulling data together on the other guys who died. I've got quite a file. Hey, how's your friend Kirk doing? You said he was on board trying to help, too."

AJ was finally beginning to relax. "He's doing fine. But he's traveling so much he hasn't had much time to devote to the mystery. Having your help puts my mind at ease."

Emile Bouhler walked rapidly away as AJ and John finished their conversation. Bouhler was formulating a plan for the next few days. He had the fake ID's to rent the vehicle he needed. Too bad this Clark woman had a case of the curious. A terminal case.

CHAPTER 41

G regory Krug knew it was time. Time to unveil his creation. Time for him to show the world what he had developed. Time to display the centerpiece of the research started during the Third Reich.

Krug sat in his walnut paneled office with a soft sea breeze blowing through the open French doors. He looked at the date circled on his calendar and smiled. The Gardener was discretely cleaning up loose ends, so all Krug had to concern himself with was preparing for F-Day.

F-Day denoted the Final Day. It was the culmination of six decades of research and development. Six decades of secrecy and sacrifice. Six decades of living as someone else.

Rickie Armendariz had easily qualified for the Olympics in the Central American/ Caribbean Trials. Krug orchestrated a strong performance, being careful not to clear a height so high as to draw undo attention. The last thing needed was a wave of publicity prior to the Chicago finale.

Krug needed to go to the testing center this afternoon to check on the electronics. Everything worked to perfection at the trials. But in Chicago, the controller would be further away. The controls had to be checked at a greater distance to be sure there were no signal distortions which could affect the speed of the synapses.

Rickie's body was honed to a razor sharp edge with controls to match. Krug had spared no expense in acquiring state of the art electronics and programming. His perfect plan would soon meet the perfect opportunity.

Gregory Krug was also riding the chemical euphoria of his morning shots. By upping the dosage Gertrude administered, Krug found his body reacting differently. He was concerned his body was developing immunity to the anti-aging serum.

While he found the reaction not without pleasure, he worried about unknown side affects. He was, after all, going where no man had gone before. But he pushed that out of his mind as he thought about the triumph of Rickie's success.

Krug picked up the one-foot tall gold hourglass from his desk. It represented everything he held dear. The gold casing represented wealth and power, while the white sand stood for time. The glass containing the sand told mortals that time could be observed, but not changed. You could see, but not touch.

Until now. Josef Mengele, Doctor of the Third Reich, had solved the riddle of aging. He could defeat Father Time. He made a young man strong and quick. And he made an old man younger and more vibrant.

Standing, Mengele held the hourglass above his head. In his mind, he heard throngs cheering. They were cheering for him. Not for the Fuhrer. Not for Jesse Owens. Not for Rickie, his prized creation. No, they cheered for him with a deafening roar as one voice.

CHAPTER 42

S mash dug his name. It had power, it had grace, and it jumped right in your face. He had christened himself Smash four years ago as a new beginning. His folks and his old friends were stifling him. Now everyone saw him for what he was.

Bernard Ware, the name bestowed on him by his parents, had always grated on him. It was so white bread. When he was fifteen, he had seriously considered killing both his parents. He would have claimed mental abuse as the cause for his flipping out.

His anger stemmed from being born in the wrong decade. He'd entered the world too late. He was a child of the 60's. He loved the music, the clothes, and the culture. He read about it, watched old movies, and wanted to be part of something that made his soul soar.

So he changed his name and left home. Dropping out of high school had been a trip. Mom and Dad hit the roof. What would the people at the country club say? His parents were more worried about how things looked than about what actually happened to their son.

He remembered screaming at them. "What have you ever done for the world? All you care about is the stock market and trips to Europe. You sat out the cultural revolution. I want to be part of it!"

Smash experimented with drugs and grooved on rock and roll. Nothing made him feel as good as rocking to the 60's music. It spoke to his soul and made him whole. It was his religion.

After fifteen job changes —a guy had to eat, even in the 60's — Smash found a job he really dug. He was the Marlboro Man! He drove a truck route to restock cigarettes at gas stations, liquor stores, and grocery stores.

His route covered the area north and west of Madison, Wisconsin. He had freedom. He was on his own, as long as he made his stops and made his deliveries. He'd developed camaraderie with his customers, giving him his greatest feeling of self-esteem. To them he was Smash, the smokes man. No more, no less.

Customers didn't mind his hair or his attire. He wore faded wide flare jeans, tire tread sandals, and a woven headband to hold his long hair in place. He had to wear a company shirt with his name on the breast patch. But even that was cool, because his boss put Smash on the patch. The boss didn't even seem to mind that Smash cut the sleeves off the shirt at the shoulders and only fastened the bottom two buttons.

His territory was the best! Lots of small towns like Black Earth, Prairie du Sac, and Baraboo. The drive time between towns gave him time to play his music. On his route, he was totally in charge.

After three months on the job, his boss even let him install a Pioneer twelve CD player and killer speakers in his truck. When he was alone in the truck, with the volume jacked up, Smash would look at the Wisconsin countryside and believe it was 1968. The revolution was getting ready to start.

Today, Smash was working Highway 12. Roadside stops on the way to Sauk City, then north to the Dells. It was a beautiful day for a beautiful drive.

As he was saddling up to leave the Wisconsin Pit Stop, a pump and pop place, a woman getting out of a red Jeep made him pause. The tall, pretty woman in tan slacks and a blue blazer scanned her charge card at the pump and began to fill up. She expertly washed her windshield and then squatted next to a front tire to check the tread.

When she stood up, she brushed her hair away from her face and made eye contact with Smash. He instinctively smiled. There was something so friendly about her.

She smiled back, gave a little wave, and then turned to finish gassing up. Smash slid into his warehouse on wheels and suddenly felt warm. A pretty woman who wasn't stuck up. That's one for the record books.

Pulling out on Highway 12, he looked into his rearview mirror to catch a glimpse of Jeep woman. The truck jerked as he let off of the clutch too fast. *Haven't done that in months. Eyes on the road, Dude.*

Skipping over a Credence Clearwater Revival CD, Smash punched up Crosby, Stills, Nash, and Young. Time to rock. Fast forward to song four. "Teach Your Children Well".

Smash knew all the words and sang with gusto. The next song was even better. "O-HI-O" ! Four dead at Kent State. We'll change the world. Smash knew he was going to get in a mood. Today was the day to change the world.

He might have to toke up today. It was looking like a day to bring everything you had.

Smash needed a hit. He dug in the glove box for his stash.

Smash knew deep down you've got to love things in life. You've got to love your music and your pals. Someday he hoped to have a girl he could love, a girl who would love him back.

He loved his music because it spoke to him. His exposure to religion had been fleeting. His folks had taken him to Sunday school a few times, but then Sundays had become country club or mall days.

Maybe serious religion was only for the poor and the sick — a safety net for those who needed it. He had his music. It was his Alpha and his Omega.

His music made him whole. He didn't feel like he was driving a crummy old truck on a crummy old job. He felt like he was accomplishing something. He filled a need on this spinning mass of mud we call earth.

He was the Smash Man! Road warrior. Cigarette minister to the masses.

When he saw the red Jeep appear in his mirror, he smiled. Pretty lady is going to Sauk City. There was a stretch of road here where she could pass him, but after that it was all winding road to the river.

As she gained on him on the two-lane asphalt ribbon, Smash eased back on the gas. He saw clear highway ahead, so he waved out of the window with his left arm for her to pass.

She passed him carefully, throwing him a smile and a wave. After pulling in front of the truck, AJ gave a final wave and gradually pulled away. Smash gave the raised fist salute and downshifted as the grade of the road increased.

The world could use a few more polite, pretty women. He had a quick mental picture of Miss Jeep in a tie-dyed tank top and Daisy Duke short shorts. She'd look great in the sixties.

A few minutes later, a yellow rental truck came barreling up from behind. The 14 foot parcel van dwarfed the cigarette delivery truck. Van Man rode Smash's tail, swerving back and forth, looking to pass. Smash knew the double yellow line extended for miles, the stretch of road ahead yielding nothing but curves and hills.

Just to stick it to Mister In A Hurry, Smash slowed down just a bit. He could see the frantic expression on the driver's face. Van Man began laying on the horn and waving for Smash to pull over. The shoulder was narrow, and Smash wasn't about to get over for this guy.

They entered an S-curve as close as two Nascar racers, and Van Man made his move. He gunned it to pass on a blind curve. Even in a low traffic area, it was the dumbest, most dangerous thing Smash had ever seen.

Van Man mouthed an expletive as he flew by on the left, causing Smash to have a random thought. *That guy is no Packer fan!* He was wearing a brand new Green Bay Packer cap. Smash had a Packers' sticker on the back of his truck. No Packer fan would treat another Packer fan like that!

Something was up with Van Man. The guy was too focused on getting past the delivery truck to be up to any good. Smash goosed his truck to keep up.

CHAPTER 43

A J sensed the approaching vehicle before she saw it in her mirror. With a start, she realized the crazy yellow van was going to hit her. Impact came just as she entered a curve. The van struck the Jeep on the right rear and threatened to shove her over the cliff on the left as the road curved to the right.

Stomping on the brake, AJ twisted the steering wheel to the right with all her strength. Then hitting the gas, she shot around the curve on the left shoulder, spraying gravel over the cliff.

Pine trees flew by on her right as she accelerated. As she was braking for another curve, the van caught the Jeep a glancing blow from behind.

AJ saw the face in the rear view mirror, and gasped. It was Bouhler/ Cox! The look on his face was one of pure hatred. AJ didn't know what she had done to incur his wrath, but she knew he meant business.

The state of Wisconsin had an inadequate budget for guardrails, so there were none along this dangerous stretch of road. A tree branch scraped the Jeep as AJ hugged the right shoulder on the next curve. She screamed, "What are you doing?" as if Bouhler/Cox could hear her — or even care.

Another bump and the crunch of metal infuriated AJ. "My Jeep!! You're wrecking my Jeep!" she shouted.

Smash saw the yellow van attacking the red Jeep. His first thought was Van Man had the world's worst case of road rage. The dude needs a downer.

As the attack continued, Smash realized Jeep Woman was in deep trouble. He decided to get into the mix. Stomping on the gas, he pushed his old truck forward to help the damsel in distress.

With a war whoop only he could hear, Smash shifted and kept the pedal to the metal, aiming for the yellow van. How often do you get a chance to be a knight in shining armor?

While the two vehicles in front separated for a moment, Smash accelerated and caught the left rear of the van. Startled, the driver looked into the mirror and spun his van to the right. Smash jockeyed for position behind. He faked left, and then went hard right, catching the back of the van again.

While those two were battling each other, AJ was able to pull ahead of them. She pushed the Jeep forward, looking for an escape route.

Smash kept close behind Bouhler. Suddenly Bouhler braked, forcing Smash to instinctively brake also. After the bump from behind, Bouhler cut across and drove in the left lane.

Smash gave the volume knob on his radio a quick spin. Music blared as the silver cigarette truck made a final run. He was going to end this game.

Crushing the gas pedal to the floorboard Smash steered across the lane toward Van Man. He had a perfect shot to hit the antagonist in the side and disable the rampaging van.

As Smash bore down like a torpedo, Bouhler hit the gas and spun the wheel to the right, causing the van to spin clockwise. It crossed back across both lanes and into the right shoulder, throwing turf and gravel, as it completed a 360-degree rotation.

Smash miscalculated the speed and angle needed to hit the van. What looked like a sure broadside hit, turned into a clean miss as his truck passed left of the van. Twisting to the right Smash looked at his outside mirror to see where the the yellow van stopped.

Suddenly his mind did a flip-flop. He felt weightlessness. Riding the Tilt-a-Whirl at the county fair popped into his head. The not so unpleasant sensation of his stomach rising told the story. Snapping his head forward, his eyes confirmed it.

His truck had left the highway. *Elvis has left the building. Thank you, ladies and gentlemen. We hope you've enjoyed the ride. Please fly with us again.*

Gravity overtook the forward thrust of the truck and the nose turned downward. Smash could see the horizon, then the valley spread out before him, then grass and rocks a hundred feet below.

He realized he was squeezing the life out of the steering wheel and pressing on the brake for all he was worth. You can't brake or steer a flying truck. With a fatalistic laugh, he took his foot off the brake and held his hands over his head. *Roller coaster time.*

Smash thought of Jeep Lady. *Hope she got away.* His last thoughts were about his parents. *I did my best. I hope it was good enough.*

The truck hit the slope of the hill and pin-wheeled down to the bottom.

Each bounce sent truck parts and cigarette cartons flying. The final crash came as the truck wedged on its side against a tree.

AJ had been able to find an old logging road turn-off, and pulled onto the overgrown path into the thick woods. Killing her engine, she peered back toward the road.

She heard the horrible sound of a crash that seemed to go on forever. Then she saw a flash of yellow as the van raced past on the road to Sauk City. AJ sat still in the eerie silence, wondering what she would do if Bouhler/Cox returned.

AJ decided she should go back the way she came and call the police. She started the Jeep and eased back onto the highway. As she slowly rounded the third curve, she saw smoke rising from the valley below. Pulling off on the shoulder, she looked over the edge.

Grabbing her cell phone, she dialed 911 and started to climb down the steep embankment. The shattered silver delivery truck was visible far below. The LED display on her phone showed 'lost signal'. *Great,* she thought. No cellular service.

Shoving the phone in her blazer pocket, she slowly picked her way down toward the truck. Her thoughts of Bouhler/Cox were replaced with concern and dread for the truck driver. He had literally saved her life. At what price?

Bouhler looked for the Jeep as he sped along Highway 12, with no results. Had the woman turned off? He hadn't noticed any side roads. Or had she gotten so far ahead that he couldn't catch her?

He continued driving frantically, but when he reached Sauk City without seeing the red Jeep, he knew he was done for the day. He needed to dump the rental truck and decide what to do next. It looked like he would have to tell Krug. That was one phone call he dreaded making.

AJ was glad she was wearing slacks and low shoes today. In a skirt and heels, this would have been a much tougher task. The brambles and bushes tore at her slacks and jacket as she half slid, half climbed down the side of the hill.

When she reached the vehicle, she could see the driver lying by a sapling, his legs and neck at unnatural angles. Kneeling next to him, AJ felt his neck for a pulse, and found none. The truck driver was dead.

Leaning back, she sat with a thud. She looked at the dead body before her. It was the longhaired kid from the gas station. He had colored friendship bracelets tied around his right wrist. She remembered his smile as she was filling up the Jeep.

His shirt, unbuttoned almost to the waist, made a soft flapping sound as the breeze moved it back and forth like a battle weary flag. AJ looked at the nametag sewn on the shirt. Smash.

Thanks, Smash. You saved my life. I am so sorry it cost you yours.

AJ said a prayer for Smash. She prayed for his family. She prayed for his friends. And then she wept.

She wasn't sure how long she cried. But she finally realized it was time for action. She'd thought she was paranoid, but now she knew Bouhler/Cox was a real threat.

AJ had been afraid. She had been deathly afraid, but she knew fear would do her absolutely no good.

She remembered Dad's rule number ten: "Don't get scared, get mad." Dad was a firm believer in righteous anger. He preached to her, be slow to anger. But when pushed to your limit with right on your side, let the anger give you power. Don't let fear sap your will.

AJ stood up and wiped her eyes. Taking her cell phone from her pocket, she gently laid her blazer over Smash's chest, and then she softly touched his cheek. A dead hero deserved some dignity.

Clawing her way up the incline, AJ was mad. Oh, yes, she was furious. Who were these people, and what right did they have to threaten her life and destroy the lives of others? They had to be stopped!

AJ knew she was right. She was onto something big, and Bouhler/Cox was the key. *Thanks, Dad, for helping me focus.*

CHAPTER 44

While AJ was under attack in Wisconsin, Kirk was in Atlanta undergoing an attack of his own. At five foot one and one hundred five pounds, Dr. Deirdre Walling was a tightly wound package. And she knew it.

She rose to the position of assistant director of the Drug Enforcement Agency section on research by being professionally aggressive. She used every mental and physical tool to her advantage on the job. She used the same aggressiveness in her personal relationships.

When Kirk Vail walked into her well-appointed office for his scheduled meeting, Deirdre Walling immediately liked what she saw. Tall, athletic men were high on her list of interesting activities. And Dr. Walling usually got what she wanted. In her early thirties, she believed men were like business. They were there for the challenge.

As she showed Kirk the relevant reports, she made a point to brush against him. When she talked to Kirk, she made long eye contact, occasionally playing with her short, jet-black hair. She leaned close to Kirk as he reviewed the data.

Kirk found the attention of Dr. Walling disconcerting. He was trying to get data to unravel the mystery of Jimmy Wickland. He also needed to follow up to help AJ. But being near this woman made him feel guilty, even though he wasn't doing anything wrong. He found her attention flattering, but also dangerous.

Deirdre was proud of her body and her mind, and enjoyed using both. She realized she was making Kirk uncomfortable, which gave her greater power over him. Leaning closer, she pushed for the kill.

"Mr. Vail, will you be staying in Atlanta this evening? There are a number of wonderful restaurants I can recommend."

Kirk knew a come-on line when he heard one. While Deirdre was quite

131

attractive, there was the air of a predator about her that turned him off. And of course, there was AJ to think about. "I'm flying back to Wisconsin this afternoon. It will be peanuts and a soft drink on the plane for my dinner."

Deirdre smiled and touched Kirk's hand. "Well, maybe next time you're in Atlanta?"

Kirk let the question hang in the air without a response. "Back to the data you've compiled. What's the major significance?"

Pointing to the chart on the table, Deirdre explained her results. "Using the national data from the year 2000 census, I found a quadrant in northwest Tennessee with a higher percentage of citizens over the age of sixty-five than any other area in the United States except Florida. Knowing Florida's data reflects retirees moving in, I've quantified that area of Tennessee as having the longest life expectancy in the United States."

Kirk nodded as he looked at the bar graph.

"We further analyzed the data on the number and ages of those who wear glasses or corrective lenses. We cross referenced that information with the insurance industries' national data base on eyewear and with data from sales of glasses and contact manufacturers."

Kirk gave her a smile. "Quite thorough, aren't we?"

Deirdre flashed her pearly whites back. "I'm thorough in everything I do." She put the emphasis on everything as she smiled at Kirk. "To finish my corollary, we found that northwest Tennessee has the lowest percentage of vision failure in the country, even when adjusted for mean income."

"Well, Dr. Walling," replied Kirk. "Maybe I'm dense, but what does the number of people wearing glasses have to do with what Dr. Jacobs and I discussed at the Olympic trials?"

Deirdre leaned very close to Kirk. "The significance, my dear man, is the fact that the eye is the first part of the human body to suffer the affects of aging. Studies have determined the eyes are a significant determiner of overall tissue aging of a person. This data intrigued me, so I used the government data base to check military and hospital records."

Kirk leaned back just a bit to give himself some breathing room. "Nice having those kinds of resources."

"Exactly. I discovered northwest Tennessee had by far the highest percentage of expert marksman in the armed service. Even accounting for an environment where hunting is common, the numbers speak to something physical. Possibly great eyesight. And hospital stays in this area were shorter than the national average for surgeries."

Kirk stood up and leaned against the bookshelf. "OK, so what are we concluding here? Sounds like you have lots of data. Have you developed a hypothesis?"

Deirdre turned her chair to face Kirk and crossed her legs, showing lots of leg below her short skirt. After carefully settling herself, she looked up at him.

"The point, Mr. Vail, is that I don't think it's genetic and I don't think it's a coincidence. I think there is something in the environment in northwest Tennessee that has people seeing better, living longer, and healing faster. It could be the water, it could be the air, or it could be plants or animals in the local diet."

Kirk pondered Dr. Walling's hypothesis. "So you think Jimmy Wickland is a manifestation of this local phenomenon?"

Deirdre uncrossed, and slowly recrossed her legs. "Dr. Jacobs was involved in a confidential conference where I detailed my findings a month ago. When he called me from the Olympic Trials to describe the miraculously fast healing of the pole vaulter, we both felt it was significant that Wickland is from northwest Tennessee. Jimmy Wickland is the poster boy for health miracles."

"Maybe Tennessee should use him in their tourist advertising," offered Kirk. "Come to Tennessee and live longer!"

Deirdre stood up and laughed. "That's cute. Maybe you should join a Madison Avenue advertising firm." She touched Kirk's forearm as she spoke.

Kirk wished Deirdre didn't smell so good and he wished she wouldn't stand so close to him. "Quite honestly, Dr. Walling, my first concern was the possibility of steroid use or some other performance enhancing drug. When something out of the ordinary happens to an athlete, it comes to our attention."

Deirdre smiled up at Kirk. "So you're the undercover protector of purity in sports? You're the Secret Agent Man. Maybe I should call you Sam, for Secret Agent Man. And you can call me Dee Dee."

Kirk had planned on discussing AJ's theory about Bouhler/Cox and AJ's performance enhancement, behavior control ideas, but this meeting wasn't going the way he'd planned.

"Well, Dr. Walling, you've certainly been most helpful. Could I have copies of your reports to take with me to analyze?"

Deirdre knew when a fish wasn't taking the bait. Kirk Vail may prove to be quite a challenge. That was just fine with her. She liked challenges. Especially tall ones. Landing a big fish was half the fun.

"You can have whatever you want from me." Kirk understood her not so subtle emphasis. "I'll have my assistant make copies for you."

While they waited for the copies, Deirdre asked Kirk about his job. She seemed interested in Green Star Athletics and his investigative work. Kirk found himself telling Dr. Walling much more than he ever told anyone about what he did for a living.

Deirdre was well practiced in the art of male entrapment. "I'm sorry you're not staying this evening in Atlanta. I would love to show you the local sights."

Kirk had to admit Dr. Walling was persistent. She certainly was attractive, qualifying as a local sight herself. She finally wore him down into calling her Dee Dee.

"Dee Dee, I have to get to my plane. I have lots to do back home before I go to the Olympics."

She touched Kirk's arm again. "Kirk, maybe we'll run into each other in Chicago. I'm going to the Olympics, too."

Kirk carefully phrased his response. "It's a huge venue. And I'll be working the whole time. Not much chance we'll run into each other."

"Oh, don't worry," replied Deirdre. "We'll run into each other. You can count on it."

With the report copies in hand, they walked through the lobby and outside onto the concrete landing. As they said their goodbyes, Deirdre held onto Kirk's hand. "I'm really looking forward to seeing you in Chicago."

All Kirk could manage was a weak smile as he turned to walk away. After he had gone down the seven steps to the asphalt parking lot, he turned and glanced back toward the DEA building. Dr. Walling stood at the top of the steps. She posed with one hand on her hip, the other hand raised in a wave.

It's as if she knew he would look back. Kirk thought of that old song that went, "I was looking back to see, if she was looking back to see, if I was looking back to see, if she was looking back at me." He gave a quick wave, and turned back toward the parking lot. Man, this trip hadn't gone as he thought it would.

CHAPTER 45

I t was mid afternoon and AJ was mentally tired after dealing with the police and Allstate Insurance. She had rescheduled customer appointments and brought her company up to speed on what happened.

As she sat in her Madison apartment, she had two calls to make. She had to call Grandpa and Kirk.

Part way into her description to Grandpa of what had happened, he interrupted her. "Baby Girl, you just sit tight. I'm on my way."

"No. It's fine. Really, I'm OK."

"Honey, this is what your Dad would do. This is what I'm doing. I'll be there in an hour. No discussion."

"But Grandpa..."

"I said, no argument. Keep your door locked and don't leave your apartment until I get there. Promise me?"

AJ knew when Russell Clark made up his mind, there was no changing it. "OK, I promise. But drive carefully. There's no hurry."

Russell Clark let out a laugh. "I've been driving tractors, trucks, and cars since I was nine years old. I reckon the interstate to Madison won't present too many problems. Now you sit tight."

After hanging up the phone, Russell strode into the mudroom of the old farmhouse and opened the door to a small closet. Leaning in the corner of the closet was his twelve-gauge shotgun.

He picked up the gun by the barrel, hefting it in his right hand. He liked the feel of this gun. It was a Remington pump action model he'd gotten over sixty years ago.

He had painted a white C on the stock when he was nineteen because there were two other guns just like it at the gun club. When the gun club met to shoot clay pigeons, the shot guns were lined up against the wall of the corncrib like soldiers, waiting to be called to action. The last thing young Russell Clark wanted was for someone to use his gun without asking.

He dug a box of shells out of the locked cabinet in the closet. Setting the shotgun and shells on the kitchen table, Russell went to the bedroom to pack a bag. A few clothes and his shaving kit went into a small, weathered duffle bag.

He added the shells to the packed duffel, loaded it and the gun into the back seat of the dark blue Ford F-150 pickup truck. He covered the gun with a blanket. Returning to the house, he donned his blue cloth coat and pulled his John Deere hat over his thinning hair.

Only then did he walk around to the side of the house where his wife, Betty, was humming as she hung out the laundry. Betty gave her husband a quizzical look. She had both hands on the clothesline holding a wet sheet, and clothespins in her mouth.

Reaching over the clothesline, Russell took the clothespins from Betty's mouth and pinned the sheet to the line. Then he pulled the clothesline down and leaned over to give Betty a kiss. After the kiss, Betty looked into her husband's eyes. "What's going on?"

"AJ called, and I'm worried about her. I'm going to Madison."

"Need me to come along?"

"Nope. It's something I need to do. I'll call you when I get there and explain. But I have to leave right now."

"Russ, do what you have to do. Let me know how AJ's doing."

As he turned to leave, Russell remembered something and turned back toward Betty. "Honey, call Otto and tell him I won't be over tonight to look at his Angus bull."

"Sure thing. Remember to call me when you get there."

Betty leaned over to get another sheet from the wicker laundry basket as her husband disappeared around the corner of the house. Russell Clark had a strange thought as he drove down the gravel farm lane. The adrenaline pumping through him reminded him of Iwo Jima. He hadn't killed a man in a very long time. But he would to protect AJ.

CHAPTER 46

Two sharp raps on the door were followed by a voice AJ recognized instantly. "Open up. It's Grandpa."

Upon opening the door, AJ was struck by the thought she'd had many times before. Grandpa Clark looked like a Norman Rockwell painting. He was tall with square shoulders. His strong chin and clear eyes showed strength and intelligence.

From his worn work boots to his John Deere cap, Grandpa looked like what a farmer/Grandfather was supposed to look like. He had a duffel bag in one hand and a long object covered by a blanket in the other.

Grandpa stepped into the living room of the apartment, quickly placed his things on the floor, and jostled the head of Freethrow, who was dancing around his feet. Giving AJ a hug, Russell Clark said, "Are you all right, honey?"

"I'm fine, Grandpa. Really I am."

As Grandpa Clark hugged AJ's head to his shoulder, he felt the vise around his heart loosen a notch. Nothing in this world compared to touching his loved ones. Holding AJ was a way for him to touch his lost son. He wished he could stand here and hold his granddaughter forever.

Finally turning AJ loose, Grandpa took both of her hands in his. "Let's sit down and sort this out. I want to hear exactly what happened."

"Okay, Grandpa. Let me put your things in the guest bedroom."

Letting go of Grandpa's hands, AJ stooped to pick up the duffel bag and the blanket. Startled, she stepped back. "Grandpa, you brought your shotgun?"

Picking up the gun, Russell answered. "You're in danger and you never know what else might happen."

"Well, let's put the gun in the closet with your hat and coat. I think we're safe for now."

Relinquishing his gun, hat, and coat, Grandpa seated himself on the couch. "If you'll make me a cup of coffee, I'll call your Grandma to let her know I made it here in one piece."

After his phone call, Russell sat at the kitchen table with AJ and sipped his black coffee.

"How's Grandma?" asked AJ

"She's doing just fine. I told her I was probably going to spend the night here to be sure you're safe. Said that's fine with her. It will be the third night in the past sixty some years we haven't slept together. Said she could use a break," Grandpa Clark added with a twinkle in his eye.

AJ laughed.

"The old woman told me to get out on my own some, anyway. Said I'm a pest since I retired."

As she poured more coffee, AJ laughed again. AJ knew farmers never truly retire. They just throttle back a bit.

It was nice having Grandpa here. He may have a few years under his belt, but he was still a rock and a great source of strength during a crisis.

AJ explained everything that happened, but continually assured her grandfather she was safe. As she recreated the chain of events, she hoped her theories sounded plausible. Sometimes, the more she talked about her conspiracy theory, the less she believed it.

After a hint from Grandpa that maybe she should eat something, AJ went to the kitchen to work on grilled cheese sandwiches. There was something calming about performing a routine task. AJ needed normalcy after the day she'd experienced.

There was a knock on the door and Russell Clark was on his feet in a flash. "I'll get it," he said, as he was halfway to the door.

Looking through the eyepiece at the person in the hall, Mr. Clark called, "Who is it?"

"It's John Cline. I'd like to see AJ." After a pause. "I work with her."

AJ gently pushed Grandpa aside so she could open the door. "Hi, John. Come on in."

John stepped into the apartment and gave AJ a quick hug. "Are you OK?" He looked into her eyes, searching for an honest response.

"Oh sure, I'm fine. A little roadside mayhem sure gets the adrenaline flowing, though."

AJ introduced John to Grandpa and the three of them sat down in the living room. AJ began to fill John in on the details of the attack while Grandpa held Freethrow and scratched his ears.

The conversation was interrupted by another knock on the door. "I'll get it," Mr. Clark said. "Kinda like Grand Central Station here." He went to the door with Freethrow under his arm.

Mr. Clark's "Who is it?" was answered by Kirk Vail. AJ again came to open the door and gave Kirk a hug. When they unclenched, Grandpa looked at AJ. "Should I just leave the door open, in case there are any other men in the neighborhood who want to drop by?"

AJ softly punched Grandpa in the shoulder and rolled her eyes. She made the introductions of Kirk to Grandpa, and Kirk to John. Grandpa gave Kirk an appraising look up and down as the introductions were made.

"Well, AJ," Grandpa interjected. "Now that we have our fourth for bridge, why don't we sit at the kitchen table? Gentlemen, AJ and I were about to eat. You're more than welcome to join us."

They settled into the kitchen, with Kirk and John helping set the table while Grandpa and Freethrow observed. Grandpa gauged the mannerisms and character of AJ's two visitors and decided they would both pass muster.

Both men seemed intelligent and sincerely interested in the well being of AJ. He could tell AJ liked them both, but in different ways. Russell Clark was content to listen to the three of them discuss the day's events, only interjecting when asked a direct question.

The conversation in AJ's kitchen revolved around the attack on AJ and what to do next. They discussed possible motives for Bouhler/Cox wanting to harm AJ.

Russell listened a while longer and concluded that he wasn't needed here after all. AJ seemed comfortable and safe. The shock of the morning's trauma had faded. She had two friends here to support her, and her special relationship with Kirk was quite evident.

Having made his decision, Russell Clark wasn't one to dillydally. Standing, he interrupted AJ in mid sentence. "Honey, time for me to go."

AJ, a bit surprised, stood up also. "Grandpa, you don't have to go."

Giving AJ a hug and a kiss, Russell looked her in the eye. "I can see you're doing fine. I had to be sure you were OK. You sit and talk to John. Kirk, walk me to the door." After a quick handshake with John Cline, Russell turned and left the kitchen.

Since it was a command, not a request, Kirk followed Grandpa Clark toward the door. Russell stepped into the spare bedroom to fetch his bag, and opened the closet door for his coat, hat, and shotgun.

As Kirk eyed the gun, Russell spoke in a low tone. "Kirk, AJ's depending on you. You take care of her."

"I will, Mr. Clark," responded Kirk.

Russell hefted his shotgun. "Son, do you own a gun?"

Kirk gave a half smile. He liked Mr. Clark, and he liked the fact that he cut to the chase. "Yes, Sir, I do. And I know how to use it."

"Good. Keep it handy. Whatever AJ has stumbled into has put her in danger. I expect you to protect her with your life."

Kirk responded in the same solemn tone. "Mr. Clark, I believed AJ from the beginning and I will do everything in my power to protect her."

Russell nodded his satisfaction and pulled a scrap of paper from his pants pocket. With a battered ballpoint pen emblazoned with Garst Seed Corn on the barrel, he scrawled something on the paper. "Here's my phone number. Anything happens I need to know, anything jeopardizes her safety, you call me."

"Yes, Sir. You can count on me."

Holding out his weathered hand, Clark took Kirk's large hand in his and gave it a firm squeeze. "Son, take care of my granddaughter. She means the world to me."

"I will, Sir. She means the world to me, too."

CHAPTER 47

K irk sat at the table with AJ and John. "Your Grandfather is quite a man. I like him."

"I like him, too," chimed in John. "You've got a real supporter there."

AJ stood to clear the dishes and nodded her agreement. "He and Grandma are all the family I have. They've been my anchors since I lost Dad."

The mention of AJ's father had a sobering effect on Kirk and John.

Looking at his watch, John said, "Whoa, look at the time. AJ, thanks so much for the food. I really need to get going."

After multiple goodbyes and assurances from AJ she was feeling fine, John Cline made his exit. After closing the door, AJ turned to Kirk and held out her arms. He stepped forward and they hugged tightly.

"I'm so glad you're here, Kirk."

Kirk held her close, and stroked her hair. He wanted to feel the warmth of her body forever. "You really had a rough day. Are you sure you're OK?"

AJ leaned back, holding Kirk's waist and looking up into his searching eyes. "I'm still confused over the whole situation. What have I gotten involved in? I need to know."

"Time enough for that." Kirk's concern right now was for her safety. "Are you sure you weren't hurt at all? Your Jeep was pretty banged up."

"Actually, my neck is a little sore from being hit from behind. But what hurts is my ankle. I twisted it going down the hill to check on the truck driver. I think I need to give it a little therapy. Let's go out on the deck."

Kirk followed AJ through the sliding glass door to the deck of the apartment. He wondered what type of therapy she could do on a deck, but he had learned not to question AJ's decisions.

Scooping two cushions from the lawn furniture, AJ tossed one to Kirk. "We're going to do L therapy. Great for the feet, ankles and legs."

Kirk laughed. "OK, Dr. Clark. I'll bite. What is L therapy?"

"I'll show you." AJ went to the side of the building and sat down on the deck. She swung her legs up in the air and scooted her bottom next to the building until her body formed an L. Her back lay on the deck with her legs extended skyward, resting against the wall.

AJ positioned the cushion under her head and laid her arms along her sides. "Come on, big boy. Assume the position, and I'll explain the benefits of L therapy."

Kirk struggled to get down on the deck next to AJ. After some grunting and groaning, he lay next to her with his legs pointing up. Turning his head to look at AJ, he smiled. "I feel silly. Is that part of the therapy? To humble me?"

AJ laughed. "Any humbling effect is simply a side benefit. L therapy drains the blood from the legs, promoting reduced swelling. It reduces stress on the lower extremities."

Kirk could already feel his feet beginning to tingle as the blood supply lessened. "So, is this something you developed yourself as some sort of yoga exercise?"

"No. Dad taught me this years ago. He and I would sit like this and he would tell stories. The athletic trainer at Kansas, called Deaner, would have anyone with ankle or leg problems do this in the training room. Dad said he would sit like this and listen to Deaner tell stories about Wilt, Gale Sayers, and the other great Kansas athletes."

"One thing Dad said was that Deaner allowed no complaining. Injuries happen. There was always a way to attack the rehabilitation. Deaner said elevation, ice, and a strong mind would overcome any injury. Bellyaching had no place in his training room."

Kirk felt the conviction in AJ's voice.

They were both silent, lost in their own thoughts. AJ looked at the sky and reflected on the attack on her and on the loss of her father. Life was so fragile. We're all subject to the actions of others and to events beyond our control.

AJ slid her hand across the deck until the back of her hand just came in contact with the back of Kirk's hand. She felt the warmth of his hand as he returned the pressure.

"Kirk, tell me about your family."

After a moment, Kirk replied. "There really isn't much to tell. My folks divorced when I was young. Mom did the best she could raising me in California. I went to Pepperdine on a volleyball scholarship. Got the job with Green Star out of college, came to Madison, and here I am."

AJ probed, and was able to get Kirk to open up more about his childhood and college days. As they talked, Freethrow made himself comfortable, lying on the deck with his head resting on AJ's stomach. Stroking Freethrow's head with her free hand, AJ listened as Kirk talked.

"I wish I had a father like yours, AJ. You had someone to count on."

AJ admitted she was extremely fortunate. She told Kirk about her dad's success as a boys' high school basketball coach. And how, when AJ got to high school, her dad had successfully pushed to get the job as the girls' coach in order to coach his daughter. Sam Clark encouraged AJ to excel, without destroying their father/daughter relationship.

When AJ had gone to the University of Wisconsin, her dad attended all of her home games and many of the road games. She also told Kirk about her cooking classes with Dad. Sam Clark thought it was important for his daughter to learn to cook, so he took cooking classes with her. He would not ask her to do something he wouldn't do himself.

"Actually, my Grandmother didn't really want my dad to go into coaching."

Kirk turned his head to look at AJ. "That surprises me. I thought your grandparents supported everything your father did?"

AJ chuckled. "Grandma wanted Dad to be a dentist or a doctor. She wanted to have a professional in the family. Dad was smart and could have been whatever he wanted to be. He loved sports and history, and he wanted to work with kids. He wasn't money motivated."

"Like those of us in sales?" said Kirk.

AJ smiled. "Your words, not mine. Anyway, Dad bought a dentist's chair at an auction and put it in our house. When Grandma came over, he would ask her to sit in it so he could look at her teeth. Grandma would laugh and tell Dad he had made his point."

"Whatever happened to the chair?"

"I've had it since Dad..." AJ hurriedly began to get up. "We've been doing L therapy long enough. C'mon, I'll show you the chair."

"You may need to help me up," said Kirk. "I think my feet are asleep."

With AJ's help, Kirk rose and followed her into the apartment. Freethrow followed at their heels as they went down the short hallway and into the master bedroom.

"There it is," said AJ. Sitting in the corner of the bedroom was a vintage brown leather upholstered dental chair.

"What a neat piece of furniture!" Kirk exclaimed.

"Dad thought the same thing. I sit in it and read. The small tray table for dental tools works great for holding snacks and drinks."

"AJ, do you mind if I sit in it?"

"It's all yours."

As Kirk stretched out and made himself comfortable, AJ stepped to the side and said in her most professional voice, "Now, Mr. Vail, this won't hurt a bit."

Kirk took AJ's hands and pulled her down to his lap. He looked into AJ's eyes. "You appear to be just what the doctor ordered. I'll take whatever you're prescribing."

AJ leaned toward Kirk. As their lips touched, AJ felt her heart jump. They kissed deeply as Kirk wrapped his arms around her and held her close. When their lips parted, Kirk kissed her cheek, her nose and her forehead.

With a sigh, AJ began kissing Kirk on the lips again. When they parted this time, Kirk placed tiny kisses along the ridge of her chin. Feeling light-headed, AJ leaned back and slowly stood up.

"Rule Number Six. Cows and barn doors. Don't open the barn door unless you're prepared to chase the cows."

Kirk looked at AJ with an affectionate smile. "Somehow I don't think I want to know how Rule Six applies to me."

"Rule Six means don't start something you're not prepared to finish. This isn't the time or the place to continue what we've started. I hope you understand."

With a twinkle in her eyes, AJ continued, "But that doesn't mean it will always be that way."

"In that case, I will honor Rule Six until a future date. I look forward to that magical moment." Kirk unfolded himself from the dental chair.

"How do you keep your rules straight? And how many are there?"

AJ laughed. "I know I invoke the family rules at inopportune times. Dad and I developed the rules and wrote them out together. He wasn't one to lay down the law, but he had a strong sense of right and wrong. I keep a framed copy of the rules on the wall."

AJ pointed to the wall of the bedroom displaying framed pictures and documents she held sacred.

A simple, black frame held a sheet of lined paper with a handwritten credo. The penmanship looked a bit juvenile, and Kirk guessed AJ had written it as a child. Kirk read the rules and smiled as he remembered his first lunch date with AJ, when she had mentioned Rule Number One.

SAM and AJ CLARK
RULES TO LIVE BY
1. The Home team MUST wear white.
2. Don't Foul Out.
3. Bottled water and the Weather Channel.
4. Face your currency.
5. Touch all the lines.
6. Cows and barn doors.
7. Unlock both doors.
8. Keep a pen in your car.
9. On time is late.
10. Don't get scared, get mad.

Kirk finished reading and turned to AJ. "Pretty cool rules, I think, although I'm not sure what they mean."

"Dad was big on doing the right thing," AJ explained.

"I think it rubbed off on you." Kirk looked back at the wall. "I have to ask about Rule Number Three. Bottled water and the Weather Channel? What's the moral of that one?"

AJ smiled. "That was one Grandpa Clark helped with. Dad and I were at Grandma's and Grandpa's for Sunday dinner, and I was talking about the rules we were working on. We were trying to come up with something that meant "all things are possible.""

AJ couldn't help grinning as she recalled that day. "When Dad and I were brainstorming, Grandpa piped up. He said, 'Bottled water.' I asked, Grandpa, what do you mean?"

He answered, "AJ, if you would have said twenty years ago people would pay as much for a bottle of water as they do for pop or beer, people would have said you'd lost your marbles. When the French first came out with that spring fed bottled water, old Paul Harvey said that Evian is naíve spelled backwards, and the French are just trying to pull a fast one. They want to see if Americans will pay for something that's free out of the tap. I figure if people will buy bottled water, then anything's possible.' "

Kirk laughed out loud. "I can see your Grandfather saying that, and when you think about it, it's true."

AJ nodded. "And Grandma chimed in with the Weather Channel. She said if they could have a channel that shows weather 24 hours a day, nothing would surprise her. So we decided to use bottled water and the Weather Channel to remind us that nothing in life is impossible."

"So if nothing is impossible, what the heck is Rule Number Two? Don't foul out?"

AJ smiled at the memory. "Dad hated profanity. In high school, a wise man told him that profanity is the attempt of a feeble mind to express itself forcefully. That man was his basketball coach and I think he influenced Dad to go into coaching. Using foul language puts you out of any reasonable conversation and you can never take back something hurtful you've said."

Kirk put his arm around AJ and hugged her shoulder. Her head leaning against his shoulder was a perfect fit. He wanted to stand like this forever. "I like your rules. I like them a lot."

He took AJ's hand and walked her out of the bedroom, sitting her down on the sofa in the living room. He sat beside her and looked into her eyes.

"AJ, I have to admit I'm a bit jealous of your relationship with your father. I know you've had a terrible loss, but his memory will influence you forever."

After pausing to organize his thoughts, Kirk continued. "Speaking of forever..."

AJ looked at Kirk as he continued to hold her hand. She was touched by his sincerity. "Forever is a long time," she said.

Rising, Kirk continued, a bit uneasy by where this was taking them. "Now, down to business." He pulled a notepad and pen from the end table. "Let's get to work."

As they put their heads together and outlined the chain of events, AJ couldn't help but let her mind roam. She loved his willingness to step in and get involved. He accepted her theories and respected her opinions. He showed her that he was someone she could count on. He was acting more and more like a Gretzky every day.

CHAPTER 48

"That's enough. Time for a break." Kirk stood and stretched his arms above his head. They had dissected the Bouhler/Cox experiences for the past hour. "What you need, girl, is some comfort food. And being the kindhearted, sympathetic guy I am, I'll join you."

AJ stood and rubbed the back of her neck. "How considerate of you. I think you're right about taking a break. How about ice cream?"

Kirk smiled. "You're reading my mind! The Mad Town Ice Cream Shoppe! Let's hoof it."

Saying goodbye to Freethrow, AJ locked her apartment. As she and Kirk began their walk down the street, they talked of the weather, news, and sports. Anything, but the attack on AJ.

Entering the ice cream shop, Kirk took AJ's hand and led her to the counter. Amid the hundreds of choices, she chose a sugar cone with two scoops of Moose Tracks ice cream. Spotting an open table, Kirk sent AJ to save them a seat while he waited in line to order.

Watching Kirk in line, head and shoulders above those around him, brought AJ's thoughts to her Dad. Growing up, she often thought how nice it was to have a father who was tall. She could pick him out in a crowd and spot him in a mall easily. He was the one she looked up to literally as well as figuratively.

Scanning the crowded ice cream shop, AJ made eye contact with a young girl and smiled. The girl, with flowing brown hair, smiled back and gave a timid wave. It warmed AJ's heart when children responded to her.

Then she noticed the dress the young girl was wearing. It was a sleeveless white dress with a wide, multicolored collar. The collar was red with a green border. Teardrop shaped black spots were evenly spaced in the red area. The black spots represented seeds. It was a watermelon dress.

Seeing that dress brought back a flood of memories. Five-year-old AJ Clark wanted a watermelon dress. A girl in her kindergarten had worn a watermelon dress to school, and Sam's daughter had her mind set on having one, too.

But the search proved daunting. After four stores and no watermelon dress, Sam tried to persuade her to change her mind. But she would have none of it. She was displaying a focus and determination admirable in athletes, but unbelievably frustrating in a little girl.

With no luck at store number five and closing time fast approaching, Sam could feel his heart sinking. He would rather die than disappoint his daughter. But he was at the end of the line today.

"Honey, it's too late tonight to keep looking. We can try again tomorrow."

Little AJ, in pigtails and with the face of an angel, scowled up at her father. "Daddy, I have to have a watermelon dress. I can't believe you can't find one!"

Coming from his daughter, the words were like a punch in the stomach. Sam Clark felt the frustrations of the past months boiling over. He had promised himself he wouldn't break, for AJ's sake. But on this day, his spirit was overcome.

He sat down on the curb, put his head in his hands, and began to weep. He cried for his wife, he cried for himself, and he cried for AJ. He knew the world would never be the same, but he had told himself it would be OK. He thought he was strong. Who was he kidding?

Little AJ stared at her dad. She had only seen him cry once. At her mom's funeral, but not like this. He had held her tight at the funeral and cried, but it was controlled. Now, her dad was shaking and crying, and it scared her.

She knew it made her feel safe when her father hugged her, so AJ leaned on her dad's back and put her arms around his broad shoulders. Squeezing him, she rested her head on the back of his neck and whispered. "It's OK, Daddy. I don't need a watermelon dress. I love you, Daddy. I love you Daddy. I'm sorry I'm such trouble."

When the shaking and crying stopped, AJ could feel her dad breathing as she held on for dear life. After a minute, Sam spoke. "Honey, you're no trouble. You're my life. Do you know how much I love you?"

AJ knew what came next, and she couldn't wait. "No, Daddy. How much?"

Sam twisted his shoulder to get an arm around AJ and scooped her onto his lap. "This much!" He kissed her on the neck and cheeks and forehead, making loud smacking sounds. They both laughed and they both knew life was going to be all right. That was the day AJ Clark learned a valuable lesson. Material things don't matter. People matter.

AJ looked up as Kirk called her name. She was no longer a five-year-old and Dad was no longer here. Sometimes that irreversible truth slapped her hard. Not realizing she had been crying, she stood up, and stammered, "I've gotta go." As she stumbled out the door, she knew Kirk deserved better than this, but she didn't have the strength right now.

Standing in the Mad Town Ice Cream Shoppe with a cone in each hand, Kirk didn't know what to do. He glanced around in confusion to see what could have upset AJ. Not seeing anything even remotely disturbing, his eyes met those of a wide-eyed young girl in a multicolored dress.

Kirk handed the two cones to the girl. "Treats on me, honey." With that, he headed after AJ.

CHAPTER 49

A J stumbled out of the ice cream shop in confusion. She was angry, hurt, and frustrated. Angry with herself for not controlling her emotions, hurt by the continuing thoughts of missing her father, and frustrated by her inability to communicate with Kirk on the deeper level she craved.

Rubbing the tears from her eyes, she walked briskly. She needed fresh air and she needed to escape. Glancing across the street, she stopped in mid stride. Standing on the sidewalk with his hands in his pockets and staring right at her was a man. It was Bouhler.

It took a moment for reality to sink in. Bouhler turned and was quickly walking away. AJ yelled, "Hey!" She sprinted across the street.

With a glance behind him, Bouhler took off running. The race was on.

Bouhler had a half block head start, but AJ was the better athlete and she was fueled by angry determination. Horns honked as Bouhler crossed the street against the light. AJ zigzagged around an SUV, sidestepped an elderly couple, and threw it into high gear. She was gaining fast.

Hearing the pounding of AJ's feet, Bouhler turned sharply into an alley. He ran along the cobblestones, flipping over trashcans. Hurdling the cans, AJ drew close and lunged at Bouhler. She caught him by the coat, dragging him to the pavement with her.

As they landed, Bouhler kicked at AJ's head and shoulders, causing her to lose her grip. Rolling away, and standing, Bouhler reached for something to throw. AJ was coming to her feet when the bottle whistled past her head.

"Hey, Bozo! Watch it," she shouted. "I want to know what's going on."

Bouhler's answer was to launch a Heinz 57 ketchup bottle her way. It splattered against the brick building. AJ tossed a tin can in the air to distract him, and charged full speed ahead. Bouhler backpedaled down the alley.

He wasn't ready for the perfect soccer slide tackle AJ executed. Her legs swept across his ankles, knocking him to the ground beside her. Sweeping her right elbow at his head, she caught his cheek with a glancing blow as he tried to lean away.

Groping as he fell, Bouhler grabbed an old two by four. He swung it hard, striking AJ in the abdomen. Holding her stomach and gasping for breath, she could only watch as Bouhler stood, ran down the alley, and disappeared.

Emile Bouhler was infuriated with himself. He'd let the Clark woman see him, and she almost caught him. Now he wasn't sure what to do. After the truck accident, he had notified Krug to confess he had a major problem. Krug sent a cryptic response: the problem would be eliminated.

But Bouhler couldn't resist the temptation to follow the woman. And now this! She had gotten a close-up look at him. It was time to clear out. He'd let Krug take care of this problem. His job was to get to Chicago and do the preliminary setup.

The operation was finally reaching its climax. Bouhler thought about his payoff and smiled. As the field agent for Krug in the United States, Bouhler had taken the greatest risks, so he deserved the greatest rewards. Working with Krug had its perks, but the boss was seriously psycho. Bouhler was glad he wasn't called to the island much. Krug's temper prompted him to set up his own retirement plan by placing bets on Rickie Armendariz in the Olympics.

After a moment of coughing, AJ slowly stood and walked to the end of the alley. She saw what she expected — no sign of Bouhler. Slowly walking back through the alley, she felt dejected. *Why is this man following me? What have I done to deserve this? Why couldn't I hold him once I'd caught him?*

As she came to the spot where she had tackled Bouhler, she noticed a folded piece of paper lying where they had struggled. Picking it up and opening it, AJ began to smile. It was an Internet receipt for tickets to the track and field events at the upcoming Olympics in Chicago.

This whole crazy scheme had something to do with the Olympics! Stuffing the paper into her pocket, she walked back to the main intersection. Stepping out of the alley, she spotted Kirk across the street. When AJ called his name, he spotted her and jogged across the street.

"What's going on?" Kirk was shocked by her appearance. He noticed the dirt on her clothes and her disheveled hair. "AJ, are you OK? What happened?"

"I found Bouhler! I tackled him and I had him, too, but he kicked me and got away. But I know what's going on and I know where he's going!" AJ was talking a mile a minute.

Kirk put his hands on AJ's shoulders. "Whoa, Nellie. Slow down, I can hardly understand you. You fought with Bouhler? Are you all right, and what were you thinking?"

AJ resumed her staccato delivery. "I saw Bouhler across the street and chased him. I caught him in an alley and I had him. But he got away." AJ's hands were gesturing as she gave her animated response.

"You can't just take off chasing someone," Kirk said.

"But Kirk, I know what's going on!" Pulling the paper from her pocket, AJ held it up like a straight A report card. "Look what I've got. He's going to the Olympics. They're going to control athletes in Chicago!"

Kirk looked at the paper. "The Olympics?"

"Yes, the Olympics! Track and field events. Bouhler was getting research information on food supplements, electronic muscle stimulation and growth hormones from GF Products, Fermi Labs, Eli Lilly and who knows how many other companies. Then he killed the guys he got the information from so they wouldn't interfere with plans for using it at the Olympics."

It was all starting to make sense. Kirk nodded. "I see your point." He pulled AJ to him and hugged her. "But AJ, you just can't go running after guys and fighting with them. It's dangerous."

"I know, I know. But I'm fine." AJ was wired with adrenaline and held Kirk tight. "I had him, Kirk. I had him."

"I know. But I'm worried. What were you going to do with Bouhler if you held on to him? He could have hurt you."

After a pause, Kirk pushed on, "AJ, just tell me why you were crying in the ice cream shop. Was it the Dad thing again? Is your Dad always going to be with us?"

Kirk felt AJ stiffen. She clenched her teeth and stared up at Kirk. "Oh. Is my Dad always going to be with us? Lord, how I wish he were with us! Oh, Kirk!"

With a grunt of disgust, AJ pushed away from him and began walking away. Kirk took three giant strides and turned to block her path. "Please, AJ, I want to help."

Stepping around Kirk, AJ shook her head and said, "You can go to Red Grange Walter Payton and flip upside down, for all I care." With that cryptic parting shot, AJ turned and began to jog away.

"AJ, wait!" called Kirk. His words fell on deaf ears as AJ broke into a sprint toward her apartment. With her back toward him, Kirk couldn't see the hot tears streaming down her cheeks.

CHAPTER 50

K irk was about to run after her when his cell phone rang. Snatching the phone from his belt holster, he looked at the caller ID. Not recognizing the number, he opened the phone to make the connection. He gave an automatic, "Hello, Kirk Vail," as he began walking after AJ.

"Hi Kirk. This is Dee Dee."

The lilting voice didn't register. Kirk's mind went blank. *Dee Dee? Do I know a Dee Dee?* "Hello."

"Well, you don't sound very excited. I thought you'd be glad to hear from your Atlanta connection."

The bell went off in Kirk's head. Atlanta. Of course, Deirdre Walling. "Sure, Dee Dee. I'm glad to hear from you. I was just in the middle of something, and you caught me off guard." Kirk looked both ways before crossing the street as he talked.

"Kirk, I'm going to Chicago next week. I didn't know if you would be in the area, but I'll have some free evenings. If you're available to discuss... whatever you want to discuss."

Kirk's concentration was split. He was thinking about what AJ had said while he half listened to Dee Dee. *AJ had said Red Grange Walter Payton. That was 77 for Red Grange and 34 for Walter Payton. 7734. But what did that mean?*

"Kirk, are you listening to me?"

"Yeh, sure, Dee Dee. Go on."

"Well, I thought if you were going to be in Chicago, we could get together and..."

Kirk again tuned Deirdre out as he thought about AJ. She had said something about flipping upside down. Maybe the number was flipped upside down. "Dee Dee, I've got to put you on hold."

Putting her on hold before she could protest, Kirk pulled a piece of paper from his pocket and his pen. He wrote 7734 on the paper and turned it upside down. He looked at it closely. hELL. AJ had told him to go to Hell! Kirk laughed out loud and punched the phone line back to Dee Dee.

"Sorry about that. I'm going to be in Minnesota next week, so I guess we can't get together. But if you have any pertinent information, you can e-mail it to me."

There was a petulant tone in Dee Dee's response. "That's too bad, but I'll be looking for you at the Olympics."

Kirk pictured Dee Dee at their meeting in Atlanta, and carefully framed his reply. "The Olympics for me will be all work. Fifteen-hour days."

Dee Dee's laugh told Kirk she didn't believe him. "All work and no play, you know what they say," Dee Dee teased.

"I'll be busy. I have some leads to follow up on, and I think there is something worth investigating with the pole vaulter Jimmy Wickland."

Dee Dee's voice was laced with sugar. "Kirk, let me know if there is any information you need."

Kirk had the feeling Deirdre Walling got what she aimed for, and Kirk was in the crosshairs of her sights. Delaying was his best strategy. "Dee Dee, I've got to go. I'm in the middle of a crisis."

With a sigh, Dee Dee gave in. "Fine. You can go, for now. You have my number. I expect to hear from you. I need to know where you'll be staying."

Kirk thought, *I've got your number, all right.* "OK. But I have to go. Bye." Kirk closed his phone and slid it back into the holster. Did I say OK to Dee Dee about letting her know where I would be in Chicago? Man, that woman comes on strong.

He started walking slowly toward AJ's apartment. Suddenly he was in no hurry to see AJ. She pushed him away and expected everything to be just fine. Well, maybe Kirk Vail had other options.

Kirk felt an inner struggle. Dee Dee was certainly attractive and obviously available. But she wasn't what he was looking for. It was AJ who was important to him. With everything AJ had gone through, she may not be able to handle another letdown.

Her overemotional episodes were becoming more frequent. She needed Kirk more than ever. He really better go check on her. Kirk trudged onward, then had a thought that made him stop.

What would AJ's Dad do?

AJ said Rule Number Five, "Touch all the lines", was her Dad's favorite. It made perfect sense after AJ explained it. When you run suicide sprints in basketball, you run from baseline to free throw line, back to baseline, to half court, etc. You run as hard as you can and you touch the lines every time. Not some of the lines, some of the time. But all of the lines, all of the time.

Like the Golden Rule, it encompassed all behavior. If you know what is right, then do the right thing. If you know to touch the lines, then touch them. No debate. No excuses. No gray areas. No rationalizing behavior.

The right thing was to give comfort to AJ. Even if she acted like she didn't want or need his support.

Kirk walked on with the stride of a man on a mission. He was going to AJ's to touch all the lines.

CHAPTER 51

Tony took another bite of his thick crust pepperoni pizza. There was something intoxicating about pizza. The texture, the smell, the taste. He could eat pizza every day, and it showed. As he leaned back in his swivel chair, he absentmindedly scratched his ample stomach.

His mind had been wrestling with a problem for weeks. He felt a nagging emptiness and struggled to discover the root cause. Self-evaluation wasn't something he normally spent much time doing. Typically, the day-to-day routine was enough to keep him going.

But, he was bored. Not short term bored for an afternoon, something he could get over it by going to see the Cubs kick a baseball around. No, he was bored out of his mind. He was tired of work, home, and life.

Tony Massetti made book for a living. Some people called him a bookie, but he thought of himself as the guy who made book. He didn't just take wagers. He set the odds.

He looked at the green metal desk he had worked at for years and grimaced. He was sick of being around cheap furniture. Papa taught him to never be ostentatious. Dress down, act like the lower middle class. Even though he had money to burn.

Standing, he looked out one of the two picture windows in his office. The windows were a bonus when he purchased the building. One gave an unobstructed view of the parking lot so he could monitor anyone coming. The other window looked into the warehouse so he could watch his employees.

To call Tony corpulent would be kind. In his early forties, with black thinning hair greased flat against his skull, he moved to the warehouse window with surprising grace. He peered at the pallets that represented his import/export business. The legitimate business practically ran itself, and provided a wonderful vehicle for money laundering.

Tony's attire completed the picture of a small time Chicago businessman — cheap short sleeve white shirt, tie off the discount rack, polyester navy slacks, and black dress shoes sorely in need of polish. He knew he looked the part he played. The front allowed him to live in anonymity as he rose through the ranks of his true profession.

Tony's passion had always been gambling. He learned there were suckers who would bet on anything. Sometimes the more outrageous the bet, the more excited the better.

Working for his father, he discovered his penchant for sports. Not the ponies, which were fixed anyway. But Tony found he had an understanding of the sports where human gladiators pitted themselves against one another. Football, basketball, baseball, tennis, and track became his life. He immersed himself in the glorious statistics.

He was uncanny at predicting the mental and physical side of a contest. He knew which teams would come back and which would fold like an origami bird. He knew which athlete could dig deeper and which one had already overachieved and was on the wrong side of the bell curve of success.

Tony had a knack for the creative wagers that set the blood of the fan boiling. When Michael Jordan made his comeback in the NBA, Tony knew the Chicago fans coveted Michael more than the Bulls. So he set up a series of options for betting on the Wizards and on Michael. Tony brought in truckloads of money from fans betting on his Jordan matrix. You could bet on Michael's first shot, his percentage, his steals, etc. Fans betting with their hearts, not with their heads, were easy pickings.

But lately the thrill wasn't there. Now he was setting the spreads for most of North America and losing his competitive edge. He used to care if Notre Dame scored on their first series of downs. But really, did it matter to the world?

Shaking his head, he tried to clear his mind. Was he going soft? He'd made his mark taking money from the weak-minded gamblers of the world. He created a betting empire bringing millions of dollars into the organization. It was no time to lose his drive. But where was the spark?

Finishing the slice of pizza, Tony wiped his hands on a paper towel and let himself fall into his chair. With a protesting creak, the chair reluctantly accepted its load. Fingers danced across the keyboard as Tony called up reports on the betting for the week.

The light betting on the Olympics was disappointing. Tony set up a huge array of betting options, but the initial response was soft. This Olympiad lacked the charismatic athletes of previous years. There was no Carl Lewis or Michael Johnson going for multiple gold medals. It appeared to be a lackluster betting competition.

As he scrolled through the betting log, he noticed something interesting. There were an inordinate number of bets being placed on the pole vault. Tony had set up a line of bets on each event with detailed odds on world records being set. The hundred meter and the other glamour events normally led in wagers placed.

But from all over the country, sizable bets were coming in on a new Olympic record and a new world record in the pole vault. Bets from Atlanta, Boston, Dallas and St. Louis. Bets were also coming in picking a vaulter from the Caribbean to win the event. All of these bets carried long odds.

Tony began to add up the wagers. Then he calculated the payout based on the odds. Then he calculated the payout again. And again one more time.

Leaning back in his chair, he chewed on the tip of his thumb. His thoughts weren't on the taste of tomato sauce he was getting. Suddenly, the boredom was gone.

Tony kept staring at his calculator and thinking of the implications of the number staring back at him from the LED display. 22,000,000. Twenty-two million dollars. He could almost hear his dear departed Papa's voice saying to him, "This is money to die for."

Everyone else had left the south Chicago building as Tony Massetti sat staring at his computer screen. He worked his calculator enough times to know the numbers weren't going to change. The only sound in the office was the low hum of the ancient fluorescent lights.

Tony scratched his head along his thinning hairline and spoke to himself. "Somebody thinks they've got a sure thing. There's half a million bucks on some pole vaulter from a dinky nothing island to win the gold medal. And another 300 G's bet that a world record will be broken in the pole vault."

Tony leaned back and clasped his hands behind his head. Looking at the ceiling, he continued to think out loud. "So the fix must be in. These smart guys spread their bets around and think they can take us for twenty-two mil. Ain't happening. Not in Chicago. Not in My House!"

He needed information and he needed muscle. There wasn't much time till the Olympics. He had no time to waste.

Tony opened his bottom desk drawer and looked at the pile of cell phones. Grabbing one, he turned on the power. He used clean cell phones as the most untraceable way to communicate. Dialing a Miami number from memory, he walked to the window to look outside.

All was quiet in the parking lot as Tony waited for the connection to take place. The deep voice answering the phone couldn't hide the Bronx background in the one word response. "Talk."

"You still play baseball?" asked Tony. His code word verification was baseball, requiring a response using summer.

"Only in the summer."

"The Cubs will take the Yankees."

The laugh from Miami was long and hard. "You got some nerve talking trash like that. What's up?"

Tony was smiling now. Maybe it was the weather down there, or maybe it was the women. The Miami connection always laughed. "You know the two sure things in life?" Tony asked.

"Definitely. Death and taxes."

"Right," said Tony. "I got somebody who thinks there's a third sure thing. Could be an expensive one."

The laugh came again over the cell phone. "I hope he's paid his taxes. You want this sure thing should be permanent, or just painful?"

"I need information first." Tony outlined where the bets were coming from and gave the information about the pole vaulter from the Caribbean.

"No problem. I got a nephew with an island fetish. He flies a small plane. We'll find out what gives."

"Thanks. I need to know fast. This sure thing would be bad for business."

Miami laughed again. "You're the King of the Point Spread. We can't have your image besmirched."

Now it was Tony's turn to laugh hard. "Besmirched? Where did you pick up that word?"

"My sister, Maria, is on this Reader's Digest Word Power kick. She's quizzing us and telling us to speak more refined. Like we're from Long Island or something. I think she wants to marry a senator."

Tony thought about that. "Wouldn't be a bad move."

"Nah. I don't mind paying them, but I don't want politicians in the family. Then what can we talk about over Sunday dinner?"

Tony agreed and said his goodbyes. With the cell phone back in the drawer, he turned his attention back to the computer screen. *OK, Mr. Sure Thing. We'll see just how smart you really are.*

CHAPTER 52

Florida in the 1960's enjoyed a real estate frenzy not seen in America since the Oklahoma land rush. A burgeoning peacetime economy created a mobile society with the greatest disposable income in history. Disposable income and leisure time created the desire for the three indispensable elements of the perfect vacation paradise — sun, sand, and surf.

As investors, speculators, and snowbirds descended on America's 27th state, many saw the tropical peninsula as the answer to their prayers. Others saw it as the loss of innocence. Sleepy seaside towns would soon become inundated with fast food chains and urban sprawl, as the Florida population increased by 145% in two decades.

The population explosion brought houses, stores, and cement. Miles and miles of cement. Roads, bridges, parking lots, and retaining walls zigzagged across the Florida landscape. Economic growth required dry land, which, in Florida, meant draining swamps and lowlands.

From Jacksonville to Miami, the east coast of Florida changed. A pond near St. Augustine, which had been slowly shrinking for four hundred years, was drained so the adjoining twenty acres could become a strip mall. A nail salon, a souvenir shop, and a mini-mart would replace the habitat of the greatest healing plant the world has ever known.

When the bulldozers finished covering the low spot with dirt, the operators leaned against their hulking machines for a smoke. Compacted under tons of earth were leaves of the ancient healing plant, destined to suffocate and die. Buried beneath the booted feet of the dozer operators was the miracle answer to aging.

Lou Groves saw the pickup truck coming first. The battered red Chevy truck with "Peters Construction" stenciled on the side bounced along the gravel road, fishtailed through the turn into the construction zone and barreled across the open field toward the men. Pointing with his cigarette, Lou alerted the others. "Hank's got a burr under his saddle."

The other three men turned to watch the pickup careen toward them. As the truck skidded to a stop in a cloud of dust, the door flew open and a short stocky man leaped out.

Hank Johnson was a tough construction manager. He'd boxed his way through the Pacific Fleet during his stint in the service, pausing to fight in the Battle of the Coral Sea. At 44 years old, he could still throw a punch if provoked, which caused the dozer drivers to stand at attention as he approached.

Lou noticed Hank wasn't just scowling. His eyes looked like he'd been crying. Lou had an immediate thought. *You could cut off old Hank's legs and he wouldn't cry. Hank was tougher than high school algebra. What could make the man cry?*

"Men, the president's been shot," blurted out Hank.

The blank stares told Hank the news hadn't sunk in. "Don't you hear me, the president's dead!"

Lou spoke for the bewildered group. "Hank, slow down. You mean somebody shot Old Man Peters? Was there a robbery or something?"

Hank shook his head. "No, no. President Kennedy. I heard it on the radio. The president was killed in Dallas. Right in front of hundreds of people!"

No one knew what to say or do. They all threw their cigarettes into the dirt and ground out the butts with their boots. Lou spit and kicked at the ground. Hank leaned against the dozer and slapped its side, somehow needing to punish something for the tragedy.

Each man was lost in his own thoughts. The enormity of the event short-circuited the thought process. Finally, Lou spoke. "Hank, was it an attack? How many guys were there and why did they do it?"

Hank kept slapping the dozer. "Don't know." Slap. "Don't know." Slap.

The men had never seen Hank act anything like this. "Well Hank, what do we do?"

"Don't know." Slap. "Don't know." Slap

Lou motioned with his thumb and whispered to the men, "Go home." They nodded and drifted toward their personal vehicles, still dazed by the unbelievable news.

Lou wiped his arm across his face and looked out across the Florida fields. He felt empty in the pit of his stomach. Like hope had been taken away. He stared at the land he knew so well and wondered what happens now.

The only sound was the rhythmic slap, slap, slap of Hank's hand on the side of the yellow dozer. Lou had to get Hank to the office or home. He couldn't let him stand here slapping the bulldozer.

"Hank, Buddy, we've got to go. Come on, man. Let's go to the office and find out what's going on."

Hank turned and looked at the younger man. "It's just like December seventh in '41. The world won't be the same. That's only supposed to happen once in a lifetime."

Lou patted Hank on the shoulder. "Yeh, sure Hank. Let's go."

Hank stood rooted to the spot. "You'll always remember where you were when you heard about Kennedy. November twenty-second, '63, will be remembered fifty years from now."

Lou nodded. "Sure, Hank. I'll always remember you gave me the news. I was two when Pearl Harbor was hit, so I only know what my folks told me. But my gut's telling me I won't forget this moment."

Lou began walking slowly to see if his boss would follow. Hank fell in step next to him and the two walked shoulder to shoulder across the freshly graded field. Their thoughts were on the death of the president. A beacon of hope for the nation had been snuffed out.

Both men were oblivious to the fact they had unknowingly perpetrated as great a tragedy. Without fanfare or national mourning, the plant that could speed healing and retard aging had been obliterated. Bulldozed under, the plant that could have cured legions would wither and die.

On November twenty-second, 1963, the Peters Construction Company killed the last remaining Florida descendents of the Native Americans' "Plant of Forever Young". The only remains of what Ponce de Leon had sought as the Fountain of Youth were the plants growing in northwest Tennessee.

The final vegetation of hope against aging quietly grew along the banks of Reelfoot Lake. The nation was filled with outrage and grief over the assassination of President John Fitzgerald Kennedy, unaware it was a day of double tragedies.

CHAPTER 53

Timetables and deadlines didn't mean much to Bubba. He couldn't believe sawed off Jack Ward treated him like he couldn't read a calendar. Bubba knew the Olympics were breathing down their necks. He knew the mayor had a parade and other shindigs planned when Jimmy Wickland came back.

Bubba also knew he was the one doing all the work. He saw Ward and the mayor walking the streets, planning where the reviewing stand would go. He saw them in the coffee shop, talking like big shots. And he knew he was the one killing the kudzu and building the reviewing stand.

The building assignment actually worked out well. Bubba ordered extra wood for himself and stashed it in his garage. He figured he'd make his own bonus for all the work he was doing.

His kudzu concoction was working like a charm, too. There was brown, dead kudzu all over the place. Granted, there were a few dead bushes and dead patches of grass, but that was the price you had to pay. In war, there were casualties. General Bubba was waging a war to the death on kudzu.

As he drove out of town to do more spraying, he checked the cooler on the seat of the truck to be sure he had a few brewskies. It was another hot one and he needed liquid refreshment. He'd make one last swing to spray along the lake.

Tomorrow he'd start on the reviewing stand. Maybe he could talk the mayor into putting indoor/outdoor carpet on the platform. That way he could order some extra and do his screened-in porch like he hoped. *Thank You, Lord, for giving us a genuine local sports hero.* Bubba smiled. *The Olympics have been very, very good to me!*

CHAPTER 54

Jimmy gave Grams a final hug. "I wish you could come with me,Grams. It's going to be the greatest!" Jimmy was so excited he could hardly stand still. Years of training and mental concentration had given Jimmy Wickland the opportunity to represent his country in the grandest sports' venue in the world.

Grams held Jimmy's face in her hands and looked him in the eyes. "Honey, you do me and Billy Mills proud, you hear? We've been talking about this since you were a baby." Lily Morales' eyes began to fill with tears.

Wrapping her arms around Jimmy's neck and pulling him to her, she whispered in his ear. "Who's gonna make it?"

Jimmy practically squeezed the air out of Grams as he held her tight and whispered back. "WE'RE gonna make it!"

Finally letting go of her grandson, Lily turned to pick up a plastic thermos. "Here's the last of my plant juice."

"Thanks, Grams. That's plenty to help me bring home the gold. My shoulder and leg feel great. You work miracles."

Lily waved her hand as if to say, "It's nothing". Then she opened a kitchen drawer and took something out, hiding it in her hands. "I know you told me I couldn't make you a warm up suit because they give you those nice ones with USA on them. But I had to make you something."

Opening her hands, she held them out toward Jimmy. He took the offered object and looked it over. It was a sky blue cloth bracelet with the words KISS THE SKY embroidered across it in white. Each end had a leather thong attached, decorated with dark blue beads and a tiny feather.

"I want you to jump so high you kiss the sky when you clear the bar." Lily looked at Jimmy expectantly.

"I love it, Grams! Thank you. Will you tie it on for me?" Lily saw the genuine appreciation in the eyes of her grandson.

She carefully tied the bracelet around Jimmy's left wrist. Patting his hand when she finished, she said, "You better go. You can't miss the bus or you'll miss your plane."

"You're right." Jimmy put the thermos in his large duffle bag, then slipped the strap over his shoulder, hoisting the bag off of the floor. He'd be walking into town to catch the bus.

As he walked away from the house, Lily stood in the doorway to watch his departure. Jimmy turned to give a last wave, and Grams Morales called out, "Kiss the sky, you hear me? Give it your best!"

Jimmy gave a thumbs up signal, then blew a kiss to the woman who'd given him everything. "Never a doubt!" he called back. They both smiled as Jimmy turned toward his destiny. Grams went inside, closed the door, and hurried to the kitchen window to watch as he walked away from her and toward his goal.

CHAPTER 55

A J drove her Jeep hard. Bouncing over hills and plowing through creeks were just what the doctor ordered. Her arms ached from fighting the steering wheel, and she loved it. Her vehicle wore a mud badge of courage, proving they were competitors. The dents in her back end gave the Jeep a battle-scarred appearance.

The Saturday Jeeping competitions were informal, but fierce. The men cut the women no slack, and AJ wouldn't have it any other way. Steep grades and hairpin turns challenged even the most proficient drivers. Finishing her run, AJ pulled under an ancient cottonwood tree and killed the engine.

Jumping out, she tossed her helmet on the seat and yelled toward the small group in lawn chairs twenty yards away. "Lois, how'd I do?"

Looking at her stopwatch, the heavyset woman frowned and pushed her black cowboy hat further back on her head. "If this was the Rose Parade, you would've won."

Leaning forward in the lawn chair that threatened to collapse, Lois studied her clipboard intently. "Clark, if you had a Wrangler, stead of your Cherokee, you'd do better on the turns. 'Cuz you can drive some."

Lois paused to spit a stream of brown tobacco juice into a red plastic Miller High Life cup. "As it sits now, you're hanging in fifth."

Smiling, AJ tied her hair up as she walked to the cluster of chairs. "I'm making my move, Lois. This will be my best finish." Leaning down, she grabbed a bottled water as it floated in a galvanized washtub.

"Sure you don't want a beer to wash away the dust?" The speaker held up a can as he looked up from his webbed lounge chair. His graying ponytail hung over the chair back as he looked up expectantly.

"Thanks, but not today, Clete. I've got to get back to town. No drinking and driving for this girl. Too many Smokies out."

166

Lois chimed in. "They see you in that red Jeep and they'll pull you over just to talk!"

There were hoots from the men. Just then a Green Wrangler with a yellow lightning bolt etched across the hood roared past.

Lois checked her watch and dutifully recorded the time. "Your sixth now, Clark. Want to ante up again and make another run?"

"Naw, gotta hit it." The top three times of the day split the pot held by Lois. She charged by the run and took her cut out for refreshments, the rest going to the winners.

Lois made one last offer. "Clark, if you can toss your empty water bottle into that trash can from there, I'll give you a free run."

AJ looked at the rusted 55-gallon drum wired to a wooden post. She gauged the distance as 24 feet with the drum leaning to the left. "Too easy," she said to Lois. As she spoke, AJ began walking to her left. She was lengthening the shot, but improving the angle.

As she walked, AJ tightened the cap back on the bottle and let her right arm drop to her side, holding the bottle by the neck. There was an ounce of water left in the bottle, giving it better weight than if it were completely empty.

"Make it two runs," she called over her right shoulder.

"You got it," responded Lois.

Spinning to her left, AJ raised the bottle behind her right ear. Pivoting on her right foot and stepping with her left, she looked like a second baseman turning a double play.

She figured thirty feet to the drum, negligible wind, a slight drift to the left because of the pivot. Her arm snapped forward as she aimed for the right edge of the drum opening.

There was a quick pop and then a metallic rattling sound as the bottle hit the inner wall of the drum and banged around inside.

"Bingo!" crowed Clete. "I believe we have a winner."

AJ smiled at Lois and the appreciative spectators. "I'll take a rain check and use my free runs next time. Thanks for the challenge."

Lois shook her head and smiled. "OK, Clark. Next time the first two are on the house."

AJ tipped an imaginary hat and turned to leave. "But Clark." Lois called after her. "Throwing ain't driving. You might try giving us a lot more Jeff Gordon and a little less Randy Johnson next time."

There were good-natured catcalls and hollers as AJ walked to her Jeep. She could hear the laughter as the mention of Randy Johnson generated a quick reference to his nickname, The Big Unit. The humor of the Jeeping group ran from suggestive to gross, creating locker room type camaraderie.

On the drive back to Madison, AJ had the windows down and the CD player blaring. She certainly needed the diversion today. The Bouhler scuffle had upset her more than she cared to admit. And her explosion with Kirk in the street had left her feeling alone and guilty.

But not as guilty as Kirk had made her feel. He had come to her apartment and acted so sweet. When AJ refused to let him in, he talked to her calmly from outside her door. So she had turned her stereo up to drown him out.

He called from his cell phone and spoke to her soothingly. She hung up and shut off the phone. AJ thought that would send him away.

But a few minutes later, she heard the sound of pebbles hitting her deck. Looking out through the sliding glass doors, she could see a white poster board being marched along her railing on a stick. Kirk was down below holding a six foot long 2 by 4 with the poster board nailed to the top.

The poster board had the single letter "I" written on it in black marker. After the poster disappeared from view, another poster appeared with the word "CARE". It too paraded across her field of view. A third poster followed this with the word "ABOUT" written in huge black block letters.

AJ couldn't resist a smile. Kirk wasn't accepting the rejection she was throwing at him. As the fourth poster appeared with "U!" written on it, AJ walked out onto the deck and went to the railing.

"Hey down there. Do you have a permit to picket here?"

Kirk looked up. "I think it's part of the First Amendment. Freedom of speech, freedom to be a jerk, and freedom to apologize. I'm sorry.

The guilt hit AJ like a hammer. Kirk HAD been there for her. She knew she acted irrationally sometimes and she never wanted to totally open up.

She told him to give up picketing and come back around so she could let him in. They had a long talk, held hands, and made up.

A week had passed since then and life had still not returned to normal. Nightmares about the car attack disrupted her sleep. And with Kirk gone all week in Minnesota, she felt strangely alone. As she and Kirk grew closer, being apart became more difficult.

That's what made driving today so great. She needed the mental and physical exertion to clear her system. She was going to zip through the car wash when she got to town and then pick Freethrow up from Sarah's. They could go for a nice long run after she went home to change.

For the first time in weeks, her mind was free of mysteries, mayhem, and murder. Rolling into Madison, her mind floated along with the music.

CHAPTER 56

While AJ's mind floated, the Gardener focused. He hated quick jobs. He liked to have time to carefully study the subject and plan in detail. He knew success was assured by leaving nothing to chance. Plus he enjoyed the preparation.

The joy was in the plan. The thought process and the stalking brought a heightened sense of oneness with the target. Understanding the hopes and dreams of the victim made the climax that much sweeter.

But Krug messaged there was no time to waste. One attempt had been botched, so the first string was called in to finish the job.

As he followed the filthy red Jeep into Madison, the Gardener reviewed a dozen potential scenarios for the death of the attractive young driver. It was really too bad he didn't have more time on this one. It had been a long time since he had put his hands on anyone this beautiful.

But he didn't have the luxury of a leisurely stake out. He was going to do this job today and get out of America. He'd scouted her apartment last night and followed her to the crazy country race. He watched from a hill with his binoculars as Clark traversed the irregular shaped course.

Now, as he followed her into town, the Gardener felt a stab of joy. The Clark woman was pulling into a full service car wash. It was one of those where you got out as the car went through unattended. There was a long line of cars waiting to enter, which would play right into his hands.

He drove past the car wash and turned into the McDonald's parking lot next door. Putting the rental car in park, he dug into the cheap duffel bag and found what he needed. Slipping the two credit card size blocks of wax into the pocket of his jeans, he casually walked to the car wash.

As he walked, he pushed his black hair forward so that it hung just above his eyes. He shuffled, appearing lackadaisical as he sauntered into the back of the car wash as his eyes took in every detail. A row of dark blue jumpsuits hung on pegs along the wall. Snatching one off a hook, he quickly stepped into the restroom.

He'd hit the jackpot. The jumpsuit was large enough to fit over his clothes, but not so huge to look unnatural. There was a dirty black baseball cap in the pocket. Putting it on, the gardener looked in the mirror. The bill of the cap was rolled in a tight half circle the way kids wear them.

Hunching his shoulders forward slightly and hanging his head to the side, he liked the look. He was going to play the part of a young Hispanic worker who's tired and bored. No English required.

The car wash was busy. Sunny Saturday's were the biggest payday and everyone was humping. When he exited the restroom, the Gardener knew the key to blending in was to never stop moving.

He walked along the wash area toward the customer waiting room, stopped, and headed back. He was in a hallway with a glass wall on one side where you could see the cars going through the wash, rinse, and dry areas. The customers dropped their vehicles at the back, where the vacuuming was done. Then the customers walked down this hallway to the waiting room.

A couple with a small boy was looking through the glass at the cars as the father explained what was going on. Walking toward him was a short man, mid fifties, in a gray suit and sunglasses. His stride said I've got places to go and things to do. He went past the Gardener without giving him so much as a look.

Next came two high school girls, chattering about who knew what. He heard one say, "Whatever!" while they passed him as if he were a piece of furniture.

Next came the victim. Miss Clark was walking toward him and looking him right in the eyes. She wore faded jeans that fit her like a glove and a short sleeved orange top with thin blue stripes. She was very attractive with a confident, athletic walk.

The Gardener noticed she didn't carry a purse. Her arms swung freely as she walked. He met her gaze from under his cap as the distance closed between them. He knew his plan, and he would stick to it.

They were about six feet apart when AJ smiled at him and said, "How ya doin?"

A thought flashed through the Gardener. *I can take her right now. Right here. Sprint out and be gone before anyone even knows what happened.*

Instead, he responded with a rapid stream of Spanish. He said, "Hello, beautiful Miss. I hope you have a wonderful day."

As they passed, AJ replied in Spanish. "Thank you, kind Sir. I wish you the same."

Surprised at her response, the Gardener smiled. "Many thanks to you. Your kindness has made this a day to remember." He liked the cadence of Spanish and was enjoying the chance to use his skill.

AJ gave a last smile and a "Gracias" as they parted, She headed toward the waiting room, and he continued on his way to the back of the car wash.

The Gardener fought an almost insurmountable urge to reach out and touch the victim. Her friendliness and openness were engaging. *But the innocent die, too. What was that Billy Joel song they had tried to ban in Italy years ago? It talked about Catholic girls and the Vatican was up in arms.*

"Only the Good Die Young!" That was it. Well, this Miss Clark seemed to have some good in her. But she had learned something she shouldn't have, so she had to go. She was good and she would die young. I, on the other hand, have done so much bad in my life that, according to Billy Joel, I should live forever.

Momentarily lost in his thoughts, the Gardener was startled when his shoulder was grabbed. He was looking into the pimply face of a young man in a blue jumpsuit. "Who are you?" he was asked.

The Gardener rattled of a few sentences in Spanish, waving his arms for effect.

"Oh, man. You telling me, you no hablo English?"

Another steam of rapid Spanish followed.

Shaking his head in disgust, the young man tried once more. "Who hired you, man? Was it Big Steve? He's a great big guy." The young man held his hand above his head for emphasis. "Great big dude. Steve. Ring any bells, Jose?"

Needing to move on, the Gardener played along. "Si, senior Steve!" Smiling effusively and nodding his head, the Gardener then threw another long stream of rapid fire Spanish at his confronter.

Putting his hands up as if surrendering, the young man stopped him. "Okay, Okay. I'm Paul, the shift manager. Enough of the taco talk already." Pointing to the back of the car wash, he gave the Gardener a shove. "Go vacuum. Zoom, zoom." He made a back and forth motion with his hand. "Go suck some dirt, Pedro. Zoom, zoom. Got it?"

Moving toward the back, the Gardener nodded. Smiling the whole time, he told the young man in Spanish that he had a face that would scare a mother into celibacy and that, as a favor to his ancestors, he would cut his heart out and feed it to the crows.

The young man just nodded and turned to head to the front, muttering under his breath.

CHAPTER 57

The Gardener needed to move quickly. He saw the mud-covered red Jeep being vacuumed by two workers. It would then be driven forward and parked on the conveyor that would carry it through the wash.

Moving to the opposite side of the conveyor, he pretended to work on a piece of equipment as he kept his back to the glass wall. He watched out of the corner of his eye as the Jeep was driven from the vacuum area to the conveyor.

As the Jeep approached him on the conveyor, the Gardener squatted and pretended to manipulate a hose nozzle. When the Jeep reached him, he turned, opened the passenger door and was inside. Ten seconds later water began blasting the vehicle from all sides.

Knowing he couldn't be clearly seen, he removed the key chain from the ignition. It was a quick deduction to determine which was Clark's apartment key. Spinning the key around the ring, he removed it completely.

Soap was now being sprayed on the Jeep, further hiding the Gardener from view. He reached inside his jumpsuit to his pocket and removed the two blocks of wax. Carefully, he pressed the key against one block. Then he placed the other piece of wax over the key and squeezed the blocks together.

After holding them together for five seconds, he pulled the wax apart. Rinse water was now cascading across the Jeep. The wax disappeared into his pocket and the key spun back on the ring.

He made sure the apartment key went back next to the ignition key, keeping the same order. The key chain was replaced in the ignition just as the whine of the dryers began.

Pulling a shop rag out of the jumpsuit pocket, the Gardener busied himself wiping off the dash board and the inside of the doors. As the Jeep slowly rolled off of the conveyor, Paul, who questioned him previously, opened the driver side door.

"What are you doing in here?" he screamed above the noise of the dryers. Jumping into the driver's seat while staring at the Gardener, he started the vehicle and drove it forward sixty feet to the finish area.

"You stupid moron!" Paul yelled as he put the Jeep in park. "I told you to vacuum, not joyride through the wash." After waving at two boys in jumpsuits to wash the windows, he quickly walked around the Jeep and jerked the passenger door open.

"Out, pea brain! Get in the back and vacuum!"

The Gardener smiled and nodded as he quickly headed into the building to avoid further abuse and attention. As he neared the door he made eye contact with AJ, who stepped outside to claim her vehicle. She had seen the exchange with the supervisor and gave the Gardener a sympathetic smile.

"I'm sorry you are in trouble. Better days will come if you keep working," she said in perfect Spanish.

Glancing back at the supervisor, the Gardener responded in Spanish, "His mother is the one we should feel sorry for. It must be a burden to have raised a son with neither a brain nor a conscience."

AJ laughed and her eyes sparkled. "Well put, my friend."

Her beautiful smile, considerate attitude, and fluent Spanish caused the Gardener to have a momentary pang of regret over what he must do.

AJ retrieved her Jeep while the Gardener moved quickly through the car wash to the men's room, removed the jumpsuit and hat, and went out the back to his car. He watched from the McDonald's lot as AJ pulled out into traffic. Pulling out five cars behind her, he began tailing her again.

After six blocks, AJ turned into a mall parking lot. This was working out perfectly. This would give him time to make the key and arrive at Clark's apartment ahead of her. The woman appeared to enjoy life. Little did she know she had only a few hours to live.

CHAPTER 58

A J didn't find what she was looking for in the mall, so she left to swing by Sarah's place and pick up Freethrow. Her friend was great about watching him. Since AJ left early to go Jeeping today, Sarah had taken Freethrow yesterday afternoon. Sarah didn't have any pets, but AJ was able to reciprocate by watering her plants when she was gone.

With Freethrow happily riding in the passenger seat, AJ made the final turn into the apartment complex parking lot. Past the sand volleyball pits and the pool, she turned left and parked in front of the two-story building with the large blue "4" painted on the side.

Her dog jumped out of the Jeep and ran back and forth as AJ grabbed her racing helmet and Freethrow's overnight bag. The backpack was used to transport Freethrow's small blanket, food, bowls, and toys when he stayed at Sarah's.

With Freethrow at her heels, AJ walked up the sidewalk to the building entrance, slipping her arms through the backpack as she walked. Inside, she took the stairs two at a time as Freethrow raced her to the landing.

Walking down the hallway to her apartment, she held her helmet in her left hand and twirled her key chain in her right, talking to Freethrow all the way. She found the correct key by feel and had it ready to unlock her door. But something didn't feel right.

She subconsciously did an inventory of her keys every time she handled them. There was a specific order to her key chain. Ignition key, apartment key, office key, filing cabinet key, locker key, petite Swiss army knife. The order was correct. But something was wrong.

AJ hesitated as she inserted the key in the lock. What was wrong? She turned the key unlocking the deadbolt and turned the doorknob, hesitating again before pushing the door open.

The apartment key was facing the wrong way! AJ kept all of her keys on the key ring so the teeth all faced the same way. But the apartment key was turned the opposite way.

The Gardener choreographed his jobs. He used his copied key to enter AJ's apartment undetected. A quick look in the kitchen showed what he hoped to find. Miss Clark had a gas range, which would develop a fatal leak.

He brought a short piece of heavy rubber hose to subdue Clark. His plan was to strike her on the back of the head as she entered the apartment. He could knock her out with a properly placed blow with the hose without leaving an obvious mark.

He checked to be sure the windows were all closed so fresh air wasn't entering the apartment. After disabling Clark, he would sit her on the living room sofa, start the gas leak and let himself out.

Her death would be painless and would be blamed on a faulty gas connection. The loss of this beautiful young woman would be viewed as an unfortunate tragedy, but certainly not as a homicide.

As he stood waiting for the door to open, the Gardener wondered what Clark was waiting for. He'd heard her unlock the door and saw the knob turn. But the door still didn't open.

He was poised with his feet spread wide, knees flexed, and the hose in his right hand. When Clark opened the door and stepped in, he would grab her left arm with his left hand, strike her behind the ear and kick the door shut with his right foot. It would only take two seconds and she would never see what hit her.

"*Open the door!*" he screamed inside his head

Freethrow could stand the wait no longer. He pushed on the door causing AJ to let go of the knob as the door swung into the apartment. Freethrow was around the door with a growl and yelped as the Gardener swung the hose down on him.

AJ stepped in and the Gardener swung the hose up at her face with a backhand. Reflexively bringing her left arm up, she blocked the blow with her helmet and kicked at her assailant with her right foot.

Her kick was blocked and she was propelled backwards with a punch to the jaw that sent her sprawling on the floor. The Gardener leaped toward her, holding the hose in both hands, hoping to choke her and muffle any cry for help.

AJ raised both feet just in time to catch her attacker in midair, kicking to vault him over her head. He did an awkward summersault, landing hard and sliding into the kitchen.

Both scrambled to their feet, breathing hard. Neither had spoken a word during the physical exchange. In a flash, the Gardener pulled a chef's knife from the kitchen counter. The eight inch long tapered stainless steel blade gleamed in the afternoon sunlight.

"Fun's over," he said. "Time to finish the job."

He stepped forward with the knife held low, blade side up, preparing to make a sweeping uppercut swing guaranteed to inflict maximum damage. As he took one more step and began his thrust at the stunned AJ, he picked up a blur of white coming at him from between her legs.

The blow from the hose had stunned Freethrow. Regaining his bearings, he immediately knew AJ was in mortal danger. He could smell anger and fear in the air. With a burst of adrenaline, he sprinted in the most direct path toward the danger, which took him between the legs of his master.

Leaping with all of the ferocity he could muster, Freethrow bared his teeth with a guttural growl. Extending his front legs forward in an attack posture, he flew toward the midsection of the Gardener.

Startled, the Gardener shortened the arc of his stroke, catching the dog in the chest with the kitchen knife. The knife carried Freethrow higher, where he bit and clawed at the Gardener's face, even as his own life-blood pumped out through his wound.

Screaming and staggering back, the Gardener pulled the animal off of his bloody face, throwing the body on the floor and extracting the knife. AJ turned to run for help, knowing she must escape or die.

Seeing his target about to exit through the open apartment door, the Gardener stepped and threw the knife with all his might. His aim and skills were as sharp as ever. But his luck was not.

AJ felt a thud in her back as she reached the door, but she never broke stride. Once in the hall, she turned and sprinted to the stairs, leaping down them four at a time.

Bursting outside, she shouted for help as she sprinted toward the apartment complex office a hundred yards away. She didn't slow down until she crashed into the counter in the small office, sending papers flying.

"Help me, help me. I'm being attacked!"

The girl behind the counter gave AJ a terrified look and shouted, "Mr. Petry, get out here now."

AJ stepped behind the counter as the girl shrank away from her. "Call 911, call 911," AJ kept repeating.

A tall white haired gentleman stepped out from the back room, making an immediate assessment. Taking AJ by the shoulders, he looked her in the eyes and spoke quickly. "It will be all right, Miss. Sue, call 911."

Seeing AJ trembling uncontrollably, Mr. Petry pulled her to him, giving her a hug. He heard Sue talking to the police, knowing they would be there soon.

Andrew Petry held the sobbing Miss Clark. As he had his arms encircling her, he was careful not to touch the bloody knife buried up to the hilt in her backpack. He didn't want to disturb the evidence.

CHAPTER 59

AJ stared at the floor dejectedly. Kirk was unreachable. He was in meetings in Minnesota and couldn't get messages until Sunday. Grandpa and Grandma were in Iowa on a Farm Bureau sponsored trip. A group of Wisconsin and Illinois farmers were touring John Deere manufacturing plants, with a special stop at a riverboat casino.

As she studied her living room carpet, AJ had a sudden random thought. *My life has turned into a country song. My dog's dead and my man isn't here. If I lose my job, I'll hit the country song trifecta.*

She felt like there was no tomorrow. The attack on her was overshadowed by the murder of Freethrow. He was her family. Grief, anger, and frustration swirled inside her, all fighting to take control.

Looking around her apartment, it hit her how little material things really mattered. Nice furniture, new clothes, and more gadgets paled in comparison to the love of family. If she could wave a magic wand and trade all of her things for Freethrow, there would be absolutely no hesitation.

And what about Dad? What would she trade to have him back? What about the Mother she hardly knew? What would she trade to have them both back? *Everything! Take my money, my job, and my possessions!*

Her psychology professor asked in a class discussion, "What would you give up or do for a million dollars?" The discussion that followed had been heated and wide-ranging. For money, people seemed willing to do the undignified and give up their pride.

But AJ knew mere money did nothing for the soul. It couldn't bring love and happiness. It couldn't cure heartache nor dispel fear and loneliness.

AJ closed her eyes and tried to go to a place long ago. She strained to hear her Mother's voice, to see her Mother's face in her mind. Folding her hands in her lap, she concentrated with all her might.

A policeman came in from the deck and watched AJ for a moment, then went into the kitchen where another officer was still looking for fingerprints. "Hey McNamara." Cocking his head toward the living room, he continued,

"She all right?"

McNamara stood up and stepped to the doorway to look into the living room. "Yeh, she's Okay. Leave her alone."

The police had interviewed AJ, dusted for prints, and searched within a ten-block radius. They believed the assailant opened the sliding glass doors, exited to the deck, jumped to the ground, and escaped along the common grassy area between the apartment buildings.

The grass was dry, leaving some markings, but nothing close to a usable shoe print. The doorknobs, kitchen counter, knife handle, and deck railing were all clean of usable prints. The assailant must have worn gloves.

When interviewed, AJ told the police she thought it was a Hispanic man from the car wash. She told them a rapid fire tale of being attacked before while driving, and about a plot to kill her because she knew too much about their plan to sabotage the Olympics.

Which caused one interviewer to roll his eyes. "*The Olympic sabateurs have come to Madison*," he thought, but fortunately he held his tongue. He had been reprimanded before for sarcastic comments during interviews and had vowed to keep his nose clean.

The description of the man was of marginal help. Average height, average weight, dark hair, and no discerning features. Why didn't really tall guys with huge noses commit crimes?

The officer pushed AJ, asking if she was absolutely positive she had seen the man before. When AJ admitted that it was possible it was a different man because everything happened so fast, the officer had snapped his book shut. He knew this was probably going into the unsolved pile.

At AJ's insistence, an officer had been dispatched to the car wash to follow up on her comments about a worker there. But it was looked at as a courtesy check. The woman was close to delusional when she began spouting something about a conspiracy.

The immediate judgment of the detective was it was a typical crime of an attractive woman being attacked in her home during an attempted robbery or rape. Luckily she escaped. But a worldwide conspiracy? Not hardly.

AJ squeezed her hands together as hard as she could. Why did Freethrow have to get killed? He'd been a living link to her parents. Freethrow was a constant reminder of what was good in life. He was unquestionably loyal and trusting.

And now he was gone, leaving AJ feeling like an orphan. Freethrow had willingly given up his life to save hers. He'd made the ultimate sacrifice.

For what? Why had she stumbled onto this scheme? Why couldn't she have just ignored Bouhler when she first saw him acting suspiciously? Why did she have to keep pushing deeper into something that was none of her business?

AJ snapped back to reality as a hand touched her shoulder. Startled, she looked up into the concerned face of John Cline. Jumping up, she gave him a hug.

"AJ, are you all right?" John felt this was his opening line every time he saw AJ. "I can't believe what happened."

Letting go and stepping back, AJ gave John a quizzical look. "How do you know what happened?"

John replied with a sad smile. "I must admit, I fall into the category of old bored guy with a police scanner. When I heard about the disturbance in your apartment complex, I called your apartment to check on you and a policeman answered. So here I am."

As they both sat down, John asked AJ what happened. After a pause and a sigh, she recounted the tale of the attack. When finished, she gave an involuntary shiver.

"John, there was a knife stuck in my backpack. It would have killed me. The man was here to kill me. This wasn't a robbery gone bad, as the police are saying."

AJ crossed her arms, hugging herself to ward off the what if's.

"What if I hadn't had Freethrow?" she said, strain showing in her voice. "He saved my life by attacking this guy. And what if I hadn't had Freethrow's backpack on with his blanket and toys inside? The knife would have killed me. Freethrow saved my life twice!"

John sympathized, making comments about what a wonderful dog Freethrow had been. Stunned and bewildered, they sat in silence for a few minutes.

AJ glanced around her apartment, and then looked back at John.

"What am I going to do? I know this is related to Bouhler. I can't just forget about it and act like I don't know there's something going on."

"Course not," said John clenching his fist. "We have to fight."

AJ's weak smile told him he had hit the mark. "Look AJ," said John as he leaned close to her. "There's something going on, and you've somehow been thrust into the middle of it. I'll do whatever I can do to help you."

John's support allowed AJ to focus on the present and somehow push the attack to the back of her mind. They huddled together as AJ recapped her theory again for John. "I'm more convinced than ever that this has something to do with The Olympics, John. I want to go to Chicago. It's where I need to be."

She could tell by the look in his eyes he thought her reaction was a bit extreme , but he didn't say anything. At that moment, AJ appreciated his friendship more than ever.

"I need to find out what's going on. Kirk will help us when he gets back."

"I trust your instincts, AJ. You were right about what happened to the others. But what do you think you can accomplish at the Olympics? Shouldn't you leave that up to the authorities?"

AJ looked at John and hesitated for a moment. "I want to be there. I must know enough to put the pieces together, or why would they try to kill me twice?"

John couldn't argue with her logic.

"We know they've killed before," she continued. "We know Bouhler is going to Chicago. Based on the companies they're involved with, I believe it has something to do with a performance enhancing product or procedure. The Olympics have to be the goal. By process of elimination, we can narrow our investigation down to a manageable set of athletes."

"Okay," John said. "Even if you can do that, or if you THINK you can do that," he corrected himself. "You have to be able to get to Chicago, get a hotel room, and get tickets to the right events. All that is probably impossible to pull off. "

"I've heard that even the parents of participants can't always get tickets to the right venues, so how are you going to do it?"

John recognized AJ's determined look. Her mind was made up. "John, don't worry. I can take care of the details." He found himself believing her. " I'll need a plan and I'll need some help.

John leaned back and looked at AJ. "Girl, you've got a tiger by the tail. And you're not going to let go, are you? You're going to drag that tiger down, or die trying."As soon as he said die trying, he regretted his words.

"I mean you're not going to give up, are you."

She looked at John. "No, I'm not giving up. Freethrow died to save me. I can't walk away now because it would be safe for me or convenient. That's not the way Dad raised me."

AJ was once again warming to the challenge. "We need to ride this one to the end, John. When I get off, I want to know what happened and why. And I want to know I did everything I could."

John looked at AJ with admiration and said, "I'll help any way I can." He wasn't sure what he had committed to, but he had committed.

"So," AJ said. "You'll go to Chicago with me? You'll help?"
John shrugged. "In for a penny, in for pound. Let's take it a step at a time and see what we can do. When does Kirk get back?"

"Tomorrow night. He told me he couldn't even pick up messages until Sunday morning. He's on some sort of a Green Star Athletics team building retreat."

CHAPTER 60

E veryone in the group wanted to retreat. They wanted to retreat into the tents where there was protection from the wind and some semblance of comfort. But they knew from previous lectures by the General, that retreat was not an option. Forward ever, backward never.

The General was lecturing, or more specifically, haranguing, about the need for increased effort and greater results. He paced in front of them, fervently expounding on the goals of the program. Their resolve must not waver, even in the face of a society constantly loosening the already lax rules governing moral and legal behavior.

The Green Star team understood the message, but not the choice of locations. The recipients of the General's admonitions would have been surprised to learn that Matthew Brady was the reason they were sitting on canvas camp chairs on a windswept bluff overlooking the St. Croix River, a hundred and twenty miles northeast of Minneapolis.

Brady's haunting black and white photographs of the Civil War made him famous. His portraits, group shots, and battlefield scenes captured the imagination of generations as they tried to understand the bloody conflict that pitted brother against brother.

It was a collection of Matthew Brady photographs that inspired the General as a grade school boy: a picture of an outdoor Union field staff meeting; General Ulysses S. Grant leaning against a tree with a cigar in his mouth; President Abraham Lincoln standing tall in his stove pipe hat; and various meetings with generals and majors sitting in camp chairs or standing. The serious poses with the tents in the background spoke of monumental decisions in the making.

The General wanted his group to experience the camaraderie he had seen in the photographs decades earlier, so he brought his team to meet outdoors in rural Minnesota. He knew this would be more effective than meeting in the typical antiseptic conference room.

In the semicircle before him sat the Green Star brain trust and the key field operatives. Physical challenges and adversity would build character in the group and forge their resolve. He knew this silver spoon MTV generation needed baptism by fire.

The General stood ramrod straight and looked at the assembled group. They were bright, all right. They had been recruited for their intelligence. And a few had shown competitive fire. But he wished the whole group had more grit.

"Chuck," the General said, "come up here and give us an overview so we can discuss our objectives."

Charles Franklin Wadlington hated being called Chuck. He detested Chuck, Chuckie, and Charlie. His name was Charles. His parents had christened him Charles, he went by Charles, and everyone called him Charles. Except the General.

But rather than protest, he dutifully responded, "Yes Sir," and rose to stand in front of the dry erase board. He steadied the board with one hand as it threatened to blow off of the easel.

"The major emphasis for the next month will be college football, the Olympics, and professional baseball." He made a few notations on the board. "The BCS bowl series football championship is the greatest travesty in sports." This brought a laugh from the group.

Charles continued with a smile. "We suspect money is changing hands under the table. Why else would a playoff not be instituted? We have a lead indicating organized crime may be involved in influencing the bowl selection process. By controlling which schools participate, they can fill up their hotels and have additional influence in the point spreads. Our investigation hopes to yield results yet this fall."

Charles pointed to number two on the list — The Olympics. "The focus is on the use of performance enhancing drugs. Kirk Vail," Charles nodded toward Kirk, "has uncovered some interesting data on a pole vaulter from Tennessee. We don't think drugs are involved, but we will be tracking this young man. Our sources on gambling have reported large sums being bet on two Olympic events, the women's hundred meter dash, and ironically, the pole vault."

Looking at the expectant faces, Charles asked a rhetorical question: "Does the attention on the pole vault seem too coincidental to anyone else? I believe where there's smoke, there's fire. So we'll be giving all of the participants in the pole vault special attention."

Pointing to number three, Charles continued. "Our third focal point, professional baseball, will concentrate on the west coast franchises. There may be some changes in ownership, which concerns us. We will be investigating all of the prospective purchasing groups for ties with undesirables."

The General stepped forward. "Good overview, Chuck. Now give out the assignments and let's break into small groups for strategy discussion."

As Chuck listed the groups on the board, the General looked out toward the horizon. He would love to take this group on a twenty-mile hike with full packs, but that wasn't part of the agenda. As much as he kept telling himself he enjoyed what he was doing, it wasn't like the old days. Guess it never would be.

CHAPTER 61

Gregory Krug woke with a start. He'd dozed off, dreaming in his easy chair. The sounds of cannon and rifle fire rang in his ears. And the smell. He wondered why smells were so strong in his dreams.

He'd been running through the forest, dressed in the uniform of a private. His hair was clipped short, and he carried no identification. He knew what his fate would be if the Angel of Death were captured.

In his dream, Auschwitz burned on the horizon, belching pungent black smoke skyward. The odor of gunpowder, blood, mud, and death filled his nostrils. Worse, he smelled fear on himself like cheap cologne.

Krug paced back and forth across the study, physically trying to shake the dream. Why, at his finest hour, was he haunted by nightmares of the war? Why must his memories harass him now?

Sitting at his desk, he unlocked the top drawer, extracting a knife with an ivory handle topped by a carved skull. It welcomed his touch like an old friend. It was a death's head knife of the Waffen-SS. In Nazi Germany, to be presented with such a knife was a high honor.

Krug gazed at the knife and thought back to the glory days of the Reich. The absolute power and authority. The omnipotence of a Caesar.

Josef Mengele wanted to bathe in the glow of that feeling again.

He yearned to be praised and glorified. In the modern world, dominated by sports, he was going to shine. He pushed the ugly memories of the fall of the Reich into a locked closet in the corner of his mind.

The future is all that counts. He looked out the window at the brightness of the sunshine, and his heart was lifted. His day was coming.

CHAPTER 62

What a beautiful day! The Caribbean sun and constant sea breeze created the perfect temperature. As he sat in the shade watching the entrance to the Krug compound, Anthony "Deuce" Cacciatore understood why they called the islands paradise. You didn't have the humidity of Miami. Or the crowds of New York.

Deuce hated crowds. Growing up in New York, he felt his life had been one giant crowd. People pushed and shoved all the time, and everyone was always in a hurry. When he turned twenty and started in the business, he'd done some strong-arm work. Things got hot for him and he needed to disappear for a while, so he moved to Miami to live with Uncle Victor.

He loved Florida: warm weather and lots of sports. He still wasn't crazy about the crowds in Miami, but he had found the love of his life there — flying.

He loved piloting his plane. When he was flying, he was in control and at peace. No crowds to contend with and no expectations to live up to. The freedom of leaving the ground was exhilarating each and every time he took off.

Deuce loved his family, but flying allowed him to to get away from them for a while. Back north in The City, he could hardly keep his relatives straight. Even his name got confusing.

His Papa was Anthony. He had an uncle Anthony who went by Tony, and he had at least five cousins who had Anthony or Tony as first or middle names. When Deuce was a kid, his Papa wouldn't let anybody call him Little Anthony. It was Uncle Frankie who started calling him Deuce, and it stuck.

In his straw hat, flowered shirt, and baggy shorts hanging past his knees, Deuce was the symbol of island cool. He was so glad Uncle Victor gave him this job. Maybe he could find more reasons to come to the islands.

He hit a speed dial on his cell phone and spoke in a quiet tone.

"The fox has left the lair. Repeat, the fox has left the lair."

"Cut the crap, Deuce," barked Victor. "Just tell me what's going on." Victor and Deuce originally discussed possible code words to be used in case the cell phone transmissions were monitored. Fox stood for Krug, who they determined ran things in the compound. But the codes were supposed to be used in a conversational way, such as, "I saw a foxy chick moving out of her apartment."

The codes were not to be stated in a 1950's Cold War monotone. Victor realized Deuce had too much Maxwell Smart in him, so he scrapped the code idea. He had two perfectly clean cell phones and figured, with all the air traffic, they could just talk.

Deuce responded in a hurt voice. "Okay, chill. I get it." Glancing at the road, he gave the update. "Big Old Ugly is on the move. We have four vehicles rolling. Two black limos and two blue panel trucks. Heading north along the ocean road, probably headed for the airport."

Victor glanced at his watch. "Keep a tail on them. I want to know when they leave and how. Private or commercial plane. You know the drill."

"Roger, wilco, Blue Leader. This is Little Red Riding Hood heading for Grandma's house. I'll keep the pedal to the metal and catch you on the flip-flop."

Victor laughed. His nephew was irrepressible and irreverent, which played better in Miami than New York. "Okay, Li'l Red. Just do a good job and I won't have to hang you by the family jewels. Capiche?"

Deuce could tell by Uncle Victor's tone that everything was cool. Papa, on the other hand, could never take a joke. "Reading you loud and clear, Blue Leader. I'm on it. Anything to save the jewels."

Deuce clicked off and kicked his motorcycle to life. He would follow the convoy and report on their progress.

Victor dialed a Chicago number from memory. When Tony Massetti answered, Victor gave a quick update. "Looks like our bird is about to fly north. The migration will be monitored."

"Good," replied Tony. "I'm going to prepare a welcoming committee."

They said their goodbyes, and Tony looked back at his computer monitor. Way too much money to be left to chance. He needed to be in the stadium to control the outcome. He still couldn't believe anyone had the audacity to put all that money on a pole vaulter and think they could get away with it.

It took some work, but Tony traced the bets on the Caribbean vaulter. The wagers were placed in multiple cities through various bookies. His contacts revealed the money had been funneled from Atlanta and Houston to all of the betting sites.

The real revelation came when his boys twisted a few arms and found out the money coming to Atlanta and Houston came from the same city — Caracas, Venezuela. A reliable source in South America confirmed the final link. The money from Caracas was being directed by a contact on the island of St. Lucia.

Someone on the island was planning to make twenty-two million from the performance of the St. Lucia pole vaulter, Rickie Armendariz. It had been simple to find out that the owner of the compound where Armendariz trained was an old man named Gregory Krug.

Tony's plan was two-pronged. First, he would set the stage to assure that young Armendariz did not win a gold medal or set a world record. For Tony, that was the easy part. He could do it with bribes, intimidation, or violence.

The second prong of his attack was to follow the entire St. Lucia group. He would determine who controlled the bets. Once that was discovered, the person or persons would be handled accordingly. He looked forward to that day.

They were thumbing their noses at him. As his nephew would say, they were talking smack. *They were talking trash, thinking they were dealing with a bunch of two bit bookies that could be suckered on a big play. Well, they aren't Paul Newman and Robert Redford and this isn't the Sting.*

Tony loved sports and looked at his betting business as a game, akin to the sports for which he set the odds. What he hated most in sports were the players who trash talked and did chicken dances, especially over entirely mediocre performances. He wouldn't let them get away with thinking he was an easy mark.

He wouldn't give up the money. He was going to make an example of the offenders. He knew twenty-two million dollars was money to die for. In fact, he would bet even money someone was going to die over these wagers.

CHAPTER 63

A J and Kirk made it over another relationship hurdle. Kirk was furious over the attack on AJ. But AJ thought he was just as angry because she had turned to John Cline in his absence.

When she told Kirk she was going to the Olympics and had invited John, Kirk came unglued. He stomped around her living room in his size sixteen sneakers, waving his arms like a traffic cop. When she could stand it no longer, AJ's relief valve popped.

She stood toe-to-toe with Kirk and unloaded. "You're upset? You're upset? Who was attacked and almost killed? Who saw her dog brutally murdered?" She stared into Kirk's eyes with the veins on her neck standing out like dew worms.

Kirk was too startled to breathe. After a pause, AJ broke the silence. "ME! I'm the one they're trying to kill."

AJ stood with hands clenched into fists, her jaw jutting forward, challenging Kirk to disagree. Realizing AJ was right and he was selfishly jealous, Kirk responded with the only words possible to defuse the situation.

"I'm sorry, AJ. I am so sorry." AJ's aggressive stance softened as she felt the sincerity in his voice. "I'm acting like a fool," he said. "Please forgive me."

They wrapped their arms around each other. AJ squeezed Kirk hard, pressing her chin into his shoulder. For a few moments at least, AJ blotted out everything that had happened and focused on Kirk.

Reluctantly they separated. Both knew they had work to do. It was time to plan their strategy. AJ called John Cline and asked him to come to her apartment. The three of them brainstormed over pizza and beer.

First they worked on the logistics of the trip. Kirk already had a mini-suite booked in downtown Chicago by Green Star. An online search confirmed their fears. There were no other rooms to be had near the Olympic events.

It was decided that AJ and John would drive down together. Kirk suggested they all stay together in his suite. AJ could have the bedroom, and John and Kirk could make do with the couch and chair.

AJ and John agreed, at Kirk's insistence. He argued that with AJ's life in danger, it would be best if they stayed together.

Tickets to the venues would be tough to come by, but Kirk would work to get some extras. AJ and John said they could talk to their key manufacturers and customers to call in favors for Olympic tickets.

So far so good. That was the easy part.

The hard part came as they labored to put a strategy on paper. Pulling out her notes, AJ gave a quick review of the chain of events. They discussed various theories about performance enhancement, and what could be gained. Kirk shared his information concerning large bets on the pole vault and the women's hundred-meter dash.

AJ lit up like a sparkler on the fourth of July. "That's it! It has to be one or both of those events. They think they've got a lock. That's where we'll focus."

In her excitement, AJ didn't question Kirk's source of information. When he added the information about Jimmy Wickland healing extremely fast, AJ could hardly contain herself. "Maybe he's getting special shots or pills. He could be getting some fancy electronic shock treatment to enhance muscle growth."

Kirk couldn't reveal that the Company had Wickland under surveillance and Jimmy Wickland's only contact was with his grandmother in Tennessee. Nor did he want to divulge the statistical data he'd been given by Dr. Deirdre Walling. He couldn't share his real occupation with AJ and John.

"I don't know about Wickland," said Kirk. "His performances have been adequate at best. He qualified for the Olympics, but he's not an obvious favorite to win a medal."

It was agreed they would research all the contestants in the men's pole vault and women's hundred meter dash before they left for Illinois.

CHAPTER 64

The attack in her apartment, Freethrow's death, the outburst with Kirk, and the planning session all swirled in AJ's mind like a Texas twister. Doubts flew in and out of her mind like bats on caffeine. Concentrating on work was a huge challenge.

AJ looked around and reality hit. She was standing in the maintenance shop of a meat packing plant in Jefferson, Wisconsin. The maintenance man had left her waiting while he went to get the plant engineer.

The room was filled with metal cabinets, shelves, and tables. Disassembled valves and pumps were haphazardly strewn on the tables and the floor. Calendars with girls in bikinis were taped to cabinet doors. Open wall space held posters of Hooter girls and Harley babes. Political correctness had yet to penetrate this small company in rural Wisconsin.

One constant in all maintenance shops was the smell of oil. In some shops you could almost taste the oil in the air. During training, her boss asked her the question on her first sales call.

"Clark, do you smell that?"

"Yes," she replied.

"Know what that is?"

Having been in her share of garages, AJ said, "Oil."

"Wrong," he said. "That's the smell of money. Don't ever forget that. You'll come to love that smell. It means equipment is being fixed and the customer is spending money!"

The vibration of her cell phone interrupted AJ's memories.

"Good morning. AJ Clark, Ultra Valve," she responded automatically.

"The answer is no," a voice boomed back. AJ searched her mind to recognize the voice. The connection was faint, making recognition difficult.

"I beg your pardon," she said. "This is AJ Clark of Ultra Valve. Do you have the correct number?"

An electronic crackle was followed by, "No, no, no. Against company policy."

AJ thumbed the volume on her phone to the highest level and strained to hear. "To whom am I speaking?" she asked.

The signal cleared as AJ walked out of the maintenance shop and into a hallway. "Clark, this is Dick Stiles. I'm in the Pittsburgh airport and don't have much time."

"Hello, Mr. Stiles. I can hear you better now. What were you saying?"

Stiles' voice came through loud and clear. "I saw your vacation request and the answer is no. You know you must put in a request for personal time off 30 days in advance. I can't have you gone next week."

Caught off guard, AJ wasn't sure what to say. "But Mr. Stiles, you heard about my being attacked, didn't you? I need some time off, and I have vacation time."

AJ could feel the heat of impatience coming through the phone.

"Listen, I was mugged in LA three years ago, but didn't miss a day of work. Sure, it's upsetting, but the best thing is to keep busy and keep working."

She couldn't believe what she was hearing. Stiles compared getting robbed to attempted murder! Taking a deep breath, AJ leaned against the wall to steady herself. Looking down the hall she saw the maintenance man coming toward her with the plant engineer right behind.

In a calm voice, she spoke into the phone. "My appointment is here and I can't talk now. I am taking the time off. No way around it. Have a nice flight." With that, AJ shut off her phone and turned to face her customers.

AJ was stuck in the middle. Maintenance and engineering disagreed, and she was supposed to be the tie-breaking expert. She had tap danced around the question diplomatically for a while, but finally had to give her opinion.

The plant engineer was wrong. He was wrong in his assumption of how the signal from the level transmitter would be utilized by the digital control system to modulate the control valve on the inlet of his process vessel.

The maintenance man tried unsuccessfully to hide a smirk as AJ gave her analysis to the plant engineer. "Hugh is right, sir. Just let him wire it his way and everything will be fine."

The plant engineer looked at AJ as if she were road kill. Telling him he was wrong and the maintenance man was right was the same as calling him stupid. In an effort to save face, he attacked AJ's credibility.

"Miss Clark," he said coldly. "Have you been in the industry more than twenty years?"

AJ raised an eyebrow at a question to which he obviously knew the answer. "Well no, sir."

"Have you ever designed an entire control system?"

As a representative who supplied system components, AJ knew this was another obvious no question. "No, sir. We supply the final control element, the valve."

With a smug glance at Hugh, the plant engineer kept attacking. "And Miss Clark, are you a double E?"

AJ knew a double E was an electrical engineer, an ME was a mechanical engineer, etc. But she had put up with enough of this pompous engineer. The gloves were off. Besides, she didn't know if she'd still have a job next week.

Raising her voice with as much righteous indignation as she could muster, AJ looked him squarely in the eyes. "Sir, I'm offended! You'll hear from my lawyer. What kind of a question is that? Am I a double E! I don't give my bra size out to anyone!"

As the engineer's jaw dropped, AJ turned on her heels, giving a quick wink to Hugh, and stormed out of the building, never looking back. She heard Hugh's laughter echoing through the hall as she stepped into the Wisconsin sunlight.

Standing by her Jeep, AJ looked up into the clear blue sky that stretched forever. "Dad, I need a little help here. Feel free to send in the cavalry any time now."

In the distance, a lone cloud seemed to turn in the wind ever so slowly. Standing on the hot asphalt with the smell of processed pork hanging heavily in the air, AJ stared as the cloud turned toward her. The sun gleamed on the dove white sides of the cloud as the profile of a llama became clear.

Blinking back tears, she opened the Jeep door. With a nod toward the cloud, she whispered, "Thanks for the sign. We'll stop the bad guys, Dad. Count on it."

CHAPTER 65

K irk held AJ's hands in his and looked into her eyes. He saw trust and strength. He wanted to take her into his arms right there in the Madison airport terminal. But he held back.

Kirk couldn't totally let go and commit. Deep down, he knew it was fear of rejection. He cared for her so much, which made him afraid of losing her. And he felt guilty.

He felt guilty about hiding the truth about his job. He felt guilty about being jealous. He felt guilty about failing to protect her from the attack in her apartment.

And now he felt guilty about flying off to Cleveland and leaving AJ to make the trip to Chicago with John Cline. AJ was risking her job and her life, while Kirk was leading a life of deception. He wished she were coming with him.

"You better get going," she said. "I can't come to the gate with you and I won't be held responsible if security takes too long and you miss your flight."

Kirk smiled and gave her hands a squeeze. "Okay, Miss Amanda Julie Hawk Clark. As soon as my Cleveland meeting ends, I'll be on a plane to meet you in Chicago. I'll call later. Any rules to travel by?"

AJ pursed her lips in an exaggerated show of deep thought. "Numbers eight and nine."

Thinking about AJ's rules, Kirk reached into his pocket and pulled out a pen. "Eight. Keep a pen in your car, or in this case, on your person."

"Very good. Be prepared." After glancing at the long security line, AJ turned to Kirk. "I think Mr. World Traveler better think about Rule Number Nine."

Impulsively, AJ pulled Kirk to her and kissed him hard. When their lips broke free, she whispered, "On time is late. Now git."

Not wanting to let her out of his grasp, Kirk gave AJ another quick kiss. "You're right. Gotta go. I'll see you in Chicago."

Picking up his Green Star carry on bag, Kirk gave AJ's hand a last squeeze. "Be careful." He turned to wade through the layers of security on his way to the departure gate.

As she walked through the terminal toward the parking garage, AJ realized she missed Kirk already. And he wasn't even gone yet.

Her cell phone vibrated. Duty calls. The customer waits for no one.

CHAPTER 66

With the Olympics approaching, athletes, officials, and spectators streamed into Chicago, by plane, by train, and by car. Illinois poet Carl Sandberg's "City of the Big Shoulders" put on its' best face for the Olympics as hotels, restaurants, and shops filled to capacity.

Colorful banners snapped in the breeze along every thoroughfare. Street vendors hawked Olympic souvenirs as cash registers gobbled up the recently converted currency of the foreign visitors.

With his prize athlete, Rickie Armendariz, delivered to the Olympic Village, Gregory Krug and his entourage settled into their string of suites in the high-rise hotel. Bill Schultz assured Krug the equipment had been moved into the rented office space without incident. All was in order for the pole vault. Gregory Krug would enjoy unparalleled success while Bill Schultz and Emile Bouhler reaped millions off of their bets on Rickie.

Krug was jovial as he looked out over Lake Michigan from his balcony window. Years of work would soon yield results. He could still picture the saying over the steel entrance gate to Auschwitz. Arbeit Macht Frei. Work Brings Freedom. The Reich had been correct. His hard work was going to set him free to reveal his scientific advances.

"Gertrude," he called. "Time for my shots."

CHAPTER 67

Tony Massetti set up his Olympic operation off North Lake Shore Drive in the area known as the Gold Coast. Chicago's wealthy families had been building mansions there since the late 1800's. Massetti's group was ensconced in a private mansion of a business partner who was more than happy to provide shelter for the men from the South Side of Chicago and his associates from New York and Miami.

From this base of operations they were close to the Olympic activities with plenty of room and privacy. The 24 room home with expansive brick-fenced private gardens provided the security needed to plan their operation.

Tony was going to deliver justice with a dash of vengeance to those who were trying to cheat him out of his money. Stacking the deck against him was a violation of his gambling code. For this, the violator would have his ticket punched.

The Olympics were his personal arena for quashing those who would rob him of his money and his pride. Come cheat me in My City? Leave in a body bag!

CHAPTER 68

K irk arrived in Chicago exhausted but excited. He checked into his hotel, then started examining various venue sites. He heard every language imaginable as he worked his way through the throng in front of the new Olympic Stadium that had been constructed along the lake in Washington Park.

The Chicago Star logo was everywhere as the city worked to brand their first ever Olympics. The six points of the white star represented hope, respect, harmony, friendship, excellence, and celebration. The bands of orange and gold radiating above the star represents the Chicago skyline reaching toward the sun. The bands of green and blue radiating below the star stood for the beauty of the many parks of the city and the glory of Lake Michigan.

Kirk stood on the edge of the crowd and read from the Olympic program he had just purchased from a street vendor at an outrageous price. The blend of colors in the multicolor logo was meant to symbolize the diversity of races and cultures involved in the Olympic Games.

The sparkling white Doric columns circling the Olympic Stadium were an inspiring exhortation for the athletes to perform their best. As the mob of humanity flowed past him, Kirk could feel the pulse of the city as it embraced the greatest athletic event in the world.

The Olympic program stated that athletes from 200 countries were competing in 296 events. There were almost 11,000 male and female competitors, accompanied by their support group of 5,000 coaches, trainers, and physiotherapists. It truly was an event of monumental proportions.

Many indoor events were being held in McCormick Place, the second largest convention center in the world.

Chicago's first Olympics would make up for the slight the city had experienced in 1904 when Chicago unanimously was chosen to host the

Summer Olympics, and then the International Olympic Committee relocated the games to St. Louis to coincide with the 1904 World's Fair. Having the Olympics taken away is a stigma Chicago is glad to forget.

The program said that the first recorded Games were in 776 B.C. Celebrated continuously for almost 1200 years, the Olympic Games became the most enduring institution of the ancient world.

After a fifteen hundred year hiatus, the Olympic Games were resurrected. The world embraced the concept once again as competition and athletic camaraderie lifted the spirits of rich and poor nations alike. Once every four years, everyone was equal on the playing field.

At least that is the way it was in the beginning. Unfortunately, competition doesn't always bring out the purest instincts. The "amateur" athletes in Europe were given apartments, cars, and salaries. Anabolic steroid use was rampant as coaches pushed their athletes to develop greater strength and speed. Gambling reared its ugly head. All in the name of sport.

Also, the non-political athletic event became political. Communist bloc judges gave American gymnasts unreasonably low scores. The referees gave the Soviet basketball team three tries to defeat the US team in 1972. Olympics were boycotted and demonstrations staged. Terrorists murdered participants. All because this was the center stage.

Those thoughts and more ran through Kirk's mind as he stood before the entrance to Olympic Stadium. As a spectator he would be excited to be here. But as an undercover agent with a dangerous assignment, he was on edge.

Kirk scanned the crowd with a practiced eye taking in familiar sights and looking for anything out of the ordinary. His eyes stopped. Forty yards away stood Tony Massetti, the Chicago kingpin of gambling. Kirk had seen Massetti previously in a gambling parlor in St. Louis, and he recognized Massetti's face and Alfred Hitchcock build.

Massetti, his gold pinkie ring flashing in the sun, pointed down the boulevard as he talked to three men. The group in dark suits and ties didn't look like they were simply on a sightseeing stroll. In Kirk's mind, the presence of Massetti and his cronies meant trouble.

As Kirk stared at Massetti, AJ and John Cline were working their way along the boulevard toward the stadium. They were scheduled to meet Kirk in an hour at the hotel. They had arrived early, making better time than they had expected coming into downtown Chicago via the Kennedy Expressway.

When they finally found a parking spot near the hotel, AJ told John they should go for a walk. They couldn't get into the room without Kirk, so they may as well stretch their legs and explore.

The trip had been a good one. AJ and John further bonded as they shared stories about their backgrounds. AJ divulged some of her emotional problems since the loss of her father and John opened up about his failed marriage. AJ also told John how she felt about Kirk.

John liked AJ. In fact, he liked her a lot. Why else would he be burning vacation time and possibly risking his life? He knew she was someone special.

He wondered if he were younger if he would have a chance for a serious relationship with Miss AJ Clark. But given the circumstances, he resigned himself to being the big brother figure she needed now. He refused to even think about being a father figure. Those were shoes he knew could never be filled in AJ's eyes. Besides, he didn't feel that old.

AJ and John soaked up the sunshine and the festival atmosphere. Spotting Kirk's head above the crowd, AJ nudged John. "Look, there's Kirk!" she said in an excited voice. "Kirk!" she shouted. But he couldn't hear her over the noise of the crowd.

Zigg-zagging through the throng like a broken field runner, AJ worked her way toward Kirk with John Cline in tow. She noticed Kirk staring to her left with a concerned look on his face. Following the line of Kirk's gaze, she saw a group of dark haired men in suits talking and gesturing with their hands. She wondered who they were and why Kirk was watching them so intently.

CHAPTER 69

The crowd jostled AJ and John as they closed the distance to Kirk. AJ stepped around a woman with a huge carry-on bag hanging from one shoulder and a video camera case hanging from the other. She was just about to call to Kirk when he turned to face an attractive smiling woman.

"There's my Sam," the woman said as she stepped quickly to Kirk and gave him a hug. The picture of the two of them embracing burned into AJ's brain in a flash. AJ stood with her mouth open, ready to shout, but no sound came out. Her mind was trying to compute what she was seeing.

The petite, vivacious woman hugging Kirk had short black hair, a sleeveless white top, and a bright red mini-skirt. She was on her tiptoes, pulling Kirk to her as they embraced.

AJ's world began to spin. She caught bits and pieces of their conversation as the synapses in her brain fired like a Fourth of July fireworks finale.

"Dee Dee..."

"No, I can't..."

"Maybe we..."

"I don't know..."

John Cline was at her side, holding her arm for fear she would faint. He felt the tension in her body as AJ walked stiff legged toward Kirk. "Maybe Kirk has a sister, AJ, and this is a family reunion," he whispered, hoping for the best.

The woman had one hand on Kirk's bicep and gestured with the other as she talked. Her focus was totally on Kirk Vail.

Taking AJ by the elbow, John propelled her forward. "Come on, AJ. Let's crash the party."

Kirk was in mid sentence when he felt AJ and John enter his personal space. "Now Dee Dee, I think ..." He turned, saw AJ and smiled instantly.

"AJ! You're here!"

Disengaging himself from Dee Dee, he stepped forward to give AJ a hug. She stepped back and held her hand out against his chest, stopping him cold.

"Hello Mr. Vail. Fancy meeting you here." The look in AJ's eyes was as cold as the tone of her voice.

Confused, Kirk looked at John, who nodded his head toward Dee Dee. "Oh, yes, oh," Kirk responded, stammering. He struggled to make proper introductions. "Dr. Deirdre Walling, this is AJ Clark and John Cline."

Giving her best southern belle smile, Dee Dee replied. "Now Kirk, you needn't be so formal, honey. It's Dee Dee to y'all. Any friends of Kirk's are friends of mine. Welcome to the great city of Chicago."

AJ did something she hadn't done in a long time. She sized up the shorter woman as an adversary. AJ knew she had the advantage of height and reach. She was sure she had speed and strength on her side. *I can take her out in a heartbeat!*

Then she had a brief pang of guilt. Dr. Dee Dee Walling probably didn't know tae kwon do. AJ couldn't let her temper get the better of her.

Taking deep breaths, AJ fought to regain her mental balance. She suppressed the urge to wipe the sugary sweet smile off of Dee Dee's face.

"Pleased to meet you, Dr. Walling," said John.

"Likewise," added a stone-faced AJ.

John looked at Dee Dee. "AJ and I were out for a little walk to see what surprises my kind of town has for us on our first day in Olympic city."

Tension filled the air like static before a rainstorm. Dee Dee was the only one enjoying the moment. "Well, Kirk, honey, we should get together with your friends while we're here in Chicago." Her emphasis on WE almost drove AJ over the edge.

Dee Dee shifted her weight slightly to lean against Kirk, the physical contact running from shoulder to hip. Kirk made a small sidestep in an effort to disengage.

"Deirdre, I have to go with AJ and John. We'll see you later." Kirk regretted the use of the standard parting line as soon as he said it. His innocent goodbye sounded like a promise of another meeting.

Dee Dee looked at AJ and John with her best high wattage smile. "Y'all have fun." Turning to Kirk, she batted her eyes. "I'm at the Ritz-Carlton. I know you have my number on your speed dial. Let me know when you want to get together to go over the data. Bye now."

Without a glance at AJ, Dee Dee turned and walked down the sidewalk, swaying her hips in what AJ saw as a deliberate provocative move. AJ remembered an old Marilyn Monroe movie she had watched with Dad in which Marilyn worked her hips as she walked away from the camera. Dad had called it sashaying. He said when a woman sashayed, she was strutting her stuff.

Dr. Deirdre Walling was definitely strutting her stuff for Kirk. It was obvious she was pitching. What AJ didn't know was if Kirk was catching.

"You must have made great time to get here early," said Kirk. "Man, am I glad to see you two."

AJ had her arms tightly crossed. "Not half as glad as you were to see *Miss Dee Dee*," she said with hurt and anger. "Kirk, how do you know *Miss Dee Dee*?"

As Kirk struggled for an answer, John Cline intervened.

"Children, let's play nice. Let's go sit somewhere and get comfortable. It's been a tough day, and I could use something to eat."

Taking them each by the shoulder, John steered them in the opposite direction of Dr. Deirdre Walling.

CHAPTER 70

The three of them walked in silence. "There," said John as he pointed to a café with sidewalk seating. "We can sit in the sun and eat."

John flagged down a waiter who seated them at the last open table. AJ and Kirk still had not spoken a word, so John tried to break the awkward silence.

"Have I ever told you my favorite prayer?" he asked. AJ and Kirk both looked at him curiously, but neither spoke.

"It goes like this. God grant me the senility to forget the people I never liked, the good fortune to run into the ones I do, and the eyesight to tell the difference."

Kirk laughed and AJ showed the hint of a smile. "That's funny, John. Maybe Kirk should have his eyes checked to help him remember Miss Dee Dee."

Kirk let out a low sigh. "AJ, she's just someone I met through work. That's all. I really don't know her at all."

Leaning forward with her elbows on the table and both fists under her chin, AJ looked hard into Kirk's eyes. Kirk felt her looking right into his soul.

"It's answer time," said AJ. "Honest to goodness, no holds barred total honesty, or I'm out of here. Gone, never speaking to you again." Her voice lowered to a whisper. "I thought we had something special. And nothing special can be built around secrets."

Kirk nodded, meeting her gaze. He wanted to take her hand, but feared she would pull away. John sat quietly watching the two of them, not sure how things would play out.

"One. Who are those people in the group of Sopranos you were staring at. They look like extras from *Godfather 4*. Two. How do you know Miss Deirdre Walling and what is her job? Three. Why did she call you Sam?

And don't try to tell me I'm wrong about anything. I know what I saw and heard."

AJ continued, keeping Kirk in her gaze. "I have the feeling you know a lot more about what's going on here than we do. John and I are sitting here feeling like see no evil and hear no evil. My life's in danger, and you're keeping us in the dark." Standing, AJ bit off her next words. "I'm going to the restroom. When I get back, I want the truth."

After AJ was gone, John looked at Kirk. "You messed up, man. What are you doing? She was thinking you walked on water. But you just sank to the bottom of the sea."

Kirk groaned. "It's not what you think. There's nothing going on with Dee Dee, or any other woman for that matter."

"Hey, don't tell me," said John. "In AJ's eyes, you've done her wrong. She counted on you and you let her down. You've got heavy duty explaining to do."

When AJ returned, she sat down and crossed her arms. "Truth or consequences. Kirk, who is the woman?"

Kirk knew this was break point in their relationship and he couldn't hold back. "She is a doctor with the Drug Enforcement Administration. When I was in Memphis for the Olympic trials, a friend of mine said she had research data I might find interesting. So I went to Atlanta to meet with her and review the data."

AJ continued her interrogation. "Why does a shoe salesman care what kind of data the drug enforcement agency has? And why didn't you tell me why you went to Atlanta?"

Kirk plunged forward. "Green Star keeps track of athletes' performances so we know who's hot and who's not in order to decide who may be a good investment as a shoe or apparel spokesman. The pole vaulter from Tennessee, Jimmy Wickland, was injured in Memphis. But he healed amazingly fast and Dr. Walling had some data on injury recover I wanted to see."

AJ was unconvinced. "You told us about him healing fast. But you never said where you got that information. I still don't see why you'd be that interested in his injuries." AJ paused. "The thing that's baffling me most of all, is why did Walling call you Sam?"

Kirk knew AJ had heard correctly. Her Dad's name was Sam, so he knew that name carried extra sensitivity for her. There was no sidestepping he could do now.

Kirk looked at AJ and John. He had to be honest with them. "The truth is, I have two jobs. You know I'm a sales rep for Green Star. That job takes up half of my time and is used as a cover for my main job. I'm an undercover agent for the government, specializing in drug and gambling violations in sports."

There was a stunned silence as this revelation sank in. Kirk charged forward. "Dr. Deirdre Walling had information I needed. She found my dual jobs humorous, so she called me SAM as an acronym for Secret Agent Man. She thinks she's funny. I've only met with her once. She is interested in me, but I am absolutely not interested in her. I think I am irrevocably attracted to one AJ Clark."

Kirk continued. "The Sopranos are exactly what they look like. One of them is Tony Massetti, gambling guru here in Chicago. Lot's of money is placed on the Olympics, but for him to be here in person tells me something big is going down."

AJ shook her head. "You must think we're stupid. You told us large bets were placed on the pole vault and the women's hundred-meter dash. I didn't ask where you got your information. Did you really care that I was attacked, or was I convenient bait to help you and your James Bond buddies figure out what was going on?"

Kirk was hurt. "AJ, of course I cared that you were in danger. And I wanted to tell you about my job, but I couldn't. You don't know how hard it's been for me keeping it secret."

AJ clenched her fists. "That secret cuts both ways. I feel like I don't even know you."

The waiter took their orders and left them sitting in silence. No one seemed to know what to say. AJ stared out into the street, watching the smiling faces go past. Kirk looked at John for a reaction and only got a shrug in return.

After their food arrived, AJ finally broke the silence. "How do I know you were telling me the truth about anything, including your feelings?"

Kirk fought the embarrassment of talking in front of John and the guilt of having deceived AJ. "I think you know how I feel about you. I know you do. I wouldn't throw that away."

AJ looked into his eyes. "I want to believe you."

Kirk made another pitch to sway her feelings. "AJ, if I could do it over, I'd handle it differently. I would tell you sooner."

AJ picked up her fork. "Forgiveness takes time."

John picked up his cheeseburger. Hanging out with AJ and Kirk certainly wasn't boring.

CHAPTER 71

Kirk didn't feel loved. He didn't even feel liked. He sat on the couch in the hotel suite wrestling with uncertainty. AJ had remained cool toward him the past three days and they had made little progress in their inquiries concerning the athletes. Dee Dee had been calling and pressuring him to meet with her, but he put her off.

John came out of the bathroom dressed to go out. The sun had set, and a warm breeze blew in through the open balcony doors. "Kirk, don't you want to go out with me and sample the night life on Rush Street? It beats sitting in here all night while AJ sits on the balcony."

"John, does she say anything to you about me?" Kirk asked.

John grunted. "She hasn't said much since you told us you were a double naught spy. It's quite a shock, you know, to find out someone you care for has a secret life."

"Don't you understand? I couldn't say anything. I've told you both everything now."

"Doesn't matter, man. You held out on her. She meant what she said. Forgiveness takes time."

"I must have looked like the biggest jerk the world has ever seen."

John nodded. "You got that right. I thought AJ was going to faint when she saw Dr. Walling pawing you. I don't know what was worse, the act of omission or the act of commission. But, she'll get over it."

Kirk sighed. "I hope you're right."

John checked his pockets to be sure he had his wallet and money clip. "Kirk, I'm going to do a little individual research on Chicago. You're not the only one feeling a bit uptight. Don't wait up for me."

After John left, Kirk paced around the hotel suite, constantly stealing glances at AJ sitting on the balcony. He fiddled with the radio on the end table. On his second trip around the dial he heard a voice that wasn't, for once, talking about the Olympics.

"We're bringing you all the hits from the 90's and today. Jeff requested the next song. Hey Jeff, we're playing this one for your special girl. I hope she's listening, man. Because if you're listening, Carol, my man Jeff thinks you're all that. So give the Dude some play, okay?"

Kirk adjusted the volume. "Jeff hates it that you go to different schools, but that's not the end of the world. He wants to let you know how he feels. Here's the hit song from a few years back by Nine Days, called Absolutely. But I prefer the subtitle, Story of a Girl."

The words of the song jolted Kirk. As much as he cared for AJ, he had never used the L word. What was he afraid of? Rejection? Of course. Wasn't every guy?

Kirk walked to the balcony doorway and looked out at AJ. Her back was to him as she sat on the wrought iron chair. Forearms on the railing, she looked out over the lights of Navy Pier. The 15-story Ferris Wheel exuded a joy and vibrancy she didn't feel.

Kirk knew he had to tell her now. His senses were acute with hope and anticipation. The soft breeze tickled his skin and flooded him with pleasant sensations. The sounds of the lakefront and the fragrant flowers of the park below set the stage.

And he could smell AJ. He wasn't sure if it came from his olfactory nerves or from recent memories, but the sensation was real. The scent of her hair and perfume filled his nostrils.

Kirk crossed to AJ and stood behind her. He put his hands on her shoulders, thrilled that she didn't pull away. He gently massaged her shoulders and felt her relaxing under his touch.

Softly, he spoke into her right ear. "AJ, I absolutely love you."

Kirk held his breath. He dared not breathe or move or even think, for fear of breaking the spell.

AJ leaned back to look up at Kirk. She reached up with both hands and pulled his face near hers. And she smiled. "I know." Their lips met as the final line of the song drifted out to them.

CHAPTER 72

Tony Massetti finished his glass of Chianti, setting it on the coffee table next to the coaster, to the chagrin of his host. Making himself at home was one of Tony's skills.

"Gentlemen, I want to be sure you all understand what must not happen."

Every man in the room remained still, cigars and half filled glasses in their hands. "In two days the most important event of the Olympics will take place. The pole vault has huge financial implications for us." Tony paused for effect. "I don't care who wins the competition, but who will not win is Rickie Armendariz from that island in the Caribbean."

"You can bet on that," commented the host. One thing he knew about this group was their determination. A pledge by them was a promise made in blood.

Tony outlined the plan to neutralize Armendariz. Security in the Olympic village was tight, but their host had acquired a pass for one person to enter the village. The plan was to plant drugs in the room of Armendariz and then notify the authorities. A credible source had been set up to leak the information that would disqualify the Caribbean pole vaulter from the competition.

Deuce had been chosen for the task. His age gave him the best chance of being inconspicuous in the village full of athletes. Chicago's Olympic Village was a billion dollar complex of lakefront apartments built specifically for the Games. There were four entrance points where security personnel checked identification. Tomorrow Deuce would stroll among the world's most elite athletes. He could hardly wait.

Tony held up his glass, wagging it from side to side to motivate his host to fetch more wine. "Deuce, you've got a big job to do. Do it right and you might just get that new airplane you've been hoping for." Deuce grinned and nodded at Tony, knowing failure carried as grand a punishment. "And then," continued Tony, "we'll flush out the rats to find Mr. Smart Guy who's behind the bets. He must be dealt with for trying to screw the house. Nobody sets us up!"

There was a chorus of agreement around the room as each man contemplated how an appropriate punishment for Mr. Smart Guy should be carried out. The imaginations of the men in the room would have made the Marquis de Sade blush.

CHAPTER 73

Jimmy Wickland knew life couldn't get any better. The sun warmed his back as he jogged in place. His thoughts were on tomorrow as he high-stepped. In twenty-four hours he would be competing for the ultimate athletic prize, an Olympic medal.

The practice area filled with athletes going through their training routines. Jimmy's USA teammate from UCLA was favored to win the gold, with the French and German vaulters picked to win silver and bronze.

But Jimmy knew something the press and the Olympic officials didn't. He felt fantastic. It was a feeling hard to describe to non-athletes. Jimmy was at the peak of his physical and mental readiness. His muscles practically vibrated with energy as he worked out. As he glanced at the bracelet Grams had made him, he knew he would do his best. It was his destiny.

The competitor Jimmy considered the other dark horse was the kid from St. Lucia. His strength and speed were obvious as he glided effortlessly around the track. What impressed Jimmy most was that he seemed to have another gear. During the practice vaults, Armendariz looked like he had been zapped with a cattle prod as he hit his last steps and planted the pole. He cleared his training heights with ease, almost like he was holding back.

Jimmy knew he had to perform his best because Armendariz and the rest of the field would be pushed by adrenaline as they competed in front of 100,000 fans. Jimmy did an extra set of sprints before he called it a day.

CHAPTER 74

D r. Deirdre Walling gave Kirk her best pouty face. "Oh, Kirk. I certainly didn't mean to cause any problems for you. If I were you, I'd question the stability of your friend if she misinterpreted our relationship."

They sat on a couch in the lobby of Dr. Walling's hotel. Kirk had wisely declined the offer to meet in Dee Dee's room. He worked to keep his notebook between them as she tried to slide closer.

"Dee Dee, you and I don't have a relationship. We're just ships passing in the night, okay?"

Leaning toward Kirk, Dee Dee made her final pitch. "Ships can't stay at sea indefinitely, Kirk. I don't see any harm in docking occasionally, do you?"

Kirk couldn't help but laugh. When he told AJ he was meeting with Walling, he knew his resolve would be tested. "Dee Dee, there are plenty of ships out there for you. But the SS Vail will not be left bobbing in your wake. I'm steaming full speed ahead on a separate course." His tone was firm. "Let's talk business."

With a shrug, Dee Dee responded, "Have it your way." Pulling a printout from a folder, she handed it to Kirk. "Here are the urine and blood test results for all of the pole vaulters. I've highlighted the two you asked about, Wickland and Armendariz."

Kirk looked over the report for two minutes in silence. When he looked back up at Dee Dee, she was smiling at a young blond man sitting on a loveseat twenty feet away. He was dressed in an expensive white linen suit with an official Olympic pass hanging around his neck by a thin chain. Kirk realized Miss Dee Dee had moved on to new prey.

Kirk needed to ask about the report. "Dr. Walling, I have a question."

Still smiling at her new target, Dee Dee answered without turning.

"Ask away, Mr. Vail."

"I don't see anything unusual, but I'm not sure exactly what I'm looking for."

Cocking her head slightly and batting her eyes at Blondie, Dee Dee expounded. "Nothing illegal shows up in either of your guys. What's unusual is that they both have the highest mineral concentrations of the group. Not out of acceptable range, mind you, but I find it interesting that your two are the highest."

Dee Dee continued. "Kirk, there is a trend which most athletic organizations are fighting. There is a fear that athletics may become an exercise in human bioengineering. With cloning and cartilage regeneration experiments, we know genetic engineering is creeping into sports. There is no accurate test to detect a genetically juiced athlete."

Kirk thought about that for a minute. "What about electrical impulses or electrical stimulation?"

"Unless it was strong enough to upset the chemical balance of the body, it wouldn't show up. It's not my area of expertise, but I think the only way to detect that would be to have an EKG while the impulse was sent."

Kirk had a thought, which he didn't share with Dee Dee. Her attention was elsewhere. Kirk stood. "Thanks," he said, holding out his hand. "I appreciate the help."

Remaining seated, Dee Dee shook Kirk's hand as she looked up at him. "I wish you luck with your voyage, Kirk. But if the wind blows you off course, give me a call. Atlanta is nice any time of year."

As Kirk walked across the lobby toward the ornate gold and glass exit doors, he glanced back. Blondie had moved to sit next to her on the couch and Dr. Deirdre Walling was giving him her full attention. As he stepped into the revolving door, Kirk thought about the differences between AJ and Dee Dee. He knew he'd made the right decision.

CHAPTER 75

A J sat on the balcony, enjoying the sun as she listened to Kirk's story of blood and urine tests. "AJ, the key element has to be the pole vault. There must be a link between Bouhler, the scientific data, and the bets on the pole vault. I think Armendariz is juiced up somehow, and it's all staged to win the bets."

AJ nodded. "You said there was a lot of money on the women's 200 meter dash, too. But that was yesterday, and the sprinter with the heavy bets on her came in fourth. That was just reckless betting."

AJ was holding Kirk's hand, playing with his long fingers. "I'm glad Miss Dee Dee didn't get her hooks into you when you went to pick up the report."

Before Kirk could respond, John stepped out onto the balcony. "Is it all right if I join you? I don't want to interrupt a family discussion."

Kirk waved John to a seat. "I watched the vaulters work out today," said John. "Our two guys look pretty good. Armendariz has an entourage led by a white haired old man who is definitely in charge. Wickland works out kind of on his own."

"John, the urine and blood tests didn't come up with anything on either one," Kirk responded, "but I really think Armendariz is juiced up, judging from all of the betting on him. How do we prove it?"

John, AJ, and Kirk discussed courses of action. They decided that at the competition the next day, one of them would watch the vaulters closely, while the other two watched the Armendariz entourage. Kirk wanted AJ close to him, so they agreed that he and AJ would watch the support group while John stayed close to the athletes.

"I'll get a field pass for you," said Kirk to John. "That's where the company pull comes in handy."

John and AJ stayed at the hotel while Kirk went to arrange the pass. Whatever happened tomorrow, it would be a relief to end the waiting and the suspense.

CHAPTER 76

C harles Wadlington looked at Kirk incredulously. "Are you nuts? You told your girlfriend and another guy what you really do? You told them about Green Star? Are you insane?"

Kirk shifted his weight from one foot to the other. He hadn't been dressed down like this since junior high school. He looked at the wallpaper in the hotel room, not willing to make eye contact with Wadlington.

"Vail, do you remember the oath you took when you were sworn in as a member of the team? The oath of loyalty, the oath of obedience, the oath of secrecy? This isn't a kids' game."

Charles paced back and forth. What bothered him most was not what Vail had done, but how the General would react. Vail was an excellent operative, and Charles trusted his judgment about the discretion of his girl and his friend. But he knew that meant nothing to the General.

Charles looked out the window at the street full of tourists from all over the world. In his blue blazer and tan slacks, Charles knew he could walk into any party and play the part of the vague official from somewhere else. He used his chameleon-like abilities to gain access to countless groups in Chicago as he sought information.

Now he faced a major decision. The strength of Charles Wadlington was his ability to make decisions quickly and effectively based on the information at hand. This case was no exception.

Turning back to Kirk, he gave him a withering look as he delivered his verdict. "First, consider this a verbal reprimand. Second, I'm not telling anyone else right now. This operation is based on information you have provided, so I'm giving you the benefit of the doubt. Third, I will be outside of the stadium during the competition tomorrow with two additional operatives. I'll have special resources on me, if they are needed."

Kirk had been nodding as Wadlington ticked off the points. "Fourth, I will provide a field pass to go with the stadium tickets. I expect you to maintain contact with me via cell phone."

Charles Wadlington, mid thirties, slightly balding, and bachelor not by choice, softened his visage a bit. "Fifth, " he paused to look into the eyes of the taller man, "Vail, is she worth it?"

The question took Kirk by surprise, but he could tell by Wadlington's tone he wanted a sincere answer. Breaking into a smile from ear to ear, Kirk replied, "Yes, sir, most definitely!"

Wadlington gave a wry smile. "I hope so. For your sake and mine."

CHAPTER 77

Frankie and Deuce stood before Tony Massetti under the linden tree in the mansion's back yard. They had their hats in their hands, begging for forgiveness. Frankie made a plea for understanding.

"It wasn't Deuce's fault. The security was unbelievable. They had checkpoints with metal detectors and dope sniffing dogs. You'd a thought they had gold and jewels in those apartments in the Olympic Village."

Tony didn't comment. "Deuce did great just to get into the place," continued Frankie. "We had the dope wrapped and descented so the pooches wouldn't squeal on him. But when he got into the building, it was crawling with cameras and reporters."

Deuce picked up the tale. "See, Mr. Massetti, it went like this. I get in the hall to the guy's room, and there are camera crews from a couple TV stations filling the hall. I knew the pole vaulters would all be out practicing, 'cuz it was their time."

He paused to take a breath. "But some dude from Mexico won a bronze medal, and he's staying right across the hall from my target. So the stinking Spanish TV stations are showing the guy's room and talking to him in the hall. They're, like, camped out. I can see they're telling the dude's life story and I'll never get into the room."

Frankie jumped in. "And there were cops in the hall, too, weren't there?"

"Yeh, yeh," agreed Deuce. "The place was lousy with blues. I figured I'm packing blow and a bogus ID, so I better split before the whole deal is blown sky high."

Tony looked at Frankie. "You're telling me there was no way he could make the drop? Absolutely no way?"

Frankie had known Tony forever. He knew he was tough but fair.

"Tony, no way in the time frame we had to work with. Just wasn't possible."

Tony picked up a twig and picked the leaves off. "All right. You come up with a new plan for tomorrow. I don't care what, I don't care how. But if Armendariz wins the gold medal tomorrow, somebody dies."

Tony snapped the twig, looking at them both. Then he threw it on the ground and walked into the house, leaving Frankie and Deuce alone with their thoughts.

CHAPTER 78

This was the day Rickie Armendariz had been made for. He was nourished and trained for this moment. Special food supplements and special training techniques had given him a body envied even among elite athletes. But that wasn't enough.

Tiny electrodes had been implanted in the muscles of his thighs, hips, shoulders and arms to improve the explosiveness of his movements. He knew this was to help him be the best, but he wondered if it was right. Nobody asked him what he thought. He was treated like a racehorse, not an athlete.

Rickie loved working out and competing. The thrill of physical exertion brought him the only true joy of his life. His existence of isolation in the compound on the island was contrasted by his experiences during the past week in the United States. The unabashed joy exhibited by the athletes and the fans was affecting him.

Rickie wanted to feel that camaraderie and joy. But he knew it wasn't meant to be. He dutifully wrapped the red flag with the black swastika inside of the blue, black, and gold St. Lucia flag. Mr. Krug had instructed him to take the flags out of his bag after winning the vault. As he ran a victory lap, he was to unroll the flags, drop the St. Lucia flag, and hold the Nazi flag aloft.

He always did what he was told. He was taught to speak when spoken to and follow instructions to the letter. He responded to instructions with immediate obedience. But now he wondered to what purpose. He was told the Fourth Reich was coming, and his athletic prowess would be the cornerstone of a new world order.

Mr. Krug had shown him a list of countries where rallies were to be held to celebrate his Olympic victory. The United States, Argentina, Brazil, Venezuela, Germany, Austria, Hungary, and more. Racial purity and superiority would be the touchstones for a worldwide political uprising. After he won the gold, Rickie would shout to the world his real name — Richard Krug.

In his whole life, he had never called Gregory Krug father or dad. It was always Mr. Krug or Sir. It was not until he was seventeen that he learned he was not an orphan. He was the product of a petri dish union of Mr. Krug's genes and those of an unknown woman of racially pure German descent.

He'd been instructed to be proud of his German heritage and his opportunity to excel. He carried his head high as he competed, knowing that on his shoulders rode the hopes and dreams of legions of true followers. He had always looked forward to his day in the sun. Until now.

A long distance runner from Kenya had been widely quoted as saying his "heart took wings" when he competed in the Olympics. Rickie wanted that feeling of a heart bursting with pride. But his heart had no wings. He felt only the dead weight of deceit and doubt.

His life was a lie. His name, his achievements, even the country he represented, were all deceptions. He used illegal means to gain a competitive edge.

It was with a heavy heart he zipped his bag closed and prepared to go to the stadium. He wasn't happy, he wasn't excited. But he was raised to be a good soldier. He would do his duty and perform to the best of his ability.

CHAPTER 79

A J and Kirk didn't know what to expect. Sitting in the Olympic Stadium, they observed the Krug entourage in the section below them. The pole vault was about to begin as other events continued on the track.

Kirk had a small radio in his pocket with an earpiece so he could listen to the comments of the announcers and event results. The stadium announcements were almost impossible to hear above the crowd noise. The Bushnell 27X binoculars made them feel like they were on the field.

AJ zoomed in on John. He was with a group of reporters standing near the pole vault pit. AJ saw him chatting animatedly with a pretty young journalist.

Scanning the stadium, AJ watched Wickland and Armendariz warming up. She realized she was sitting on the edge of her seat, bouncing her legs nervously. She'd much rather play than have to sit and watch. The tension was mounting.

A track and field meet is a kaleidoscope of sights and sounds. The eyes feast on the action, with changing colors both on the field and in the crowd. Starters' pistols, bell laps, and crowd noise challenge the ears. It borders on stimulation overload.

AJ and Kirk looked at each other and smiled. He wanted to freeze-frame her just the way she looked now, with the sunshine on her face and her hair blowing in the breeze. Her eyes, her smile, her perfectly shaped lips — Kirk swallowed and felt a tightening in his throat.

He gave AJ's knee an affectionate squeeze. *Man, if this is love, bring it on.* His thoughts were interrupted by AJ.

"The vault is starting!"

Glancing down, Kirk saw the competitor from Italy hoist his pole. Here was the reason they were in Chicago. Picking up his binoculars, Kirk looked to check John's position on the field. Time to focus on the action.

CHAPTER 80

G regory Krug was euphoric. The time of triumph was at hand. Soon Rickie would possess a gold medal and the world would know the power of the Reich and of Josef Mengele. Gertrude had given him a double dose of shots today and he felt marvelous.

He needed the track success to pressure ODESSA to increase their financial support of his work. His anti-aging research could truly develop a Fountain of Youth serum and give him thirty more years of life. What he learned working on Rickie and the others would help him reach his ultimate goal of self-preservation.

William Schultz sat next to Mengele, lost in his own thoughts. He did the mental calculations of the winnings he would enjoy from his bets. He and Bouhler had hatched the plan to place the bets on Rickie. He figured they would each clear over ten million dollars after payoffs and transfer charges.

Emile balked at first. He was deathly afraid of Mr. Krug. But Schultz had pressured him until he finally agreed to place the bets in the United States. Schultz told him it was a sure thing. By spreading the bets around, there was no way the money could be traced back to them.

Krug had told Bouhler to stay away from the stadium, which suited him just fine. He was the one who had spent the past two years in America, and Krug would take no chances with someone recognizing him.

Bouhler leaned against the wall and admired the setup. It was amazing what money could buy. They were on the thirty-second floor of an office building a quarter mile away from the Olympic Stadium. The three scientists from the island were adjusting the computers and transmitters arranged on a conference table pushed in front of the large picture window.

Next to the table, two telescopes on tripods pointed toward the stadium. They had the perfect vantage point to look over the rim at the competition.

On each side of the conference table was a desk with a 36" flat screen TV tuned to the Olympic coverage. The room looked like the bridge of the Starship Enterprise. Bouhler could almost hear Captain Kirk say, "Beam me up, Scottie."

The scientists, looking like triplets in their matching black slacks and short sleeved white dress shirts, performed their final tests of the equipment. Bouhler idly watched a TV as the vault began. He was wrestling with fantasies about what to buy with his winnings. *A yacht or a mansion? Maybe both.*

CHAPTER 81

The pole vault moves at a snail's pace in the beginning. While the favorites pass on the lower heights, the unknowns happily vault away, enjoying the chance to compete on the world's largest stage. Some of them work to extend their fleeting moment in the spotlight by taking as long as possible before each jump.

The stars of the show spend this time in mind games. Some strut and preen while others feign indifference and boredom. The tactical game involves deciding when to tell the officials you're ready to participate. Begin too soon and you use up valuable energy on too many low jumps.

But wait too long and you become a sports media joke; a favorite who misses all three attempts at his first height and finishes last with no jumps completed.

As the field thinned, the top six began vaulting. Races were finishing, and more and more spectators focused on the pole vault. As heights rose, misses increased. Then there were five competitors remaining.

A Frenchman, two Americans, a Saint Lucian, and a Russian remained. Sitting for an interview by Olympic sportcasters in the Olympic media broadcast center was Sergei Bubka, the retired pole vault great.

"With us for the finals of the pole vault is the former Russian and Ukrainian great, Sergei Bubka," effused the broadcast host. "Bubka set 35 world records and has one Olympic gold medal to go with his six world championships. Sergei, what do you think of this year's Olympic field?"

"It looks like a very strong field. I was disappointed that our Ukrainian champion struggled today and has been eliminated, but such is the nature of the Olympics. There is so much pressure for four years and then it comes down to one day's performance."

"Indeed, there is pressure, Sergei. And speaking of pressure, do you think there will be a challenge to your world record today? For those who don't know, Sergei Bubka currently holds the indoor record of 20 feet 2 inches, and the outdoor mark of 20 feet 1 3/4 inches. Quite a remarkable accomplishment for someone over forty to still hold world records in track."

Bubka smiled into the camera. "You are kind to mention my record."

The stage director was giving the stretch it out sign. "I see that we have a delay in the pole vault. It seems there's been a slight injury on the track near the vault pit that is holding up the competition. Speaking of injuries, Sergei, what are your thoughts on pole vault safety."

Bubka looked straight into the camera. "Technology advances and superior training methods have been double edged swords. Poles have gone from bamboo to fiberglass to composite resins that propel the vaulter harder and higher. Athletes are stronger and faster, creating more torque and strain. But as heights increase, the risk of injury increases if a fall isn't controlled."

The interviewer nodded in agreement. "You're so right. We all remember the tragedy at the 2002 Big Ten Championships when the young man from Penn State died after landing on his head during the pole vault competition."

Sergei nodded gravely. "That was a horrible accident. Since then additional padding has been added on the periphery of the pit, as well as additional spotters to check the vault box and poles after every jump. A few competitors have also opted to wear protective helmets."

He paused. "But falling from twenty feet in the air is like jumping off of a two story building. You're punished for landing wrong."

On the prompt from the director, their attention returned to the live action. "We have Rickie Armendariz, representing tiny St. Lucia, making his first attempt at 5.6 meters, or 18 feet, 4 7/16 inches. Armendariz is attempting to break the stranglehold the United States and Europe have had on this event. He also hopes to become the first ever medal winner from his small Caribbean island nation. Let's watch his approach."

Rickie looked down the runway at the rubberized surface, rocked back and forth, and ran toward the pit with his pole held aloft. Halfway down the runway he picked up speed, practically leaping from foot to foot. He planted the pole in the metal box and catapulted skyward.

There was a moment when he seemed to be suspended vertically, his feet pointing up and his hands on the pole like an upside down fireman ready to descend the pole. Then he gave a tremendous push with his arms, sending him over the bar and sending the pole crashing back to the runway.

Emerging from the billowing landing pad with his arms in the air, Rickie savored the cheers. He had cleared the bar easily, a good omen for the rest of his jumps.

CHAPTER 82

G regory Krug applauded with the rest of the fans. He was enjoying the well-deserved success. It wouldn't be long now. Sitting on the aisle, he had a perfect view of the competition. Next to him sat Schultz, his two bodyguards, and Gertrude.

Coming down the aisle toward Krug was an American couple who'd been trying desperately to get into the track venue. Mr. and Mrs. Bernie Kerman came to Chicago to celebrate their wedding anniversary. Their children had surprised them with airline tickets and hotel reservations, making this a truly memorable anniversary.

The New Jersey couple had been trying to scalp tickets to events all week. They had seen badminton and fencing, but Bernie was determined to see some of the track events. He decided to bite the bullet and pay whatever it took to get into the Olympic Stadium.

Over fifty years of marriage was something to celebrate, especially for someone like Bernie, who was lucky to be alive. Born in Hoboken in 1932, Bernie's parents had moved back to Germany in 1937. The depression had bankrupted the business of Bernie's father, so they packed up and went to Europe to live with Bernie's grandparents in Schwerin. The small town in northern Germany held promise of work and the support of family.

Bernie's father felt safe when the war broke out since his entire family were American citizens. That was until the Gestapo swept through Schwerin, herding them into the streets. His protestation that they were Americans meant nothing to the SS lieutenant.

"Are you Jews?" he asked while looking at their papers.

"Americans," answered Bernie's father.

With a snort, the lieutenant pointed to the trucks that would begin their relocation process.

After a series of moves, the Kerman family ended up in a cattle car destined for Auschwitz. Emerging into the sunlight from the darkness and stench of the overcrowded railroad car, eleven-year-old Bernie held his mother's hand as huge German soldiers prodded them forward.

Someone on the train had told the children to stand tall and lie about their ages. "Say you are fifteen," a man said to all of the children. "They want children who are old enough to work."

Bernie's mother was fighting a dreadful cold and a body-racking cough. As the line moved forward, they could see two officers standing on the platform directing the human flow.

When they reached the front, Bernie's father spoke up. "We are Americans. We don't belong here."

He was cuffed behind the ear for his insolence, tumbling to the ground. The officer in charge looked at Bernie and his mother. Bernie stood tall and pulled his shoulders back, trying to stand at attention. A smile crossed the officer's face.

"To the right," he said pointing at Bernie and his prone father.

Just then Bernie's mother erupted with a violent coughing fit, doubling her over and sending phlegm spraying onto the pant leg of the officer.

Striking her on the back of the head with his riding crop, the officer growled. "Move to the left, you cow!" The venom in the officer's voice made Bernie very afraid. A guard pushed Mrs. Kerman to the left toward the showers.

As the lines pushed on, Bernie kept looking back, straining to see his mother. His helplessness and hopelessness shamed and angered him. The face and the voice of the officer were burned into young Bernie's mind forever. He pledged revenge on the Angel of Death. His resolve gave him strength to survive the nightmare of the concentration camp.

After the liberation of Auschwitz at the war's end, the Red Cross helped Bernie and his father return to New Jersey. Bernie cared for his father, who was physically and mentally broken by the prison camp experience and the murder of his wife by the Nazis.

When Bernie Kerman married his lovely Louise, he had almost put the war behind him. The nightmares became less frequent as the responsibilities of job and family filled his life.

Now, as he and Louise slowly made their way down the steep stadium steps, Bernie's heart was soaring. He saw an American preparing to pole vault and he gave Louise's hand a squeeze. "Look, honey. One of our boys is about to go."

They stopped on the steps to watch, inadvertently blocking the view of the fans on the aisle.

"Move to the left, you cow!" snarled Gregory Krug at Louise.

Bernie's head snapped around. That voice! Bernie looked into Krug's eyes and was transported back to that day in Auschwitz. Spoken in German then and in English now, the voice and syntax were unmistakably identical.

Without hesitation, Bernie Kerman shouted, "Mengele!" and sprang at the seated old man.

A bewildered Louise watched as her husband was pulled off of the white haired man and punched by his bodyguards. Her husband was knocked into the aisle, bleeding from his nose and mouth.

Bernie lay dazed as Krug and Schultz started up the steps toward an exit. The two bodyguards held Bernie while Gertrude leaned over him. Looking up at Louise she spoke reassuringly. "It will be all right. I'm a nurse."

Wiping the blood from his face with one hand, Gertrude stuck a hypodermic needle into Bernie's chest with the other. She used her body to shield her action from Louise and the other spectators.

Slipping the needle into her jacket pocket, Gertrude used both hands to clean up Bernie. "I think he fell on our group and we thought he was attacking us," she said to Louise. "I'm so sorry. Let's make him comfortable and we'll get a doctor."

The bodyguards placed Bernie in the seat vacated by Krug and folded his hands in his lap. His breathing was shallow and labored.

"We'll be right back," said Gertrude. With that, she and the bodyguards headed up the steps. The whole exchange had taken less than a minute.

There was a roar from the crowd as Louise sat down next to the love of her life. She held his hand and looked onto the field. If she was reading the scoreboard correctly, the American Wickland had just cleared 5.7 meters.

Looking back at Bernie, she shuddered. His eyes were dilated and his mouth hung open. His breathing was barely detectable. She was afraid he had suffered a heart attack. Frantically, she called for help.

CHAPTER 83

K irk nudged AJ and pointed to the stands below them. "Krug's leaving. Something happened down there and he's heading for an exit."

AJ looked below as Kirk thumbed a speed dial on his cell phone. "CW, this is KV. We may be leaving the stadium. Probably west exit. You have an eye on JC?"

"Roger that, KV. You're man's covered. I may say hi to you as you pass."

Kirk was up and had AJ by the arm. "We're on it. Out." Kirk hit end and holstered the phone. They excused their way to the aisle amid annoyed looks as Krug and Schultz disappeared into the cement hole of an exit. Gertrude and the bodyguards made it to the exit as Kirk and AJ worked their way down the steps.

Taking the steps two at a time, Kirk and AJ reached the exit, turned and went down the next flight of stairs. As they reached the landing below the stands, they could see Krug and his associates walking quickly out through the columned exit.

Krug's group loaded into two taxis that quickly pulled away from the curb. As Kirk and AJ stepped onto the sidewalk, the bright sunlight forced them to squint as they peered at the departing vehicles.

"Excuse me, Sir," said the man as he bumped into Kirk. As his eyes met those of Charles Wadlington, Kirk felt his shirt being pulled up as the Beretta was shoved into the waistband of his slacks. Instinctively rearranging the pistol to fit it more comfortably, Kirk pulled his shirt out so that it hung loosely covering the butt of the weapon.

"You're excused," answered Kirk as Wadlington walked away. Kirk whistled for a cab and smiled at AJ as she stared at his waist. "Tools of the trade, my dear. Rule Number Eight, keep a pen in your car, or as the Boy Scouts say, 'be prepared'. I find the Beretta is mightier than the pen in a crisis."

Kirk slid into the backseat of the cab after AJ and instructed the cabbie to head straight up Martin Luther King Drive.

Kirk leaned forward, his eyes intently following the two taxis. "When we see where they're going, I'll get out and follow while you to stay in the cab. I want you to go back to the stadium and meet John after it's all over."

AJ looped her arm through Kirk's, holding on tightly. "Not on your life. I'm going with you."

"You can't," said Kirk. "It's too dangerous."

AJ's grip tightened. "No way we're separating, and that's final." AJ pointed ahead. "They've pulled over."

Kirk held his hand to his ear, cocking his head slightly, listening to the Olympic announcers. "Only three competitors left. Wickland, Armendariz, and LaBeau from France. They've all cleared 19'5" to tie the Olympic record. The Russian and the American from UCLA are out."

Kirk barked at the driver, "Pull over here." He handed the driver enough cash to cover the short trip as the Krug group entered a high-rise office building. AJ and Kirk walked quickly toward the building entrance. "Wait outside," Kirk ordered.

AJ's response was to walk faster and beat him to the door. "Middle elevator," she noted as they spun through the revolving door. The lighted panel above the elevator door indicated the floors as the elevator rose up the shaft.

The number thirty-two remained lit for fifteen seconds and then the elevator began to descend. Kirk and AJ walked across the lobby to observe from a distance if anyone got off of the elevator. The stainless steel door opened. The elevator was empty. Grabbing Kirk's hand, AJ pulled him in. "We're on. Let's take a ride."

Kirk punched number thirty-one and the doors closed. "We'll check out the floor below first. It's Saturday and there's not much going on in this building. We need a plan before we go to thirty-two."

"What's going on with the pole vault?" asked AJ.

Kirk paused before replying. "Wickland just missed at nineteen nine, which is the U.S. record. He gets two more attempts. Good thing the announcer converts the metric for me. He's making a big deal that they are at 6.02 meters. To Europeans, the six-meter mark has the mystique of the four minute mile."

The elevator opened onto a deserted hallway. "Go left," said Kirk. "That side of the building faces the stadium."

They went down the hallway and around the corner. In the center of the adjacent hall were two large glass doors. International Mortgage was etched across both doors in ten inch tall letters.

Kirk scanned the hall for video cameras, finding none. "This looks like a good place to start." Pulling a small zippered case out of his back pocket, he prepared to work on the lock. He gave AJ a wink. "Don't try this at home. Acts of espionage are being performed by trained professionals."

CHAPTER 84

J ohn Cline used body language to help Jimmy Wickland over the bar, but it didn't help. Jimmy's hip grazed the bar on the way up, and he and the bar fell to earth together. The groan from the crowd told John he wasn't the only one hoping to see a new U.S. record.

John was enjoying his up close and personal view of the Olympics. Being on the field was an experience to remember. He looked at the press corps gathered around him. All faces and cameras were focused on Jimmy Wickland as he prepared for another vault. Except one.

One young man was looking at Rickie Armendariz as he sat stretching on the grass. The man was fiddling with his camera and looking hard at Rickie. There was something not right about this picture. John's sixth sense told him there was danger here.

As he stepped closer, John saw the man manipulate the lower housing of his camera. He wasn't inserting a memory card or new battery. Whatever he was doing was strange and John didn't like it. From five feet away, John spoke. "Hey, what're you doing?"

The look in Deuce's eyes told the whole story. Guilt and fear flashed like a neon sign. Turning quickly back toward Rickie he raised the camera for the shot.

"No," shouted John as he lunged for the camera. He grabbed Deuce's arms as the camera spit a small stainless steel dart in the direction of Armendariz. John's quick reactions caused the projectile to bury itself harmlessly in the Olympic grass.

Deuce brought an elbow up into John's chin and swung the camera at his face. Leaning back, John blocked the blow with his left forearm, ducked, and delivered a right uppercut, stunning Deuce.

Two men in dark blue shirts with SECURITY stenciled on their backs in four inch high white letters tackled John and Deuce with moves that would have made an NFL coach proud. Muscle encased shoulders drove into John and Deuce's midsections and rammed them to the turf.

A split second before Jimmy Wickland went airborne, there was a roar from the crowd at the melee on the field. In later interviews he would not blame the sudden noise for disturbing him, but it did.

The eruption from the crowd caused him to tighten his grip on the pole. This caused undo tension in his forearms a millisecond prior to his push off.

The result? A botched jump. With his timing off, Jimmy passed under the bar. Under the bar? He hadn't done that since high school.

He walked back up the runway, dragging his pole in disgust.

He noticed the commotion in the infield as security and Olympic officials sprinted to the area. Just what he needed — a delay before his final attempt.

CHAPTER 85

"Fans, I don't know what's happening in the infield, but it looks like the pole vault has been halted." The sportscaster looked earnestly into camera number one. A teleprompter scrolled in front of him while the producer chattered through his earpiece.

"There appears to be a scuffle between two of the press corps." The producer told him it may be a security issue, but Olympic personnel had asked the media to play it lightly while the situation was controlled. "I wish my co-journalists would realize that we're reporting the action, not creating it. Maybe two photographers were fighting for the same shot."

The producer indicated they were staying with the pole vault and not showing the security force dragging the two men from the infield. "Sergei, do you think a break will help or hurt Jimmy Wickland?"

Bubka picked up on the cue. "I think it will help him. He was totally out of sync on his last vault. Wickland realized it and just let his body go under the bar, which is the safest path on a bad jump. Now he has some time to get his head together for his final attempt."

The announcer was getting the stretch sign. "Do you think the pressure of going for the United States record got to him? Was this a choke?"

"No, not a choke. Just a slip. When an athlete pushes the personal success envelope, the unknown challenges his confidence. Outside of the comfort zone of past performances, slips become more likely." Bubka was enjoying the chance to explain the psyche of the elite athlete.

"Sergei, what defines a choke?"

Smiling with the recollection, Sergei looked into camera two. "Years ago at a meet in Paris, there was a man paralyzed by emotion on the runway. He was attempting a personal best in the vault, and he stood with the pole on his shoulder for minutes, staring straight ahead at the bar."

"Did he ever jump?"

Sergei shook his head, no. "The official walked up to him holding a stopwatch and called a forfeit on his first attempt. He stood next to him and called a forfeit on his second attempt. By now everyone in the stadium was watching to see if he would forfeit his last jump. The rest of the vaulters had lined the runway and were shouting for him to go. Some clapped and others whistled, trying to move him. But there he stood."

"How did it end?"

"The man's fiercest rival walked to within a few feet of him and spoke softly. 'Procrastination robs you of opportunity. You must try. Don't let me win this way.' These words moved the man to action and he thundered down the runway before a final forfeit was called."

"Did he make the height?"

"Yes," smiled Sergei. "That was the day I set the first of my world records."

CHAPTER 86

During the delay, the United States coach told Jimmy to forget about the last vault and think positively. Of course, having someone tell you to be positive and actually being positive under pressure are two different things.

Jimmy closed his eyes and turned his thoughts inward. He took deep breaths and pictured Reelfoot Lake on a quiet summer afternoon. He filled his mind with soothing blue water and green trees.

His fingers played with the bracelet on his wrist. *Kiss the Sky. Kiss the Sky.* He knew Grams was watching on television.

Reaching into his bag, he pulled out the squirt bottle and took a long drink of the green liquid. A second swig finished off the last of Gram's plant juice. It was now or never.

"Wickland, we've gotten the okay to restart." The official was from Australia and had worked many meets where Jimmy had competed. He liked the polite young American. "Make it a good one, mate."

"Thank you, Sir." Jimmy was ready. You only had to clear each height once. It didn't matter if it was on the first, second or third attempt.

CHAPTER 87

K irk placed a chair on top of a desk and removed a panel from the drop ceiling. He stood on the chair with his head hidden in the ceiling as he tried to hear something from the floor above.

"What's going on?" whispered AJ as Kirk climbed down from the chair. He held his hand toward her, palm out, asking for silence. He looked at her without responding as he listened to his radio plugged into his ear.

After what seemed an eternity, Kirk spoke. "Wickland missed on his second attempt and some sort of commotion happened with the journalists on the field. They stopped the competition while they settled things down. I'm going to call John to see what's really happening."

Kirk dialed John's cell phone. After four rings, it went to voice mail. "John, it's Kirk. Call me. What's going on?"

Snapping his phone shut, Kirk looked at AJ. "He's not picking up. And I can't hear anything from the next floor. I put my ear next to the air duct in the ceiling and couldn't hear a thing. We have to go upstairs."

"All right. What's the plan?"

"We'll see if we can go up the stairs and maybe get into the room next to theirs to listen. We're so close. We have to do something."

AJ agreed and watched as Kirk replaced the ceiling tile. She wanted to know what this was all about. What did she know that warranted these maniacs trying to kill her twice? Kirk called Charles Wadlington to tell him where they were and what they were doing. Getting his voicemail, he left a curt message. Hanging up, he looked at AJ. "Nobody's answering their phones. I don't know what it means, but I don't think it's good."

"So, in other words, the cavalry may not be on the way." AJ paused. "Let's hit the stairs."

Kirk took her hand. "My sentiments exactly."

Gregory Krug looked through the telescope and spoke with glee. "Wickland is ready for his last attempt. He went under the bar last time, so who would expect him to make it over the bar set at the United States record?"

Bill Schultz knew the correct answer. "No one, Doctor Krug. They should stick a fork in him, because he's done. And Rickie has already cleared it."

Schultz looked at Emile Bouhler and smiled. Bouhler rubbed his thumb across his index finger in the universal sign for money and smiled back. It wouldn't be long until they were both millionaires.

"Here he goes," said Krug.

The scientists were playing with their computers and transmitters in preparation for Rickie's next jump. Schultz, Bouhler, Gertrude and one of the bodyguards watched the two televisions as Wickland sprinted down the runway.

Jimmy planted his pole and it bent under the strain. The pole straightened and sent him skyward. He arched his back and passed cleanly over the bar. He pumped a fist in the air as he fell to earth as the new United States record holder.

No one in the room dared speak. They thought Krug might explode with anger. But he didn't. He stepped away from the telescope and addressed the group.

"Excellent. This will make Rickie's success more dramatic."

The room breathed a collective sigh of relief that Krug hadn't unleashed his anger. While they were all confident Rickie would win, they didn't want anyone else making his gold medal run difficult.

Just then the door to the office flew open and two strangers were shoved into the room. "Look what I found sneaking up the stairs," explained the bodyguard. He had been watching the hallway when Kirk and AJ made their move. He held his gun on them and had Kirk's pistol shoved in his belt.

Bouhler strode toward the captives. "Well, well, Miss Clark. We meet again. Has being nosey paid off? You may wish you had minded your own business."

AJ responded defiantly. "You tried to run me off of the road and killed an innocent young man. Then you sent someone to kill me at my apartment Were you afraid to try again yourself?"

Bouhler cocked his arm back to slap AJ, when Krug shouted, "Enough! Guard them so they can see the wonders of my work. Then we will eliminate them."

Kirk spoke up. "You'll never get away with it. Your scheme won't work. You won't get out of Chicago."

The bodyguards pushed AJ and Kirk into chairs facing the windows.

"On the contrary, young man," Krug said. "We are succeeding, and we will safely leave America, which is more than I can say for you and Miss Clark."

"In a way, I'm glad you're here," Krug continued. "My accomplishments deserve an audience. Watch the television as Rickie easily covers the next height."

The scientists adjusted their instruments. Armendariz stood on the runway, poised to begin his vault. As he began to run, one scientist called numbers off of a computer monitor while another hammered at a keyboard.

Kirk and AJ watched Armendariz moving gracefully down the runway. He planted the pole smoothly and rose high over the bar. Kirk could hear the announcer in his earpiece raving about the ease with which the St. Lucia vaulter had cleared this difficult height.

Krug had been looking through the telescope as Rickie performed. Turning to his captive audience, he smiled with pride.

"Remarkable, isn't it? I've created the perfect athlete."

"At what cost?" challenged AJ. "Ever since I stumbled across Bouhler at GF Products I've seen nothing but death and destruction. What makes Armendariz so perfect?"

Krug looked at AJ and Kirk. "You're like all the rest. You don't understand. I've been working for years on human body enhancements. I've learned how to nurture the body and activate the muscles to produce flawless performance. I've also produced huge advances in aging retardation. Haven't I Gertrude?"

Gertrude smiled and nodded dutifully.

"How old do you think I am?" challenged Krug. He ran his fingers through his thick white hair and asked again. "How old?"

Kirk looked at the man standing before him and figured he was mid to late sixties. Not wanting to compliment him, he threw out an age. "Seventy-seven."

"And what do you think?" Krug asked AJ.

He wasn't as big a man as Grandpa, so he didn't have the same muscle mass. His skin looked considerably younger and his hands didn't show the knotted knuckles she associated with old men.

"Eighty," she said, thinking like Kirk.

Krug smiled delightedly. "I know you are both guessing high to try to anger me. Well, not high enough. I'm over one hundred years old and planning on twenty-five more good years."

Kirk couldn't pass up the chance to throw a verbal barb. "If you don't let us go, you won't last twenty-five more minutes."

Krug's reaction was swift. He reached onto the desk and backhanded Kirk with a metal object. Kirk's head snapped back and blood ran down his cheek.

"You Americans!" hissed Krug. "So arrogant! You think you own the world. You use your wealth to insulate yourselves from hardships. You buy victories in wars fought on the homeland of others. Our cities were destroyed while your families slept safely in their warm beds."

As he spoke, he gestured with the object he held so tightly. AJ strained to see what it was. It was a knife in a scabbard. As Krug waved it back and forth, AJ saw a scull cast into the hilt.

Kirk made eye contact with AJ. "I'm okay," he mouthed. They both returned their attention to Krug, not wanting to incite him further.

"The American and the Frenchman are next, Sir." Bill Schultz hoped to divert Krug back to the task at hand.

Krug calmed himself. "Fine. Let's watch the inferior specimens fail. The American is worn out, and the French have been spineless and undisciplined for a thousand years. Their Maginot line was a paper tiger. We crushed them in weeks. Just like Rickie will crush this LeBeau."

Krug returned to the telescope as everyone else focused on the televisions. A rejuvenated Jimmy Wickland cleared the height on his first attempt. The announcers gushed over the ability of Jimmy Wickland to push to new heights.

It was obvious from the first attempt that LeBeau was stretched to his limit. None of his three vaults seriously threatened to clear the bar.

"Then there were two!" exclaimed Krug. "Soon the American will fail and Rickie will stand alone as the world champion."

AJ and Kirk had been whispering to each other. Kirk hoped Wadlington was coming to the building, but he wasn't getting his hopes up.

AJ was still curious about the reason for all of this effort over the pole vault. "So why the pole vault?" She directed her question at Krug. "Really, who cares about one event in the Olympics? So you stole a bunch of technology and made a super athlete. Big deal. You think you're some kind of hero because you think you're going to outlive the rest of us. But you're not sharing your discoveries? Again, big deal."

Krug paced in front of AJ and Kirk, looking down at them in the chairs. He couldn't resist talking about his success, since these two wouldn't live to tell anyone.

"This is only the beginning. My work proves our superiority. We Aryans truly are the Master Race. We will have demonstrations in every major country in the world. What you call a no big deal pole vault is the beginning of a new world order."

Krug picked up the hourglass from the desk. He'd brought it from the island as a reminder that times have changed. He turned it over and placed it back on the desk.

"Watch the sand flow from top to bottom. The irresistible force of gravity pulls the sand irreversibly downward. Your weak governments will be pulled down by the power of the New Reich."

AJ challenged Krug. "Aryan. Master Race. What century are you living in? Did you invent a time machine, too, so you can goose step back to Nazi Germany and World War II? Were you one of them, and now you're having a Nazi flashback?"

Krug's eyes blazed. "You impertinent sow!" His fists were clenched at his sides in rage. "I only wish I had time to experiment on you. Then we'd see how long your disrespectful attitude would last."

Schultz interrupted again. "Wickland is up, Sir. The bar is at 6.1 meters, just shy of the world record." He couldn't contain the excitement in his voice. He was close to becoming a millionaire.

Krug wanted to expound further on his greatness, but he had to see Wickland fail. He returned to the telescope and Bouhler turned the volume up on one of the televisions.

CHAPTER 88

"This has been an extraordinary event. The young American from Tennessee and the powerful competitor from the island nation of St. Lucia have turned the pole vault into a western hemisphere shootout." The sportscaster looked into the camera and delivered his words with the sincerity of a sermon.

"Both men have broken the Olympic record. Both men have cleared the United States record. Now they both have an opportunity to be the first non-Europeans to break the magical twenty-foot barrier, equal to 6.1 meters. I don't know about you, Sergei, but my heart is racing."

Sergei nodded in agreement. "This is the ultimate in track and field. Two great competitors battling for a gold medal."

"Sergei, if they move past this height, your record will be eclipsed. I know you enjoy watching excellence, but it becomes bittersweet when it's your record that is broken. Wickland is poised to make his first attempt. Sergei, why don't you call the action?"

"I'll do my best. Wickland is checking something on his wrist. Every athlete has superstitions and personal rituals that must be honored. He wipes his hands on his shorts and grips the pole. Routine is tremendously important before each attempt. He looks very ready as he holds the pole aloft and flexes his knees."

Jimmy Wickland filled the television screen, staring down the runway. AJ and Kirk leaned forward to see the picture as Jimmy began to run with the pole.

"He looks good on his approach, running hard but smooth. It's a clean plant and he's well back to make maximum use of the pole's flex."

Wickland, outfitted in red, white and blue, jackknifed skyward. Sergei's voice raised an octave. "It's a strong release, he has the height! He's over! Jimmy Wickland has cleared 6.1 meters, setting a new Olympic record."

The sportscaster chimed in. "Jimmy Wickland, of the United States, has just become the first man to clear the phenomenal height of twenty feet in Olympic competition."

Kirk and AJ whooped with joy. The next sound was the door to the office suite being kicked in. "Hands in the air!" shouted Frankie waving an Italian submachine gun. Two men entered close on his heels and targeted Krug's two bodyguards, disarming them quickly and forcing them to the floor at gunpoint.

Everyone but Krug had their hands in the air. Tony Massetti entered the room once the situation was secure. "Nice place for a party." He walked up to Krug. "So, how do you control your boy Armendariz? We were going to give him a little negative help, but Deuce couldn't get the job done."

"Who are you?" asked Krug.

"I'm the one you're trying to steal money from. Which is not going to happen. So how do we keep your boy from making the next jump?"

Bouhler and Schultz looked at each other at the mention of money. Krug noticed the look and frowned. "I have no idea what you're talking about. I'm not stealing anything from anyone."

Frankie pressed his gun to Schultz's chest. He'd noticed the same look Krug had seen. "Tony, I think these two are our pigeons." Frankie motioned with a nod of his head to Bouhler and Schultz.

Krug's voice rose as his eyes burned into those of Bouhler. "What are they talking about, Emile?"

Bouhler fidgeted under Krug's intense gaze. "It was his idea," said Bouhler pointing at Schultz. "He said it was a sure thing and the bets could never be traced back to us. We knew Rickie would win."

Krug unsheathed his dagger and stepped toward Schultz with murder in his eyes. Tony reacted with speed and agility belying his size, chopping Krug's wrist, sending the dagger clattering onto the floor. Twisting Krug's arm behind his back, he shoved the older man's face and chest against the picture window.

"I'm in charge now, not you." Tony gave Krug's arm an extra twist.

Frankie shoved Schultz and Bouhler in front of the window next to Krug. "Tony, the kid's getting ready to go. We need to stop him." The televisions showed Armendariz stretching on the runway in preparation for his first attempt.

Massetti spun Krug around and poked a finger into his chest. "How do you help him? What do you do to make him win?"

Krug only glared in his face. His eyes showed rage and frustration. He was so close to the goal he'd worked toward for decades.

"These guys control Armendariz," shouted Kirk, pointing at the scientists sitting at their computer terminals with their arms in the air.

"Silence!" shouted Krug. "You have no right to interfere."

While Frankie covered the three men by the window, Massetti walked over to Kirk and AJ. "So, kid. What's the deal?"

"They use the computers and transmitters to help Armendariz run faster and jump higher. They've got something implanted in him that they control from here to make him win."

AJ jumped in. "We found out what they were doing and they tried to kill me. We followed them here and they caught us. Please let us go."

Massetti smiled. "Sure, honey. Maybe later. First, we gotta make sure Armendariz flops."

Pulling a snubnosed .38 caliber revolver from his jacket, Tony stuck it under the chin of the scientist sitting in the middle. "Make the kid miss, or I give your head a sunroof. Then I do your partners."

The scientist nodded and began tapping on his keyboard. He instructed the others to cooperate as Tony held the gun under his chin.

"Ladies and Gentleman, if you've just tuned in, don't go away. We are witnessing one of the most exciting duals in Olympic track and field history. Jimmy Wickland of the United States has cleared 6.1 meters, setting a new Olympic record. Rickie Armendariz, the relative unknown from the small Caribbean island of St. Lucia, is ready for his first attempt to stay in the race for the gold medal."

"Sergei, we couldn't have scripted a more exciting pole vault finish. Two men having the performances of their lives at the Olympic Games."

"It couldn't be better. Armendariz is ready. He looks confident as he begins his approach. Oh, he's wobbling! His steps are off. He plants the pole but looks awkward. He's trying to push off. Oh no, he crashes across the bar, hitting it with his chest. He wouldn't have cleared fifteen feet with that jump."

"Sergei, we're going to show that attempt in slow motion while the bar is being reset. Let's see if we can determine what went wrong."

The image of Armendariz slowly running filled the television screens. "There it is. His left leg kicks forward too far and he grimaces in pain." The slow motion replay continues. "There it is again. His leg jerks out of sync."

"Sergei, it almost looks like he was suffering from a cramp. Or could an insect have stung him? I remember a meet in California when a bee stung one of the hundred meter contestants. He hopped wildly halfway through the sprint."

"I don't know what the problem is. But something obviously happened to disrupt Rickie Armendariz."

CHAPTER 89

Massetti complimented the scientists. "Nice job, gentlemen. Let's do that twice more and you just might live." He held his gun at the back of the head of the scientist to be sure he didn't lose his motivation.

Kirk and AJ whispered to each other. "It's amazing how they control Armendariz, AJ. I wonder how high they can make him go?"

"My concern is what happens to us? Will they let us go when this is over?"

Frankie didn't like whispering. "Hey, you two. Shut-up. We don't need you're yapping." Frankie waved his gun at Krug's two bodyguards sitting on the floor in the corner. "And don't you two get any ideas."

Gertrude was standing by the window next to Bouhler, Schultz and Krug. She licked her lips nervously and addressed Frankie. "Can't you let me go? I'm just a nurse. I don't know what this is all about. Please, let me go and I'll disappear."

Frankie moved closer to Gertrude, looking her up and down. "Maybe we can work something out." His voice dropped to a whisper as he spoke to Gertrude.

AJ used the distraction to talk to Kirk. Massetti could hear them, but she knew he wouldn't understand. Looking straight ahead, she spoke softly. "Kirk, remember when I said Joe DiMaggio and Babe Ruth were the greatest Yankees ever? And how important their numbers were to the dominance of the Yankees?"

Kirk's mind was racing. DiMaggio and Ruth. Okay, they wore number five and number three respectively. Kirk stole a sideways glance at AJ, and she cocked her head slightly to the left. Kirk looked past her head and saw the large clock on the office wall. It was 5:01, with the black second hand just beginning another 360-degree sweep.

AJ spoke in a low monotone. "I would take the Bambino and I bet you would take Joltin' Joe."

The hair on the back of Kirk's neck stood up. AJ was saying at 5:03 they should make a move. She would go after the heavyset leader holding the gun on the scientists, a Babe Ruth type build. And Kirk would jump the taller slender man talking to the woman. The other two men were out in the hall, securing the floor.

Kirk considered the options. He didn't think Wadlington was coming to rescue them. With surprise on their side, maybe he and AJ could both disarm their targets. Then they'd have to contend with the other bad guys in the hall, as well as worry about everyone else in this room.

Rational thought told him their odds of success were slim. But that was unproductive thinking, and this was no time for negativism. AJ was right. They had to act. Kirk gave AJ a nod of agreement.

The sweep hand hit the apex of the clock, making the time 5:02. Tony Massetti, with his gun pressed to the base of the scull of the lead scientist, turned to look at AJ and Kirk. "Mickey Mantle. I don't care what anybody says, the Mick was the greatest to ever wear pinstripes."

AJ and Kirk nodded woodenly as Massetti turned back to look at the TV. He had been listening to their conversation. They both had the fleeting thought that they might have only a minute to live.

The television showed Armendariz readying for attempt number two. Massetti pushed his gun forward. "Let's see an ugly attempt. Don't let me down."

It was a repeat of the first attempt. Rickie started down the runway and his legs went helter skelter. He looked like a marionette whose puppeteer had gone mad. Again, he missed badly.

Massetti relaxed just a bit. One more missed attempt by Armendariz and Tony's money would be secure. He was debating what to do with his captives. He had no beef with the young man and young woman sitting in the chairs. He wasn't sure where they fit in the equation, but he didn't see them as threats.

The second hand hit twelve and a shooting pain in his forearm interrupted Tony's thoughts. AJ hammered down on his gun arm as she kicked at the back of his knees. Tony fell backwards, grabbing at AJ on the way down. They crashed to the floor, jarring the pistol from Tony's hand.

Kirk caught Frankie with a roundhouse punch to the cheek, snapping his head back. Kirk grabbed at the gun, but Frankie's grip held firm as he swung at Kirk with his free hand, growling angrily.

The first rifle shot interrupted the beginnings of the melee. The shattering glass and a grunt from Krug were simultaneous. Krug fell forward with blood pouring from his chest, glass from the shattered window filling the air.

A scream died in the throat of Schultz as he caught the second shot in the back of his neck. His limp body fell to the floor. Bouhler dove to the floor as the third slug from a high-powered rifle ripped through his side.

The carnage jolted everyone to action. Those not on the floor scrambled for cover. Kirk crawled across the floor toward AJ as she and Tony separated.

Screams filled the room as everyone's thoughts centered on survival. "Tony, who's shooting?" yelled Frankie. Bullets riddled the computers, sending plastic pieces flying.

Tony was hugging the carpet as tightly as he could. "I don't know. Are you hit?"

"No. I'm okay," answered Frankie.

Kirk picked up the gun dropped by Tony and pushed AJ along the floor toward the wall. He pulled a filing cabinet over, crashing loudly as it fell on its' side. He and AJ lay behind the small barricade seeking protection.

Frankie turned a desk on its' side, hoping to shield himself and Tony from bullets entering through the shattered windows. He had a random thought of John Wayne in an old movie shooting at Indians over the side of an overturned wagon. At least the Duke could see what he was shooting at. Frankie, on the other hand, didn't know how or why they were being attacked.

The shooting stopped and the silence was broken by the commentary coming from the television. "Rickie Armendariz is starting his final attempt at 6.1 meters after two of the most ungainly attempts I've ever seen. If Armendariz fails, Jimmy Wickland of the United States wins the gold."

Tony peeked over the desk at the television. The computers were totally destroyed. He knew they couldn't hinder Armendariz now. But neither could they help him. Surely, the Caribbean vaulter wouldn't clear the bar without the help of the computers.

As Rickie prepared for his third attempt, Jimmy Wickland wished him luck. It was a sincere gesture in a world of trash-talking athletes where mind games were the norm. "Shake it off, Armendariz. We all have bad jumps." Jimmy pumped his fist. "Give this one your best and kiss the sky. You can do it."

Rickie was touched by the gesture. He nodded thanks to Wickland and stared down the runway.

Jimmy looked on, knowing this jump determined his fate. He hadn't said a word to the judges, but he was done for the day. He twisted his left wrist on the last jump and it was screaming in pain. It would be days before he could hold a pole comfortably.

If Armendariz cleared 6.1 meters, he'd win the gold medal by virtue of fewer misses for the day. Jimmy would get the silver. If Armendariz missed, Jimmy would hear the Star Spangled Banner as he stood at the top level of the awards platform.

Rickie knew something was drastically wrong with the computer-controlled transmitters. It had been all he could do on the last two jumps to keep from falling as he ran. The electric impulses were timed wrong and way too strong. If the problem wasn't corrected, he had absolutely no chance of making the jump.

No more time to think. He started down the runway. No shocks to his muscles. He neared the takeoff point. No shocks yet. He planted the pole. No shocks. A thought flashed across his mind. *It's all on me. I'm the one making the jump.*

Rickie soared with an adrenaline rush of his first unassisted jump in years. His feet were over the bar. His hips were over the bar. His body curved as his shoulders cleared the bar.

Cleanly over the twenty-foot height, Rickie's elbow brushed the bar on the way down, causing the bar to bounce. The television close-up showed it bouncing once, twice, and a third time. With each bounce, the bar moved closer to the edge of the horizontal pins marking the height.

The third bounce caused one end of the bar to slip off of the supporting pin. Like an arrow falling to earth, the bar plummeted straight down. Rickie could see the bar falling, but he had a truly joyous thought. *I cleared twenty feet!* He knew he'd made a good jump. The bad luck of the brush with the bar couldn't take away the personal satisfaction of a quality effort.

Pandemonium erupted. Some photographers rushed to snap Rickie in the agony of defeat as he exited the pit, while others worked to freeze the image of Jimmy's face in the ecstasy of victory as the gold medal winner.

"What an effort by Armendariz! After two disastrous vaults, he pulled himself together and easily cleared the bar. But for a slight bump on the way down, he would still be competing."

The sportscaster looked directly into the camera. "This pole vault competition is now history. Jimmy Wickland from Tennessee, unsung coming into these games, has won the gold medal for the United States."

Television screens across the world showed Wickland conferring with two Olympic officials. "Sergei, Wickland can now make an attempt at a height of his choice, which may be your world record. I must say, he looked so strong at 6.1 meters, he may be able to clear 6.15."

Wickland walked away from the officials and knelt down next to his equipment. The TV camera zoomed in, showing a piece of tape with CHICAGO written on the side of his bag. Jimmy ripped off the tape, revealing tape with OLYMPIC RECORD on it.

He pulled this piece off and reattached it next to the piece below. The exposed tape filled the television screen with two words. GOLD MEDAL.

Jimmy Wickland had attained two of the greatest goals of his life. No one else knew, nor right now did Jimmy care, that there was a final piece of unexposed tape. WORLD RECORD was a goal for another day.

Sticking his hand in his bag, he felt for something as reporters called for him to smile. His hand came out holding an American flag, prompting a roar from the crowd.

"Ladies and Gentlemen, we have just been informed that Jimmy Wickland suffered a wrist injury on his last jump and has declined the option of trying another height. He is the gold medal winner, and he holds the new Olympic record. He will be taking the traditional victory lap in a moment."

Jimmy walked to Rickie Armendariz and shook his hand. "Rickie, you broke the old Olympic record, too, and you easily cleared the last height. Come with me." It took some convincing, but Jimmy won the argument. Rickie dug into his bag and carefully pulled out only one flag.

The voice of the announcer almost cracked. "What you are witnessing today, ladies and gentlemen, is the true Olympic and athletic spirit. Jimmy Wickland of the United States is taking Rickie Armendariz of the tiny island country of St. Lucia on a victory lap with him. Both men are waving their national flags as they jog, side by side, around the Olympic track. The familiar red, white and blue stars and stripes flutter in the breeze next to the not so familiar black and gold triangle on a blue field that represents St. Lucia."

The picture of the two athletes, proudly waving their flags, would make the cover of Sports Illustrated and countless other magazines and newspapers around the world. Wickland and Armendariz would become the poster boys for athletic competition and sportsmanship.

CHAPTER 90

T he Gardener slid his rifle and scope into the air conditioning duct and replaced the vent cover. He didn't care if they found the weapon, since it was untraceable and he'd left no fingerprints. But he didn't intend to make it quick and easy for the authorities. As he tightened the screws to the vent cover he thought about Lee Harvey Oswald.

Hitting a moving target from the window of the book depository in Dallas had been quite a feat. Today's shots, by comparison, had been target practice. He'd had a straight line of sight from one building to the other. Krug had been kind enough to have all three targets standing by the window.

ODESSA had contracted him to eliminate Krug if his Olympic scheme became a risk. The Gardener received the message that Krug, Schultz and Bouhler had to go. There had not been time for anything quiet or subtle. For the fee he was receiving, he would have shot them at midfield of Olympic Stadium.

Gregory Krug, alias Josef Mengele, had become a liability to ODESSA. His developments in physical performance were welcome, but his attempt to steal the limelight at the Olympics had been roundly opposed. ODESSA was an organization with worldwide contacts that made inroads by working in the shadows through subterfuge and quiet negotiations, not by drawing attention to itself.

The new leadership of ODESSA had lost patience with the small group of surviving original Nazis. The ODESSA leaders decided to make an example of Krug. Eliminating the infamous Mengele would certainly keep the remaining low level Nazis in line.

The Gardener took a final look across the street at the shattered thirty-second story window. It had been almost too perfect, having targets lined up in plain sight in front of the window. Almost as easy as that St. Valentine's Day shooting many years ago right here in Chicago.

He was able to hit all targets — people and computers — in one quick burst. One of the easiest fees he'd ever made. He was surprised to see the Clark woman sitting in a chair. She wasn't on the list for this hit, so he gave her a pass. For now.

Straightening the employee badge hanging on the pocket of his blue maintenance jumpsuit, the highest paid assassin in the world headed for the elevator. It was time to leave the unequaled freedom of the good old U.S. of A. He needed to perfect the details for his next contract in Amsterdam.

CHAPTER 91

Tony and Frankie watched the television as Armendariz missed his last attempt. "That's it," said Tony. "I don't lose the bets and it looks like someone else took care of our personnel problems." He looked across the floor at the bodies of Krug, Schultz and Bouhler. "Let's get out of here before the cops show up."

A voice called from the hallway. "Boss, you all right?" Tony's other two men were peeking around the doorframe, guns drawn.

"Yeh, we're fine. Get the elevator," called Tony.

Frankie had his gun trained on Kirk and AJ behind the filing cabinet. The scientists, Mengele, and his bodyguards lay scattered across the floor. Sirens began to wail in the distance.

Tony spoke loudly. "Listen up." He paused. "Here's the deal. The two of us are going to back out of here and nobody else gets hurt. You wait ten minutes, then you leave." There was steel in his voice.

"You never saw us. Understand? I don't know who shot the place up, but we had nothing to do with it. Believe me, you don't want to know me or drag me into an investigation," Tony threatened.

"Elevator's here," called the man from the hall.

Frankie kept his gun pointed at Kirk, who was peering over the cabinet holding Tony's gun. "Toss the piece out where I can see it," commanded Frankie.

"No can do," answered Kirk. "These people were holding us captive. I feel better knowing I've got some protection. I'm not keeping you from leaving." Kirk set the gun on the filing cabinet and rested his hand next to it.

"Yo, boss. We going, or what?" came the shout from the hall.

The elevator's warning bell was ringing, announcing that the door was being held open longer than allowed. The sound of sirens grew louder.

Tony stood up. "Let's go." He gave a quick nod to Kirk and AJ, who were peeking over the cabinet. Frankie stood and backed toward the door, shielding Tony with his body in case there was trouble.

When they were through the door, Kirk picked up his gun. "AJ, check the bodies to see if anyone survived."

AJ quickly went to Bouhler, the closest body. She checked for pulse and breathing. "Dead," she pronounced. She checked Schultz next, with the same result.

It was the same with all except the last body. Feeling the neck of the old man, AJ detected a faint pulse. "Got a live one here, but just barely."

AJ knelt and gently pressed on the wound in Krug's chest to stem the flow of blood. "Kirk, we need an ambulance," said AJ.

Kirk punched the speed dial for Charles Wadlington. He was rewarded with Charles' voice. "Kirk, are you okay?"

"Never better, Charles. But we need an ambulance. Now. One badly hurt and some for the morgue."

"What happened?"

Kirk knew time was of the essence. "Long story. And I think you'll want to keep a lid on it." Kirk told Charles where they were and stressed the need for speed.

Slowly, Krug's eyes opened, his lids rising like an opening night curtain on Broadway. His gray eyes fixed AJ with an icy stare.

"Lucky," he whispered. "You got lucky. I was going to change the world." A cough racked his chest.

AJ returned his stare. "Who are you?"

A trace of a smile played at the corners of his mouth. "I'm a dead man come to life. I could make a man invincible. I was creating my own Fountain of Youth." Another cough shook his chest.

AJ remained silent, waiting for him to continue as they focused unblinkingly on one another.

"Your own Thomas Jefferson summed it up correctly. He said some people arrive into the world with saddles on their backs, while others arrive with boots and spurs. We are the Master Race and are meant to rule the rest of you." His chest rose as he took a labored breath. "I am Josef Mengele, doctor of the Third Reich."

An electric shock of recognition surged through AJ! Dr. Mengele? The horrible monster from World War II? She'd read about his infamous experiments at Auschwitz. But he had died in South America years ago, hadn't he?

Mengele's eyes danced as AJ wrestled with the incomprehensibility of the situation. He savored the bewilderment on her face.

"Believe it," he hissed. "I was so close. So close. But I was betrayed."

While Mengele talked, AJ monitored his pulse in his left wrist. She was so intent on what he was saying, she didn't notice Mengele slowly inching his right hand toward the dagger lying on the floor.

The monumental absurdity of sitting on the floor talking to the war criminal known as the Angel of Death had AJ mentally disarmed.

Mengele's fingers reached the hilt of the knife and he ever so slowly pulled it toward his palm. "You Americans are so egotistical. You think you are smarter, richer, prettier, stronger, faster than everyone else. You want the world to march to your beat, but you are amazed when not everyone is willingly Americanized."

Mengele had his hand firmly on the hilt of the dagger. "But for a few tactical mistakes and luck on your part, you would all be speaking German today. The entire Western Hemisphere would be a giant German colony." Mengele gritted his teeth against the pain in his chest.

"Your blind obedience to the rhetoric of your leaders is admirable, but I'm afraid the end result remains the same." Mengele paused to look deep into the eyes of AJ. "You lose."

Mengele swung the dagger with all the strength he had left. Only AJ's quick reaction to lean back saved her life. The dagger slashed across the left side of her ribcage as she stretched away from the blow.

Mengele followed up with a backhand swing at her face. Kirk shouted and pointed his gun at Mengele, but AJ blocked him from a clear shot.

Twisting her head sideways, AJ's right cheek was caught by the tip of the dagger as it whisked by. Mengele grunted from the effort, while adrenaline surged through AJ. She grabbed Mengele's wrist with both hands and turned the dagger toward him.

Her instinctive reaction drove the dagger deep into Mengele's right side. The tempered German steel slid easily between the fourth and fifth ribs, burying it up to the hilt in the chest of the Nazi doctor.

As she looked Mengele in the eye, AJ was oblivious to her surroundings. Kirk leaped to stand directly behind, his gun pointing down at the forehead of Mengele.

Time stood still as the Angel of Death pursed his lips to speak. But no sound came out. The life light began to fade from his eyes.

Josef Mengele, the infamous Nazi concentration camp doctor, exhaled as his eyes glazed. His head slumped to the side. AJ's hands still gripped the dagger.

She felt Kirk's hand on her shoulder. "It's over, AJ. It's all over. You can let go now."

CHAPTER 92

AJ awoke with a start. *What time was it? What day was it? Where was she?* She frantically looked around the room and nothing registered. White walls. Green linoleum floor. Strong disinfectant smell.

The fog in her mind began to lift. She realized she was in a hospital. She tried to sit up, wincing in pain as her left side screamed in protest.

"Hold on there, girl. You're supposed to take it easy." John Cline rose from the chair in the corner and stepped into AJ's field of vision.

"Oh, that hurts," said AJ as she tenderly touched her left side where the bandage covered her wound.

John took AJ's hand as he stood by the bed. "Well, Kiddo. They tell me you have a new career as a one woman wrecking crew."

AJ laughed, and then groaned. "Don't make me laugh. It hurts." She looked up at John. "After they stitched me up, they gave me happy drugs so I'd go to La La land. I feel like I've been hit by a truck." AJ paused to slow her breathing. "Nobody told me where you were. I'm so glad to see you."

John pulled his chair next to the bed and sat down. "I've been sitting here for three hours waiting for you to come to. The reading material in this hospital leaves something to be desired. And their television? Forget it."

AJ laughed again, groaning with pain. "Thanks for being here, but no jokes." She practiced shallow breathing to quiet the throbbing in her side.

John gently squeezed her hand. "I wanted to be sure you were all right. Thank goodness for that Wadlington friend of Kirk's, or I'd be in a Chicago prison. I stopped a man posing as a photographer from hurting Armendariz, and they hauled us both off the field. I kept saying I was a good guy, but the security people cuffed us both and were sending us to the police station."

Recognition hit AJ. "So you were part of the commotion that held up the vault?"

"Part of it?" John shook his head. "I was in the center ring. That's more attention than I ever want. But Wadlington has some stroke with the local police and he made it right. They were coming down on me like it was the 1968 Democratic Convention all over again. Those men know how to use their nightsticks."

AJ fingered the bandage on her right cheek and had a quick thought, wondering if she would have a scar. "Kirk and I could have used Wadlington a little sooner in that office building. It was crazy."

John nodded. "I got the whole story. All I can say, AJ, is Wow. Too bad we can't tell anyone about it."

AJ tried to sit up, but decided the pain wasn't worth it. "What do you mean?"

John held up two fingers in a Boy Scout salute. "I had to promise, on my honor, not to ever mention the details of the events of today. If I should fail to keep my vow, my government shall, with all due haste, throw my rear end in the slammer and throw away the key."

John could tell by the look on her face AJ didn't believe him.

"No kidding, AJ. They're screwing the lid down tight on this whole thing. As soon as they know you're awake, they'll be in here having you sign your life away. It scares them that we don't work for them. Kirk is getting debriefed right now, and you can bet they own him."

CHAPTER 93

K irk looked at Charles Wadlington and shrugged again. "Charles, what else can I say? I've told you over and over, I don't know who fired the rifle shots. I don't know why the mob was there. I'm sorry about the mess, but I'm glad AJ, John, and I made it out alive. What else do you want from me?"

Charles leaned on the table with both hands. The Chicago police had helped him commandeer the small conference room on the first floor of the hospital. He and Kirk were alone, except for the constant noise in the hallway.

"What I want, Kirk, and what I need, are answers for the General! He wants this fiasco tied up with a bow like a Christmas present so he can present the results to the financial committee and justify our expenditures."

Kirk snorted. "It all comes down to money. Doesn't he care that we risked our lives? We stopped a plot to use the world's premier sport's event as a showcase for resurrecting totalitarianism, brutality, and master race madness. Doesn't that count for something?"

Kirk's voice continued to grow louder. "We're out there busting our tails, and all anybody worries about is the General. He doesn't wear a uniform anymore. So, was he in the Army or the Navy, or what? And who made him King?"

Neither Kirk nor Charles heard the conference room door open, but they both heard it slam shut. The General stood ramrod straight, jaw clenched, his dark eyes glaring under salt and pepper brows. His carotid artery visibly pulsed with each beat of his heart. His tanned face topped with brush cut gray hair remained perfectly still.

Kirk realized he was holding his breath. He tried to let it out and breathe quietly. Though the General was in his late sixties, he looked like a recruiting poster in his khaki slacks, white shirt, regimental striped tie, and blue blazer with gold buttons. To Kirk, he looked very military and very scary.

After an intimidating full minute wait, the General marched three steps forward, bringing him directly in front of Kirk. "First, the only thing keeping me from pulling your stomach out through your throat is the fact that you made a few correct decisions. Don't think I can't take you apart with my bare hands because, make no mistake, I can."

The look in the General's eyes left no doubt in Kirk's mind on that score. "Second, I was not IN the Army, or IN the Navy." The General's jaws clenched and unclenched as he paused. "I AM a Marine. Was, am, and always will be. Is that clear?"

Kirk's reaction was instinctive. "Yes, Sir."

"Third, you get to play secret agent at my discretion. If I hear any disparaging words from you about the organization or anyone associated with it, you're through. No employee review, no appeal, no discussion. Understood?'

"Yes, Sir." Though never in the military, Kirk was giving a pretty good impression of standing at attention.

"Fourth, this was a covert operation, and as such, the details can never be divulged to anyone. Not by you or by your two sidekicks. I'm holding you responsible for their actions, so I hope you convey the seriousness of the situation to them."

This time Kirk merely nodded.

The General turned to Charles, who was also standing at attention. "Chuck, I'm leaving before I do something you'll both regret. I want you to personally tie up loose ends and button this up. I want a daily report sent to me detailing any developments."

Turning on his heels, the General strode to the door and was gone. After the footsteps faded, Charles turned to Kirk. "Do you know how bad your timing is?"

Kirk realized he had been clenching his fists so tightly at his sides that his hands were numb. He opened and closed them to restart the circulation. Kirk hung his head, looking at the floor.

"I'm sorry, Charles. It's all my fault." He paused. "But look on the bright side."

Charles had his hands on his hips. Something about Kirk's apology didn't sound sincere. "Bright side? What bright side?"

Kirk looked up with a mischievous grin. "Sure makes you glad the General's on our side."

Charles gave a wry smile. "Why don't you and I work together just to see if we can make it to retirement. For you, Kirk, I think that's job one."

CHAPTER 94

The past days had been a blur. AJ leaned back against the headrest of the rental car and closed her eyes. She had replayed the struggle with Mengele a thousand times in her mind, yet some of the details were still unclear.

Why hadn't she noticed him reaching for the dagger? He was old and critically wounded, so why couldn't she have subdued him without killing him? Had she wanted to? Even though he was a monster, she hated the thought that maybe part of her had relished seeing his life extinguished.

She kept telling herself it had to be done. She and Kirk helped prevent an international incident. She just happened to be the one who faced Mengele at the end. It could just as easily have been Kirk confronting him, or Mengele could have died instantly from the gunshot wounds.

But that's not the way it ended. AJ Clark had been the one talking to Mengele. Arguing with him about America's moral makeup. AJ Clark was the one attacked by the Angel of Death. AJ Clark was the one who stabbed to death the self-proclaimed architect of a new world order.

The gentle squeeze of her hand pulled AJ back to the present. "We're almost there," whispered Kirk. "Were you asleep or just thinking?"

AJ turned to look at Kirk. He was steering with his left hand while his right hand held hers. The Tennessee countryside spread around them like a patchwork quilt of green hues. As the road curved, they suddenly had a view of a slice of placid, deep blue water.

"Reelfoot Lake," exclaimed Kirk. "Land of milk and honey, home of the miraculous regenerating man. Bane to salesmen of eye glasses and dentures, because everyone lives forever but no one gets old."

AJ played along. "Better than OZ," she injected. "A Technicolor fantasyland, where all dreams come true."

Kirk pointed to the car ahead of them. "We'll ask the wizard for a heart for Wadlington. Heaven knows he could use one. But what for John Cline? He's got courage and a brain already."

AJ thought for a moment. "We'll ask the wizard for a home for John. I know he misses his wife and the life they had together. John's a very good man. Maybe the wizard can find him a home that will bring him peace."

Kirk braked as the vehicle ahead of them slowed. "What about you, AJ? If the wizard of Reelfoot Lake exists, what would you wish for?"

AJ answered without hesitation. "No wish for me. I believe my wishes have been answered." She gave Kirk's hand a squeeze.

Kirk had a lump in his throat as he kept his eyes on the road. "Mine too."

CHAPTER 95

The celebration parade was over. Jack Ward stood on the reviewing stand as the mayor and the other township dignitaries milled about politicking.

Sheriff Ward was mighty proud. The grandstands and storefronts along Main Street were resplendent, covered with colorful bunting and streamers. The streets and sidewalks were spotless as a result of his cleanup campaign.

Ward had reveled in the compliments. The mayor thanked Jack and said because of his efforts, the three TV stations covering the parade for Tennessee's own gold medal winner would show a beautiful town anyone would be proud to live in. Or vacation to.The mayor hoped to use film clips of the parade in upcoming tourism ads.

This was the proudest day of Jack's life. The roadsides and campsites looked the best they ever had. Bubba had taken on the kudzu with a vengeance, with fantastic results. Even his over zealousness down by the lake could be overlooked on such a successful day.

Jack noticed Bubba sitting on a wooden chair in front of the barbershop across the street. He'd been hard on Bubba. Maybe it was time to give him a compliment and thank him for a job well done.

Jack went down the reviewing stand steps two at a time and walked across the street with a bounce in his step. As he reached the opposite side, Bubba spit a stream of tobacco juice, splattering on the sidewalk and narrowly missing Jack's freshly polished boots.

"Bubba, watch it." Jack felt his good mood dissipate.

"Hey Jack. How do you know?" Bubba was leaning his chair back against the barbershop, his bulk making the chair almost invisible. The front of his stained tee shirt carried the logo of a local bar.

"How do I know what?" Jack regretted falling into Bubba's trap as soon as he responded.

Bubba smiled in anticipation of his own punch line. "How do you know when the mayor is going to stop walking so you don't stick your nose up his behind? If you kiss up to him any more, he's gonna have to get you a friendship ring."

Jack clenched his teeth. So much for a compliment for Bubba. As Jack worked to frame an appropriate response, a white sedan pulled up to the curb, with a black clone pulling in next to it.

Charles Wadlington got out of the first car and walked over to the sheriff. "Hello, officer. Could I trouble you for some directions? I'm looking for Jimmy Wickland."

Bubba spit between Charles and Jack. "If you'd a been here an hour ago, you could've seen him riding through town in one of them convertibles."

"Bubba!" exclaimed Jack. "That's enough." He escorted Charles down the sidewalk, out of Bubba's hearing.

Jack apologized for Bubba and asked Charles his business with Wickland. After a plausible explanation from Charles, Jack explained that Jimmy lived with his grandmother and gave directions.

"Thank you, officer. And if you don't mind, I need directions to one other spot."

Jack found the request a bit incongruous, but gave the gentleman directions to his second request. After shaking hands and thanking him again, Charles returned to the car.

After conferring with John Cline, he walked to the black car Kirk was driving and climbed into the back seat. AJ and Kirk turned to look at him. "This is it. Let's go see Jimmy Wickland," ordered Charles.

John Cline had pulled away in the white car and turned down a side street. "Where's John going?' AJ asked.

Kirk and Charles exchanged a conspiratorial look as Kirk answered. "He has to pick something up. He'll meet us at the Wickland place."

AJ knew they were up to something, but she was too tired to press them on it. "All right. Let's go."

Kirk pulled onto Main Street and followed the directions Charles gave to the home of Lily Morales and Jimmy Wickland.

CHAPTER 96

L ily Morales was happy. Jimmy had made her proud with his performance at the Olympics. The parade and the attention Jimmy was getting were well deserved rewards for his fantastic accomplishments.

While Lily worked in the kitchen, Jimmy was looking over his scrapbook in his room. Grams had purchased every newspaper and magazine she could lay her hands on and clipped articles about Jimmy to commemorate his triumph.

A black car stopping in front of her house interrupted her thoughts. Drying her hands on a dishtowel, she went to the door to see what the strangers wanted. She was getting a little tired of reporters and photographers stopping by at all hours of the day.

Lily stepped outside to meet her visitors. As the two men and the woman got out of the car, she didn't think they looked like reporters.

AJ led the way to the house and quickly appraised the woman who greeted them. Dressed in a blue and white sundress, the woman was of medium height, slender, with long black hair flowing around her shoulders. Her skin was smooth and bronzed. AJ admired her high cheekbones and bright eyes. She guessed the woman's age to be in the late forties. *Was this an aunt of Jimmy Wickland's,* AJ wondered?

"Hello. May I help you folks?"

The beautiful smile and strong voice reinforced AJ's assessment. "How do you do?" AJ responded. "We're looking for Jimmy Wickland. The sheriff was kind enough to give us directions. Is Jimmy here? Or is Mrs. Morales home?"

Lily crossed her arms and looked at the three strangers. "May I ask who's looking for them?" The mention of the sheriff struck a cord of caution.

Charles spoke up. "We were at the Olympics in Chicago and observed

Jimmy's tremendous victory. I'm with the National Institute of Health and Fitness." He presented an ID card identifying him as such. "My companions are AJ Clark and Kirk Vail."

Lily nodded to them.

Charles plowed forward. "We would like to discuss training regimen and nutrition with Jimmy. Is he available?"

Lily uncrossed her arms and placed her hands on her hips. "I'm Lily Morales, Jimmy's grandmother."

"You're Jimmy's grandmother?" asked Kirk incredulously. He expressed what they were all thinking. They knew from the research file that Lily Morales was over 70 years old. The woman standing before them appeared at least twenty years younger.

For the first time, Lily smiled. She understood the incredulous looks. "I get that a lot. Don't look my age. Must be my heritage." She looked the three visitors over again. "Come on in. No sense standing outside."

When Mrs. Morales turned to go inside, AJ, Kirk and Charles exchanged wide-eyed looks. All three thought there was more than good genetics making Jimmy's grandmother look so young.

Once inside, Lily positioned her guests on the couch and love seat. She offered sweet tea, but received no takers. "Honey," said Lily, looking at AJ. "What happened to your cheek?"

AJ instinctively reached to touch the cut where the stitches remained. "Actually, Mrs. Morales, it happened at the Olympics during Jimmy's vault. When he won the gold medal, a man next to me jumped up in excitement and a buckle on his camera case cut me."

"That's a shame. You have a beautiful face. I certainly hope it won't leave a scar. I'm completely out of my homemade salve, or I'd give you some to rub on. It always worked for Jimmy when he would scratch himself."

The mention of Jimmy brought Kirk back to their mission. "You said Jimmy was home. Could we talk to him for a few minutes?"

With a nod, Lily agreed. "I'll get him."

They all stood when Lily returned with Jimmy. "Jimmy, this is Mr. Wadlington, Mr. Vail, and Ms. Clark."

Jimmy shook all three offered hands. "Pleased to meet you. Grams said you want to talk about my training?" Jimmy wore a white USA Olympics tee shirt and blue running shorts.

"Please, everyone, have a seat," said Lily. Jimmy pulled a chair from the kitchen as the group reseated.

Kirk began the discussion. "Jimmy, I was at the Olympic trials in Memphis when you were injured. And we were all at the Olympics, too.

You made a miraculous recovery and performed beyond everyone's expectations. All of America is proud of you."

Jimmy had been through enough interviews to smoothly handle compliments. "Mr. Vail, it was such an honor to compete for our country. I just worked hard and I was extremely fortunate to have my best day in Chicago."

Kirk leaned forward and clasped his hands, resting his elbows on his knees. "Jimmy, I know Dr. Jacobs. He told me your recovery from your injuries in Memphis was miraculous. His word. Miraculous."

"I'm a fast healer."

Kirk shook his head. "Jimmy, we think there's more to it. There may be something in your environment which gives you special recuperative powers."

Jimmy looked at Grams and back at Kirk. "Look, I just recover fast. I've got a very high pain threshold, so I can get back to competing quickly."

AJ took her turn. "Jimmy, if there's something that makes you heal fast or perform better, it's something we should share. We know from your regular tests that you don't do steroids or other illegal performance enhancers. So if there is something organic that helps you, we would like to know."

Jimmy again looked at Grams.

"Mrs. Morales," said AJ. "Seeing how wonderful you look for your age, we have to believe there is something very special going on here. Is it the water? Maybe there are concentrated nutrients in this area. Please, can you help us?"

The silence in the room seemed to last an eternity. No one spoke, no one moved, no one twitched.

Lily looked at AJ and made a decision. Something in AJ's eyes told her she could be trusted.

"It's not the water." Lily spoke so softly that at first no one reacted.

"What did you say?" whispered AJ.

Lily repeated herself. "It's not the water."

"Grams," said Jimmy. "You said we could never tell. You said it was our special gift, our special secret, and we could never, ever tell anyone."

Grams reached out and took Jimmy's hand. "It's all right, Jimmy. It's time. It's stressful keeping a secret this long. It's time, because it doesn't matter anymore."

Lily held everyone's attention. "There's a plant with great healing powers that grows near here. When consumed orally, it provides energy, promotes healing, and slows down deterioration."

Charles couldn't resist the obvious. "Slows down deterioration, as in, retards aging?"

Lily shrugged. "Seeing is believing. Also, the plant can be applied topically, like the aloe leaf. It anesthetizes and speeds up healing. My ancestors passed down the secret of the plant. But it doesn't matter anymore."

"I'm not following you, Mrs. Morales." Kirk was trying to grasp what was being said. "You're telling us about a generations' old secret of incredible physical and scientific significance, and you say it doesn't matter anymore?"

Lily shook her head sadly. "The plants are gone. I ran out of my plant supply and the juice I make from the plants. When I went to get more, I found the plants all dead."

There was a stunned silence. "All dead? There must be some mistake. There must be some left somewhere?" AJ couldn't believe the miracle plant was gone. It didn't seem possible to come this far and be denied the great discovery.

"Grams, let's show them." Jimmy was already standing.

Everyone stood. "It's a twenty minute walk to the lake," said Lily. "I think you need to see for yourselves."

During the walk, Lily explained how she would harvest the plants from the water's edge. She would put a few leaves in the salads she made, use the leaves like lettuce in sandwiches, and mix the leaves with water and honey to make her juice.

Jimmy said he didn't think the plant helped him perform better.

He was sure his successful pole vaulting was a result of his hard work. But he did admit that without the plant and the juice from Grams, he probably wouldn't have recovered from injuries fast enough to compete at the Olympics.

When they reached Reelfoot Lake, they stood and stared. All along the edge of the water floated dead brown leaves. Shaped like lily pads, the leaves were flat and four to six inches across. Their irregular shape gave them the look of giant four leaf clovers.

AJ squatted and scooped up a handful of leaves. She inspected the brown specimens, looking for faint signs of life. Convinced they were terminal, she handed them to Charles. "What do you think?"

Charles turned the leaves over in his hands. "I'm not a botanist, but they certainly appear dead. Mrs. Morales, is this the only place they grow?"

Lily pointed along the shoreline. "I've been all around the Lake, and this inlet is the only place. It's where my mother, and her mother, and her mother's mother came to harvest the leaves. And now, they're gone."

The finality of the situation weighed on them all. "Believe me, I've looked," said Lily. "When I saw this, I waded along the shoreline for hours, searching for a plant that was alive. My heart hoped for a miracle, but none could be found."

CHAPTER 97

T he sun shown brightly as a soft breeze rustled the grass and songbirds sang in the distance. But there was nothing in nature to lighten their mood. The vision of opportunity lost hung over the five of them as they stared at the lakeshore.

"Hey, Kirk! How about a little help here," John Cline called from up the hillside.

Kirk waved and began walking toward him. "You found us."

"I caught a glimpse of you walking away from the house as I pulled in. Two roads diverged in the yellowed wood, and lucky I took the same one you did. I thought I'd lost you."

John was carrying a shoebox and handed it to Kirk. "Mission accomplished." John looked at the group by the water. "Really an outstanding idea, Kirk. I must admit you've outdone yourself this time."

Kirk held the shoebox carefully. "I hope you're right. We need a little cheering up about now."

"How're things going with Wickland? You learning anything?" probed John.

"More than we can believe, and not all of it good. We'll fill you in, but first, let's do this."

Kirk and John walked to the water side by side. "Mrs. Morales, Jimmy, this is the other member of our group, John Cline."

John shook hands with them both, telling Jimmy what a great job he had done at the Olympics.

Kirk put one arm around AJ, holding the box behind his back with the other. "AJ, we have a presentation to make. You are the driving force of our merry band. You've shown us how to persevere, even in the face of personal tragedy. As a token of our appreciation, we would like to present you with a gift."

Kirk handed AJ the box. It was a Green Star running shoe box, way too big to hold shoes to fit AJ. She held the box, wondering what in the world could be inside.

She felt the weight of the box shift. Something moved. AJ pulled the box top up a few inches to peek inside and stared into the eyes of a tiny white furry Bichon Frise puppy.

Tossing the top aside, she scooped the puppy out, letting the box fall to the ground. "Oh, sweet baby." AJ held the tiny puppy to her cheek, whispering gently to it. She was rewarded with licks to her cheek, ear, and neck by the wiggly one-pound pooch.

"It's a girl," said Kirk.

"Thank you, thank you." AJ kissed Kirk on the cheek, and repeated the gesture for John Cline and Charles Wadlington. They both seemed embarrassed by the show of affection.

"It was Kirk's idea," said John.

Charles directed his comments to Jimmy and his grandmother. "AJ lost her dog in a tragic accident a few weeks ago. He was a great friend and companion to her. Kirk felt a new puppy would help fill the void."

"I've got just the thing for that puppy in the house," said Mrs. Morales. "Let's go see how hungry she is."

Kirk picked up the shoebox and they started up the hill. With smiles on their faces, they left Reelfoot Lake behind.

"Ms. Clark, may I hold her?" Jimmy asked as they walked.

"Sure, Jimmy. Here." AJ gently handed the pup to Jimmy, who cradled her to his chest.

"What are you going to name her?" asked Jimmy, laughing as the puppy tried to burrow into his neck.

Holding Kirk's hand, AJ thought for a moment. "Hope," she answered. "I like the name Hope."

"Yes, the puppy will be named Hope," announced AJ again. Everyone agreed it was a splendid name.

As they walked up the hill, all were lost in their own thoughts. Hope. A simple word with magnificent meanings.

The afternoon sun bounced off the silver surface of Reelfoot Lake. Under a partially submerged log in a corner of the lagoon, the reflected light found three green fronds.

Hidden from view, the leaves were softly kissed by the nurturing afternoon sun. This triumvirate represented the chance for survival.

Hope.

Book Club discussion notes and questions are
available at www.dalegreenlee.com.

Follow A.J. Clark in her next adventure when she is caught in a web of espionage as America's favorite pastime is under siege from abroad.

An excerpt from *Kiss For Luck* by Dale Greenlee follows:

The crowd was loud, and no one cared. Shouts, laughter, and curses bounced off the walls like pinging sonar. It was a beautiful spring evening, but there were no windows to allow the revelers to enjoy the impressive sunset on the river.

No view to distract, no clocks to remind. A world of no regrets and no remorse. Yet in a room all about money, none was visible. Colored chips were the currency of the realm. Men and women in starched white shirts and black vests expertly performed five-dollar multiplication as they racked bets and chatted with customers.

The Empress was a ship without a voyage, a pleasure boat permanently docked in the DesPlaines River at Joliet, Illinois. Riverboat casinos dotted Illinois rivers. Gambling in the Midwest was no longer a vice. It was taxable revenue.

Money flowed like water through the Empress as roulette wheels spun, dice rolled, and cards were dealt face up. The house never cheated. It didn't have to. The odds were in its favor. But someone in the room was cheating.

Brian Landers wanted it all. He wanted more money, more excitement, more power, and more love. At thirty-one years old, he was the vice president of his father's business empire, and his goals were set high.

At six-feet two, with thick, wavy black hair and the chest and shoulders of the football player he once was, Brian Landers looked good. And he knew it. His perfectly tailored navy jacket, expensive tan slacks, and pale blue shirt exuded the power he felt. He was a man used to getting what he wanted. Tonight he wanted excitement.

Blackjack was exciting, though not as exciting as Dora Delgado, the beautiful young woman standing behind his chair as he wagered. But tonight she was getting on his nerves. For the last ten minutes she had been chattering nonstop with complaints about Brian's behavior.

He tried to tune her out, hoping she would give it up. When she started mixing Spanish with English, he knew she was serious.

Dora challenged Brian's manhood in Spanish, then shouted the word that stopped the gambling cold. "Cheater!"

The accusation echoed off the crystal chandeliers, causing every croupier to freeze. "You're a cheater!" Dora stood, hands on hips, feet spread wide in defiance. Her dress shimmered under the fluorescent lights as her body shook with fury.

"You think you can do anything you want. You run around and you treat me like dirt." She paused for breath. "You pig."

The pit boss quickly moved toward Brian, motioning with his thumb. "Hey, Buddy. Take it outside. Now."

Brian scooped his chips into the pocket of his sports coat and rose while Dora raged on. Everyone was watching, waiting for his reaction. "Dora, knock it off."

"Oh, so Mister Big Man wants Dora to be quiet. You think you get what you want? Not this time, Mister Big Man. You cheat on me, you cheat at work. You're even trying to cheat and buy the Cubs for Asian buddies."

Brian's veins shown on his forehead. "That's enough!"

Ask for Kiss For Luck
ISBN: 978-0-910941-34-1
by Dale Greenlee.
www.dalegreenlee.com